EXIT STAGE IV

EXIT STAGE IV

BEN EMERY

Epigraph Books
Rhinebeck, New York

Paperback ISBN 9781966293132
eBook ISBN 9781966293149

Cover artist: Carmen Mateo
Book and cover design by Colin Rolfe

Epigraph Books
22 East Market Street, Suite 304
Rhinebeck, New York 12572
(845) 876-4861
epigraphpublishing.com

Dedicated to my mom, Barbara Hannah Cassidy Emery.

Exit Stage IV is a fictional story based on true industrial atrocities.

Murder is morally wrong, regardless of the perpetrator.

Corporations have no soul to save, and no body to incarcerate. —Unknown

CHAPTER ONE

THE VERDICT

NOVEMBER 23, 2010

The jury foreman stands and hands the results of their deliberations to the court clerk:

> The State of Montana versus Benjamin Brown: Verdict Count One, District Court Missoula, Montana. We, the jury, being duly impaneled and sworn, do hereby find proof beyond a reasonable doubt that Benjamin Brown is guilty of murder in the first degree with premeditation and malice.

Wordless approval is heard and felt throughout the courtroom. A chorus of sighs and gasps fills the air, loud as a scream, yet the verdict rises above it. The court clerk's voice is clear and crisp. What comes next is unbelievable.

> Considering the mitigating factors of the horrific act, we, the jury, unanimously recommend the defendant Benjamin Brown's sentence be considered time served on all guilty charges.

As the court clerk continues to read the remaining guilty verdicts, the courtroom noise fades to a faint muffle for the defendant. His eyes fill with tears. In a surreal state, he feels numb to the lawyer's grip on his arm and the gasps from the crowded courtroom. For the first time in months, the pain from excessive asbestos exposure has eased to the point that breathing feels almost unconscious again.

Succumbing to gravity, a single tear is released down his cheek, and a single thought consumes all the energy and attention of this newly convicted murderer. *Justice! Finally, some goddamn justice.*

In a court of law, the people of Montana have recognized the decades of suffering Benjamin Brown's family endured. He has achieved justice, the only way possible, for both his family and the residents of Sawpit, Montana, who were sacrificed for profits by Vermolite Mining Company.

CHAPTER TWO

HANNAH CASSIDY AND WHITE COUNTY, INDIANA

MARCH 21, 2011:

A man knocks the snow off his boots as he enters the door, and a cold breeze flows through a small-town community center in White County, Indiana. This year, March is unusually cold, and the chill enhances the smell of stale coffee and pastries as a few people wait for their meeting to begin.

"Whew! It's been a cold one. Can you remember a colder or wetter winter?" the man comments, entering the building, removing the first of three layers of clothes.

Without moving her eyes from the TV screen mounted on the wall, a woman replies, "According to the news weather report, it will be in the teens tonight."

Jokingly, the man adds, "Great. More ice and snow to shovel in the morning. Don't they know my chemo makes breathing in cold weather feel like I'm suffocating? It's tough to keep on living without breathing."

With a snort, the woman says, "Scott, we are damned if you do and double damned if you don't. Somehow, I should feel lucky. It feels like cement is being poured into every joint in my body with the Anastrozole. This is the last option. We've recycled through every treatment and we're giving it another month or so before we call it quits."

A young woman politely tries to interrupt the conversation. "Is that some form of chemotherapy? This is my first meeting, and I don't understand almost anything the doctors tell me." Her voice starts to shake with emotion. "My husband and me thought that coming to this meeting might help us learn more about what's happening before it's too late."

As the last word leaves her lips, the meeting room door opens, and dozens of people begin to exit. Some stop for coffee and donuts, while others hurriedly pull out cigarettes as they rush toward the dusk-lit glass door at the end of the hall. The scared, shaken, young woman composes herself and follows a few others into the room, where she begins to break down chairs left from what appears to have been an Alcoholics Anonymous meeting.

The young woman arranges chairs and sorts pamphlets on the back table for various topics like divorce and couples counseling. She glances at the door, waiting for the elderly woman with stiff joints to arrive. The room has changed from an auditorium with a podium to an intimate circle of chairs for their meeting, Living with Stage IV Cancer.

A few minutes pass, and the one person the young woman wanted to talk with has participated in neither the breakdown nor setup of their meeting room. Instead, she remains in the hallway, staring at the TV screen, waiting for the news story that has been dominating the global population for nearly two weeks, the Fukushima nuclear meltdown.

A 9.0 Richter Scale earthquake in Tohoku, Japan, had set off a forty-five-foot tsunami that hit the Fukushima nuclear plant. The earthquake also damaged and shut down nuclear reactors, causing them to overheat. Once the tsunami made landfall, it created the worst natural disaster in Japanese history, which included a failure and a complete meltdown of the largest of Japan's fifty-five nuclear power plants.

Who could have known the Tohoku, Japan region would be at the top of the news cycle for a month in White County, Indiana? Hell, wherever people watched TV, had computers or smartphones, or even still read newspapers, this was the story the world was paying attention to.

"Hannah, we're ready for you anytime," Scott calls out.

She sighs. "Yeah. Please apologize to the group for me, and I'll be in after this segment. I think Fukushima will cause lots more people like us."

"That's for sure," says Scott. "I'll let them know you'll join us in a few minutes."

Meanwhile, on TV:

> An extraordinary case that is still being fought out for financial compensation in the courts sees its informal leader succumb to mesothelioma just months after

the shocking verdict of guilty of first-degree murder with time served so he could spend the remainder of his life in his own home, in the town he loved, Sawpit, Montana. Sawpit is nicknamed the City of Eagles. Today, Benjamin Brown's wings are soaring over his Montana home up to the heavens. Next up—they are calling them *Kesshitai*—or "suicide squads."

Hannah speaks softly to an empty hallway. "Thank you, Mr. Brown, and I am glad your suffering is over."

The first of a series of marketing advertisements fill the hallway with an ad for an alternative drug for those suffering from irritable bowel syndrome. Next, a class-action lawsuit against the maker of Kill-All herbicide. And then, to finish it off, back-to-back ads for a potato chip and a soft drink. TV News Anchor:

They are calling them *kesshitai*—or "suicide squads." Kesshitai translates into English as "a unit that expects to die." These suicide squads are not the career risk-takers and macho men commonly seen portrayed in movies. Their meeting resembles that of a senior-citizen neighborhood planning committee, an overwhelmingly older demographic. Over 250 members are attempting to address the worst meltdowns in nuclear history. One criterion for joining the group is that all persons must be sixty years or older.

TV cuts to video and translation:

Japanese Woman, sixty-five, one of the group's cofounders, says she has many personal reasons for wanting to work at the plant. "We're doing nothing special. I simply think I have to do something, and I can't allow only young people to do this."

Japanese Man, sixty-nine, says, "My generation, the old generation, promoted the nuclear plants. If we don't take responsibility, who will?"

Looking up at the screen, Hannah says out loud, "Good for you—way to take responsibility and action. We need more people to take action." Then she takes a deep breath, closes her eyes, and whispers to herself, "Stay positive and focused." She reaches for the meeting room door and opens it.

CHAPTER THREE

MICHAEL BENNETT AND DEMONS

SEPTEMBER 12, 2010:

Early, very early—in Denver, Colorado—a telephone rings. On the other end of the line, a man stands alone on a road in rural Montana. He speaks with an out-of-breath wheezy voice. "Jesus Christ, this has to be the slowest damn phone in the country." When you're sick, deathly sick, time seems to move slower, and each pause between rings feels like an eternity.

A raspy voice picks up on the fifth or sixth ring and says, "Hello, this is Michael Bennett. How can I assist with your legal needs?"

In mid-cough, the man on the side of the road, facing away from the phone, says, "Mornin', Mikey. I need you to do me a favor."

"Wait—what? Who is this? My name is Michael Bennett, and you might have the wrong number."

"Mikey, it's Ben! Ben Brown from Sawpit."

Now a bit irritated, Michael says, "What time is it? Why in the hell are you calling me before sunrise on a Saturday."

Ben interrupts. "I need you to do me a favor, a huge favor. When explained, you'll understand why it's gotta be you."

With his body and brain synapses finally starting to function, Michael says, "Slow down for a second; let me wake up, for Christ's sake."

The sound of clanging empty bottles and cans rings loud and clear through the phone as Michael groans in what sounds like an attempt to stand up. He finally gets to his feet on the third attempt. Stretching, coughing, and farting his way to the bathroom with a chorus of sounds only an overweight, chronic smoker, and hungover, advanced-middle-aged man can make. Eventually, "Ah..."

Ben hears the sound of a man urinating for what seemed like minutes.

"Are you fucking through your morning meditation yet, or do you need to do some downward dog stretches first?"

"Okay, Ben, tell me what's going on. *Jesus*. . ."

"Are you awake, Mikey?"

"Yes, I'm awake. And quit calling me Mikey—I'm not a teenager anymore."

"This is serious. I need you to hear and understand what I am about to tell you. Are you awake? And you'll always be Mikey to me, no matter how many fancy degrees or grey hairs you got."

"Yes—fuck yes. I'm awake. What's going on?"

"I killed old man Shadwick last night."

"What! Say that again."

In a surprisingly calm voice, Ben says it very slowly and deliberately: "I–killed–Carl–Shadwick."

"Holy Shit! Are you serious? The same Carl Shadwick from Vermolite Mining Company?"

"The one and only shithead Shadwick," Ben says proudly.

The reality of the situation is now settling in, and Ben can hear Michael clambering around what he can only assume is a shithole by the sounds he heard when Michael stood up the first time.

Now, a bit more alert and anxious, Michael replies: "Before you say anything else, let me clear my schedule and get up there to see what the hell you got yourself into. Don't talk to anyone else about it."

After a frantic weekend of rescheduling clients and court dates, Michael Bennett, Attorney at Law—Denver, Colorado, pulls out of his driveway heading north to Sawpit, Montana, at 6:00 a.m. on Monday. He is no longer a young man on any level. His hairline is thinner, his waistline is wider, his eyes need a change in prescription every few years for his glasses, and his back can no longer handle the eleven-hundred-mile, fifteen-hour drive from Denver (if driving fast) to his hometown of Sawpit in one straight shot. Now in his sixties, the last decade had taken a large toll not only on his physical health but his mental health as well.

* * * *

Michael and Nicole divorced when their youngest was a junior at Denver University. Both had massive amounts of trauma from growing up in

Sawpit. Watching multiple family members suffer from the same fate has a way of sticking with a person, and mesothelioma had touched both Nicole and Michael at the deepest level.

Mesothelioma is a horrible disease and cancer that affects the lining tissue of major organs. The lungs seem to be the favorite target, causing difficulty breathing, chest pain, difficulty swallowing, severe pain caused by pressure on the nerves and spinal cord, and pleural effusion, which is the build-up of excess fluid between the layers of the pleura outside the lungs (a.k.a., fluid on the lungs).

Having to sit helplessly by while their families had to go through this living hell before either one of them turned eighteen years old, they both wanted out of Sawpit and to never come back, if possible. For years, this connection of shared misery drove Nicole and Michael in their professional careers while ensuring they lived long enough for their children. Long enough so their kids would not have the same excruciating experiences they both endured watching their loved ones struggle to breathe and deteriorate before their eyes.

Life is stolen little bits at a time until there is nothing left. Unconsciously, everyone knows this to be the truth, but it is never discussed outside the periodic moment of anger.

Michael's last, long, biannual visit to Sawpit was during his mom's final year alive—2002. Since the divorce, Michael's drinking and prescription drug use had increased to the point of a daily lifestyle. For decades, Michael would plan to visit his parents and friends who were still living in his hometown; he had a routine to prepare himself for the emotional visit. By mentally and emotionally shutting down, it took weeks to get into the correct headspace to make the trip. It would take another week or two to decompress whenever he returned. When that phone rang two days ago, and he agreed to meet with Ben in Sawpit, there was no time for the routine to shut down.

* * * *

As Michael merges onto Interstate 25, the trip to Sawpit becomes real. No matter how hard he tries or how loud he turns up the music to sing along, flashes of his childhood, sick and dying relatives, and his last visit to his mom flood his mind. *Hey, Mom, do you want to go to the store with me?* He had watched and could almost hear the calculations in her head since she had become imprisoned by her dependency on how much time the oxygen tanks, Burns #1 and Allen #2, could last. Michael's mom loved to laugh, so she named her oxygen tanks after the 1950s comedy show stars, George Burns and Gracie Allen. Burns and Allen were good memories that made her smile, instead of the harsh reality that cancer was slowly taking away her ability to breathe.

"Hey, Mom, do you want to go to the store with me?"

Calculations start: If the flow on Allen (oxygen tank #2) doesn't need adjusting. Let's see. Five minutes to the car. Walking from the truck to the store takes about five minutes unless there are no handicap spaces. Then it could be a ten-minute walk up that graded parking lot and heavier breathing. Split the difference. Seven and a half minutes. Twenty minutes walking around the cool-level aisles, and then the walk back to the car. By that time, I will be exhausted. What is today? Tuesday. Martha likes to shop on Tuesdays. If we meet up at the store that will be another ten minutes.

Michael is standing there waiting for an answer and sees his mom about to speak: "Do we got gas in the truck?"

He answers yes.

Calculations resume: Good—no stop at the gas station. Ten-minute walk back out to the truck, and then ten minutes back home, and another five back into the house. Shit—did I add the trip to the store?

She finally gives Michael the answer: "I better not. Burns is empty, and we're already running close to Allen until the next fill-up. Do you remember that day I felt so good in the park? We used up lots of my breaths that day, but it was worth it." *In a wheezy, crackling, coughing, laughing voice, she says,* "Better using them up feeling good than to extend feeling bad. Right?"

Michael replies, "You sure? I'm only here for another few days."

"Yeah, it's not a good idea. If you see Martha, please say hello and send her my love. Maybe next Tuesday we'll meet up."

Michael's mother died within a couple of months of his last visit.

Finding himself on autopilot after shaking his head out of this memory, Michael notices he has driven fifteen miles and doesn't remember any of it. He tells himself, "Concentrate, damn it." Within a few minutes, his mind drifts back to high school and Nicole.

* * * *

Nicole's father, Tony Hamilton, was one of the unlucky victims. His cancer spread through his body so fast, and it seemed everywhere. The rapid weight loss created a barrel of ribs while, at the same time, his tumors and inflamed organs were bulging into abnormal shapes. Mr. Hamilton was not the toughest man in town, but he was never known as a complainer. His wails of agony at night seemed to be worse since the neighborhood was quiet, and their neighbors were all home to hear. No matter how many pain meds were given, it did not help.

Nicole and Mikey were friends for as long as either of them can remember. On those nights when the pain was so unbearable, Nicole would go out her bedroom window and across the backyard to Mikey's house and bedroom window. He would be waiting for her; they would stay up all night talking about how they were leaving after high school and never coming back. By the time Mr. Hamilton was in his last months, Mikey had had almost two years of processing the awful death of his Grandpa Nick, his mother's father. The seemingly unbreakable bond between Nicole and Mikey was forged during those times.

Although miserable, Mr. Hamilton's experience was not uncommon. The fluid buildup and tumors pushing on vital organs naturally caused their decline in function until the day came when those organs stopped working altogether. The ambulance rides, emergency rooms, long days and nights sitting in intensive care units holding hands and trying to pretend everyone in the room did not know the outcome. These chunks of time of consciousness are reminiscing about the good times.

Times when the town of Sawpit meant good jobs, good living, and all the dreams still to come. Accidentally, within the storytelling, one by one, a name would be mentioned for someone who was no longer. Soon, those good times and dreams slowly turned into nightmares lived out. It was hard growing up in a town that was slowly dying off.

The most frustrating part is that there was no other version of how life could be for far too many people. All mining and timber towns have similar stories, so much so that nobody stops to ask why so many families stay and watch loved ones die off one by one. It seems like this was how it had always been and would always be.

Both Mikey and Nicole made promises to each other: No matter what, if either of them got cancer and it was spreading, they would help end the misery of the other. They had experienced too much and had known too many people suffering from no relief and nothing left to live for other than not to die.

* * * *

Michael approaches the Wyoming border in his 2000 Mercedes Benz-M-Class (known as Jerry) with the Grateful Dead playing on maximum volume, trying to get his mind anywhere except on his childhood and Sawpit. Jerry is still good enough; it was the last big purchase made as a couple before Nicole filed for divorce. Emotionally, Michael can't bring himself to cut that string.

With Fort Collins now in his rearview mirror, he starts seeing signs for Cheyenne, Wyoming. A tightness in his gut and chest begins to happen; Colorado has become his security blanket. Passing over into Wyoming, Michael swerves onto the side of the road. Instantly, a dust cloud engulfs Jerry, as he pours himself out of the car with hands on his knees, completely nauseous. With the Dead's "Mississippi Half Step" blasting, Michael walks further away from Jerry, and the music seems to sing into the wind and through the dust.

The idea of making it to Billings or—if he pushed it—Missoula, was no longer within his thought process. Mind racing, he thinks: *Is this a heart attack? Settle down and breathe.*

In an open conversation with himself, pacing back and forth on the side of the road: "What time is it? Seven-thirty. Shit! I've only driven ninety freaking minutes. How am I going to do this? Settle down, big guy, get yourself to Cheyenne—drink some coffee and eat breakfast."

After a few minutes of convincing himself that he isn't having a heart attack, Michael feels his heartbeat slow down. Exhausted, he slams the door just as "Truckin'" starts playing. Gazing up through the skylight, Michael takes a deep breath and says, this is going to be one long, strange trip.

CHAPTER FOUR

MEETING IN WHITE COUNTY, INDIANA

MARCH 21, 2011:

As she opens the door, Hannah hears laughter, wheezing, and coughing simultaneously. Seven people are arranged in a tight circle, sitting on uncomfortable fold-out chairs. The circle is so small that their feet are almost touching. Hannah says, "What's so funny? What did I miss?"

Scott replies in a laughing voice, "The chronicles of *HaleKaka'la*."

Hannah asks, "Is it worth repeating?"

"Nah. It blew up like a balloon as I addressed the board of the IDA (Indiana Department of Agriculture) the other day. Everyone on the panel watched this bulge develop right before their eyes, and I don't think they heard anything I said. We did get them to agree to bring the bill to the committee."

"Well, I see we have a new face in our group tonight. Welcome. My name is Hannah, and I am the unofficial leader of this group, not because of anything other than I started it and am willing to do much of the legwork of signing papers and scheduling the room. When starting this group, it was just a safe place for those of us going through Stage IV diagnosis and treatments. A place where we can talk about everyday worries, demands, obstacles, the strain on relationships—and sometimes, we need freedom to blow off some steam without judgment.

"That is what we started, going on eight years now, but we've turned it into so much more. A place that doesn't shy away from talking about integrative approaches, the resilience of bending but not breaking. And the last three are our big ones: building community, healing our physical and emotional wounds, and working towards justice."

Looking at the young woman, Hannah asks, "Do you mind sharing your name?"

Despite sitting so close, the young woman's reply is so soft—her voice cracked in fear—that her name is barely heard by the group. "Ashley—my name is Ashley."

"It is customary for me to hug our new members in their first meeting," Hannah explains. "You won't know when, but it is going to happen. Is that OK with you?" Ashley nods, looking down at her feet.

"Well, Ashley, we are all sorry to meet you in this group, but if you take away one thing from here tonight, you now have a support system in place, and your family members just grew by six. Let's all introduce ourselves to Ashley. Scott, can you start?"

After a few minutes of introducing each member, someone asks if they could take a break and stretch. Hannah agrees. "Why not? Let's take a few minutes."

Ashley remains seated, watching the others grunt and groan to their feet. Hannah approaches her and asks if she would like that hug now. Ashley's eyes tear up as she stands and wraps her arms around Hannah as she says, yes, please. The hug is that of a mother trying to ease her child's fears. "It's all very scary, but you're not alone; we are here for you now."

Ashley begins to sob, so much so that the others in the group exit to the hallway to give her some privacy. Hannah, with a very soothing soft voice, asks, "Do you have anyone that helps you at home?"

Unable to speak, Ashley shakes her head, her face buried in Hannah's shoulder. Hannah begins to stroke her hair with one hand while squeezing tighter with her other arm wrapped around Ashley. "We are here to help you in whatever way possible. It's natural to be scared and healthy to cry. Go ahead and let it out. It's just you and me right now." The sobbing gets more intense.

Eventually, Ashley releases her arms and apologizes as she wipes the tears from her face. "Thank you. I'm so sorry."

Hannah grabs some tissues, which she hands to Ashley to blow her nose and wipe the tears away. Once again, in a calm, motherly voice, she says "Oh dear, there is nothing to be sorry about."

"This is the first time I've cried since being diagnosed."

Hannah brings her in for another hug. "When did you find out?"

This time, Ashley hugs with her cheek pressed up against Hannah's chest so she can talk. The comfort of being held without making eye contact is exactly what she needs at this moment. She replies, "A few days ago." The conversation starts to flow more easily.

"Do you live with family or anyone?"

"Yes. My husband and I moved here within the last year."

"What about your husband? How is he handling everything?"

Ashley's body starts to shake—not enough for her to notice but enough for Hannah to feel. "He's not good; he's had a rough life and lots of problems. Don't get me wrong, he's a great man, and he loves me. He treats me good, but he has lots of demons. He says the best way to keep those demons quiet is to keep them to himself."

Hannah now regrips her arms around Ashley. "I see. Yes, life is harder on some, and many times, it's so hard it can't be spoken out loud for fear of losing control. Can I ask you his name?"

"Josh—Joshua Bush. He grew up in West Virginia. He comes from generations of coal workers."

The door opens, and the remainder of the group comes back in and returns to their seats. Ashley wipes her face dry, and Hannah lightens the mood to get the meeting going. "Ashley wanted me to ask the group: 'What the hell is a HaleKaka'la, and how does it blow up like a balloon?'"

Laughter echoes through the large room, and Scott tells Ashley his story. "Well, Ashley, as I mentioned earlier, my diagnosis is colon cancer that has made it into my liver. Part of the protocol was surgically removing the tumor from my liver and a good chunk of my colon. And if stuff goes in, it must come out somewhere. So they created an ileostomy, which is a little slit in my small intestine. A little piece is sown outside of my body."

Scott begins to lift his shirt, and unanimously, the group yells *nooo!* with hands up in stop motion and shaking their heads. "*We don't want to see that thing ever again!*" Ashley cracks a smile.

Scott continues. "Well, that's how I go to the bathroom. It oozes twenty-four hours a day into what I call my Bag-O-Shit. It needs to be emptied a couple of times a day. Like everyone else, my digestion releases gas into the bag. As I said, it works twenty-four hours a day, and there is no turning it on or off. So, to answer your question, HaleKaka'la is the name I gave my ileostomy the first time I saw it work. We were in the hospital after the surgery. It was quite a sight. My digestion was starting to turn back on, and it takes a couple of days with these types of surgeries.

Your gut kind of shuts down out of shock or something. Anyway, the ostomy nurse showed up to teach us how to change the ostomy bag. There was an empty bag on my side that I hadn't even looked at because it was the one thing that bugged me most about all of the side effects of treatments. Losing hair, changing taste buds, sensitivity to cold, nausea, etc. It's just part of the deal. We all have that one thing that bugs us—like losing our hair for many people. My hair was so thin already it didn't bother me at all."

"Just get to the point," says someone in the group.

"Okay, okay, the name HaleKaka'la comes from the first time my ile-ostomy worked. The nurse came in to show us how to change the bag properly. While the bag was off, a huge cramp came on suddenly, and then an eruption of liquid waste shot out of it. One spurt after another. It was gross and hilarious at the same time. Later that day, I named it after the volcano on Maui with a little twist of reality; instead of Haleakala, which erupts lava, my ostomy is called HaleKaka'la, as in *kaka* or *poop*.

"Now for the balloon answer: Sometimes gas fills the bag faster than it can be released. When this happens, it gets like a balloon. The other day, I spoke to the state agriculture board about a bill we are trying to get introduced, and my balloon kept getting bigger and bigger, making a huge bulge in my shirt. I don't think anyone on the board knows my sit-uation. So they were all a bit confused and probably scared that I would explode all over the room. They just agreed to our proposal and asked me to leave so they could get to their other items on the agenda. That's the story for this week. I call it the chronicles of HaleKaka'la, since it seems like every week an adventure is associated with my Bag-O-Shit." By the time Scott finishes his explanation, Ashley's demeanor is more relaxed, even prone to a few giggles.

The meeting continues, and they all share what is going on in their lives. Most talk about the pain and stress of dealing with all the doctor appointments. One needs help with their health insurance since their net-work doesn't have the necessary equipment to perform a procedure, and it would cost over $25,000 out of pocket to get it done in Indianapolis. Hannah volunteers to research how to get around this recurring problem.

Hannah is a retired librarian in year eight of living with stage-IV breast cancer. Competent and an absolute dynamo at research, she has learned how to navigate a dysfunctional healthcare system. She is not only the unofficial leader of the group, she is the rock and nucleus who holds everything and everyone together. Hannah organizes therapy sessions and exercises that help cancer patients and their loved ones cope with all the stresses and unknowns. She always seems to know what to say and when to say it—when to listen, when to pull a person aside, and how to balance the roller coaster of emotions each meeting brings on. Accepting this role, the one aspect she doesn't excel at is sharing her own story.

As the meeting ends, everyone held hands, and Hannah prays for inspiration and hope.

Hannah continues, "Our cancer diagnosis doesn't define who we are and does not devalue what our life means. It gives us the ability to see the beauty of life, the gift of appreciating the things that go unnoticed, and eventually, the ability to shed ones ego to the point of knowing when to let go.

"Everyone, have a great night—and see you next time. Ashley, can I talk to you before you leave?"

With a glance and a nod of her head while she is saying goodbye to her new family members, Ashley agrees. The chairs are all put onto the racks, and the room is ready for whoever needs it next. Ashley and Hannah are the last two remaining.

Hannah thanks Ashley for attending the meeting and asks, "Do you think you will continue with our little group?"

"I think so. There are so many questions I didn't get to ask, and so much I need to know. Everyone here seems nice and has so much more experience with everything."

"It comes with the territory; it's a steep learning curve. Listen, I would love to invite you and your husband to dinner. It will be just me; my husband passed away a few years ago, and I'm by myself. You won't need to talk about your diagnosis or anything serious. I'm just an old woman wanting to welcome a new couple to our community and have the luxury of hearing about life outside our county for a change."

"That sounds nice. Josh would like to eat someone else's cooking for a change. Thanks to Josh's demons, we don't get out too often."

"I'll keep the conversation light, and please steer me away from any subject that might upset him. Let's say in a couple of days, Saturday at six p.m.?

At the end of the hallway, bundling up to head outside into cold and snowy conditions, Hannah hands Ashley a piece of paper. "Here's my address and phone number. Drive carefully; it's icy out there."

"Thanks for everything, and we'll see you in a couple of days." Ashley gives Hannah another hug and heads out into the cold.

CHAPTER FIVE

MICHAEL BENNETT AND BEN BROWN MEET

SEPTEMBER 15, 2010—1:30 P.M.:

Michael Bennett pulls into the Lincoln County, Montana, Sheriff's Office within seventy-two hours of receiving Ben Brown's phone call early Saturday morning. He puts "Jerry" into park, turns off the ignition, and looks at himself in the rearview mirror. *Jesus Christ, I look like hell. I've aged five years in the last three days. Ben, this better be worth it.* He puts in eye drops, gulps the last of his cold coffee, rinses with mouthwash, spits it into the coffee cup, and attempts to brush back the remaining hair on the front side of his aging hairline. He looks in the rearview mirror and says, "And they're off; Bennett is out of the gates." It's part of his routine when he starts any new case, especially one in which he is in no way, shape, or form fit to represent his client.

The afternoon before, Michael had received a phone call from the Lincoln County Jail: "Hey Mikey, I turned myself in and need to be picked up."

"You did *what*? I thought I told you not to talk to anyone."

"Why?"

"*Why would you fucking turn yourself in!?*" Michael screams as he drives seventy-five miles-per on the highway.

Ben interrupts him with an out-of-breath voice. "Would you like for me to answer those questions, or are they rhetorical? I'm good with the Sheriff's office here. I know almost everyone who works for Sheriff Patterson—Chuck. I'm saving them and the county lots of time and money. Also, I wanted to show my friend Chuck is a good guy—good enough for a person to come in on his own to turn himself in."

"Fucking Christ, please let me handle the law side of this relationship, will ya?"

With a rasping laugh that sounds like from a lifetime smoker, "Sure, sure, you're the boss."

"I'll be there by early afternoon tomorrow. Do not speak to anyone else until I get there, and stop calling me Mikey!"

Since that phone call, Michael "Mikey" Bennett has been having an ongoing conversation with himself, trying to figure out how to begin, once he sees Ben. But he has no more time to figure it out. He opens Jerry's door and gets out. He walks up the path to the front door, trying to use every ounce of coolness and confidence his aging body can muster. He opens the door, ready to meet the receptionist, start his spiel on why he must see his client ASAP, and try to get the arraignment moved up. Instead, he sees two old men sitting on the bench; one wears a cowboy hat, and the other sits with his hat on his knee and an oxygen tank. Michael squints as he enters the fluorescent, light-soaked lobby. Whenever he removes his driving glasses, it takes a few minutes for his eyesight to adjust and see clearly. "Ben? Is that you?"

"I know I look like shit, but you don't even recognize me?" Ben replies.

Looking confused, Michael asks, "What the hell are you doing in the lobby?"

The man in the cowboy hat looks up. "Howdy, I'm Chuck Patterson. We got Ben here a quick arraignment and he posted bail."

Michael's look switches from confused to absolutely blown away. "*What!* Ben, is this true? Did you represent yourself for your own arraignment? Didn't the judge warn you not to?"

For each question, Ben has the same answer: "Yep."

"Please tell me what your plea was, since I don't have a fucking clue about what is going on here."

"Not guilty."

"Whew! Do you know who the prosecuting attorney and judge are? I need to check in with them—get some paperwork—do the meet-and-greet of lawyers visiting a new area."

Calmly and confidently, Ben says, "Alaetra Anderson's the judge. She's an old acquaintance, and I'm not sure who the prosecutor is since the district attorney sent in someone from the office. The district attorney is Champ Sanders from Sawpit. I think you know him from high school. He was maybe a couple of years ahead of you. His younger sister went to school with Arthur and me."

Unsure of what to think, Michael asks Sheriff Patterson if Ben is free to go. The Sheriff answers, "He's all yours. Good luck. Ben has the tentative court date, but we all suspect that'll change with gathering evidence and all. He can't leave the state without permission, and there is absolutely no flying out of the country. Ben, you agreed to turn in your passport, right?"

"Yep, thanks for everything, Chuck. I'll get it to you within a couple of days."

Michael hugs Ben and whispers in his ear. "This is absolutely fucking twilight zone . . ."

After stops at the courthouse and the district attorney's office, Ben says, "Shit, you must be hungry. I know I am, and you've been the one running around all day while I just sat in this fine automobile."

"Yeah, that thought crossed my mind. It's been a crazy few days. I've only had stale coffee, cigarettes, gas station junk food, and these bad boys." He shakes a prescription bottle.

Ben grabs the bottle and reads the label. "What's bupropion? Some kind of upper?"

"*Whoa!* Jesus, you're quick for an old, withered bastard. It's a type of antidepressant—and yes, it's an upper."

"Why would a successful lawyer who got out of Sawpit and who has a family be depressed? You got the world by the tail."

"Oh, I don't know; watching your brother, parents, and countless relatives and friends waste away in front of your eyes and die has a way with the psyche. Nicole and the girls are still my family, but we no longer live together. Nicole and I divorced, and that was the final straw. As usual, when it was too late, I finally went for some counseling that Nicole, for years, was trying to get me into. When Nicole filed for divorce, I just shut down and was in a bad place."

Ben sits in the passenger seat, nodding while Michael tells this story. Ben chimes in, "Yep, Sawpit did a number on all of us. My antidepressants are the forest and river. "Hang on—it's coming up." Kootenai Kafé, also known as "the Double K," is now in view.

Irritated by the lack of sleep, Michael snaps, "Yeah, I know.

Remember, I grew up here too." The Double K has been here for their entire lives. Several different owners have remodeled the inside in small ways, but the menu has generally stayed the same, and it has always kept its name. As they walk in the door, a waitress says, "Afternoon, Ben, we didn't see you this morning." On a typical day, Ben's first stop of the morning is to pick up a cup of coffee and talk about local goings on with employees and regulars. But today was no typical day. The waitress adds, "Hope everything is alright."

Calm as can be, Ben Brown smiles, rolling his oxygen tank behind him and pointing over his shoulder at Michael. "Had to meet Mikey, here, this morning. He came up from Denver to help me out with something. He's an old friend from Sawpit."

"Sit wherever you like, and your regular booth is open. And welcome home to you, Mikey."

With a smile, he politely corrects her. "I haven't been Mikey for about forty years now. It's Michael these days. And yes, it's nice to see the Kafé is still here, and it's good to meet you."

Ben walks toward "his" booth, as comfortable in this restaurant as in his own home. "Okay, thanks, Maddie. We'll grab a couple of menus on our way. I'll take my usual cup of coffee and some buttered sourdough toast." He asks Michael if he needs to wash up and if he knows where the bathroom is.

"I know where it is, and yes, I need to take a leak and wash my hands." When Michael gets back and scoots into the bench seat, a glass of water, menu, and place setting are waiting for him.

Ben says, "It was this booth that my dad, Grandpa Jack, Carl Shadwick, and me sat in after my first buck. It was before Grandpa Jack had moved out to the ranch and he still lived in Sawpit. Shadwick offered to buy me a new rifle. I remember the day but not much more after getting the buck into the truck's bed and Shadwick telling me about the birthday gift he was going to get me. I do remember both my dad and grandpa being upset with Shadwick.

"Wait, that's not entirely true. I remember the blood. This slow drip of blood was coming off the corner of the bed. I do remember that like it was yesterday. It's almost like a scene from a movie or something in my head. The image pops in at random times without any reason at all. Hell, Mikey, you just solved one case already. The origins of that memory.

Despite it flashing in my mind, I could never pinpoint where it came from."

Maddie comes back to the table with coffee and sourdough toast for Ben and asks Mikey what he would like. Not having had a chance to look at the menu, he takes an educated guess and asks, "Is rainbow trout on the menu?"

"It sure is."

"I'll take two of those, one for now—and if you can make one to go for me, that would be great. Does it come with rice or potatoes, or anything?" Maddie, with a smile, says it can be anything he'd like; it's usually served with brown rice and steamed vegetables.

"That sounds perfect. As I said, I'll take two, one for now and one to go. Thanks."

Mikey and Ben drive out of the parking lot of the Double K towards the town of Eureka, and after a few minutes, they pass a driveway with police tape across the entrance. Ben looks down the driveway and says, "That's my Grandpa Jack's old place. And that's where I took care of shithead Shadwick. The police tape is the sheriff's office investigating the incident."

"Jeez, you say that so easily. What the hell happened?"

Ben fiddles with his oxygen flow as he looks out the window. "Yeah, we'll get to that part once we get to my place. It's just a few more miles. You'll see the sign for Brown Expeditions, and that's it. Turn down the driveway for a minute or so and drive slowly. The dust this time of year is bad."

Michael pulls his Mercedes into Ben's driveway and slowly heads up to the home. Fish out of water is the only way to describe Jerry on this property. Although orderly, the property has an antique tractor, an old truck, an archery target, a chicken coop and run, and a barn/shop that appears to be on its way to dilapidation from the outside. However, once inside, it's obvious to Michael that Ben has put a ton of time and energy into this amazing workshop.

Ben sees Michael looking at the structure and says, "It ain't much to look at from the outside, but once you get inside, her real beauty comes out."

"Where is your house?"

Ben snorts. "House? Who said anything about a house? What I have is a *home*. Some might call it a glorified camper setup—everything a person needs—a place to eat and sleep while keeping the weather off your head. And nobody can beat my view from my front porch. I always have four-legged family members—that's them barking now. I need to go let them out and pet them for a few minutes." Pointing toward the barn, Ben says, "The beer is in the fridge, and I'll be right back out."

Both men are stretching, and Michael can hear the dogs barking in the distance. Michael asks as he approaches the barn. "Can I look around inside?"

"Mi Casa es Su Casa," Ben answers, walking away.

Michael swings the door open and pauses in amazement. Inside, he finds a bandsaw, a power planer, a router table, and a large workbench, surrounded by an impressive array of tools on shelves. The clean dirt floor is crowded with both finished and unfinished wooden furniture. He thinks, this person does everything with forethought—a person who takes his time to do the job right. He hears Ben enter the barn and asks, "Where did you learn woodworking?"

"Grandpa Jack taught me about timber, woodworking, and joints. Did you grab the beers?

I'll fill you in on Carl Shadwick's last few days after we catch up for a bit." Ben sits down, pops open a beer and updates Michael on Lincoln County.

CHAPTER SIX

DINNER, JOSH, AND COFFEE SHOP

SATURDAY, MARCH 23, 2011:

"Turn on the headlights, honey," Ashley tells Josh.

Focused on the blue-tinted snowy road at dusk, Josh replies, "Are you sure this isn't going to be all cancer talk where we're all supposed to be crying and making promises? Ashley, you know I'm in this for the long haul and will do whatever is needed. I simply don't like talking about it, especially with strangers.

"Hannah isn't like that, and she promised this would be a relaxing dinner—just welcoming us to the community. You're going to like her. There's something very calming but also very fiery about her."

Nervously talking out loud to no one in particular, Josh says: "So, what's for dinner? Am I dressed all right? I took a shower and shaved. What more can I do?" Should we have brought some wine or beer or something?"

Ashley laughs. "Relax honey, this isn't an interview or a court-martial." As soon as the words leave her mouth, she regrets it. "I didn't mean that. I just meant it didn't need to be taken seriously."

Josh's focus on the road intensifies, and he says softly but angrily, "I know what you meant. Don't worry about it; I won't embarrass you." "I know you won't, Josh—we'll get to eat some food we didn't have to make and meet someone new." Josh turns the volume up, and Johnny Cash sings his hit song, "Hey Porter."

Ashley turns off the radio and says excitedly while pointing, "Here it is—that's the house."

They pull up to a little yellow house with pruned rose bushes around the perimeter and several well-spaced fruit trees that look ready to come out of dormancy if winter ever ends. Smoke rises from the chimney and fills the air with the soothing smell of burning wood. What can only be the kitchen window is steamed up, and the flicker of candles is just visible through the foggy glass.

Josh gets out of the very used but still reliable all-wheel-drive SUV and tries to brush out any noticeable wrinkles on his shirt. He licks his hand and plasters down his "Superman cowlick," as Ashley calls it. A short, round, grey-haired woman waves from the doorway. Hannah yells to her guests: "You made it right on time—dinner just got out of the oven. I hope you both like lasagna!"

As they approach the door, Josh says, "Sorry, we didn't bring anything—we didn't want to bring something you wouldn't like."

Hannah laughs as she touched his arm. "Don't worry, you're my guests. I should be the one concerned about serving something you'll enjoy. Did you find the place okay?"

Ashley is bursting with excitement: "What type of roses do you have? Are those fruit trees? I love preserving fruits to taste summer all year long! What's that song about Grandma putting summer into jars?"

Josh laughs. "You'll have to excuse Ashley. She gets really excited about the little things."

"That's a wonderful quality! I feel the same way—blooming flowers and singing birds excite me too."

Josh chuckles: "Great—then will we have *The Sound of Music* here tonight?"

"Maybe," Ashley and Hannah say in unison.

Josh teases, "I didn't bring my lederhosen tonight, so I'll sit my part out. Better for everybody—nobody forced to hear me sing—and I avoid embarrassment." A light laugh is shared, and everyone realizes the remark could apply to them all.

Hannah notices the change in the woman she met just two days ago. Ashley is now happy and confident, with no trace of fear. She thinks, what changed? Was it the circumstances, the people, or was it Josh? Are these two soulmates who found each other at the right moment? She sees her breath in the cold air and says, "Look at us—standing here in the cold, letting the warmth escape. Come on in.

"Yes, those are all types of roses and fruit trees. Years ago, we collaborated with my neighbor, Scott, when we planted to cross-pollinate and share the bounty of our combined orchard. You've met Scott already at the meeting. He's my neighbor. Oops. . ." She motions a zipper across her lips. "I broke my promise. It won't happen again."

"Ashley, Josh—do either of you drink wine or alcohol? If not, we also have juice, water, tea, and coffee available. We'll need to let the lasagna cool for twenty minutes to avoid burning our mouths. I hope you enjoy Caesar salad and garlic bread!"

Ashley looks at Josh and says, "That sounds perfect."

Josh nods as he notices a picture of Hannah's husband. "Who is this?"

"That's Bob. We were married for over fifty years. He passed away a few years ago from Parkinson's at eighty-five. He lived a wonderful seventy-five years and then had a decade of decline before passing." Ashley and Josh offer their condolences. Hannah continues: "He had been a truck driver for several decades, and while he enjoyed being on the road, his true passion was flowers. As odd as it may seem, he adored flowers. He took the time to plant and care for each of the rose bushes around the house. Every plant, tree, and flower you see was like a child to him."

"Did he have any brothers or sisters?" asks Ashley.

"Oh yes, they were a very close family."

Ashley adds, "How about you? Do you have any brothers or sisters?"

"Yes, I have two sisters, but we live all over the place. We mostly talk on the phone these days; traveling became too difficult when we hit our eighties."

Surveying Hannah's collection of framed photos, Josh notices there are none with children and asks, "Do you have children?" Ashley glances at him in disapproval out of the corner of her eye.

Hannah, now busy at the kitchen counter pouring some wine into glasses, says, "No. We tried, but—" The phone rings, and Hannah excuses herself to answer it.

"Hello. This is her. Oh yes, Mr. Bennett. Thanks for getting back to me. I would like to talk with you at length about Mr. Brown and the entire situation, but I'm about to sit down and have dinner with guests. May I call you back?

"Tuesday at noon—Denver/ Central time—will be 1:00 p.m. for me. I got it. I look forward to speaking with you. Thanks again for calling back. Yes. Thank you, good night."

Hannah shifts back to being a host having friends over: "So, what's new and exciting with you two in Monticello or White County? It's a small town, but it has lots of good people. Lots of—pardon my French— assholes as well, but for the most part, people try to take care of each other around here. There are only two things you don't talk about in White County: If you're not Christian and if you don't support Fulcircle Company. At this point, it's a company town where they control virtually everything, except me and a few other rebels who expose the company's history and what it actually stands for."

Ashley responds, "Luckily, we are Christian, so that isn't a problem, but we aren't big fans of Fulcircle. My father was a soybean farmer who took the science of Fulcircle as seriously as the New Testament. He was a one hundred-percent believer that Fulcircle would end world hunger."

"Oh, I'm sorry. Hopefully, I didn't offend you. I have some personal history with the company that we don't need to discuss."

Josh interrupts Ashley as she starts telling Hannah why no offense was taken: "Let's just try to make it through this evening as light as possible and enjoy great food and good company."

"Here, here," says Hannah.

As they sit down at the table, Josh says, "Canned Goods."

Hannah and Ashley look sideways at Josh: "Canned Goods?"

"When we first got here, you were trying to remember that song's name." It's Greg Brown's "Canned Goods."

Ashley claps her hands and points at Josh. "That's it!"

* * * *

SUNDAY, MARCH 24, 2011—7:00 P.M.:

"Hello—is this Hannah?"

"Yes, this is Hannah. Is this Ashley?"

"Yeah, it's me. I wanted to call and thank you for dinner last night. I can't tell you the last time Josh and I had a night out that didn't involve worrying."

"It was my pleasure, and I enjoyed the company."

Ashley sighs. "I called for another reason—and I feel guilty for asking so much from you. You've been so nice, and you've already done more for us than you can imagine."

"Honey, don't you ever worry about calling me or asking for help.

Helping others, especially young people like you and Josh, keeps me going."

Just as at the cancer meeting, Ashley asks Hannah in a soft, crackly voice if they could meet for coffee or tea to discuss her circumstances.

"Of course, but with one condition: You stop getting quiet and passive when asking for anything from me again. I loved hearing your real voice and love for life last night, and that is the Ashley I want to talk with—whether it's about gardening or working our way through cancer. Is that a deal?"

"Yes, it's a deal. I feel so guilty for putting this burden on other people—"

Hannah interrupts, "And that starts now, okay? Let's meet at the Steaming Bean coffee shop on Main Street tomorrow. How's 2:00 p.m.?" Ashley agrees.

* * * *

MONDAY, MARCH 25, 2011—2:00 P.M.:

Hannah opens the door as someone behind the counter yells, "*Dirty double chai for Karen.*" Sipping elderberry tea, Ashley smiles and waves her over, and before Hannah can sit, pops up and hugs her.

"Now that's what I want to feel and see," says Hannah. After their hellos, Hannah excuses herself to order her drink, then returns to the table and looks deep into Ashley's eyes, holding her hands out. Ashley places her hands on Hannah's and looks directly into her eyes. Hannah says in a soft, compassionate voice, "Ashley, please tell me everything about your story. Today is your time to be number one and the center of attention. This time is yours, and I will sit here and listen."

Tears fill Ashley's eyes; a slight blink sends them streaming down her face. "I am so scared, and I don't know how to behave—cry, be angry, be tough, be submissive, be aggressive, or be whatever. *Shit!* We went from expecting a child to losing a child. Within a couple of weeks, I was diagnosed with ovarian cancer. We've been in shock—completely overwhelmed. That's when I went to the cancer meeting. We moved to Indiana last year from Jacksonville, North Carolina.

"Only Josh and I know about Jacksonville and his military discharge. Between the court case and all the pressure we were under, we figured that it was God's way of telling us it wasn't the right time to start a family. Once we got here, the stress of everything eased up. That's when we got pregnant. That was the other sign, which was that we'd moved to the right place. For whatever reason, God wanted us to live in Monticello, Indiana, as crazy as that sounds. There is something here for us. We thought it was to start a family. We still believe that the universe has something here for us. We just don't know what. When Josh returned from Iraq, our time in North Carolina was tough."

Hannah sips her tea and focuses on Ashley. "You don't have to share anything you're uncomfortable with. We're here to build trust." To lighten the mood, she adds, "Tell me about you and Josh. How did you meet? We talked about your wedding at dinner last night. It sounded wonderful, especially by the lake in northwest North Carolina surrounded by fall colors."

Ashley shares that she met Josh in North Carolina in 2000. "He was just out of high school and had finished basic training in Fayetteville, which was a couple of hours away—but he would visit me in Wilmington whenever he had the chance. Josh was part of the 525th Brigade and felt immense pride in serving his country, especially after 9/11. That was also when we got married. He believed serving was his destiny, as he was trained and ready to go when everything happened.

"Of course, when he got there in 2003, it wasn't what he had expected. I was a junior in college at the University of North Carolina-Wilmington." With a big smile on her face, she continues. "Growing up in rural Iowa, I wanted to live in a city near the ocean. I dated a little bit, but my roommates made my time in school so special. We all entered school the same year and lived together from our sophomore year. We had so much fun between school and being at the ocean; it was one adventure after another. Josh was so funny and just loved having a good time. We met at a party." Ashley looks up while trying to think. "God, whose party was that? I don't know, it's not important. Anyway, at that time, more than anything, he was just glad to be out of West Virginia and coal country. Not that there was anything wrong with earning a living with coal, but he knew there was much more for him in life than working in the dark and shooting pool and drinking beer with his friends. He didn't have much of a plan when his football dreams ended. The military was a decent option.

"They told him it would teach him life skills toward a career and allow him to go to college once he figured out what he wanted to do. Josh had just re-enlisted as MOS when we met, so he was still on active duty. As we became more serious, he would finish two years of active duty, and then his time in the reserves would be spent pursuing a degree. It turns out it wasn't Josh's destiny in Iraq. It was the beginning of his nightmare.

"Josh has bad PTSD from his tours in Iraq. We call it his *dark mistress*, and it makes him lash out with fits of rage. Luckily, the rage targets inanimate objects, not people, animals, or anything else. So, what began to teach him life skills ended with him having what seemed like a life with a dark mistress he had little control over.

"Do you remember Abu Ghraib and the waterboarding? Josh was part of all that and was dishonorably discharged when he started refusing the orders. He was at Abu Ghraib at first but then transferred to a different prison, where it all took place. He says the orders weren't from his commanding officer but from some civilian hired from Darkwater who had no authority over him. When he refused, they put him in military prison until he was dishonorably discharged. He was relieved but, at the same time, lost his sense of being a patriot and the honor of serving his country. I am the only person who keeps him from going into dark places. The drugs don't work, and he has so many triggers that keeping a job is a problem."

Hannah listens attentively to every word, nods, and offers her hand once again. Ashley begins to cry, grabs some napkins, and blows her nose. "I'm sorry..."

Hannah says nothing but squeezes her hand and gives her a look that says, *we had an agreement*. Ashley gathers herself, fights back the emotions, and her voice eventually strengthens: "I feel guilty that I'm one more thing Josh has to worry about. He is such a good man but has lost so much of himself. Life has become unbearable for him outside of our marriage. He always tells me that I am his entire reason for living. I trust him to do anything that will help me get through this cancer. He seriously would give his own life in a heartbeat if it meant my life would continue. I don't know—I don't know what to think about anything any longer.

"If I die, is it going to be painful? What happens? Does it just take over, or will it be drawn out? Is it worth getting chemo and radiation and doing the surgeries? If I only have a short time left, I want to do everything I love about life. God gave us this beautiful gift called Earth, and I want to experience as much as I can before it's time to go. Does this sound crazy—or I'm overreacting and not thinking rationally? I don't know. I just don't know what to think or what move to make because it might be stealing away life either by not extending it or, with little time left, being too sick to enjoy it."

Hannah squeezes her hand a bit tighter and looks directly into Ashley's eyes. Ashley asks, "Can you please talk for a bit and tell me what to do? I don't know. I just don't know." She looks down and tries to prevent another sobbing attack, as she did at the cancer meeting.

Hannah sighs and closes her eyes to focus before she speaks. "Ashley, you are not irrational at all, and if your head weren't spinning, I would be questioning whether you're taking this seriously enough. You've been dealt an incomprehensible situation and are being forced to make enormous decisions in a short period of time. It's not fair, but little about life is fair.

"None of us in our group know if we are going to be here next week or not. Stage IV cancer is a tightrope walk, and we can fall off at any time without notice. I don't know what will happen to you, and I understand that isn't the answer you're looking for, but if we are ever going to be honest with ourselves, it is now. This cannot be easy for Josh, but this is the time for you to be selfish and put your health before everything else. This doesn't mean Josh is ignored, and I will help you both navigate what is happening. I've been on both sides of a serious illness in a marriage. My husband's illness and death were both beautiful and traumatic. Beautiful in a way that brought us closer on a level we had never consciously been. "I think most couples who have lived a long life together would have appreciated the beginning and middle more if they knew what they did at the end. Not to sweat the small things and to acknowledge the respect and love they had for each other when life obstacles got in their way. With a partner that you respect and love by your side, getting through tough times is so much nicer. Not easier, but nicer. Very few things about life are easy.

"I'm telling you all this not because Bob and I had a perfect marriage. We didn't, but we were each the perfect piece that completed the other. I have no regrets about sharing my life with him, and if he were here today, he'd say the same thing. I'm telling you all this because it is the truth. A truth that gets lost in the shuffle of all the chaos of living day to day and dealing with the rollercoaster ride we call life. When you go home from here and see Josh, try to see him as you did when you first started dating and there was no cancer or PTSD. He is the goofy guy you fell in love with, and you're the enthusiastic girl who can have fun everywhere you go.

"Ashley, what you've gone through recently doesn't make sense. Nobody deserves to lose a pregnancy and be given a terminal illness diagnosis within a period of just a few days. Especially a young, vibrant soul such as yourself. But that is what life is: a series of events all connected through you. Some are amazing, and some are downright shitty. You are handling everything as well as a person can. I'm sure this isn't what you wanted to hear today, but it is the best advice I can give you. Please promise to try what I mentioned—leave all your stress behind and enjoy your moments together now. It is not possible to do this every day, but on a day that there are no appointments, please try."

Ashley sits up straight with a face that looks determined. "I promise to try."

CHAPTER SEVEN

GRANDPA JACK, ARTHUR, AND BEN'S DEPOSITION

SEPTEMBER 15, 2010—9:30 P.M.:

The scent of beer dominates the air as Michael holds a newly opened beer bottle away from his body (and Ben's handmade wooden chair). "These are some comfortable-ass chairs, Ben. Do you earn a living making furniture or something?"

"Earn a living—shit. I try to earn just enough to pay my property taxes. All these out-of-staters wanting to come to play out their childhood dreams are pushing out all of us who actually lived those dreams. Not too bright, outsiders going into these small towns that are hanging on by a thread. The only locals still around are either too old to start a new life, or they're young and deceived by the promise of starting a family. But the outsiders don't see those as red flags."

Nodding, Michael understands both sides of that equation. He keeps the other side to himself, knowing it bears no fruit in their situation. He continues to survey the shop and gulp beer. "I'm no carpenter, but where do you finish all your work? I wouldn't think you could do that with a dirt floor."

"At my Grandpa Jack's place. He has the whole setup; mine looks like a beginner's workshop compared to his. He converted his entire barn into a workshop over the decades and finally finished it in the last few years of his life. Understanding what he had early enough, he wanted to do what these outsiders were coming to do—live out a childhood dream of hunting, fishing, building his own wood home—creating beautiful furniture, art, gunstocks—you name it. If something could be made from wood, he could make it. It was like he had a true calling to a past lifetime; maybe he was a tree or something.

"He used to talk to the timber before any cut or tool touched it—always rubbing his hands along every piece, soothing it and thanking it. It didn't matter if people were in the room or not. Almost everything he made, he felled himself and did every stage of milling, aging, and working the wood. Just imagine my Grandpa Jack talking to a piece of wood as if it were an infant. When I was little, it seemed funny to me. But tellya the truth, I've been doing it myself for years now."

Michael chimes in. "I remember your grandpa being a nice guy with not much of a temper. It doesn't seem too far-fetched."

Michael is aware that most men living in Sawpit during that time were veterans of foreign wars, working jobs that only required a high school diploma (even though many didn't have one). They went from operating million-dollar equipment, leading soldiers into life-and-death situations, and serving a higher purpose to the menial work of the mines. The community struggled with shell shock, PTSD, heavy drinking, and violent outbursts. Michael's father was one of those veterans who never missed work but often escaped to a shack in the woods for days at a time when his past became too much to bear, which was his way of coping.

Ben laughs at Michael's comment about Grandpa Jack. "For the most part, it's true—he got along with everyone, and I've seen him get super pissed only once. I don't know how old I was, but it had to be a few years after he had bought that property. I think they got it in 1958 or 1959—it was part of the inheritance when my mom passed away a few years ago. At the moment, I was signing and initialing paperwork, not paying too much attention to any of the details. Anyway, it's one of the first memories I have outside of my Grandma Mabel's funeral. She died when I was just a kid, and I'm pretty sure it had to do with the same old shit, cancer of some sort from Vermolite Mining Company. At that time, nobody was even thinking about it.

"But back to Grandpa Jack. You guessed it—he beat the shit out of Carl in front of a whole bunch of people. I don't remember why or what was said, but I'm sure it had to do with Carl saying something about how my grandpa was lucky because he was a free man who could find himself a young wife shortly after my Grandma Mabel died. I don't know if that was said, but knowing my grandpa and Carl, it must have been something along those lines. Looking down with a grin, Ben shakes his head. "Grandpa Jack was in WWII."

"Yeah, I know; almost all those guys went."

Ben looks up and straight into Michael's eyes with a mixture of pain, pride, and intensity. "NO! My Grandpa Jack was *in* WWII. He was part of the Army special forces that eventually turned into the Green Berets. Have you ever heard of the name William Yarborough? He was this badass generational military guy who came up with loads of ideas for getting behind enemy lines with specially trained forces. Grandpa Jack was in one of his first groups of guys trained for these missions. In 1942, he and Yarborough's group, and I don't know how many others, Grandpa Jack were trained extensively in hand-to-hand combat and survival skills. Not the pretend stuff he learned and we learned as kids—but real-life warfare type shit. I think they recruited eager young fellas who came from places where survival, quick thinking, and respect for authority were needed. He only spoke of a couple of missions to me once I returned from Vietnam. My grandpa eagerly jumped at the chance when he was pulled aside one day; it was a pay increase, and he had a growing family to feed. He won the Purple Heart and the Silver Star."

On his fourth beer, Michael leans forward while listening to this storyteller talk about his mentor, Grandpa Jack. Ben clearly admires the man who educated him while teaching him life skills and, more importantly, how to think—not what to think, and how to be a decent man.

Sitting there listening and soaking it all in, Michael finds himself somewhat jealous of Ben. He notices the same deep love and respect as Ben speaks of his dad, John-J.; his mom, Pat; and his aunt and uncle. Michael's parents were good, honest people, and he loved them deeply, and they loved him in return. But the entire Brown family seem to stand out—as though they had life figured out. While they didn't lead perfect lives, they managed to live perfectly within the imperfections. They possessed a kind of knowledge, a secret that seemed to be ingrained in their very being, helping them navigate the chaotic human world while remaining in harmony with the natural one. Michael had met other individuals who appeared to have uncovered this "secret," but the Browns were the only family across multiple generations whom he felt had tapped into that deep connection and unique sense of understanding.

Ben takes a few sips of beer and a few moments to catch his breath. Ben continues. "Well, he was much more than just another soldier, and the horrific things he did and saw made him into a much more peaceful human being. That was why he urged me not to go to Vietnam or join the military. He told me, 'Don't ever give your body to the government unless it is an absolute emergency. Governments have positive aspects, but they often lack a conscience in matters of war." This may explain how such an immoral action is achieved by those willing to be the most merciless.

"When I was in Vietnam, his words rang in my head constantly. That is why, when I got back, I knew two things: I needed to be near my Grandpa Jack, and I needed to take on a job that would allow me to live with dignity but would not hurt anyone."

Michael usually likes to get his clients talking to get a feel for whether they are trustworthy and who they are as people. On this occasion, he is more caught up in the story than normal, because he knew Jack Brown.

It's just after 10:00 p.m. when Ben opens his third or fourth beer and asks Michael if he is ready to hear what happened. Michael thinks for a few seconds and says, "No, let's wait until morning. I know you and I have never been close friends, but you were always like a younger brother to me since you looked after and were so close with Arthur. I want you to know how much everyone in our family appreciated it."

Hearing this, Ben takes his dirty hat off and wipes his face from his forehead to his scruffy chin. "Arthur, goddamn Arthur. . ." He stands up, walks to a cabinet, and opens the door to the top shelves. When he turns around, he's got a bottle of Irish Whiskey in his hands and says in a calm, almost sad voice, "No, I think we need to talk about it right now. I can tell you everything, however many times you need to hear it. Do you have a recorder? If not, that's okay. I videotaped most of everything except when I had to get new tapes. Like I said on the phone, it wasn't quick. I took my time, and Carl Shadwick might have had eighty-odd years of life not caring about others, but in his last day or two, he felt the pain of all those he affected over his lifetime."

Suddenly, Michael feels afraid. He knows he has nothing to be fearful of, but here he is, on a remote, heavily wooded property in a workshop with a man who has just admitted to what sounds like a gruesome murder only days ago. Michael has always thought of murder as being temporarily insane. So either he was wrong, or Ben Brown is permanently insane. He was hoping for the former. "Are you sure? It has been a helluva long week for both of us. I'm not sure if whiskey is a good thing right now or how much I'll remember in the morning. And yes, I do have a recorder."

"Okay then, hit record, and let's get this started. But first, we need to have a drink for Arthur. I promise I'll only drink one drink. Arthur was like a brother to me, and Jennifer was like a sister. I thought those two would end up getting married. If it wasn't for that goddamned cough and shitty lungs, I think it would have happened."

Ben disappears out the door without saying a word, and Michael gets more nervous, as darkness has filled the sky outside. He hasn't thought through where he would stay that night and doesn't think the glorified trailer would sleep two very comfortably. Mikey Bennett might have grown up in a Montana mining town, but Michael Bennett has grown accustomed to the city living of Denver for the last forty-plus years.

The door is kicked back open and Ben is holding two glasses, with his oxygen tank in tow. "If we toast your brother, it'll be done in clean glasses." The loud noise shakes Michael from his gripping fear and allows his racing mind to let go of his worst thoughts.

With generous pours into the two glasses, Ben hands one to Michael and raises his glass to the sky. Michael does the same. Ben says, "Arthur—I haven't talked with you in a while, but I got Mikey here with me, as you can see, and we are scheming to make your shortened life mean something more than just important to your friends and family. You were the best friend a guy could have, and we were robbed of growing old together. I miss ya and love ya till the day I die—and then I'll join ya."

Michael rarely talks about his brother Arthur's death unless it is for a legal case, and rarely talks about his childhood with anyone, so he is at a loss for words: "Arthur, we love you and will always carry you in our hearts."

Both men tilt their glasses back and sit back down. Ben pulls his tank beside him and checks the gauges to ensure he doesn't need a backup. That small act returns Michael's mind to his parents and how they ended their lives. *Life is stolen little bits at a time until there is nothing left.* That thought flashes back as he sits before another Vermolite Mining Company victim in Sawpit, Montana.

Michael pulls a recorder out of his bag and sets it down on a beautiful, small, handcrafted cherrywood table. With such mixed feelings running through him, Michael finds it difficult to stay focused. He notices the unusual grain pattern of the wood table and wants to ask what it means, what type of finish was used, how long it took from start to finish, anything and everything but what he was about to do. He has done these depositions hundreds of times but had never been so intimately familiar with or connected to the deponent. He puts his finger on the red button to start recording. "Are you ready?" he asks Ben.

"Yep" The one-word answer is punctuated by an approving nod.

Click. "Michael Bennett conducting the deposition of Benjamin Brown of Eureka, Montana, in the case of Carl Shadwick."

"Hell, Mikey! It doesn't need to be so official. I'm just going to tell you what happened."

"Ben, this is no light matter you got yourself into, and it does need to be official, since this is a legal case outside of the form of law I practice. I need to be able to recount everything for us to have a chance at putting forward the best case that doesn't land you in prison for the rest of your life."

Laughing once again, "Rest of my life? I'm a walking dead man; you know better than anybody. There is no case. I did it."

"Then why did you plead not guilty if you're going to admit to the murder?"

"Justice."

Confused, Michael asks, "How is admitting you murdered a man and spending the rest of your life in prison—*justice*?"

"Okay, okay . . . I didn't go to law school. Still, after checking out books at the library and heading over to Missoula to the University Law Library for the last twenty years, I concluded the only way to get justice for our families and the entire town of Sawpit is what we are going to be talking about over the next few weeks. I have the whole case planned out for you. Whether it is a good plan or not isn't important. You're not trained in this type of law and don't even have a license in Montana. I'm sure they'll grant you reciprocity, since we have a lifelong connection— even though they shouldn't, since you've never been to trial in a murder case. The judge will inform me of this, and I will waive my right to a public defender or any other different representation.

"Remember Chuck the sheriff, and Alaetra, who most likely will be our judge. They are only part of the plan through my lifelong good relationship with Chuck and Brown Expeditions, helping with Alaetra's husband, Chris. Also, because I don't have any criminal record. Hell, I don't even think I have a traffic violation. We'll get to this later, and we should probably erase this portion of your tape or put a new one in at this point."

Michael—a little buzzed from the many beers, a large glass of whiskey, and lack of sleep in the last three days—waves his arm in surrender. "Okay, you're the boss. But you'll have to hand the controls over to me at some point." He rewinds the tape to the beginning. "So let's hear this story." He presses the red button. "Let's try this again: Michael Bennett is conducting the deposition of Benjamin Brown of Eureka, Montana, in the Carl Shadwick case."

CHAPTER EIGHT

PRESENT AND PAST MERGE

WEDNESDAY, MARCH 28, 2011—1:00 P.M.:

As Michael Bennett's phone rings, Hannah's mind starts racing about what she is actually doing, why she is calling, what she will say, and what will happen.

"Hello, this is Michael Bennett; how can I assist with your legal needs?"

"Good afternoon, Mr. Bennett. This is Hannah Cassidy from Indiana. Thank you so much for taking my call."

"No problem. Please call me Michael. How can I help you?"

"Thanks again, Mr.—oops, Michael. I'm sure you're confused about why I'm calling you from a different state out of the blue."

"I can take a guess. Does it have to do with Benjamin Brown's passing? I've been getting lots of phone calls over the last few days about it, with callers wanting to know where the lawsuit is. If that—"

"No, no. It isn't about the lawsuit."

"Okay-y-y-y? What is it about then?"

"I just want to ask you a few questions about the original trial and case—mainly about Mr. Brown. If I remember correctly, you two were childhood friends."

"Well, that isn't exactly correct. Mr. Brown and my younger brother were best friends, and we were connected through my brother Arthur. May I ask if you are a reporter looking for a story?"

"I can assure you I am not a reporter of any kind. I'm a retired librarian living with metastatic breast cancer and temporarily the head of the Stage IV cancer group in our town."

"Okay-y-y-y? So how can I help you, Mrs. Cassidy?"

"I followed the story of Mr. Brown and Vermolite Mining Company, as I do with stories all over the country about small company towns with timber, mining, and so on. I wanted to get a bit more of the back story—nothing that would divulge client/ lawyer privilege or anything."

"Honestly, Mrs. Cassidy, you might want to talk to my ex-wife Nicole and her organization. Nicole Hamilton is her name now. I can give you her contact number if you like."

I'd like to get that information from you for other purposes, but right now I'd prefer to talk with you. And there's no need to be so formal. You can call me Hannah."

"Well, Hannah, what do you have in mind? I'm not sure what I can help you with. I feel there is something you want to ask, but you don't know how."

"Yes, Michael, there *is* something I want to ask, but I don't even know what it is yet. I guess—first, why would a lawyer from Colorado whose primary practice of law isn't criminal defense take a murder case in Montana?"

"Hannah, what you want to know will take much more than a lunchtime phone call. Answering that question alone has multiple moving parts and would take considerable time.

"If you're worried about my using whatever you say against you—trust me, that is not my intention at all."

"I can appreciate your reassurance, but this entire conversation raises red flags, which tells me to thank you for contacting me, Mrs. Cassidy. I hope you have a good day and find what you're looking for."

"Please don't say that. I know this all seems out of nowhere. Is there any possible way I might be able to meet with you off the record in person? It's important."

"Well, thank you for contacting me, Mrs. Cassidy. I hope you have a—"

Hannah yells into the phone– "*Is it possible to get the same verdict again?!*" She doesn't know where the words came from and who blurted them out as soon as she hears them out loud. Hannah Cassidy, an eighty-five-year-old retired librarian from Indiana, wants an answer to this question.

* * * *

APRIL 4, 2011—7:45 A.M., DENVER, COLORADO:

Standing at the arrival curb at Denver Airport waiting for her ride in the brisk spring air, Hannah is stuck in an internal debate. To others standing on the platform waiting for their rides, she looks like a calm, elderly woman waiting for her grown daughter or son to pick her up. But her mind is actually gripped by chaotic panic.

What are you doing? Searching for Justice.

Justice for who? For myself, Bob, Scott, Elizabeth, and all victims of these heinous crimes.

Why involve Michael Bennett? He is the only one who knows the answer to the legal question.

Who cares if it can be repeated?

Will I be viewed as a lunatic or martyr if it is pulled off? Are you actually thinking about going through with this insane plan. And who do you think you are?

A silver 2000 Mercedes Benz M-Class pulls up in front of her. The driver rolls down the passenger window and calls out, "Are you Hannah Cassidy?"

After a short drive, Michael pulls into the driveway of a modest house for a successful lawyer and turns off the car. "Well, this is where all the magic known as Michael Bennett happens. The spare room is ready for you tonight."

Very few words were spoken from the airport to Michael's home, and both were again wondering what they were doing. Hannah's internal debate is still looping itself, and Michael is unsure of what to expect. One thing is for sure—Michael's interest has been piqued since the words: *Is it possible to get the same verdict again?* were said on the phone.

"I put on coffee before I left to pick you up. Do you have anything to take care of before we start today? Do you have any special dietary needs? I have found that on days like today, time gets away from us."

Hannah shakes her head. "No, nothing special's needed. I might need to take a break occasionally, since sitting in one spot gets extremely uncomfortable. I'm sure your spare room will be just fine. Thank you again for taking the time to do this for me."

Michael snickers. "You should wait before you thank me. You haven't seen the inside yet."

The two walk into the nice, clean home, which has graduation pictures of two young women with what she can only assume are their families on the walls and a collage of photos of them hiking, skiing, on a lake, and otherwise enjoying life. An obvious proud parent and grandparent lives within these walls.

"Do you drink coffee or tea? How do you take it?" Michael calls from the kitchen.

Hannah puts her things in the bedroom and joins him in the kitchen. "I'll drink whatever you're offering. If you have it, I could take a tiny bit of honey and cinnamon in my coffee—if not, plain is fine with me. You have a lovely home. Are those your daughters and grandchildren in the pictures? They're beautiful."

As Michael searches for honey and cinnamon in the cupboard, Hannah sets up her yellow legal pad, pencils, sharpener, and a folder with articles, among other things.

Michael comes to the table with two cups of coffee and says, "Okay, just like we talked about, this is just between us, and this conversation doesn't leave this house. I did bend one rule to a higher promise made many years ago with my ex-wife, Nicole Hamilton, I mentioned her to you on the phone. She is the expert you want to talk with, but I told her you and I would speak, and I would determine whether she needs to be included or not. I hope that is alright with you. To get this out of the way now: Although I have not been retained as your lawyer, I have penciled in a consultation meeting if it were ever to go further than this table or this house. I am here giving you legal counsel—that is all."

Sipping her coffee, Hannah nods in approval. "I understand. So, let's start, since we only have a single day to talk. Can you tell me why and how you came to represent Mr. Brown?"

Michael responds calmly, obviously comfortable in one-on-one meetings talking about the law. "Let's start with you. What is your interest in this case and verdict that has caused you great expense and discomfort to fly from your home in Indiana to meet with me?"

Hannah takes a deep breath with her eyes closed, trying to focus her mind. She begins, "Fair enough. As you know, I am living with metastatic breast cancer and head up a group —a fellow Stage IV cancer family affected by an assortment of cancers. Almost to a tee, every single member of our cancer family has been exposed to an industrial toxin. I also belong to a few other similar groups."

After a couple of hours of listening to Hannah tell her story and multiple cups of coffee with only one bathroom break, Michael interrupts. "Hannah, I believe I now understand what you're asking. Nicole would be able to help your group(s), but we'll need my private folder and tapes with Ben for our conversation today. There is no simple, straightforward answer to your inquiry. I get a deep feeling that we can trust each other—but that said, this is strictly a consultation meeting, and I'm about to share it with you for nobody else to know. Only one other person, Nicole, knows this part of the Benjamin Brown story. What I am about to share with you is the summarized version of the whole story: why and how I represented Ben in his murder case."

Michael leaves the room for what Hannah can only assume is his home office. She thinks, *what am I doing? Every step is getting deeper. Am I considering this?*

Michael returns carrying a box marked "Ben Brown." He removes the lid and asks, "Do you want to see the notes or listen to the tapes first? There's a video, but I don't think there's a need for anyone to watch it ever again."

Hannah closes her eyes and takes a deep breath. "I want to get through as much as possible in the time we have. The main questions I have for you are: Why did Mr. Brown kill the retired general manager, and why did the jury ask for Mr. Brown's sentence to be considered time served? The news coverage didn't go into any detail, but the murder seemed like it was on the brutal side. So how can an innocent man in his eighties getting brutally murdered be ruled by a jury to be almost justified?"

With a fleeting smile, Michael looks directly into Hannah's eyes. "Okay, if you want to know the whole story, I will have to answer your first question of why and how I came to represent Mr. Brown. In that answer, you'll find how a jury of his peers asked for leniency toward such a brutal act. You'll also need to understand the history of our little Montana mining town and a company called Vermolite Mining Company."

"Yes, I remember that name from the news."

Michael continues. "First off, Carl Shadwick wasn't an innocent, harmless eighty-year-old man. What I'm going to tell you happened to everyone in town and many families in the region. Ben Brown's ties to the community were deep. Almost everyone on that jury had one or more experiences with mesothelioma in their family. It would be practically impossible to hold a trial in Lincoln County, Montana, and not encounter a juror's family member affected by this deadly disease. Knowing this, the prosecutors halfheartedly tried to move the trial to a different county."

Hannah takes notes in shorthand between small sips of coffee as Michael explains, "Vermiculite is a natural mineral, but ours was contaminated with tremolite asbestos. Sawpit, Montana, is known for an abundance of this heat-resistant natural mineral. It's located in the Rocky Mountains. Mining began in 1919, and my grandpa, like Ben's, worked there and eventually moved up in the company to drive haulers or take office jobs. Initially, the mines were operated by a different company, but in 1963, Vermolite Mining bought the operation and its workers.

"At this point, the town of Sawpit was booming, and by the late 1960s, like lots of kids our age, we were living the American Dream— fishing, hiking, forts, sports, and everything a kid could want. Do you know the saying that 'If something is too good to be true, it is?'

"We grew up in a nightmare, but we had no idea. That's what was happening to the people of Sawpit and even in the nearby town of Troy. It's not only associated with vermiculite. You name the mine and the resource being extracted, and I can tell you the health dangers that were kept from or entirely unknown to the workers.

"It's the same everywhere. That's what my ex-wife's organization is all about. This is also why I believe you want to talk with *her*. Communal Fund of the Rockies—*CFR*. The organization's focus is representing the stakeholders of these mining and timber towns, not the corporations, in a court of law. It's not about the money but about holding corporations accountable. In so many of these towns, the companies have a huge amount of power and own a majority of the businesses. This gives them a kind of shield that protects them against the people they are poisoning or, in lawyer terms, 'damaging.'

"Anyway, here's where it gets sick: When Vermolite Mining purchased the operation in 1963, it was known to them that where you find vermiculite, you also find asbestos. The asbestos found in Vermolite mines is Tremolite. The higher-ups of the industry knew there was a slew of known dangers associated with working in the mines and around those minerals in any capacity. But those hazards were kept under wraps from the public.

"Nicole fulfilled her sole purpose for starting CFR; she was in charge of the deposition of Carl Shadwick in 1988. Albeit professional, Nicole had the power to ask all the questions about that piece of sh__." Michael catches himself, grits his teeth, and shakes his head to get back into the moment of here and now. "Nicole could ask him all the questions she needed to be answered. Although very personal in this case, Nicole is one of the most thorough and competent lawyers regarding preparation. Her career and life goals were fulfilled that day. She came to the table with her A-game. When confronted by Nicole's strength, Carl Shadwick's sociopathic worldview collapsed and he outperformed himself, since he believed he was untouchable. Everything came together during that deposition.

"The tricky part is that no part of the lawsuit could be officially discussed while they were investigating it. So, all the workers heard rumors but wrote it off as just some environmental group causing problems. Vermolite Company would take care of it, and it wouldn't interfere with their jobs.

"Ben Brown's father, John-J, died in an accident just months before Vermolite Mining was forced to shut down the mine. They knew it was poisoning the miners, workers, and the entire town of Sawpit while this was going on, but they were going to keep it going until they were forced to stop.

"In towns like Sawpit, people who don't even work for the company are exposed to the fine particulates that coat the town daily. Vermiculite is used in attics, pavement and parks, as additives for garden soils—and covers trucks and cars, workers' clothes, hair, and lungs along with the asbestos. Residents of these communities suffer a much greater chance of mesothelioma. Vermiculite isn't the problem, it's the asbestos that comes along for the ride when used.

"During high school, I argued with my father about it many times. Noticing that many relatives and friends were experiencing similar symptoms was my only evidence. I distinctly remember my senior year, when Vermolite Company had its employees install insulation from asbestos-filled products in attics. I confronted my dad about this in front of everyone, and he let me have it. He was sincere in his position, and I bet most Vermolite employees would have supported his viewpoint.

"He told me then, and continued to say over the years, that there's always a risk working in mines, and miners understood this and took pride in the fact they were risking their lives to provide and improve the lives of their families. Being a kid during the depression, himself, my dad didn't remember times being so hard, not like other places in the country. That was because they had mountains, a tight community, and his dad had a job in the mines.

"Miners and loggers understand that their jobs are dangerous, but they also believe that the company and the town will care for their families if something happens. In fact, many workers even considered Vermolite Company to be a part of their family. Hell—my dad did until the day he died.

"What many people like my dad could not admit or even fathom is that Vermolite knew they were poisoning their entire workforce and their families. Sawpit was a company town, and all the workers and families went to Vermolite's hospital and doctors. When I was a kid, Doctor Smalls was the one everyone went to see. Only when people got so sick they needed specialist help would they be sent to the town's hospital, where Vermolite was the major shareholder. That great family member, Vermolite, would buy people's silence about their illnesses, or they would sue for breaking the employment contract. Every worker had to sign it, and few workers even read it. Even those who read it thought that no company in its right mind would allow its workers to work in unsafe conditions outside of the obvious risks of mining. Because without the workers, the mine shuts down. What they didn't know was that this exact thing was factored into the company's business model: the average time before symptoms would start to interfere with work performance and production.

"I want to add one more thing before you dive into the files and tapes. My younger brother, Arthur, passed away from mesothelioma in 1982, just two years after his diagnosis. The number of deaths in our family spanning three generations are in double digits due to this disease, including my parents and both grandfathers. Additionally, after Ben's father died, his family revealed that Ben's sister had passed away as a new born due to complications from asbestos exposure.

"Ben's father died in an accident at work. His injuries were so severe they had to transfer him to another hospital in Missoula. The Brown family heard the rumors just like everyone had in Sawpit. They also knew Carl Shadwick intimately, Ben's Grandpa Jack and Shadwick had worked together before their Vermolite days. Shadwick was always an office person educated in business, while Ben's grandpa had started in the mines right out of the military. They were polar opposites but somehow forged a friendship through the years. Knowing Carl Shadwick and hearing what the rumors were saying, plus considering their family history, they leaned towards believing the rumors over what Vermolite Mining Company and Carl Shadwick were saying publicly.

"Ben, who hated Shadwick and Vermolite the most, insisted that the family have an independent autopsy done by Saint Mary's, specifically looking for mesothelioma. Their doctors and hospital were not in the grips of Vermolite Mining Company and would have no reason to inform the company that the Browns wanted the Saint Mary's pathologist to perform the autopsy. Between the accident and the lawsuit, the autopsy flew under the radar. What that autopsy found was that John-J's lungs were filled with tumors, and he would have suffered the same fate as so many of his relatives and, eventually, his son Ben. The Brown family contacted a reporter from *The Chronicle, a Missoula local* newspaper and shared the findings of the autopsy along with the rumors of an investigation concerning the same disease, mesothelioma."

Once again, Carl Shadwick, the retired general manager, is anything but innocent. Tears run down Michael's face, but these memories and stories have been told and thought about so much that he can recount them without going into a rage. Despite saying "one last thing" again and again, for the next few hours Michael tells Hannah story after story of Sawpit, Ben, Arthur, both his father's and mother's deaths by mesothelioma, other loved ones, Vermolite Mining Company, and Carl Shadwick.

Hannah listens quietly while Michael Bennett pours his life out as they take a walk, and then at the kitchen table into the evening. Few people who know Michael Bennet in Colorado have heard much of what he tells Hannah that day. Connecting all the dots, Hannah identifies with everything she is hearing.

Michael is so engulfed in all Sawpit has endured that only when the light on the wall changes does he realize that the sun is going down.

Surprised, he says, "Holy Cow, I'm so sorry I took up so much of your time with my story. I guess I needed to tell someone other than Nicole. I'm sorry your only day here was wasted listening to it."

Without a word, Hannah stands up, and Michael follows suit purely out of reflex. She embraces him in a long hug, crying softly into his chest. "I'm so, . . . so sorry this happened to your entire town." Once their embrace ends, she says, "Thank you for sharing your story; it helps me more than you can imagine. You didn't waste my time; you gave me the information I was looking for."

Michael thanks Hannah, and they both wiped away tears. He grabs his cup of coffee and a book to read by the window while Hannah rummages through case files, scribbling notes and flipping pages. After a while, Michael hears a click and the sound of his own voice: "Let's try this again, Michael Bennett is conducting the deposition of Benjamin Brown of Eureka, Montana, in the Carl Shadwick case . . ."

Hannah starts listening to the deposition of Benjamin Brown but has to stop after thirty minutes; she takes no pleasure in hearing about the torture of this eighty-something-year-old man. She is in her eighties and is finding herself sympathizing with Carl Shadwick despite understanding that this man knowingly slowly murdered an entire town and lied about it.

Hannah now knows much more about the story of Ben Brown and Sawpit and realizes the answer to her question: How did the "timed served" recommendation come into being? At the same time, she reconfirms how much all industrial victims share similar stories. She looks up at the clock. It is 9:35 p.m. She stretches and says to nobody in particular, "It's time to call it a day."

Michael looks up from his book. "Are you getting the answers you wanted?"

"Sort of. It seemed so crazy to hear it from the outside. There were no special circumstances or any actions that would cause a mistrial. It was a shared experience by the jury, and they probably, at some point, thought about performing the same act. Well, not the same act—but killing Carl Shadwick themselves. So, what's different about Ben Brown? Why was he the one to do it, and why did he wait twenty years?"

"Hannah, to answer that question, a person would have to know the Brown family and understand Ben from childhood until his death. I've already told you about Ben's friendship with Arthur and about those who died in his family, but I didn't go into what made the Brown family different from many of the other families we grew up with.

"Ben was a man who lived his life with strict principles and convictions, much like his parents, grandparents, aunts, and uncles—to the point that it was a negative instead of a positive compared to how our society is set up. Right and wrong were different from legal and illegal. Ben was a product of generations of proud people who didn't have college degrees but were some of the most grounded and intelligent people in Sawpit. Hell, probably the most intelligent of anyone I have ever known.

"Each generation shared their history as an educational exercise rather than as a nostalgic stroll down memory lane, to the point that Ben never married; he could have but chose not to. He didn't want to have to share his traumas with another person and most definitely didn't want to have children who would experience the suffering in the world, especially the world he knew.

"One person, Linda, almost got him to go in for the family life, but ultimately, out of love for Linda, he ended the relationship. She never understood why until he killed Carl Shadwick. When the trial took place, Linda came to every court date. I think she thought it was to support Ben, but she really wanted the answer to why Ben ended the relationship without any apparent reason. I talked with Linda a few times in the final weeks of Ben's life and at his funeral. She understands now and loves him even more for it. Ben allowed her to find love and have a family without all his baggage. I reminded her, as well, that Ben couldn't have gone through with his plan if he had a family, and I am almost positive that was the biggest factor in his decision."

After a few moments of silence to allow everything Michael had just said to sink in, Hannah says, "So, you think Ben had this plan for a long time?"

"I know he did. I think it began at Arthur's funeral in 1982. You need to understand the friendship Arthur, Ben, and Jennifer had growing up. They were inseparable. The anger, confusion, and mourning were all piling up, but it was his best friend dying before he was thirty years old that pushed him to his breaking point. Arthur had so much of his childhood controlled by illness, and Vermolite's Dr. Smalls never honestly diagnosed him. Ben was just a few years removed from Vietnam, and on the night of Arthur's funeral and again during his trial, he told me some horror stories, which included his military family dying at the hands of greed and pursuit of power. Did you know Ben hadn't lived in Sawpit since he was eighteen?"

"I had no idea. All the stories on the news and in the papers always implied he still lived in Sawpit."

"The media is known for spinning stories to attract more viewers. Ben lived in Eureka, a town not far away from where the murder occurred—on his Grandpa Jack's property. Grandpa Jack passed away from mesothelioma and was also Ben's neighbor. After his grandfather's death, Ben inherited all the family properties, as he was the only surviving member. He could have sold the properties and lived a very comfortable life elsewhere, but Montana and Lincoln County were his home. There was no way that shithead Shadwick and Vermolite Mining Company were going to force him out of his own home.

"He lived a good life and was friends with everyone, which made his case even more interesting. Much of the county was on his side. For many years, he drove a truck for a timber company. Eventually, he started a fishing and river-guiding organization that primarily focused on providing therapy for Vietnam veterans. Although Brown Expeditions never made much money, he did well enough with his pension and owned all his properties outright. He was friends with the county sheriff and somewhat knew the judge presiding over his case. Interestingly, the prosecuting attorney was also from Sawpit and had attended the same high school. They didn't know each other personally but were familiar with each other's backgrounds. From the class of '64, Champ Sanders also served in Vietnam and later opposed US actions there. While not as vocal as Ben, he likely agreed with the sentiments expressed by Veterans for Peace. Champ aspired to a life in public service and knew he needed to keep his views private. During the trial, he and I had some good conversations over drinks.

"And then there's me, the hot-headed lawyer who hated Carl Shadwick and Vermolite as much as Ben did. Ben and I were more acquaintances than friends, as you probably know by now. The two big things that connected us more than anything were Arthur and Vermolite. To answer your questions, that's why I was Ben's lawyer, why I was granted reciprocity, and how we shaped our strategy and case. Our connection and Ben's lifelong relationships with those within the Lincoln County legal system gave us the leeway for Ben to tell his story with few interruptions. He explained to the jury and the media how he viewed his actions as justice and self-defense for all those Carl Shadwick and Vermolite Mining Company knowingly put through hell in order to make profits.

"So, now I am going to answer your questions directly. No, the same verdict and recommendation from the jury *cannot* be repeated. This entire case was unique in all the people involved: the judge, prosecutor, sheriff, jury, Nicole (who took Carl Shadwick's deposition), and me—Ben's lawyer."

Disappointed, Hannah virtually sags on hearing Michael's answer.

Michael continues. "That the answer is no—I do not think it can be repeated—is *lawyer* Michael Bennett's opinion. However, here is my personal opinion, as it comes from a friend and confidant: I think now is the time for more people to get justice by following Ben Brown's actions. I don't know what you're thinking of doing. The one piece of advice I will give is that justice has to be done in connection with the crime committed. Now, Ben went overboard, and even I, who hated Carl Shadwick, could not—cannot—condone what he did. But at the same time, I don't oppose what he did either.

"We've both had a long day, and neither of us will be sleeping very well tonight. Would you like some melatonin? I have some chewable 10 mg. tablets."

"Yes, I would love one and possibly a glass of wine if you have any."

Michael apologizes. "Sorry, no wine. Had I known, I would have picked some up.

"That was the unintended benefit of Ben's trial, which has been similar for so many others: We got some closure. I know Nicole feels the same way. Before Ben's trial, I buried myself in three things. My girls, my career, and increasingly self-medicating with alcohol and prescription drugs when our girls left for college. It was the main cause of my divorce. Nicole could accept being second fiddle to our daughters and even my career, but there was no way she was going to be second fiddle to drugs and alcohol.

"I was at a low point when Ben called me one Saturday morning at the crack of dawn and gave me a second chance at appreciating life. Since his trial, all of our long conversations about our lives, learning about his motives and intentions, his convictions and principles, and most of all, his love for life gave me the strength to tackle my addictions and trauma head-on. It's been months since I've had a drink or taken a prescription drug."

Hannah hugs Michael again and says, "I'm so proud of you." She feels his arms squeeze a little tighter. "Now, let's get me that melatonin and go to bed. To paraphrase Edward Abbey—since I think it is appropriate for the circumstances: Let us get 'the sleep of the just, the just plain satisfied.'"

Michael laughs, gets Hannah her tablet, and goes to bed.

* * *

APRIL 5, 2011—7:00 A.M.:

Morning dew sweat trickles down the steamy kitchen window while Michael is making coffee and listening to the news on the radio with the volume turned down low. The results of a year-long government investigation into the largest environmental disaster in human history has been leaked to the press. On April 20, 2010, an explosion caused an oil drilling rig to sink, leading to the release of 210 million gallons of oil into the Gulf of Mexico. This devastating spill resulted in significant damage to the region's ecosystem. An investigation revealed that defective cement in the well was the primary cause of the disaster. Michael has the volume so low that he is crouched down with his face beside the radio and doesn't see Hannah walk into the kitchen.

"Good morning."

Michael bolts upright. "Whoa! Good morning, Hannah. I hope the radio didn't wake you up." Hannah laughs and says she has been awake for some time, thinking about yesterday.

In a somber tone, he says, "Me too. Would you like a cup?"

Minutes later, the sun begins to fill the room. Michael and Hannah sit at the kitchen table and attempt to finish their discussion from the day before over tea, coffee, and Greek yogurt with granola. Michael wonders whether Hannah has any other questions, or whether she has gotten her answers. Given her condition, he is surprised that she could have so much energy and mentions it to her.

Hannah lies, "I wish I knew. This is not normal for me."

Moving the conversation away from herself, Hannah responds to Michael's question. "Ben Brown's life and everything you shared yesterday clarified something for me. I was focused on the wrong outcome. Me being a good"—she uses air quotes on the word *good*—"law-abiding citizen, I was focused on the approval of the legal system and society." But really, I should have been focused on the approval of the victims of these corporate murderers.

"Let me tell you a secret to being diagnosed with a terminal disease: It forces many people to deal with their mortality and their true feelings about death. Well, I've concluded that heaven and hell are lived out right here in our earthly lives.

"There are some theories on universal energy, which scientists have shown makes up the universe. This energy is consciousness, and we return to it. When our bodies die, our souls will return to this energy source and be in awe of the presence of the Creator, or God. I believe that to be true, and that is why heaven, hell, and all of it are metaphors for how we live our lives, not the afterlife. While uncertain about what comes next, I know my life has been filled with compassion, love, and appreciation. I often tell new members of our group that living with Stage IV cancer is like walking a tightrope; we can fall off at any moment."

Michael nods as Hannah speaks, and when she says her last words, he says. "You know what? That's the beauty of being a grandparent. There's a sense of something much bigger than ourselves, and it is truly wonderful. I'm unsure if it's because I'm older and less focused on my career, or if it's simply because I've gained wisdom from the lessons I've learned throughout my life. But, without a doubt, this is the most content I have ever been.

"As I mentioned last night, that morning when Ben called set me on a journey I've been needing to take for a long time but was too afraid to begin. This journey was about all the trauma our town, friends, and family have experienced. Realizing that this trauma had dictated the direction of my life for so long was a profound discovery, even though it may seem obvious to anyone on the outside looking in.

"To a certain extent, I was lying to myself. I was so focused on trying to prevent others from going through similar experiences that I became blind to the power those events held over me. The impact was significant enough to lead me to argue with my dad, (whom I loved with all my heart), to choose law as my career, to marry Nicole, and to work with CFR. I became so immersed in my career that I missed out on many moments with my daughters, and ultimately, this resulted in the breakdown of my marriage with the woman I loved and respected deeply.

"That is a lot of power to have over someone's life. The longer I ignored it, the more pills and alcohol I consumed. The more I turned to substances, the scarier the journey appeared. It created a cycle that trapped me. Everything around me was hanging by a thread, and I didn't even realize it.

"From that morning when Ben called me, to having breakfast with you this morning, my second life has been given to me. I had many hard nights and days after going head-first into what Vermolite, Carl Shadwick, and the town of Sawpit meant to my life. But you know what? I've been in this space for a little while now and I get more comfortable with it every day."

With her hand on her chest, Hannah says, "I am so happy for you and your entire family. You asked if I had any other questions. I do have one, and it is a whopper." With her eyes closed, she takes a deep breath. "All those hours of your life, your wife Nicole's life, and the lives of her organization and all the others like you: Was it worth it? Do you really think it made a difference?"

Leaning back in his chair, Michael covers his face with his hands, trying to clear his mind in order to answer a question he had asked himself dozens of times throughout his life, always arriving at a different conclusion depending on the moment. Whenever he or CFR won a case against a company, it felt rewarding, and his answer to that question would be, "Yes." However, the initial high of being recognized in the legal system soon faded as they witnessed the corporate defendant—along with its executives, board of directors, and expensive lawyers—filing appeals that dragged the proceedings out. Everyone knew they were guilty, yet attempting to hold them accountable legally was nearly impossible. He thinks, the best our system can do is monetary fines. Those who established our system are aware of this, which is why it functions as so. While

Michael wrestles with these thoughts, he finally blurts out, "No, not really."

A shocked Hannah seizes this moment and asks quickly in a soft voice, "Why?"

Michael himself is a little shocked. He had only had these conversations previously with Nicole and Ben, two people he had known his entire life and with whom he had shared experiences.

He tries to avoid answering the question. "You don't want to hear what I have to say about this issue."

"I really do. Please, I'm wrestling with a huge decision right now, which is why I came all this way."

Michael looks at her sideways and repeats, this time with more emphasis: "*No, you really don't want to hear what I have to say about this issue*".

It is now almost 9:00 a.m., and they need to leave for the airport by 10:00 a.m. At this point, the two stare across the table at each other, and Hannah whispers, "Please."

Michael stands up. "I need another cup of coffee. Would you like more tea?"

She says, "No, thank you. But I really want to hear what you think about it."

As he stands looking out his kitchen window with both hands on the counter, trying to figure out the correct thing to do, she continues. "Listen, I'll share with you something that nobody else knows other than my oncologist. Let's put all of our cards on the table. I won't tell you about that big decision, but you can add two plus two.

"I know what you're going through right now. I'm having the same battle. I'll start by saying that my last oncology appointment went as poorly as possible. The only other time the news was this bad was during my second oncology visit—the reading of the scans and my staging. Everything looked like it was a so-called good breast cancer diagnosis, which meant it was very treatable.

"When Dr. Evans told me it had metastasized to my bones, and at my age many women choose to forgo the chemotherapy that attempts to get rid of the cancer. Instead, they try to slow its progress, while keeping the quality of life as high as possible for as long as possible. He told me it was up to me, but that he would recommend the palliative approach.

I was seventy-six years old at the time and was trying to take care of my husband, who had Parkinson's/Lewy Body disease and was heading into what became the last two years of his life. I was tired and worn out. Dr. Evans said he was concerned about my ability to handle a full-blown treatment, since my energy and most of my immune system were at such a low point. I agreed and chose to try to keep it under control. And for the most part, it has worked up until now.

"My last appointment was not long ago, and my scans were not good. I had a follow-up appointment to scan my brain. My cancer is everywhere, and I was told it'd be about a month or so before the pain would increase, and shortly after that—my life would be over. I have already arranged for hospice care when the time comes. I don't have too many days left, and I want one last attempt to make Earth a better place for future generations.

"You asked me about my energy. The truth is I'm taking a steroid medication that has the effect of what I can only imagine an upper gives a person. That's how I was able to fly to Denver, stay up all day asking questions, listen to your story, and have the energy to get up this morning to continue the conversation.

"So please, tell me what you really think about people trying to use our legal system to achieve justice. If you think the system works, then I'm content knowing that my life was spent using the correct strategy toward truth and justice. But, if you think the system is faulty, then I'll have no regrets about the path I'm contemplating to take in order to try and create lasting change. I have met and worked with amazing people my entire life, and it has always been fulfilling. But I want to know if all those hours and energy I spent actually contributed to the potential change of this immoral and dysfunctional system."

Still standing at the sink, gazing out the window, Michael says, "Okay, you'll hear what I really think on our way to the airport.

"You can have a shower if you'd like to have one, get your things together, and we can leave. That'll give me time to think about how I can clearly explain my position on this incredibly complex question within a twenty-minute drive.

"But first, can I have what I will tell people for the rest of my life is the best hug from one of the best people I have ever met?"

"Of course, you can have that hug." Michael turns around, and Hannah gives him the hug he needs to find his strength. When the embrace ends, she says, "Thank you. My opinion of you and your life's work is mutual. I wish our paths could have crossed sooner in life, but neither of us would have been ready for what this brief relationship requires. We were supposed to come together at this moment."

CHAPTER NINE

ASHLEY'S INFUSION

APRIL 7, 2011:

A mural of a barn-raising depicting life in rural Indiana in the 1880s stares back at Ashley, Josh, and Hannah as they wait for their names to be called. Sitting silently and staring at the mural, the three have different thoughts going through their heads.

Ashley is thinking about her blood work, CT scan, biopsies, and the different scenarios the tests will reveal.

Josh, with his head firmly in his hands, is thinking about how he is not going to let Ashley die and praying that the test results come back as a nonaggressive form of cancer. Then, thinking about his future without Ashley sets in. What would that look like? A battle between caring for his wife and a life without her fills his head. Another thought dominating the internal debate is feeling selfish and thinking about himself instead of his wife—*What type of person worries about themselves when their wife is fighting for her life? A piece of shit type of person. Stop being a piece of shit!*

Hannah appears to be staring calmly at the mural, but in reality, she cannot stop hearing the sixty-nine-year-old Japanese Kesshitai member's comment from just a couple of weeks earlier, and Michael's final opinion during her trip to Denver. Both are influencing and shaping her scheme that is to take place soon.

> *We're doing nothing special. I simply think I have to do something, and I can't allow young people to do this. My generation, the old generation, promoted the nuclear plants. If we don't take responsibility, who will?*

These words are so simple, but they perfectly encapsulate the wake-up call for the entire global population and the multiple climate crises occurring for all life on Earth in 2011. Here we are for Ashley, a young woman fighting for her life with advanced cancer appointments when she should be getting prenatal checkups. Hannah thinks, *For what? A few companies have billions of dollars in sales year after year when their products are known to cause chronic diseases. Michael is correct: We must use the system against itself. Ben Brown was correct in taking justice into his own hands and then owning up for his actions. That's more than any corporation has done for their known victims. For them, it is part of the cost of doing business.*

The oncology nurse comes out and tells Ashley they are ready to see her now. With Josh on one side and Hannah on the other, Ashley grabs a hand of both of them and asks, "Is it okay if they come in with me?"

"Of course, I'll find another chair once we get to the room," the nurse says.

Josh butts in. "Don't worry about it, I'll stand."

Dr. Evans, a tall, thin man, whose voice is usually jovial, walks into the room. Today, he has neither a smile on his face nor a jovial voice, and everybody can feel the bad news coming. He holds Ashley's file of reports and a laptop with her scans. In a serious voice, he says, "It's nice to see the whole team here again today." He nods toward Josh and Hannah before focusing on Ashley.

"What I have here is kind of typical for someone your age and overall health, so let's dive in. These reports are not the worst, but they're not good either. What we knew and spoke about already was that you have the most common type of ovarian cancer, epithelial ovarian carcinoma. Generally, this is a more manageable form of cancer, when it comes to a cancer diagnosis, but after running a few more tests with the biopsy, we have concluded that you have a subtype called serous carcinoma that is a bit more aggressive. But it responds better to treatment, so we have a mixed bag."

Dr. Evans opens his laptop and turns it so they can see the thumbnail file with the name Ashley Bush. He double-clicks it, and the CT scan video appears on the screen. What looks like a single image is actually a paused video of Ashley's entire CT scan. "Here's what concerns me," he continues. "This is your liver. Unless you've studied anatomy and physiology, it is complicated to understand. There are eight different functioning segments. We've chosen a single view so I can give you an overall assessment of what we're looking at. I'll offer a more detailed view at the end of the appointment if you like, but we'll need to go into my office, where we can look at multiple sectional views simultaneously, which means from the top, side, and bottom. Some patients like to see the more detailed view, while others don't want to see it at all. It's completely up to you."

Hannah has sat in on these appointments many times for herself and with others. She sits quietly, taking notes, but she sees the severity of Ashley's situation in the scan and, more importantly, in the tone of Dr. Evans' voice and bedside manner.

"Yes, we'd like to see them," both Ashley and Josh say at the same time.

"That sounds good, we'll do that, but let me give you the quick version now so you'll better understand what we are looking at later. If the cancer was contained in the ovary, the form you have would respond well to treatment, but the original PT scan showed some spots in your liver with several nodes enlarged. See these spots?" Dr. Evans says, pointing at the computer screen. "Those are most likely lesions or small tumors. That's why we asked you to come back and do another round of scans with CT and biopsy so we can see the extent while confirming what the previous tests showed. So my concern, after going over it with the surgeons who most likely will perform the surgery (they're in Indianapolis), is the location and size of the lesions in the liver.

"The science of oncology has come a long way over the last couple of decades. Unless it's an emergency, we like to do three rounds of dual chemotherapy of carboplatin and paclitaxel to shrink those lesions, or tumors, before surgically removing them. This way, we can conserve as much tissue as possible.

"After surgery, you'll continue with another three rounds of the same combo chemotherapy while we keep monitoring the tumor marker CA125. We'll be testing for tumor markers with every round of blood work. There is an alphabet soup of markers, but we will focus on CA125. It will be highlighted in your blood-panel paperwork. After surgery to remove the known tumor sites, we'll determine whether or not radiation will be needed. With your age and overall health, this might be a possibility.

"As I mentioned, this is a mixed bag, and once the surgery occurs, we will know exactly what we are looking at. It's difficult to tell exactly where the lesions are situated through imaging. What concerns me is whether they are located in places that could obstruct. So far, it doesn't seem there are any obstructions happening. Therefore, your symptoms are mild and your liver is functioning, but it doesn't take much pressure or growth of a tumor to wreak havoc.

"Are there any questions so far?"

Ashley asks timidly, "Looking at survival rates, mine isn't so good. It was like thirty-three percent or so. Is that correct?"

With his best, upbeat bedside manner, Dr. Evans replies, "Ashley, you need to understand statistics when it comes to cancer outcomes. I've seen people who caught their cancer in the early stage and looked completely healthy come in and struggle with the treatments and not survive. While others who are elderly and frail-looking with advanced cancer have complete responses, which means they're cancer-free within a year. There is another aspect of survival rates, which is important to consider, so listen carefully to what I'm about to say: "You need to understand that everyone with epithelial ovarian carcinoma is lumped into a staging category, whether you're thirty or ninety years old. Most cancer patients are on the older side with one or more chronic diseases such as diabetes or any number of conditions that come with age. These percentages are there for guidelines but aren't set in stone by any means.

"But to answer your question—yes, that is the five-year survival rate. Are there any other questions about what we've talked about today?" Dr. Evans surveys the room, and as usual, everyone has questions but doesn't know how or what to ask.

"Okay, let's go into my office and take a look at those sectional scans so you can get a better idea of what we're dealing with here." As they walk down the hallway to Dr. Evan's office, he says, "I looked at your scheduling, and it looks like you're going in this afternoon to get your port inserted. Is that correct?"

Josh speaks up. "Yeah, we met with the interventional radiologist's office already—I think that's what it was called—and they walked us through the procedure. They said it's a relatively simple outpatient procedure.

"Okay, good. And yes, it *is* an interventional radiologist who does that procedure, and it *is* relatively straightforward, and you'll be home before the sun goes down. Are there any other questions you'd like to ask? I'm here now and have the time."

In a shaky voice, Ashley speaks for them all. "We have a million questions you could answer, but this whole thing is one step at a time. I just need to worry about getting the port installed and making it to my first infusion. After that, we'll worry about side effects and make it to my next appointment. Thank you for being patient—and for being willing to answer our questions. Hannah could probably give us a ballpark answer to many of them."

Hannah speaks for the first time. "Ashley is right. All we should be concerned about are the things we can control, how we perceive our situation and circumstances. We've got to stay hydrated and eat immune-building foods to give our bodies the nutrients they'll need to recover and deal with what is in front of us."

Dr. Evans listens quietly and says, "Okay, we'll leave it here then. Have a successful and smooth procedure this afternoon, and we'll see you at your next appointment, which is . . ." he pauses while he looks through his file, "April 14th to follow up on your first infusion, which happens on Monday the 12th. And Hannah, can you hang back for a minute?"

Hannah is not surprised. "Of course." She turns to Ashley and Josh. "I'll meet you two in the lobby or in the car; I might need to visit the ladies room before leaving."

As they watch the couple walk out of the room, Hannah says, looking at her, "You would have no idea that she is having a faceoff with death."

Speaking frankly to Hannah, Dr. Evans says, "Surprisingly, things can change quickly in this business, and I'm not talking about Ashley."

Hannah turns and looks him in the eye. "Listen, Richard, I looked at my last scans and blood panels. It's no longer just in my bones, which means my body is no longer responding to treatments, and the cancer is on the move again. We've recycled through the treatments once already, and I've thought about this long and hard. I'm done. No more treatments. Let nature take its course. I've had a good run, and I can't thank you enough for indulging this old woman for these last eight years."

"I figured as much. Hospice contacted our office on the day of your meeting with their social worker. As you know all too well, just because you're entering hospice, it isn't time to throw in the towel just yet. Many people can get some of their best months and even years once they stop treatments. Can you contact our office for one last appointment so we can finalize everything."

"I will."

He responds with a half-joking, half-serious warning. "You better. Remember, I know where you live."

* * * *

APRIL 12, 2011:

The infusion nurse walks into the lobby and calls, Ashley Bush? Ashley squeezes both Josh's and Hannah's hands and whispers, "This is it." All three stand up to follow the nurse into the treatment room. Then Ashley stops. "Hannah, I appreciate everything you've done for us over the last weeks, including attending who knows how many appointments and helping us understand everything. But right now, Josh and I need to do this on our own."

"Of course, I'm here for both of you and will be here until you walk out in a couple of hours." Both Ashley and Josh mouth the words, *thank you*, as they turn to follow the nurse.

The previous week of workup tests and labs has found that the cancer had spread into Ashley's liver and continues to be aggressive. She is now aware that her ovaries, liver, and a series of nodes are affected. A second round of scans and biopsies have been ordered as well as blood tests, oncology appointments, specialist appointments, surgeon examinations, and simulation—which is getting tattoo marks on the body to perfectly align radiation treatments.

Throughout all this, Hannah was ready to be Ashley's advocate at each appointment and brought a calm, like an eye in the midst of a storm, during all the stress and fear. Both Ashley and Josh looked to Hannah as a grandmother figure—someone they can trust with their lives, as the whirlwind week of appointments had shown. The new relationship between Josh and Hannah was the most surprising outcome of everything. He had opened up to her more than he had toward any of the military psychologists and doctors he had seen about his fears and experiences. Not even Ashley knew the details surrounding Josh's experiences. They were just broad explanations of why he couldn't go into detail. What Hannah did understand more than ever was, in fact, just as Ashley mentioned at the coffee shop, Josh's entire life revolved around her. She also understood what she and Josh were talking about was a form of untrained therapy, and hopefully, it did not backfire by triggering so many dark memories.

After sitting and reading a book for a couple of hours, Hannah sees Ashley and Josh come out from the infusion station. Ashley's face is a shade of grey and looks wiped out. Josh looks deeply concerned. Hannah stands and says, "It looks like it was rough. Are you okay?"

Josh looks at Ashley and then looks back at Hannah. "It went alright, but there was pain."

"Pain?" says Hannah. "Should I go ask the nurses if there are any special instructions?"

Josh replies, "I'm going to walk her around a little bit, and the nurse will be out in a minute with instructions."

The nurse comes out with a bag full of pills, prescriptions, and the appointment summary and instructions. "Are you Hannah? I was told to speak with you, and you are up-to-date on Mrs. Bush's condition. There are medications for nausea, which you should have gone over with her oncologist last week. We numbered them in the order they should be used. Numbers one and two are used for prophylactic purposes, and three is only used if there is extreme nausea. Number three is a steroid-derived medication, so it has more severe side effects. The other pills are pain medications because Mrs. Bush indicated there was some internal pain as the infusion went on. Sometimes this happens to patients whose metastasis has moved into the liver. If the pain continues to increase, please don't hesitate to contact your oncologist, and if it becomes too severe, go to the emergency room."

Hannah asks if there is any reason for concern. "This was her first treatment. If yes, how concerned should we be?"

With an understanding look, the nurse says, "I was told you're living with metastatic breast cancer yourself. As you know, none of this is guaranteed. All we can do is follow the protocol and try our best to minimize the discomfort. Be sure to notify the oncologist if the pain increases or anything alarming happens. And of course, if it seems severe enough, go to the emergency room. I see Dr. Evans is her oncologist. He is a good one, and I'll update his office on everything Ashley experienced today. She'll get a call later today and tomorrow morning to see how she is doing."

Hannah thanks the nurse and heads out.

CHAPTER TEN

BEN BROWN'S FIRST BUCK

LINCOLN COUNTY, MONTANA, 1966:

"Yeah, I could use a cold one," Benjamin (Ben) Brown hears, with his mind still half asleep. His other senses begin to wake up. There is a wetness on his cheek and what seems to be a cold wall pressed against his face. More words begin to make sense, and the voices speaking those words are now apparent: Grandpa Jack and Dad (John Junior, a.k.a. John-J).

Grandpa Jack tells John-J to give Carl a quick flash of the headlights to let him know they're stopping as usual. Carl has been hunting with John-J and Grandpa Jack since John-J returned from serving his stint in the military in '58. Despite being John-J's age, Carl was Grandpa Jack's manager at the plant in town.

Grandpa Jack, sitting in the middle of the bench seat of the Chevy pick-up, says, "Hey Ben, it's time to get up and get something to eat. Are you awake?" Ben feels a not-so-gentle shake. "You up?" As Ben's eyes slowly open, a neon light comes into focus—Kootenai Kafé. "Damn, John-J, it seems a shame, with all that venison in the back, for us to stop and buy something to eat."

John-J chuckles that the venison won't be ready for at least a couple of weeks. This conversation is more out of tradition than meant to be funny. Whenever they hunt on Backsaw Ranch, they stop at the Double K, and Grandpa Jack says, "Damn, John-J, it seems a shame with all that venison to be buying something to eat."

John-J pulls into the parking lot, the truck squeaking and clunking with every imperfection of the ground. Three generations pile out of the 1959 Chevy Apache pickup, and Ben sees blood dripping from the bumper out of the corner of his eye in the passenger side rearview mirror just before opening the door. It's October, and nights are starting to get cold. All Ben's senses are coming alive. Seeing his breath in the air, he asks his dad, "What happens to the deer when we go inside?"

With a slight laugh, John-J says, "Well, son, if those deer decide to jump up and run back into the woods, more power to them." Ben laughs uncomfortably as his dad puts his arm around his shoulders and tells him, "You did good today, son. I'm proud of yuh. Gettin' your first buck and dressing him out can be more challenging than we think. I remember my first time. I was about your age. I had so many emotions running through me that I could barely stay in my skin. So much so that, just before squeezing the trigger on the most beautiful creature I ever saw in my life, I got sick. Yep, everything in my stomach came up. I tossed my cookies."

Ben and his dad laugh, and John-J continues. "I dropped the rifle and heaved. Your Grandpa Jack wasn't too happy."

"Because you missed your shot?" Ben asks.

"Nah—I dropped his cherry wood handled thirty-aught-six onto the ground. Your great-grandpa was a woodworker, and he and your Grandpa Jack made that stock from their cherry tree when your grandpa was a kid. Your grandpa thought that was what he would do with his life: work with wood and create beautiful things for people."

By now, Ben and John-J are sitting at a table waiting for Grandpa Jack and Carl. The waitress hands them a menu and brings glasses of water.

Ben asks, "What happened?"

"What happened to what?"

"Why didn't Grandpa work with wood? Why does he work at the plant?"

"Well, that's a long story that will have to wait for when you get a bit older. The simple answer is *me*. That's what happened. Just after your grandma and grandpa graduated high school, I was born. Your grandpa had a family of three and needed to find a job real quick. At eighteen years old, he took the best option available." John-J's voice and tone turned somber. Ben heard his dad add under his breath, "—apple doesn't fall far from the tree."

Carl and Grandpa Jack are talking and laughing loudly on their way to the table as Ben asks his dad, "What does that mean? Apple doesn't fall far—"

Grandpa Jack interrupts Ben accidentally mid-sentence as he sits down. "You probably've built up quite the appetite after the long day. Been up since four—hot chocolate and some jerky all you've eaten all day—and hiked damn near ten miles, if I had to take a guess."

"I guess so," Ben answers as he drinks his second glass of water and stares at the back of the truck, where he sees the blood dripping. The drips have now turned into a small pool of blood. The Double K is conveniently located between Backsaw Ranch and the Town of Sawpit, Montana, and has been their tradition since Grandpa Jack bought fifty acres with his promotion in 1959. Backsaw Ranch and the '59 Chevy Apache were what made Grandpa Jack's dream come true—to own some land and have a new truck. But by the sixties, the only thing missing was Ben's grandma, Mabel. She had passed away just a couple of years earlier due to a problem with her lungs. John-J and his siblings were all adults and had moved on with their lives. He was the only child who stayed in Sawpit. Back in 1959, Jack and Mabel had thought they had the rest of their lives to grow old together on their new fifty acres. With Jack's carpentry skills and no shortage of timber, they would build a home and workshop. Their dream was cut short when Mabel suddenly developed lung problems and died in 1963.

"So, what can I get you, fellas?" asks the waitress. "Lookin' at you, it's been a long day—and seein' the racks sticking out of your truck bed—it's been a good one."

Creepy and condescending, Carl says, "Well, look at you, honey. I've never seen you working here before. You must be just out of high school." Thinking to himself, *please be eighteen years old.*

The young waitress blushes. Grandpa Jack apologizes. "Sorry about that, young lady. Our friend here is from a city and lost his manners when getting a degree at some fancy college. We've been trying to remind him of them for years."

Carl interrupts, "Sorry honey, I didn't mean any harm. It is just the way I talk to pretty young things."

"It's okay," she lies in a low voice, not wanting to lose her tip or get in trouble with the manager.

Coming back from washing up, John-J sits down and feels the energy around the table—*what did I miss?* Looking at the waitress's red cheeks and posture, he knows immediately. *Did Carl stick his foot in his mouth again?* "Sorry about that, miss. Hey, Ben—why don't you get cleaned up? I'll order for you."

Once the orders are taken, the waitress is gone, and Ben is still washing up. Jack and John-J call out Carl simultaneously, "*What is wrong with you?!*" Jack persists, "You're married, expecting another kid, and talking to high-school girls that way. What if a middle-aged man speaks to Lisa that way when she gets to high school? Are you going to be alright with it? She's the same age as Ben, only a couple of years away. What is she—twelve years old now?"

Not even registering that Jack and John-J are upset, Carl muses about how she is "the perfect age to get'em. At that age, they still think of grown men as their fathers and they'll listen to whatever they say—easy to shape and mold to how you want 'em to be."

Jack and John-J are getting angrier by the second as Carl rambles on. "I got Elizabeth too late; she was a Junior in college. She—"

In a matter-of-fact tone, Jack interrupts Carl. "Shut your mouth. Ben is on his way back to the table, and I don't want him to hear this shit. It's times like these, Carl, that I'm not sure how you can be a friend of our family. It's like you don't care about anyone else."

Ben takes his seat and looks at each man, trying to figure out whether they're tired or angry. *They got a couple of bucks in the bed of the truck and we're about to eat dinner. What's there to be upset about?* Tired, he knows he will fall asleep within minutes of getting back on the road to Sawpit. Once again, he peeks out at the truck and sees another drip of blood fall into the increasing pool just below the right rear end of the tailgate.

Carl breaks the silence. He has an early surprise birthday present for Ben. "Your dad says you'll be turning thirteen on the eighteenth. What would you say to a new hunting rifle? Next week, we'll go to Jacob's and pick one out. How does that sound?"

Ben's eyes open wide in disbelief, and during the entire time they are eating their dinners, he continues to ask Mr. Shadwick if he really meant it. "What type should I get? Dad, Grandpa, did you hear what Mr. Shadwick will get me for my birthday? I can't wait to tell Mom!"

Grandpa asks John-J, "What will Pat think about all this?" There are not-so-happy faces between the two at the table.

The three men and Ben stand in the parking lot, saying their goodbyes.

No longer noticing the pool of blood on the ground, the almost-thirteen-year-old boy cannot get the rifle to stop flooding his mind.

"See you Monday, Carl. We'll bag and get 'em hung and let you know when they're ready for finishin'," Grandpa Jack says as they load into the Apache.

"Okay—thanks for the great day, guys. Congratulations, Ben. John-J, say hi to the misses for me."

John-J starts the truck and lets it warm up for a few moments. Nobody speaks—their guts are full, pushing through on a few hours of sleep. The headlights flash on and he pulls out of the parking lot and onto the road. He looks at his dad and says, "Is he asleep? I don't know about letting Carl buy him that rifle. He's getting worse. Everyone knows he's sleepin' with his newest young secretary. He doesn't even try to hide it. Does Betty not know?"

"She knows, all right—ain't too happy about it either." Grandpa Jack continues, "For a young man with a daughter and wife sweet as can be, I can't figure him out. He's got everything a man can ask for, and he acts like it doesn't even matter. But he's my boss—we've known each other for a few years—what can I do? He's pushin' for me to get out of the mines altogether and into an onsite office position. It can't come soon enough. I'm not sure if it's going down into that hole every day, or what. The cough never goes away, and it keeps getting worse."

John-J looks at his dad with concerned eyes and asks, "Have you seen the doctor about it?"

"A couple of times. They said this is typical aging of a person who works hard, especially in the mines with all that dust. You know Tony, right? Tony Hamilton. He's a few years younger than I am but has some of the same issues. Fred has been at it longer than any of us, and he says it started the same for him and hasn't changed for years."

John-J interrupts. "I've been talking with some of the guys, and they've been hearin'—"

Grandpa Jack interrupts forcefully. "There are always those who talk of the worst. They've heard this or that, but they heard nothing but a bunch of rumors. Why would the company put us in danger? Without us, they don't make money. It doesn't make sense, and I don't put much stock in it. Carl is a piece of work for sure, but the company itself is all right. Carl has his sights on becoming general manger by age forty."

Laughing, John-J says, "That's some serious ass kissing to make that happen."

Sawpit is moments away, and Ben is deep in dreamland about his new rifle. John-J pulls up to their house, unloads the gear, and reaches for the bucks to finish the day's work before bagging them. Grandpa Jack says, "I got it from here. When I get home, I'll get em' hung, finish them up, and get 'em bagged. Please apologize to Pat for my keeping you guys out so late."

CHAPTER ELEVEN

ASHLEY, ATRIUM, OLGA, AND A PLAN

APRIL 14, 2011—11:15 A.M., WHITE COUNTY, INDIANA:

Ashley, Josh, and Hannah are waiting for Dr. Evans to arrive in Ashley's hospital room for an update. Josh is sitting next to Ashley's bed, holding her hand. Ashley is awake but staring at the ceiling, a tear periodically streaming across her cheek onto the pillow.

Hannah ends her phone conversation with Scott. "Everyone in the group sends you as much positive energy and as many prayers as possible. We are a family, no matter how many meetings we have together. Some of us have been where Ashley is right now." Nobody is listening, but Hannah knows it must be said anyway, collective energy can do amazing things.

There's a couple of knocks on the door, then it opens. Dr. Evans enters the room to find only two pairs of eyes focused on him. Ashley never stops looking at the ceiling. He says, "Morning, everyone. Ashley, how is the pain this morning?"

There is no answer as Ashley continues to stare at the ceiling. Both Josh and Hannah politely answer, "Hanging in there."

Dr. Evans continues and explains that the severe pain Ashley is experiencing is associated with her treatment and is due to her liver being unable to process the chemotherapy properly. "As we discussed last week, attempting the chemotherapy first was in hopes of helping to shrink or reduce the size of the affected areas so that we could proceed with surgery. However, I just got off the phone with the oncology surgeons in Indianapolis, and legally, they cannot perform the surgery. Medically speaking, knowing the advanced stage of cancer and the amount of which has metastasized in her liver renders the surgery impossible. Even removing the lesions we know of, not to mention the lesions we have yet to find, would render the liver nonfunctional."

Josh, now standing with a laser focus on the doctor, says, "I'll give her some of my liver or even fucking all of it if it will give her a better chance at living."

Dr. Evans sighs. "I wish it worked that way, but medically and legally, it doesn't. I have an order for hospice to come in today to transfer Ashley over into their care. This is not the news anyone wants to hear or give, but I would like to know if Ashley understands what is happening." Looking directly at Ashley: "Mrs. Bush, did you hear what I said? Do you understand what it means that hospice has been called?"

Hannah is standing stoically but quietly crying, wiping away the tears. Josh is pacing back and forth in the room, mumbling something under his breath, making everyone uncomfortable.

After lying down silently for the last two hours, Ashley finally sits up and responds with a voice obviously in distress. "Yes, Dr. Evans, I heard you. I understand. There is nothing left for us to do other than let me go into hospice and die."

Josh yells, "*No, that can't be it!*" He collapses to his knees with his head in Ashley's lap, wailing.

Ashley continues, "Is the pain going to get a lot worse?"

With decades of experience as an oncologist, Dr. Evans says with his best bedside manner, "The pain will get worse, but we have medication that helps reduce it. What I will suggest, but by no means do you have to follow, is to get whatever you need in order and speak with your loved ones today. Because as the pain increases, the medication helps dull it, but it also dulls the mind along with the pain. Ashley, I'm sorry we couldn't do more for you. Hospice will be in soon to transfer you over. I will have the nurse assess your pain levels in a few minutes. Is there anything else you need from me?"

"Yes, there is something I would like. First, I understand it's cold outside, but it is a clear, sunny day. I want to go outside to take a deep breath of fresh air one last time, with the sun on my face. Also, I would love to get wheeled into the atrium to see green plants with beautiful flowers. Is this possible?"

Dr. Evans nods yes, while standing at the door. "Of course, it would break hospital protocol, but we can make it happen under these circumstances."

The door closes and Josh collapses to his knees again, buries his head into the bed blankets, and wails.

Hannah says, "I'll find out about today's schedule so you two can have some privacy to process everything."

Ashley strokes Josh's hair while he cries heavily in her lap, "*Why you and not me? Why you and not me?*"

In her best attempt at lightheartedness, Ashley says, "You'll have plenty of time to miss me when I'm gone. I'm here with you now."

This simple sentence stops the crying immediately. Josh goes to the bathroom to clean up.

Ashley thinks, *Wow! Why did that work so well?*

As Josh returns from the bathroom, Ashley starts to speak, clearly in pain. "Do you remember when Hannah gathered all the necessary forms and paperwork last week? We completed them. They are all on the kitchen table, ready to go."

Now, Josh's turn to attempt humor, he says sarcastically, "I don't have amnesia; I'm just sad. Of course I remember filling out the paperwork from last week. Ashley, your only job right now is to try not to focus on the pain, and on us getting you those two wishes."

Blown away at the dramatic shift in Josh's demeanor, Ashley tells him to find a wheelchair so they can get to the atrium. Hannah enters after Josh exits the room.

"I sent him out to fetch a wheelchair," Ashley says.

Hannah replies as she heads toward the bed, "That's an excellent way to keep these times as upbeat as possible. How are you doing?"

Ashley reaches out for a hug as she begins to cry. "I'm so scared. I don't know if I lived my life well enough to go to heaven or not. I'm afraid of not breathing—scared of not waking up."

"Ashley, whatever version of heaven you believe in is your next home. Don't let any other thoughts lead you to believe otherwise. You've lived a great life. You've made the world better by being *you*. Being scared is the most natural thing to feel right now. I've been at this for a few years and have seen many of our family members come and go. I've come away from it all with one observation, for sure. A sense of well-being from each person as they pass over. It's here in our ego where fear is found. Subconsciously, we all know where we came from and where we will return. When the ego finally lets go, our souls return to consciousness, and the fear disappears. For some, it happens long before; for others, it occurs at the exact moment. Josh and I will be here with you." Hannah spoke softly into Ashley's ear as she rocked with her gently in her embrace.

Ashley, still crying: "But I want to live."

After a long hug, Hannah asks, "Are you sure there isn't anyone else you want us to contact?"

Ashley sniffles a reply. "Josh is the only one left for me. Can you make sure to notify my relatives in Iowa? They don't know how sick I am because I thought we would get through it, and I would tell them after. My college friends are everywhere. Their names are on the memorial announcement sheet, one of the forms we filled out last week. My parents are both gone. I think you and Josh are the only ones I want to see. You will take care of him—yes? I'm the only one who understands him, the only one he trusts—outside of you now. I love how much he trusts you, and how patient and understanding you are with him."

Hannah, now standing, puts her hand over her heart. "As long as I am living, I will do my best to take care of Josh. I will be here for him. He has found himself a grandmother, whether he likes it or not."

There is a thud at the door, startling both Hannah and Ashley. It's Josh backing in a wheelchair.

* * * *

APRIL 17, 2011—7:00 A.M.:

Staring at the screen with the email typed out and ready to send, Hannah says, "My dear, precious Ashley, you are pain-free, enjoying heaven now. I hope it is as lovely as you imagined, with your parents there to greet you as you passed over. I'm doing my best to keep my promise of looking after Josh. I think we can find a way to work through his *dark mistress*. I've got an idea that might give him purpose. That purpose could give him the opportunity to want to live a long and productive life. You were right about how important it was to keep him on a good path."

Hannah hesitates a moment longer before she clicks send on the list of emails for Ashley's obituary and funeral announcement. Finding herself in a tremendous amount of pain, she stares over at the shelf with the potpourri of pain medications prescribed for her. She thinks—*maybe just this morning?*

NO! Once it starts, it is too difficult to stop, and she is trying to keep her mind as sharp as possible. The opioid-derived pain medications will muddle her mind. So instead, Hannah practices some breathing exercises and takes her opioid-free two Ibuprofens and one Tylenol to get her through the next few hours. During the last swallow of ginger tea and pills, Hannah hears the tone of a Skype call coming in on her computer. The names on the Skype call are Olga and Robert. Hannah says, "Good morning, you two. I see you're up and finishing your breakfast."

Robert: Sitting in the background, tipping his coffee cup, "Mornin' Hannah."

Olga: "Good morning to you, too. Yeah, we have our routine, and you know the saying—'If it ain't broke, don't fix it.' We were discussing the plan and wanted to run a few things by you. Oh honey, please take this in the most caring way, but you don't look so good."

Hannah: "Well, it's not good news on one front but good on another. The good news will also alter your plans."

Olga: (Both Olga and Robert are now on the screen, showing concern for Hannah.) "What's going on? *Shit!*" Olga yells as she moves away from the screen with her hands on her head, "You're finished—no more treatments are available, right? How much longer do you have?"

Hannah: "Yes, you're right. My treatments have stopped working, and that was the last option. My body is going quickly. I'm not even sure if I'll make it to May 1st." (Robert and Olga are wiping away tears and blowing their noses.) "This isn't on your mind, but it's on mine now. I just sent off emails for that lovely young woman, Ashley. I'm about to go check in with her husband, Josh."

Robert: Butting in, "Can we put off Josh and the plan for a moment? How are you doing with all this news? Is there anything we can do from here?"

Hannah: "Thank you, Robert. There's nothing you can do for me, but there is something you can do for the movement. My future is pretty much settled, but this young man needs our help. He is deeply affected by abandonment from both his family and the US military as well as suffering from PTSD after multiple deployments in Iraq."

Olga: Pacing back and forth, listening to Hannah speak like she didn't just tell them she was going to be dead within the next month. "Hannah, can we back up for just a second? Tell us what is going on with you. I know we have this loose plan or idea of creating a movement, but nothing is set in motion other than a few of us talking. We want to know about you—not some kid. I'm sorry for being rude, but what did Dr. Evans say?"

Hannah: "Well, honey, I've been doing this long enough to know that when these specific tests are done, there isn't much time left. At my last appointment with Evans, we talked about it. This was the end of the road for any other treatments. Between my age and the amount of area the cancer has spread to, no trials will take me on; it's everywhere."

Olga: "You're 'pretty sure'—so you don't know yet? There are so many new studies in Europe and South America using stem cells and cannabis as possible treatments. You're my best friend, damn it. I'm not ready to give up on you yet." She looks at Robert. "Sorry, babe, but it's true."

Robert: Laughing, "No jealousy here; you two are practically sisters."

Hannah: "We are one-hundred-percent sisters. We've shared seventy-five years and then some together. Time and experience outweigh blood when we get to this point. Okay, I need you two to really listen to what I have to say. Our plan is not just a few people talking—it *will* happen. It will ignite a movement where the people take back their sovereignty that's been lost to the land barons and bankers for the last six thousand years. I might not be around to see it, but once we shake the people loose from their chains, they'll have nothing left to lose, which will spread like wildfire worldwide. I can feel it, deep in my gut, that this will be successful. "CEOs, executives, board members, and so on will be 'put on notice': Change how you do business, or we will have a Jacobin French Revolution solution waiting for you—no more corporate monarchy or aristocratic rule. The Gulf of Mexico Oil Spill, now the Fukushima Nuclear Disaster, Avidité, Fulcircle, and the list goes on. They need to settle their debts with all life on Earth. They all have spilled the blood of millions of innocent people, and we are going to use the lives of top executives as sacrificial symbols for all those lives lost."

Olga: "As you know, you're not going to get an argument about Albert from us (said in a snobby English accent)—that smug piece of shit and what he knowingly did to our Elizabeth. Who knows how many others Avidité has inadvertently hurt or killed because of their business decisions? But to think that your Joe Sinclair and our Albert Rush will start some global revolt seems farfetched." On the screen, Robert doesn't necessarily agree with Olga but shows some concern about a dying woman's wish to rid the world of evil, which will be done in less than three weeks.

Hannah: "I need you two to listen. We have Russell in San Francisco, Theresa in Dallas, Kimo in Honolulu, Skip in San Diego, you two in New York, and me in Indiana. That is who we know of. Remember, we agreed not to share with more than three other people, and no two groups share their names and target executives. Russell and Theresa have at least one other person, and we are all in contact with people who we know of in India, Japan, Germany, and England. Let's say they all have contact with three others, and those people have contact with three others. Come May 1, 2011, we will have a global May Day Revolution.

Robert: "On that note, we too, have a couple of others to add. One is with us to address Albert Rush, and the other is someone we would like you to meet. He's a hard one to read. He is a religious fanatic, but Adicta Pharmaceuticals, along with Case Brothers, has destroyed his life. His colon cancer is spreading fast. We want to invite him to the Skype meeting tomorrow. Would that be alright with you?"

Hannah: "Of course. My Josh is sort of in the same boat—kind of a loose cannon, but he is a good young man who is so angry at the world along with having uncontrollable PTSD, which I have been gently addressing since we've met. Not because I wanted to recruit him but because I wanted Ashley and him to have a long, healthy life together. With Ashley dying unexpectedly due to complications with her first round of chemotherapy, he hasn't said much more than a handful of words since we came home from the hospital. Today, I'm going to tell him my prognosis, then ask him if he wants to be my helper, since my strength is diminishing quickly.

"He was also trained in special forces in the US military. This is where my favor comes in with you two. We all know we're a bit long in the tooth, so carrying out these acts alone will be tough. But we'll be the ones who come forward with our statements and turn ourselves in. The first drafts of the statements for May Day and three others are finished. They need a few tweaks.

"If I get Josh—who doesn't have Stage IV Cancer and potentially has a long life ahead of him—on board, will it be a life of torment or a good quality of life? I've considered this for the last few days and believe he could have a meaningful life. However, it will take a few things for that to happen.

"First, I must convince him that this movement is a way of getting justice for Ashley, since her parents' farm used Fulcircle's poisonous chemical agricultural practices. I will mention the studies to him, and if he wants, I will show them to him.

"Second, if he can break free of all the bullshit he has endured over the years, it will allow him to begin to forgive himself for trying to start building a new life.

"Three and four is where you two come in. He needs a place to land where nobody knows him or his past. I know you two help people get new identities, but I am about to ask for more than that. Along with a new identity, he will need a stable place that he knows cannot be taken from him. Along with that safe, secure place, he needs access to counseling. Your Vermont property would only be available if he agrees and continues with counseling. Olga can discuss the details with him. It needs to come from you; he has a huge heart with a great respect for mother figures.

"Here is the last thing I'm asking of you both: You've mentioned another person wanting to participate with Albert. Speak to them about Josh without using his name. Explain that you two must keep your names out of the movement for the time being, just long enough for Josh to settle. Once that happens, Robert can turn himself in with the others. We need him to have as soft a landing as possible. Your name in the news will send up red flags all over the place. We'll talk more about this over the next couple of weeks. Please don't answer me now. I love you both, and we'll talk tomorrow during the group meeting. Bring your friend, and I'll bring Josh to the meeting."

Olga: "You're throwing a ton of information with changes at us, but we'll discuss it tonight. You'll have our answer as soon as possible. We love you, too, and hope you're wrong about your prognosis. Maybe Dr. Evans has one last trick up his sleeve."

Hannah: "I know this is a lot to ask in such a short period, but besides my Bob, you two are the only ones I could ever ask so much from. I need to go give Josh another crushing blow about my condition, then explain how he can achieve a small piece of justice for Ashley. Wish me luck. Love you both. Goodbye."

Hannah closes her computer and ends the call.

CHAPTER TWELVE

TIME AND PATIENCE

SEPTEMBER 16, 2010:

Just after midnight, Ben Brown hands Michael the video remote and says, "I don't need to watch it. I did it. It's time for this old man to hit the sack. Take notes, and I'll answer your questions in the morning."

Hours later, Michael Bennett sits outside Ben Brown's workshop as the sun rises. This should bring him calmness and joy, but instead he feels the exact opposite on this brisk fall morning. He sips the hot coffee Ben left in a thermos near the door. Michael wonders when Ben dropped it off, because he found it before the sunrise even began. He feels nauseous after witnessing videos of the man whom he hated more than any human on earth getting tortured for hours. He took no pleasure in hearing or watching the cries of the old man.

All he can think is—this is wrong. How could Ben have done this without allowing his humanity to put Carl out of his misery?

Michael had taken a few notes. The only questions he had were about how Ben could have committed these acts without any outward emotion. He had skinned a man alive. No legal defense could justify what Michael had witnessed on these tapes.

Written in big, dark letters across the top of Michael's notepad is:

BEN BROWN/CARL SHADWICK NOTES

1. How did he lure Carl Shadwick to the property, or scene of the crime?

2. Why did he hang him like an animal (from his achilles) while still alive?

3. What was the purpose of torturing Carl Shadwick for so long?

That was it; after ten-plus hours of footage, these were all the questions Michael could come up with, because none of it made sense from any point of view.

Ben rides over on his quad, two dogs running beside him. His oxygen tank is bungee-corded to the rack on the back. He waves to Michael as he rides up. "Mornin'. Well, I'm sure you're horrified. I figured as much." Rubbing the back of his neck to get a morning bug off, Ben says in a drawn-out voice, "Well, let's answer your questions before this day runs away from us. I made you some eggs, sausage, and toast. I'll grab it and come back. You can eat while I look over your notes and answer any questions you have written down."

"In a soft, first-words-of-the-morning voice, Michael replies. "Sounds like a plan. Let me take a piss, wash my face, and brush my teeth. Then, we'll get to it."

With tails wagging, Bula and Yabo run alongside the quad. Both dogs were rescued from the shelter of the local humane society. Ben was a volunteer dog walker before his lungs gave out. He would take dogs out on day hikes, allowing them time out of their runs and into free open space. Ben is most at home in the forests, by the river, and around animals.

Michael watches him ride off and cannot reconcile what he saw on the tapes with the man who is friendly and kind to everyone and everything. After his morning bladder drainage, Michael looks in the mirror while washing his face. It is worse than the day before. It was another night of no sleep after viewing what can only be described as a gruesome horror movie. After washing the soap off his face, he puts both hands on the sink and rests his tired body. He looks up into the mirror and asks himself, *what the fuck have I gotten myself into?*

Michael slowly makes his way back to the workshop and opens the door to see Ben sitting at the table with a plate for him while scribbling in his notebook. Both dogs sit by his side. He says, "Is this all you have?"

Michael nods. "Hell, I'm surprised I even got that much down. What the fuck did you do? I had to fast-forward through lots of the tape." As he sits down, he says in a disgusted tone, "I don't have much of an appetite after watching that shit all night."

"Come on, eat your breakfast before it gets cold. I'll let you know how we'll try this case."

Somehow, Ben takes on the role of the father despite Michael being three years older. Resembling a scolded child, Michael picks up the fork with his head down and takes a bite of sausage. His entire demeanor changes—his posture improves, his eyes widen, and there is energy in his voice when he asks, "What type of sausage is this? I know it's venison, but what spices are in it? It might be the best I've ever tasted."

"Yeah, I've fiddled around with different ingredients for years. It's typical stuff, but I do a few things differently than most people. It takes more time and patience. I'll leave you all my recipes in my will." Ben's laugh is barely recognizable through the thick gurgle. "How does that sound to you?"

With one clearing of his throat, Ben dislodges a mouthful of mucus and spits it on the dirt floor. He kicks dirt over it automatically so Yabo and Bula won't try to lick it up. This action is done several times throughout the morning. With a quick wipe of his mouth on his sleeve, he continues, "This sausage contains a wild mushroom that I gather each year, then dry or dehydrate it. The mixture of the usual seasonings and the venison with the mushrooms gets one extra pass through the grinder with a fine die. It brings out more flavor. Patience comes with making the rub, the timing of smoking, and adding different herbs with wood at various stages. Depending on the animal, I will render some of its fat. If it tastes good, a tiny bit goes a long way with pork leaf fat. This batch was good, which is why the venison taste came through."

Now eating his breakfast and enjoying his coffee, Michael takes a break to say, "Let's hear this brilliant strategy of yours since there is no way in hell you could put forward a defense if the prosecution gets hold of these tapes."

Ben shakes his head while looking down in what seems like disappointment that Michael doesn't automatically get why and how he killed Shadwick the way he did. "Slow down! I've spent many years waiting for the right moment and planning this. On paper, this defense doesn't sound like one at all.

"Look. I've spent the last few decades observing and counseling people with different personalities and how those personalities manifest themselves in people's actions. You're going to have to trust me on this one. This isn't one of your normal legal versus illegal trials. It's something much bigger than that.

"Okay, you've already met Chuck. I've mentioned Alaetra and Champ to you. The last two are not guaranteed to be assigned to this case. I suspect they will be, since they have the most seniority and sit in the highest office. Few people work in the DA's office, and we only have two or three judges handling murder cases. None of them are in on what happened. You're the only person who has ever seen these tapes, and that is how we will keep it.

"Do you remember asking or yelling at me—why did I turn myself in before you got here? This is the real reason. When I was locked up, they had already searched my home and property by the time you got here. These tapes were kept in a place where nobody would ever find them."

Michael interrupts. "I will have you play those tapes again and record the audio. I don't want anyone ever to have to *see* them again."

Ben replies, "No problem, I'll do that after we're done here."

He continues: "Anyway, this is an open-and-shut case for the prosecutors, but it is high-profile. That's why I'm damn near positive Champ and Alaetra will be the ones assigned to it. It is also why I had to wait so long before handling business with Carl. I needed to allow all Vermolite bought and paid-for judges to retire. Also, we needed people like Champ, who came up watching all their relatives drop dead of the same disease, to control the District Attorney's office. Like that sausage recipe, time and patience were needed for this plan. As I mentioned before, I studied the law in Montana and the federal system during that time.

"I know Judge Anderson through Brown Expeditions and the veterans' PTSD program; her husband was one of my clients. He served with a couple of tours from '68 to '70, deep in the jungle shit that we all wanted to stay away from as much as possible but your unit could get called to at any moment on any day. I won't go into my experiences, but let's just say they weren't good.

"Then there's Champ. I'm not sure where he was hiding, but he must have tried to become a judge somewhere else, and it didn't happen. So he came home a few years back and hung up a shingle. He was taking care of his sister in her last couple of years of mesothelioma. Once she passed, he threw his hat in the race for District Attorney. That was the break I was looking for. I don't know Champ too well, but *you* might know him since you're a few years older and you two were in high school at the same time.

"So, to keep this moving along—what you witnessed on those tapes—the Sheriff's office will only see the crime scene as I left it. It wasn't pretty, but they'll have difficulty deciphering how it all went down. It was brutal and bloody, and Carl Shadwick suffered lots of pain. I'm pretty sure he died of a heart attack from all the distress he was under.

"Once he died, I cleaned up the work area but left behind all the evidence. The bloody tarps are all folded, and a labeled bucket of Carl's blood has a lid on it. I had wrapped his body in an old hide from an elk that came out too shitty to use for anything or even give away. But I kept it in one of my chests just in case it could be used for something one day. It was a bit stiff, so I took out my torch and heated it for a few minutes to soften it so I could wrap it properly around Carl's body. Then I smudged the workshop and left everything that the Sheriff's office would look for behind so they wouldn't tear up the place. To make it too easy also served the purpose of disrupting the investigation."

With a mouthful of food as he finishes his last bite of eggs, Michael says, "Why would you want to make it too easy?"

Ben replies, pointing at his head, "It's nature at work to take the path of least resistance. A complicated murder investigation would create lots of digging around. I didn't want my grandpa's place torn up or them coming to my place to dig around for more proof of my guilt. So, I gave them a guilty verdict, all wrapped up with a bow.

"As you saw in the video, I hung him up and dropped him down several times. I didn't want to give shithead an easy way out. This wasn't about revenge—it was about justice. Giving Carl a quick death would have been revenge, which he did not deserve. I needed him on some level to understand why he was being skinned alive. This morning's look on your face told me everything I wanted to know. You were, or are, horrified at how I took him down."

"No shit!" Michael exclaims.

"The first half-day or so, as you saw, I just talked with him, and he was the same old shithead Shadwick. I'm not sure if he was dropped on his head as a baby or was just born with a lack of ability for compassion for anyone or anything other than himself. He felt no remorse for all of our family members, including me, from getting sick from the shit

Vermolite had the entire town mining. You know better than anyone since Nicole did the deposition with him. Vermolite Mining Company knew before they bought the fucking company that all of it was insanely toxic. Shadwick just had his sights on being general manager and didn't give a second thought to all the babies, kids, and innocent people living in town being exposed. It's one thing for the miners and company employees to get sick, but not caring that town people, from infants to elderly, were going to die from the exposure is evil in my book.

"You moved away and protected yourself from seeing the collateral damage Shadwick and Vermolite left behind. Every day, I met another person who either got diagnosed or knew someone who had just gotten diagnosed. At least once a month there is a funeral for this plague Vermolite Mining brought to our town. Every one of these experiences justifies how I treated Shadwick, old man or not."

Feeling like his experiences of suffering were being reduced, Michael shot back, "Listen, Ben, I know I got out of Sawpit a long time ago, but don't forget I lost almost my entire family to this disease."

Ben seemingly ignores Michael's statement and continues. "So, I know you're horrified at what I did to that motherfucker, but what I did forced him to feel pain and suffering—something he seemed incapable of when it came to others. He was incapable of feeling emotional pain, so physical pain needed to be used. If it ever sank in or not, I cannot say." With a snort, "It wasn't from the lack of trying.

"When his heart was giving out, I dropped him down to the floor and left him there so I could grab that rifle he bought me for my thirteenth birthday. As he was gasping for air and dying of a heart attack, I sat there right in front of him, holding the rifle, reminding him of the day I shot my first buck. I could tell in his eyes that he heard me. Then he was gone.

"That's when I cleaned up the workshop. As you saw in the video, there were tarps up, and I had him dripping into a pan. I poured all his blood into a bucket and wrapped his body up with a ceremony. This ceremony was a different type, not out of respect, but trying to cleanse the area of his bad energy along with the energy of the action. I had invited lots of bad energy into my grandpa's workshop, which I could not live with. I needed to correct that flow and acknowledge why it needed to be done."

Michael had finished breakfast some time ago, and sits silently, trying to process everything being said.

Both men stand up and go outside to enjoy the Montana morning. Ben continues to explain, rolling his oxygen tank trailer, which he had fitted with an off-road wheel setup, alongside. Once out in the fresh, chilly air, Michael tells Ben, "I'm following you on everything, but I'm not so sure this is the best way forward. You're going to spend the rest of your life in prison."

Ben laughs as he gestures down his body. "What life? A life in which I can barely breathe, can't enjoy a basic beginner hike outdoors and can feel my vital organs working. Think about that—can *feel* my organs working.

"Hear me out, and you'll see the bigger picture. So, let's stand here and enjoy the here and now while I talk for the next few minutes. Interrupt me anytime you want.

"To answer your questions—I lured Carl to Backsaw Ranch by invitation. Once Champ Sanders got elected, I tracked Carl down to see if he was still alive. He was, and I gave him a call. He was in excellent health and mind, outside of a mild heart condition. I told him my Grandpa Jack had some nice things from their time together, and he might want to pick them up for one last trip to Backsaw Ranch. Knowing who Carl Shadwick was, I knew he would make that trip since he didn't see any reason why I would be upset with him, but more importantly, Grandpa Jack's woodworking would be worth a lot of money.

"The hanging of Carl was symbolic of our relationship and for effect. It was about reversing who controlled the other person's life. For decades, Shadwick controlled our family's life by having authority over the decisions of the Vermolite mine in Sawpit.

"Also, he was there for my first buck, bought me my first hunting rifle, and we hunted together with Grandpa and Dad for years. A couple of quick slits hooked him up with the gambrels and flipped on the pully. Not much blood and easy to control. I could drop him to let him lie down and recover before hanging him back up. I sharpened my straight draw in front of him."

Michael stops him. "What's a straight draw?"

"A straight draw is a tool to shave the bark off fallen trees."

"Oh shit, okay, I know exactly what you're talking about. I never knew what it was called and probably fast-forwarded through that part of the tape."

Ben, in his standard retort: "Yep! That's what was used and is how and why I could take my time. Skin off just enough to hurt like hell but allow his blood to coagulate enough to stop the bleeding.

"And for your last question, this is what we talked about—Carl and me. He didn't understand. No amount of explaining could get that man to empathize with anyone. He was one of those ambitious sociopaths—or psychopaths. The only way to get him to understand the pain and suffering of hundreds, even thousands, of people over the decades was for me to slowly show him physically. I know that he couldn't connect those dots mentally since those neurons and synapses in his brain didn't exist. So, I reminded him several times that his physical pain was going to be great but short-lived. At the same time, his victims weren't so lucky. Long, drawn-out suffocation or painful organ failure while your loved ones sit by and have to experience the feeling of helplessness is a much crueler way of dying.

"Did that answer your questions well enough? I don't care if you agree or not. There is nothing to debate. The job is done."

Silence. Michael sits there silently while Ben waits for a response. Nothing.

Ben takes that as approval because he knows Michael can't say it out loud, so he does: "Arthur's anniversary is creeping up to thirty years now, and I will join him soon, with the exact same cause of death. I'm not sure if you remember, but I vowed the night of his funeral that we were going to hold Shadwick accountable for Arthur's death and numerous other deaths in our families. Time was running out. Hell, part of me wished Carl had died already. But I think his not being dead, Alaetra being a judge, and Champ becoming the DA in his sixties meant something much bigger was at hand.

"Do you have anything else before I tell you the strategy?"

"Yeah," Michael says, "I have one more question: Since you have this all figured out, why involve me?"

"I figured you'd ask that. I've thought about it for years, long and hard. This addresses your statement of just a few moments ago. I heard you, and trust me, I do not minimize the suffering you've been through. That's exactly why you need to be my lawyer. This entire thing is about the big picture. In the end, you'll see it, and that's why I've asked you to help me with all of this.

"You and Nicole were some of the only kids growing up who

connected everything happening in our so-called *American Dream* town early in your lives. Then, you both went on to do something about it.

"We need more people who do things. I'm tired of people wanting change but not doing anything about it. It took me longer than you two did to see everything for what it was since my grandpa and Dad still worked for Vermolite and seemed content with their lives. I knew but couldn't admit it until I went to Vietnam and got away from everything. There, I experienced too much horrible shit before I had the guts to be honest with myself.

"It took my experiences in Vietnam for me to see the strategies companies deploy all over the world on innocent people. The Vermolite Mining Company was no different, but they were the company that killed my family, my best friend, and the town I loved.

"We did it all the time in the military; the difference is that we did it in short intervals instead of decades-long business strategies while hiding all the evidence. The difference, from what I can tell, was in Vietnam. We thought of them as the enemy, whereas in Montana (or wherever the business) the people being killed off were thought of as the labor and profit generators. The people were dispensable beasts of burden. In the military, we justified our immoral acts because our enemy was known and shared, which is more acceptable. However, Carl was a so-called friend of our family, and he knew what the asbestos was doing to everyone. That is straight-up evil.

"When I chose to sign up, all I knew was that I didn't want to spend my life in a mine or an office. I wanted to spend it outside. I might not have become a lawyer or some top professional—still, I've dedicated my life to healing those who have been injured in one way or another and to try and stop any more killing of innocent foreign men and women for resources. Or for geopolitical jockeying that forces countries to allow multinational corporations access to those resources with little opposition in the name of profits. Sometimes, that violence is through debt; other times, that violence is with bombs. They are both deadly weapons. One is just quick, while the other slowly kills off a culture by putting so much pressure on the people to the point that they throw their hands up and say, save us—we are dying.

"Sawpit was no different; we were sacrificed so Vermolite Mining Company executives and shareholders could reap the profits. Their orders were: With a lying smile on your face, tell these people this is safe and we all can live the American dream. They were compensated generously for selling their souls to that company.

"Our grandpas and dads took all the risks with their lives; the white-collar bean counters received all the benefits. You, more than anyone other than maybe Champ Sanders, understand what I am saying right now.

"So, to answer your question: One, I thought you would want to participate in letting the world know Carl Shadwick was held responsible for hiding evidence for decades that resulted in the killing of an entire town.

"Second, I might have found holes in the legal system, but reading about laws and understanding how to navigate a trial are two very different skill sets. Navigating a trial is a skill set I do not possess: when to object, the order of witnesses and evidence, and everything else that comes with a trial. Hell, I wouldn't even know how to address the judge to start the fucking thing.

"Third, as I mentioned yesterday, my plan might not be good, but it is mine. The goal isn't to be found innocent or not guilty, although that would be nice. This action aims to expose what Vermolite Mining Company, especially Carl Shadwick, knowingly did to everyone in Lincoln County and throughout Montana, even in other towns where the company has set up shop. If they could do what they did in our town, they could be doing it in those other towns right now.

"Fourth, this is the strategy part. I'll tell you what I believe will happen and how I want our defense to be to the jury. Your input will create the actual strategy for achieving it. You know things about the law and Vermolite Mining Company and Shadwick that I don't. Feel free to insert whatever you want. This action was for all of us, not just me."

Michael remains quiet while listening to every word, gesture, and exclamation—trying to feel what Ben was attempting to accomplish. The problem is that our brains are not meant to function with little to no sleep, gas station coffee, super-processed packaged snacks, enormous stress, and complicated plans with multiple threads weaving together.

Minutes pass without either of them speaking. Both have taken a couple of sips of their second cup of coffee in deep thought, looking out into the trees, when Michael breaks the silence. "Okay, I got it so far. I'm running on fumes here. We've both dove head-first into the pool's deep end on this one. I'm so fucking exhausted—let me go sleep the day away. Then we'll pick up again this evening. Is there any place to find a room in Eureka that is nice and quiet?"

Ben responds with authority. "You're not getting a place in town. You'll stay in my guest cabin, which has everything you need. You go lie down. I still have chores to do. My middays usually consist of just trying not to use too much energy and oxygen."

Something has shifted since yesterday morning. When he picked Ben up at the Sheriff's office, Michael heard Ben's combination of wheeze and hiss. Somewhere along the way, possibly due to the fatigue and stress that Michael had experienced in the last few days, Ben's gasping for air and hisses while talking had faded into the background as they drove around and talked deep into the night. This morning however, when Ben talks, the wheeze and hiss are back. This time, it triggers something in Michael. It is an unconscious feeling of indescribable emotions, and the one emotion he can identify is guilt. The guilt of not hearing it until this morning.

Michael now stares blankly past Ben, his mind unable to release itself from his thoughts. *How could I have not heard it? Was it because I'm so goddamn tired?* After that last question to himself, all the memories of his parents and Arthur come flooding back into his head.

Ben has seen this look many times when dealing with domestic violence victims or veterans. He interrupts Michael, who is trapped in his thoughts, and says loudly, "I have a few cottages."

Yanked from his nightmare, Michael shakes his head and apologizes. "What did you say?"

"I was saying, some of my cottages run alongside the river. They're part of the Brown Expeditions organization. I haven't winterized them yet, and they're just sitting there, ready to go. You see that trail and sign just ahead?"

Michael replies with a tired, "Yeah."

"All the cottages are ready. Pick one. You can walk back out when you're ready to continue. I'm not going anywhere today. I'll drop off a cooler of food and something to drink later. When you first walk in, flip the power on. The box is to the right of the door. Then you should be ready to go."

After a few minutes of walking along the wooded pathway, Michael hears the soft sound of rapids. *Ben said you can't miss it once you reach the big rock.* Sleep-deprived, cranky, slumped in exhaustion, and slowly dragging his bag behind him, Michael mumbles, "Where is this big fucking rock?"

Within moments, a massive rock that seems out of place in the middle of this wooded area appears. "Holy shit!" he says as he approaches it and sees a series of cabins with a big fire pit centrally located that looks like it belongs in a Hollywood studio.

He steps up to the first covered porch, thinking that this week is one surprise after another. He opens the door and sees exactly what Ben described. A guest cabin that has everything he would need for as long as he wants to stay. The power switch is inside the door on the right side. He flips it up, and instantly, the cabin comes to life; lights and the hum of a small motor from the refrigerator kick on. Outside, he hears what he can only assume is a pump as air simultaneously spits out of the sink faucet. Eventually, there is a solid water stream. The hum turns into white noise as he plops onto the bed and rolls over.

Within minutes, Michael is snoring, and somewhere in that deep sleep throughout the day, he dreams of his childhood and remembers those who he considers old-timers dying from the same illness. He tries to help them, telling his friends and family not to go into the mines, but nobody hears him. They all go about their business as though he isn't there.

In desperation, he turns to look for help. He sees Nicole and Arthur clearly, with a blurry figure in the background. Nicole takes his hand while he puts his other arm around Arthur. They walk toward the blurry figure. Michael hears his youthful voice saying, "Why won't they listen?" As they approach the specter, it becomes much clearer. It's Ben, not as a teenager like Michael, Nicole, and Arthur—but as an old man dying of mesothelioma.

Michael awakens screaming, "*No!*" The white walls from the morning now have a long shadows with a pinkish hue as he recovers from the dream. He is breathing hard, searching for his glasses. His eyes adjust. "Jesus, how long did I sleep?"

Between exhaustion from four days of little or no sleep, Ben's insane plan, and the overwhelming pressure of anticipating defending a homicide case, the sleep he just experienced can only be described as deeply satisfying. Now dressed in jeans, a long-sleeved flannel shirt, and a hand-knitted cap from Nicole, Michael slowly makes his way back to the workshop. Dusk has set in, and the colors of the sunset have faded. In a slight breeze, Michael picks up the smell of BBQ, and his nose becomes his guide. Taking a right where the trail forked instead of left, which would have led him back to the workshop, Michael walks along the river and sees Ben's glorified camper with a BBQ grill smoking away.

The walk to the cabins seemed to take forever, but the walk back only takes a few minutes. Michael yells, "Evenin'" to the vacant scene.

Both Bula and Yabo start barking from the trailer, and within a few seconds, the door swings open and Ben yells back, "Howd' yah sleep? Like a baby, I bet."

As Michael approaches the trailer: "You're not kidding. A bomb could have gone off, and I wouldn't have heard it."

Ben bends down, opens a cooler, and pulls out two beers. "Want one?"

"Yeah, I'll take one, but first, I need to drink some water."

Ben hands Michael his beer, stirs the briquettes, and asks while he steps back into the trailer, "How do you think the trial will go?"

"What do you mean?"

Ben hands Michael a 32-ounce mason jar of water, sits at the table, and flips the notepad around. He shows Michael what he has been scribbling since he grabbed Michael's notes. Michael sees a Venn diagram of circles on a page. Each circle has a name representing each category that will make up the court and trial. Using word prompts, he writes in each circle and explains how he sees each circle acting throughout the trial. In the middle, where all circles overlap, it is labeled: Jury.

"I'll make this as easy as possible," says Ben. "The overall defense is going to be self-defense."

Michael starts laughing and apologizing at the same time. "I'm sorry—the guy who can barely breathe and who looks eighty years old defending himself against an actual eighty-something-year-old struck me as funny."

Now laughing, they start giving the trial joke headlines: "Geriatric Murder Trial of the Century," "Dying Man Fears for His Life after Threats from Eighty-Year-Old Visitor.

After they both throw out a few more headlines, they settle down, and Ben continues. "Your opening statements will be about the damage that Vermolite Mining posed in Sawpit, Montana by knowingly poisoning the entire town." Out of reflex, Ben starts presenting his version of the opening statement to an invisible jury. He pauses for gasps of breath between points, and with each gasp, there is a hissing sound.

He continues. "The defendant, along with so many others" (pointing to Michael as if he is Ben sitting in a courtroom) "experienced witnessing multiple family members succumbing to the horrible effects of mesothelioma, (gasp) which has been scientifically proven to be the result of mining and exposure to asbestos (gasp). This self-defense wasn't a direct threat but an existential threat to wherever companies like Vermolite Mining Company do business. Ben Brown acted as the protector of innocent life to which he had dedicated his own (gasp).

"Returning from Vietnam gave him a profound sense of life's preciousness. The threat that companies such as Vermolite Mining or people like Carl Shadwick, pose to society is immeasurable. Ben Brown doesn't necessarily think of himself as a vigilante, although this act might give that appearance (huge gasp).

"Decades of hiding known scientific evidence that the mining, processing, and exposure to asbestos was cancer-causing had never been held accountable outside financial liability, and Vermolite Mining Company did everything in its power to reduce the compensation to its victims with out-of-court settlements (gasp). Then, once exposed or caught, Vermolite Mining Company disregarded its responsibility for the safety and cleanup of their sacrifice zone. Once again, Vermolite Mining Company disregarded their responsibility to the town and people of Sawpit, passing the buck to the workers to deal with on their own or to taxpayers as a Superfund site (gasp)."

By now, Ben's voice barely forces out a wheezing whisper compared to just a minute ago. "What I intend to demonstrate is Mr. Brown's lifelong commitment to protecting life by supporting veterans with PTSD through the founding and management of Brown Expeditions, an organization that has assisted veterans for decades (gasp). And he has expanded this organization to help domestic violence victims by becoming a certified counselor. Further, Ben Brown has been a volunteer at the animal shelter, toward rescuing abused and abandoned animals (gasp). He also works to educate the public about military objectives through Veterans for Peace, and helps friends or individuals in need within his community in any way possible. This is not a man of extreme violence; rather, he is a person with strong convictions and principles dedicated to protecting the innocent from predators in his community (huge gasp)."

With his hands on his head while coughing out the phlegm that has built up, Ben tries to catch his breath. He feels lightheaded, as though he is suffocating. Knowing the offer will be declined, Michael offers to help Ben, who waves him off: "Give me a moment, or something along those lines," he manages, once he finally catches his breath.

Now, they both are looking at the diagram while Ben recovers.

The Defense Circle: Character witnesses, my story.

The Prosecution Circle: Found evidence, will allow me to speak without objection.

When Michael sees that last element in the prosecution circle, he has to interject. "The prosecutors will not allow you to speak without filters. Let's say, for the sake of argument, Sanders doesn't object; Judge Anderson will not allow you to filibuster in her court."

"Hold on," Ben says. "You're jumping to conclusions before I lay the entire thing out.

"The prosecution holds all the cards to the physical evidence and the fact that I turned myself in. That's it; the evidence was given with the least resistance. I can almost guarantee that Champ Sanders isn't going fishing for anything else. But at the same time, he will be sympathetic to my circumstances. Remember, he just went through his sister's death of mesothelioma less than eighteen months ago. He knows what it sounds like, what it looks like, the emergency calls and stays at the hospital, and all of that shit. I haven't looked into his family history, but I bet my bottom dollar she is not the only victim in his family.

"Now, for Alaetra, I helped her husband, Chris, with counseling through the non-profit for some heavy PTSD. She, too, is from Lincoln County. She'll give me a long rope, and if I get out of hand, she will give me a hard tug to remind me I'm in her court. She is a decent woman known to be fair on the bench to everyone before her court."

Judge Circle: Alaetra, Chris, fair, from Lincoln County.

Michael is not convinced this is a good idea and lets Ben know. "Are you basing this entire thing on the hunch that you'll get a judge and district attorney to sympathize with you, ignoring the law and trial protocol?"

Ben snaps back: "No, that's not it. Listen! Will you stop being a goddamn lawyer for a minute and see the case through the jurors' eyes, the eyes of our entire childhood town that is now a Superfund site. This isn't about getting a verdict in our favor. It's about exposing the world to the truth, goddamn it!

"It's a slam dunk case; they have their conviction already. No jury will see that evidence and find me *not guilty*. If verdicts were our goal, the best we could hope for, which is almost impossible, is that they'll see me as insane. But that isn't what we are trying to get. Not only do I want them to believe me sane, I need them to see and hear me being the most sane person in that courtroom.

"We will not challenge the prosecutor's evidence—since I organized it for them to find. They will present it in a neat little package that is easy for the jury to understand.

"Remember, this trial isn't about me. I'm a walking dead man—I've already been given my death sentence. This case is about exposing Carl Shadwick and Vermolite Mining Company to the general public. The action is to hold them accountable in a way that would get all this information that has been kept secret for all these decades into public records and in the news.

"It is here that we determine whether our case is won or lost. Guilty or not guilty is a foregone conclusion: I'm guilty. We need the public to see these companies as the perpetrators of crime and mass murderers, not as innocent victims (gasp)—change the narrative: I'm guilty of trying to protect myself and the community from corporate predators." While Ben is recovering and catching his breath, Michael thinks and tries to wrap his brain around this entire idea.

Ben continues. "Just like Alaetra and Champ, I'm friendly with the local papers and many of their journalists. Our local paper has interviewed me ten times—more for good community-building events than for controversial articles against war or my affiliation with the Timber Drivers Local 2. Without my long friendships with people in the entire region, we couldn't get the journalists or papers on our side. Through my connections with different chapters around the nation, we'll try to get this story covered by multiple news outlets. It will only take one online outlet to pick it up, and then we'll be a national story."

"Jesus, Ben, when you say it, it seems so easy, but I don't see it playing out that way."

Once again, Ben says a drawn-out "Wel-l-l-l—we can eat some dinner and continue, or just eat some dinner. It's up to you."

"Let's eat some dinner, and maybe throw our lines in the water in the morning and talk some more. I'm here for a few more days before heading back to Denver. From there, we'll communicate by phone. Let's make tonight about catching up on life. It seems you have lived a good one, and I suspect it's not short of interesting stories. We'll pick up on the case again in the morning."

"Do you want another beer? We have steak, potatoes, and some cooked greens for dinner."

"Sounds great to me. But first, please, I need more water."

CHAPTER THIRTEEN

BREAKING THE NEWS AND THE PLAN

APRIL 17, 2011—10:00 A.M.:

Since Ashley's passing, Josh is inconsolable and in a very dark place. He hasn't left the house since he came home from the hospital. He was given some medications to help calm his anxiety and allow him to sleep. Hannah's daily visits are the only thing that gets him out of bed. He hasn't eaten a bite of the food left for him.

Knock, knock! "Josh, are you here?" says Hannah as she pokes her head in the doorway. "I'm coming in." She enters the kitchen and finds that the food she left the day before is still untouched on the table. "*JOSH?*" she says louder, hoping to wake him if he is sleeping.

"What time is it?" says Josh as he exits the bedroom.

Hannah opens the curtains and answers him without looking. It's around 3:00 p.m. We need to get some light in here. Have you gone outside at all? Fresh air and sunlight are great for clearing our heads and keeping us healthy. It's beautiful outside today."

Angry, Josh replies, "Is it! Is it fucking beautiful outside! Just another day Ashley would have loved, and she isn't here for it. How can I possibly go outside and smile!"

Hannah stays busy around the house and doesn't look directly at Josh. "I took the list of friends for the memorial service and sent an email announcement right before I came over."

"Whatever. I don't know any of them, and I'm the reason Ashley lost touch with them all. Her disgraced, crazy, military husband needed to be kept away from others, don'tcha know. I'm not going." Hannah stops what she is doing and stares at Josh with the biggest stink eye she can muster. "*What!* What do you want from me?" He says in a loud voice.

Hannah sighs and closes her eyes to focus. "It's not what I want but what I need from you right now. I need you to get out of your head. I need you to be present and keep moving forward. We all mourn differently, and I can't even comprehend the grief and pain you're in right now. I didn't lose my spouse in my early thirties. We were blessed with fifty-eight years together."

Josh is screaming now, "—And you're right. You don't know how it feels. It feels like I don't want to live anymore!"

Hannah would be frightened in normal circumstances, but she has mentally prepared herself for Josh's anger. She responds calmly, "You're right. I don't know, but I will say this, Josh—" She walks over to him and looks directly into his eyes. "—I have lived a long life and have experienced a hell of a lot of hard times and loss. More than you might think. I have also learned to find joy and love in the world despite those hard times and pain.

"You can miss Ashley and still go on living your life. That is what she wanted most for you—to live your life with a purpose and passion. She told me what a great sense of humor you have, your love for kids, and your love for sports and the outdoors. What both you and I need is for you to get up and eat, shower, and go outside."

Josh's expression and posture soften as he perceives an old woman and hears her voice filled with love. He grabs her and hugs her for a long while. Tears are shared, and when they separate, he says, "I'll shower, and maybe we can go for a walk."

"That would be nice," Hannah replies.

As soon as Josh leaves the room, out of exhaustion, Hannah collapses onto a chair and mumbles, "I don't know if I have enough strength to get through all of this." Her dexamethasone still dulls the sting of her increasing pain but no longer gives her the magical extra energy. Her complexion has a hint of grey, her eyes have lost that sparkle, and her shoulders are slumped forward for much of the day now. She notices that her appetite has diminished to almost not eating at all.

She hears the bathroom door open, letting out a cloud of steam with the scent of soap, and straightens up as Josh, with a towel around his waist, heads into his room to change. As soon as his door closes, she slumps back down in the chair.

Wrapped up in his own grief, Josh doesn't have a clue about Hannah's declining condition, but today will be the day he finds out—the day he finds out the only other person he trusts will leave him soon—the day that person is going to propose a way he can get justice for everything and start a new life if he wants to keep on going. For Hannah, this is the day! And she needs to be strong enough to present her plan so that Josh can understand the ultimate goal, instead of it being just another trust broken by asking him to do something everything at his core he knows is wrong.

Josh is ready to go and tries his best to put on a good face for Hannah. He doesn't want to disappoint her. Inside, he still feels incredibly selfish and like a piece of shit for being so angry about Ashley being taken from him, instead of mourning the fact Ashley had her joy of life stolen from her at such a young age. His rage blinds him to everything else. Forcing a smile, Josh says, "Are you ready to go?" Hannah slowly stands, and for the first time, Josh notices that she looks ill. His rage lessens, and he rushes over to help her out of the chair. "Are you feeling all right? You don't look so good."

"Walking always makes me feel better. Let's go for a walk—there are some things we need to talk about. There are some things I need to ask you."

All the energy of Josh's rage switches to a knot in his gut because he knows what Hannah is going to say—her cancer has gotten worse and she is about to die, and there is nothing he can do about it. "Yeah, let's take a walk, and maybe that will make you feel a bit better."

Josh lives in a guest house on the back of his landlord's property in a neighborhood of small parcels of five and ten acres. Many people called these properties "hobby farms," but they were more for people who wanted to avoid the expense and worry of having vast acres to maintain and cultivate so they could have chickens, large gardens, small orchards, possibly some livestock—and most of all, have extra time to enjoy it. A few years earlier, the Hickmans had sold their four-hundred-acre farm, where they grew Kill-All Ready corn. They are a lovely couple who tried to care for Ashley and Josh once they learned about Ashley's condition. They, too, much like Hannah, see the anger in Josh and have stayed away since Ashley's passing.

Looking out the window, Mrs. Hickman has seen Hannah come and go for the last few days. But on this day, she sees the elderly woman and Josh walking down the long driveway. Sipping her cup of tea, she silently thanks Hannah for caring for that boy. Within a minute of her thinking this comforting thought, Josh screams and starts throwing punches in the air. At first, Mrs. Hickman starts to call her husband out of concern, but after the first round of punches, the elderly woman goes in for a hug. Amazingly, Josh is hugging back, and Mrs. Hickman can only assume he is sobbing, judging by the movement of his shoulders. Mrs. Hickman silently says a prayer and watches the old woman and the mourning young husband.

What Mrs. Hickman actually witnesses is an elderly mentor and her young follower slowly walking down the dirt roadway sharing the news that Hannah's cancer has become resistant to treatment and has spread throughout her body. Josh stops in his tracks as his anger builds and boils over into a scream. Then he reaches down and picks up a handful of stones. Without looking at Hannah, he throws stone after stone at nothing specific and asks her how long she has to live. She waits for the last to be thrown, then walks over to Josh and hugs him again, saying quietly, "Not long, not long at all."

Squeezing her tightly, Josh begins to cry uncontrollably, not only for Hannah's imminent death but for the entirety of the last few months. A lost pregnancy, the death of his wife, and now the death of the only friend left on earth. Josh can't hold it in any longer, mask it in anger, or dive into a depression. The emotion is too much for his body to hold inside. It is a massive release of energy in the form of crying that Josh, in a million years, would not have thought he had within. His love for Ashley is so deep that he cannot understand the existence of this outburst.

After a few moments, they begin to walk again. As Josh regains his composure, both of them stare at the ground, Hannah says, "Can I ask you some questions?"

"What type of questions?" Hannah's apprehension and the length of time she has been thinking before speaking make Josh anxious.

"Questions you probably don't want to answer—questions about your past and your future."

Josh, now extremely nervous, begins to kick at stones in the road, mumbling over and over, "I don't know."

Hannah reaches out and grabs his hand. "If it weren't important, I wouldn't ask. I don't have time to wait if we are going to make it happen."

Josh looks at Hannah and says, "We?"

"Yes, there is a group of people who all have Stage IV cancer, just like Ashley and me, who want to hold the companies who put the poison in the environment accountable—whether it's pesticides, herbicides, bombs, or drugs—to steal resources from different regions of the world. This process creates a system that kills people and all life on Earth in pursuit of profits. We have an idea, but it will take people putting their lives on the line."

In a desperate, concerned voice, Josh asks, "Was Ashley part of this group?"

Hannah says a long no-o-o and continues: "This group is made up of older people, like myself, who supported this system that's doing all this damage for various reasons and now want to try and make amends before we shuffle off this mortal coil.

"I was hoping with all my heart Ashley was going to have many more years ahead of her, and because she needed to use all her energy towards that goal, I wouldn't have ever even mentioned it to her. The only reason I'm bringing it up with you is because you now need a reason to live, and I think this might get justice for both Ashley and me. At the pace my cancer is moving, I'm not sure if I can handle this by myself. I need your help."

Josh shakes his head. "I don't think so. That's what I was told before being shipped off to Iraq—how horrible the people were there and how much they supported Saddam Hussein. I was going to get justice for 9/11 and what Saddam Hussein, along with Al Qaeda, did.

"I just wanted to serve my country like my dad, my uncles, and grandpa. I wanted to protect the world against dictators and advance democracy so the people of the world could have power over their own lives." Josh's voice trails off, and he shakes his head again. "No, I don't know . . ."

Hannah feels an urgency to get Josh's head out of being betrayed and back towards serving a higher purpose. "Josh, it would be easy to say that Ashley would like you to join us, but I honestly don't think she would want that. She would want you to get on with your life and enjoy it enough for both of you. I know that's what she wanted. She told me so. The beauty of Ashley was that her primary vision was focused on all the good on Earth, which is admirable."

Pointing at Josh and back to herself, Hannah continues, "But some of us have experienced too much of the bad. We've been used for the gain of wealth and power of others at the expense of our well-being. I think you know what I'm talking about. Some of us have inner demons and dragons we need to slay before we can move on. Up until recently, I didn't think these demons and dragons could be slayed, at least not in the foreseeable future. This group has given me hope for a future that our dragons, which I suspect are the same type, can no longer control the way the world operates.

"Ashley never really told me much about your time in the military other than that you protected the sanctity of the US Constitution and were then punished for it by the very government whose entire oath is to serve and protect it from enemies—foreign or domestic.

"Well, we have a domestic enemy that is killing tens of thousands of innocent Americans every year and raking in hundreds of billions in profits in the process. These victims include children, women, the elderly—and even the unborn who never make it out of the womb because the mother's internal organs have been altered by chemical exposure. Year after year, these murders are studied, and the results are published. Every election cycle we have new candidates who want to hold these criminals accountable, but they can't because these criminals are the entities who fund the major political parties. With that funding comes great influence over the policies they support and the legislation they write and pass into law.

"Almost all Americans agree about this enemy, but legally, there is little we can do to impose justice for their crimes. That is what this group is all about and trying to achieve: Justice for all people, not just those of us who are sick."

Confused, Josh replies, "I don't know, that sounds so much like what we were told after 9/11—what with weapons of mass destruction and Saddam's use of mustard gas on his own people. Everybody got it wrong. They never found WMDs, and it turned out the mustard gas and its delivery system were US-manufactured and given to Saddam by the Reagan administration to fight Iran, just like they did with the Mujahadeen and Osama bin Laden in Afghanistan to stand up against the Soviets. That allowed Darkwater to come in and give me the orders that got me dishonorably discharged—and everyone from home not wanting anything to do with me."

Worried that Josh is about to get sucked into a bad place, Hannah tries to interrupt. "Josh, everything you're saying is about the same people—the demons and dragons—the people who told you those lies and then profited by it."

"*Stop!*" yells Josh. "Let me get this out. Nobody ever lets me talk—not the military, not my dad, my brothers, or my hometown. My mom and Ashley were the only ones who would listen to my side. I write my mom once a month and send it to a separate PO box to let her know what's going on in our lives—my life now. I haven't written her yet to tell her about Ashley's cancer or her—" Tears stream down his face when he gets to the word dying. He skips it and continues with an increased intensity, "That's how much my fucking family and friends hate me. I can't talk to my own mother without her having to defend me. It's not fair to her, so I write her in secret. I don't want her to know about Ashley yet because it will mean she'll have to let others know we've been in touch. She loved Ashley, and I believe that whenever she receives the news, she will feel the need to be by my side. It will create problems for her at home. As much as I would love to see her, I don't want her to see me like this."

Hannah tries to figure out how to let Josh know that no matter what words are said, his father and family still love him. "I'm sure your father and family would understand and maybe this could be part of a good thing, I think Ashley would have liked that her life brought you and your family back together."

Josh screams, "*No!* My dad made it perfectly clear that I was dead to him, and my brothers stood behind him. Serving our country honorably is one of the only things that brought any sort of importance to our family. Otherwise, we are a bunch of hillbillies who just mine for coal. What I did to get disfucking-honorably-discharged took away the only thing that separated us from the hillbilly label and transformed us into citizens with honor. No matter how many times and in how many ways it's been explained to them, in the end, it's the same result—I'm a torturer and traitor. They say, 'I can talk until I'm blue in the face, but that doesn't change anything.' I've tried many times to reach out to my dad and brothers since, but I have never even received a response."

Holding one hand over her heart and the other over her mouth, Hannah says, "That's horrible, and it's wrong."

"I'm not finished. Once I was put into prison or a pretrial confinement facility, I started reading lots of books. You can get books in there, and my mom would bring and send me lots of reading material. She would come down and stay with Ashley. That's when they became so close. In the beginning, most of it got confiscated, but then she got wise to the system. Neither of us knew they would not allow any books that tell a different history than the ones we are taught. So, we agreed I needed to learn why the American Revolution took place.

"While waiting for my court martial, I read everything about American Revolutionary history and military codes I could get my hands on. No matter what I found and showed to my JAG rep, he didn't care. I was going to lose and probably end up in prison for the rest of my life. At this point my parents hired a private lawyer to work with the JAG. I don't know where they got the money, but that was the difference between my being dishonorably discharged and me being in prison. The private lawyer put the JAG's feet to the fire and created a plea deal. The JAG finally came clean with me and the private lawyer. They said that there needed to be someone held accountable for the prison's abuses.

"Almost everyone has heard of Abu Ghraib, but there were other facilities—many others—and I was stationed at one of them, Camp Bucca near Umm Qasr."

"I don't remember hearing that name before."

"Yeah, nobody stateside has heard of it either."

"I don't want to interrupt, but does your father know your side of the story?"

"Yes! He knows the whole goddamn thing, but he cares more about his standing in our town than about his son. No matter what evidence he saw or believed, the decision was Dishonorably Discharged. He tried to explain to everyone back home that I was being used as a fall guy, but nobody was buying it. He lost a few lifelong friends over it, and then he started being left out, losing overtime shifts and spending more time alone. That's when he changed his tune. He disowned me in front of anyone and everyone. The same was true for my brothers.

"He told me that I had a life outside of Logan County, West Virginia, but our entire three generations of grandparents, uncles, aunts, cousins, and brothers did not. I could not come back home or even contact anyone for the family. He told me to think about what they are all going through for doing nothing other than being related to a torturer and disgraced soldier.

"I screamed at him, what do you think *I'm* going through, *I'm* the one who didn't follow orders from Darkwater to interrogate for entertainment and not find out any real information. We rarely got good information. If you interrogate or torture someone long enough, they'll tell you anything you want just to make it stop. At first, I followed orders from my superior officer to get insurgents to talk. If we were going to get information that would save the lives of my brothers in battle, I would get that information. When all the information we were getting was terrible, Darkwater was brought in. I was honoring my oath to uphold the US Constitution and military codes, which got me in trouble. Dad didn't care. I told him I don't give two shits about what people think and he should stand by his son, who did the *honorable* thing. That's when he said to me that his son died in Iraq, and he didn't know who I was."

Now Josh is on a roll and what he wants more than anything is for Hannah to understand he isn't just some hillbilly—in fact, he is actually smart and knows his history: "Do you remember in 1980 when the hostages were taken in Iran? Yeah, that was a result of a CIA coup over Iran's democratically elected leader in the 1950s that allowed a pro-Western leader to be put in charge. That's what led to the religious revolution in Iran.

"The other part of all this, many people still think, is some conspiracy theory, despite it being exposed that Ronald Reagan's campaign had indirect ties with those holding the US hostages, and a deal was made with them to keep them until the American presidential elections were over.

"Once in office and the hostages were released, the Reagan Administration took Saddam Hussein off the terrorist list. Then they began to arm and release intelligence to the Iraqi dictator about Iran. What a few people figured out early and had their careers ruined for was that the Reagan Administration was dealing and selling military weapons to Iran through Israel, at the same time. There are many reasons for doing this, but a big one was that Reagan wanted a war against the communists in the Americas, and Congress refused to give him the authority to do so. That's when they needed to fund the war covertly and in the process made a deal with the devil that reverberated throughout the US. It's called Iran Contra Affair."

Hannah is well-versed in the Iran Contra Affair, money laundering, and the cocaine connection to the US interests' Panamanian puppet Manuel Noreiga—forces that fueled the crack cocaine epidemic that ravaged inner cities across the United States in the 1980s. She sits quietly admiring Josh's knowledge of recent history. He continues. "Ironically, it was First Lady Nancy Reagan who led the anti-drug campaign of 'Just Say No' to the very policies—both Iran Contra-related and domestic— of her husband's administration that created the drug problem."

Then he embarks on a lecture about what led directly to 9/11. "A private group of neo-conservatives pushed Clinton administration first into sanctions and bombing of Iraq, and then dozens of them were in office of the George W Bush administration in, 2001. Have you heard of them? You might have, but most people don't have a clue!" Then switching to how George H. W. Bush, whose dad was a banker and then US Senator, tried to overthrow FDR during the Depression and was a nazi sympathizer. "You can't make this stuff up.

"George H. W. Bush, the former head of the CIA, Vice President in the Reagan administration, and then President in 1990, gave permission for the US ally Saddam Hussein's government to diagonally drill into Kuwait's deepwater oil reserves, which set off another war.

"That's when the US declared to NATO that Iraq was an enemy and went in to stop Saddam from doing what the Bush administration had permitted them to do. I forget the exact words, but it was something along the lines of 'The US has no opinion on Iraq's future intentions with Kuwait.'

"That began the first Gulf War, which started a chain of events of economic sanctions, bombing campaigns, and military bases that our buddy Osama bin Laden didn't like, so he declared war on the USA in the 1990s, bombed the USS *Cole* in October 2000, and attacked the World Trade Center on September 11, 2001.

"During the 1990s, the Clinton administration pushed for an embargo and sanctions on Iraq that were responsible for half a million innocent people's deaths. Their only crime was living in a country that was the enemy of US interests.

"I didn't know any of this when I joined the military. I was promised an education and some experience to learn what I wanted to do with my life. Then 9/11 happened, and the propaganda to avenge innocent lives pumped up all the enlisted and created a boom for recruits. We all wanted to prove to our dads, uncles, and grandpas that we would do our job and have our war to tell our kids about. What most veterans don't tell their kids, nephews, or grandkids is how much war changes and damages our loved ones and a person's soul."

By the time Josh finishes, both Josh and Hannah have been standing at the mailbox for a while. Hannah has been quiet, looking at the ground and listening since they reached the mailbox. She notices what she thinks are daffodils popping up through the soil. After a long pause, she finally breaks the silence. "Everything you just talked about is the demons and dragons I'm talking about. There isn't any political will to correct all these issues that dominate our lives today in industrialized civilization. The worst part about all of it is that a bunch of wealthy corporate business people have convinced the entire world to join their disgusting game of 'profit by death.'

"Josh, I met with a man in Colorado a couple of weeks ago. We talked indirectly about what our little group is attempting to do. He said something very profound: The one piece of advice I will give is that justice has to be done in connection with the crime committed. I want to share everything with you if that is alright. I'm tired. Let's go back inside, and we can talk some more."

Hannah holds Josh's arm as they slowly walk back down the driveway towards the house. By the time they reach the house, Josh is deeply concerned about Hannah's health and even questions her mind. Opening the door and helping her to a chair, he asks her if she would like some water or anything else.

"Water would be great. And please eat the food I brought you—you need to eat."

Josh hands Hannah a glass of water, grabs a fork, and sits with her at the table. After a couple of bites, his hunger comes to mind. "How many days has it been since I ate anything?"

Placing her empty glass on the table, Hannah replies, "It must be at least three days and maybe even more. I'm not sure how much eating you were doing leading up to everything. I know I've lost a few pounds over the last week." As Josh continues to eat at a faster pace: "Slow down.

You don't want to choke, and it's better for you to chew your food thoroughly. Listen, I know you don't want to talk about all this stuff any longer, but as I mentioned, time is running out for me. So please, keep eating and listen to what I have to say. Then I'll be on my way, and we'll talk tomorrow about everything you heard today and what you think about it. My childhood friends might join us on a computer, and you can hear from them that this isn't just the crazy idea of an old woman. Can we do that? Would that be alright with you?"

"Okay, I'll listen and think about everything." He continues eating. In reality, he is thinking of the effects of her cancer but letting her get this important idea out if she believes it will help.

Hannah closes her eyes, takes a deep breath, and begins. "Let's get my condition out of the way first. It is what it is—not much can be done at this point. What I want most before it's over is to positively impact the world towards change. That change will be determined by who controls human-made systems and who are the primary beneficiaries of these systems. So far, civilization has had the same recipe: A small few control almost everything and receive a vast majority of the benefits. At the same time, the rest of the people serve the system in whatever capacity they can and still survive. This needs to change. The problem is that the laws created are for people with the least in society to follow. Do you understand what I'm saying? Kind of like your experience in the military—there's a hierarchy, right? Until your parents brought in a private lawyer, the JAG served the system, or military machine, not you. The same is true within our government and governments worldwide at this point."

At this remark, Josh begins to listen more intensely. Hannah continues: "In all your study of history, do you remember what the definition of *fascism* is? The merger of public and private interests is what predatory capitalism represents in the twenty-first century—a form of fascism. The more powerful corporations get, the closer we get to a feudal society.

"A small few own and control everything, and the people have no say in how society is set up. It has gotten quite sophisticated—and with computers and cell phones, so has the propaganda that tells us our story. That story is that we are choosing all of this violence and suffering by the way and where we spend our money. It is simply not true. It is an illusion of choice, with the same corporations owning everything and having the same goal: profits and influence.

"I'm going to talk specifically about the corporation Fulcircle to show you what I am talking about. I could name multiple pancake mixes and syrups, cereals, cookies, and so on. We believe they are all competitors because that is how they are marketed to us, but they are all owned by the same corporation. So, do you understand what I'm saying?"

Josh has finished his food and at this point is just listening. He leans forward and puts his elbows on the table to get a little closer. "You're saying Fulcircle owns all those companies, which I assume grow the ingredients using Fulcircle seeds and products. What is the big deal about that? I like lots of those products. Ashley's parents were soybean farmers for a Fulcircle-owned company." With this statement, he begins to choke up and says, "No. I'm not going to do this. I can't do this right now."

Hannah finds the energy and stands up quickly. In a loud and firm voice, she says, "It's got to be now. You have to hear this if you want to find any sort of justice for Ashley." She sits back down and asks for another glass of water. As Josh takes her glass to fill it up, she continues. "This will be painful for both of us, but we need to push through it. Did you ever meet Ashley's parents?"

"No, they were both gone before we were serious enough for me to meet them."

Hannah explains, "I looked them up online and learned about their farm and how they lost it to the company that paid them to grow Kill-All Ready soybeans. The story didn't go into this much detail but it is the same as so many other cases I have looked into over the years. Ashley's family had a small farm until they were convinced that if they purchased a larger harvester and more land, with the new GMO seeds they could make much more money without much more work. They just needed to take out a loan for the larger combine and land—and follow the Fulcircle formula of synthetic fertilizer, pesticides, and herbicides timed applications: spray Kill-All herbicide four times yearly from cracking to flowering. The last application is used to speed up the drying out process of the plant; you cannot harvest and process the soybeans until the plant reduces to a specific moisture level. Utilizing the herbicide helps speed the process up.

"According to an article I read, Ashley's parents, like their neighbors, got so far into debt that they had to sell their farm. The best deal they could get was to sell it to, you guessed it, a Fulcircle-owned company that would allow them to still live in the same house and run the farm just like before. The difference was that they no longer owned it. So, by the time Ashley reached her senior year in high school, they were living a share-cropper's life, and she didn't know about it. That's why her getting an education was so important to them both.

"Oh—I forgot to mention the GMO seeds and the patents that made it so farmers can no longer save the seeds to replant the following season. If they do save the seeds, Fulcircle Company sues them in court and wins every time. That has also led many farmers to bankruptcy.

"Then Ashley's mom signed Ashley's dad up in a class action lawsuit against his wishes. Non-Hodgkin's lymphoma is cancer directly linked to Kill-All herbicide. He was quoted as saying he didn't like the fact that she did it but came to realize Fulcircle needed to understand that people using their products were getting sick. He didn't think they understood how serious it was, and this lawsuit was a way to bring this information to the company scientists.

"I followed up with anything else, and I found his obituary. It said he had lost his battle against non-Hodgkin's lymphoma. Within a short period, her mother died, and it didn't give any cause of death. Ashley was their only child."

Josh yells, "*STOP!* I don't want to hear any more of this shit. She told me about her parents and how her dad died, which is one of the big reasons she was so afraid of the pain. No more—"

"I'm sorry, but there is just one more thing, and I promise to move on. Ashley's ovarian cancer was probably linked to being exposed to all those poisons, which is why her body refused the pregnancy. Studies have proven it is the third-generation and chromosome disruptor that mutates cell development, and that was your pregnancy. I'm so sorry to have to bring this up, and I swear no more about Ashley."

By now, Josh is up and pacing the kitchen, trying to contain his rage. "Those motherfuckers—those motherfuckers! Do you think they knew?"

"Of course, they knew. The entire history of Fulcircle is about killing and death. The atomic bomb dropped on Japan, and Fulcircle played a part in it. Their pesticide, used to try and slow the spread of malaria also affects other animals' neurological health. Dioxin was used heavily in Vietnam as an herbicide, and it is a Fulcircle product. Over and over again, Fulcircle's business history is about death through chemistry and poison. They've added food production control in the last fifty years.

"Have you ever heard the name, *Joe Sinclair*?"

Still pacing back and forth, Josh replies, "No—never heard of the guy."

"He was the CEO of Fulcircle and now sits on many boards of directors. While CEO of Fulcircle, he doubled their profits and took the company to the next level. Under his leadership, Fulcircle's lobbying efforts were to change the laws and get insiders to head regulatory agencies. That was the beginning of what happened to so many farmers in the 1980s. You were just a little kid, but a bunch of entertainers put on a festival called Farm Aid that was put together to help small family farmers and bring attention to the issue of industrial agribusiness crushing the "culture" out of agriculture.

"Mono-industrial farming is dependent on chemicals, and with each generation, the soil, water, and produce become more toxic. Have you ever wondered why so many people are now allergic to wheat or gluten or have irritable bowel syndrome? Fulcircle and herbicides not only kill the weeds; they also kill our gut health, and we can no longer digest their poison grains.

"I'm almost positive my cancer and my husband Bob's Parkinson's are linked to living in this county and being exposed for so many years to Fulcircle's products. Enough about Fulcircle for the moment. Do you understand what I've said so far?"

"Fulcircle is pretty much evil, and they make a profit killing people or making them sick," he says.

"Yeah, that's about it. Enough of that for now. Have you been following the Fukushima disaster in Japan?"

Daylight is fading fast, so Josh walks over to turn on the kitchen light. "Of course, it's all over the news. No matter how they look at it, there isn't a good solution."

Hannah has gotten an adrenaline second wind, and her voice is strong. "Okay, I saw a news broadcast about a group called Kesshitai, which translates to 'unit that expects to die.' They are all sixty years and older, volunteering to work the shifts inside the crippled nuclear plant right now. Since they promoted nuclear power and have lived a long life, this is why they volunteered. The intense radiation exposure means they will most likely die in a short period of time. But if they are going to get any control of this disaster, they need people to work inside the radiation zones. Those who benefitted from the dangerous power source the most are the ones sacrificing for future generations.

"Our group is taking this premise and applying it to another story about a man who killed the general manager of the main corporation of his small Montana Rocky Mountain town. The man and his lawyer had experienced and witnessed over a dozen family members die of the same disease, which was known by the corporation Vermolite Mining Company and the executive and eventual general manager who worked for the company for decades. The convicted killer was Ben Brown, and his lawyer was Michael Bennett, whom I visited in Denver recently. Ben Brown died from the same disease as his family members about a month ago.

"Around 1999, Vermolite Mining was found guilty of their crimes, and the company filed for bankruptcy as the civil lawsuits began to pile up. Nobody went to jail despite the death totals being in the high hundreds and probably into the thousands if we go far enough back in time. What makes it worse is that the people still living in this town all know what their fate most likely looks like and cannot sell their homes to start somewhere new. The entire town is considered a Superfund site, or so toxic that the federal government needs to come in and clean it up properly.

"Ben Brown was dying of mesothelioma when he killed the former general manager, Carl Shadwick, who he had known since he was a child. He was found guilty, but his jail time was waived due to all the pain and suffering the company had caused his entire family and town."

Engulfed in the story, as if it were a movie or an audiobook, Josh stops pacing. Hannah has done the job she came to do. She sees his concentration and goes on with the story. "The reason I'm telling you all this is because of the group we have formed in different cities around the US and even in as far as India. We're going to get justice the only way we can since these industrial murdering corporations have captured the political and judicial system. Fulcircle, Wasser, Adicta, Avidité, and other major industrial corporations have all knowingly put profits before life for decades, and we will hold executives and, preferably, CEOs of all these companies accountable on May 1st—Ben Brown-style. Whoa! I have never said this out loud before. It sounds a lot harder when I say the actual words out loud."

Josh butts in. "Do you mean May 1st—like a couple of weeks from now?! Have any of you ever killed another person or trained to kill anything? It's way harder than you might think. I've never killed anyone, but I've been trained to do it. Even in the middle of urban warfare, I never killed anyone. I did the stuff at the prison, but nobody ever died. I don't think this is a very good idea—and not a good plan."

Heart sinking, Hannah asks, "Why?"

"I'm not saying the motives and intentions aren't well thought out, but to kill another person not in self-defense will shred a person's soul into bits."

Hannah jumps in. "It is in self-defense! That's the whole point. If a person knew another person was trying to poison them or their children to death slowly, and they caught and killed that person, it would be self-defense. Look at it this way: If I were to pull a gun out and shoot you, that would be murder. Or if I knew I was poisoning you and it would kill you, that is also murder. It is just slower."

"That's true, but I don't think the law will see it that way."

"*BINGO!* That's the ultimate problem: It's the get-out-of-jail-free card corporations and executives have in this predatory system!"

Josh asks, slightly puzzled, "What is or does the "get-out-of-jail-free card" mean? I don't know what you're talking about."

Hannah laughs. "I guess Monopoly wasn't big in your family. It's a reference to a board game we all used to play before five hundred channels of TV and computers were invented. The object of the game was to own everything, which meant you controlled the entire game, and everyone was in debt to the winner. One of the game cards was 'get-out-of-jail-free,' which you could use if your token landed on the square that would stick you in jail. Today's large corporations have that card in their pockets all the time with Limited Liability. The people who own, run, or control the corporation cannot be held personally liable for the corporation's wrongdoings or debts."

"Yeah, I know about Limited Liability, but that doesn't give them a free pass to murder people."

"Are you sure? If we're talking about a mom-and-pop shop, you're correct. But we're talking about large corporations that own dozens of other companies and have teams of lawyers who specialize in finding loopholes in the laws or who write the laws themselves to make what they are doing legal. How do you think no banker went to jail in 2008 over the financial collapse?

Here's the messed-up part: The loopholes are put into laws on purpose."

"Wait a minute. You're telling me the laws our elected officials create have loopholes on purpose?"

"That is exactly what I'm saying. The problem is that, depending on the district or state, US senators or congresspersons can spend up to 60–70 percent of their time fundraising for both their political parties and, more importantly, their next election. They don't have time to do the research, meet with experts, and really flesh out a piece of legislation that serves the people any longer. They spend the majority of their time fishing for large donors. I'll give you an example: Generally, they are called bundlers. These high-powered lobbyists can bundle a group of people to donate the maximum to the political party and specific candidates anywhere in the country. Bundlers can bring in hundreds of thousands at a time.

"Here's a specific example: George W. Bush, the Commander-in-Chief you served under. His bundlers were called different names depending on how much money they brought in. Pioneers brought in $100,000 to the campaign, Rangers brought in $200,000–$299,000, and Super Rangers brought in $300,000 or more to the campaign and the Republican Party. The Democratic Party works the same way."

Sitting there with his mouth open, Josh is trying to wrap his head around how open the corruption is right in front of us.

Hannah keeps going. "I looked it up on a watchdog website that only tracks campaign funding and spending. In the sixteen-year period from 1976 to 1992, the average for presidential campaign spending increased by 10 percent. But in the next sixteen years, from 1992 to 2008, it increased by over 400 percent. In many districts and states, those percentages tracked the same way for both the US Senate and House campaigns. Roughly 90 percent of incumbents win elections in the Senate and House in every election cycle.

"Get this: Only twice since congressional approval ratings have been followed have the people of the United States held a majority favorable rating of Congress. Right now, congressional approval ratings dip into the teens and rarely get out of the twenty-percentile ranges. And yet, 90 percent of our incumbents retain their seats. It doesn't add up."

Josh quietly interrupts, with a question: "How is this legal?"

Now as animated as Hannah can be, she responds in detail: "Both the Republican and Democratic party members have been captured by special interests. Representatives must go through all the large funders to compete in their next campaign. In return for the money to guarantee election, these funders have prewritten pieces of legislation from corporate lawyers, lobbyists, and think tanks for the representatives who submit it to the committees they belong to in Congress. More than ever, corporate lobbyists write the bills, and Democrats and Republicans propose them and vote them into law. It is one big shell game. Big lobbying firms and think tanks write corporate-friendly laws that make it almost impossible for ordinary people to hold industrial giants accountable. "Here's another example that has happened in the last few years. It started in 2003 and went into effect in January 2006. The Republican House Majority Leader was a guy from Texas named Tom Delay. While he eventually did get in trouble for laundering money, Delay and another Representative from Louisiana named Billy Tauzin exemplified everything wrong with our federal government. They were wolves in sheep's clothing. In other words, they were corporate lobbyists elected to the House who were pushing for a Medicare drug plan that would lock the federal government into paying the highest prices in the industrial world for prescription drugs.

"If you come away with one thing from this long rant of trying to explain something that took me decades to understand, it is this: *They are raking in hundreds of billions in profits by making us sick and hundreds of billions in profits treating our illnesses.*

"Back to the Medicare Part D vote: When they held the vote in the middle of the night, they thought it was going to pass easily because Big Pharma had been donating and taking elected officials on junkets or vacations dubbed official meetings like crazy, and had hundreds of lobbyists in Washington, DC. We must remember there are just over 500 elected officials in our federal government. So, in theory, industries only need to be able to buy 270 votes to get a law passed.

"Anyway, they held the vote for the Medicare Part D Drug program, and as the totals were coming in, they didn't have enough votes to pass it. Tom Delay had to call back a representative who was permitted to vote no and went home to his district before the vote closed. Delay called him, and he had to fly back to Washington to change his vote. They kept a vote that is normally fifteen to thirty minutes open for hours longer than normal. In the meantime, they were handing out checks like they did with the tobacco vote in the 1990s on the House floor, trying to get people to flip their *no* votes to *yes*. Ultimately, the vote passed, and George W. Bush signed it into law. Then, guess what happened?"

"What?"

"Billy Tauzin announced he was not running for reelection the next term and became a pharmaceutical-industry lobbyist for millions of dollars in salary. Compared to the $175,000 salary of being a US Senator or House member, that's a big incentive. It's called a revolving door.

Before you ask why can't we just vote for Democrats to get these corrupt politicians out of office—that is exactly what Barack Obama campaigned on, and the Democrats won everything in a big way. The people spoke: We want government done differently.

"President-Elect Obama's first action was to surround himself with investment-banking insiders, the largest funders of his presidential campaign of 2008. Three years later, we are still experiencing the aftereffects of the housing subprime loan depression. Obama's Attorney General, the most powerful lawyer in the country, was a high-priced, investment-banking lawyer with a very powerful law firm. The Attorney General didn't prosecute any big banks or bankers. I can go down the list of Obama's cabinet appointees and we'll find the same story. Lobbyists or insiders of the industry will head up the cabinet position or regulatory agency overseeing their business interests.

"The People have no way to redress our grievances. So, with all this said, we need to understand that all these so-called mistakes or bad decisions are anything but accidents. The bills and laws are written to work exactly the way they do. The return on investment in government is enormous. Invest a few million here and there, and you'll receive hundreds of millions, if not billions, in return.

"These Industries are not innocent; they know they are killing people but there are very little real-life repercussions for their actions. Our group is focusing on specific corporations like Fulcircle. Corporations that pollute our water and our air, kill the life in the soil and our guts, and eventually kill us. They call them all externalities. They leave it up to society to clean up their mess or, at best, suffer the punishment for their negligence with the increased social damages such as asthma, upper respiratory diseases, irritable bowel syndrome, birth defects, cancers, and so on. Or at worst, it is the grotesque business model, as general manager Vermolite Mining Company and their Carl Shadwick did in Montana. They were the number-one employer in town and had their own doctors covering up what was going on. That's why Ben Brown took action and got justice, which was the only way he could have done it before he died.

"Now, take what Joe Sinclair and Fulcircle are doing worldwide. We are told they are upstanding global citizens who employ huge numbers of people and grow food better. But in reality, their business model factors in the cost of polluting and killing people versus lawsuits and fines. If they ultimately are still profitable, they continue to do it. They spend money on public relations and buying off political parties and elected officials instead of the safety of their products."

Josh's eyes are wide open and intense. He is laser-focused on what Hannah is saying because this is similar to how the military works. "You're right—in war we call it collateral damage. The US defense has contracts with private weapons manufacturers who receive all the profits while soldiers do all of the dirty work. If something goes wrong, they do an investigation, and usually, a soldier will get demoted or put in prison. That's what they tried to do to me."

"Exactly! That's what our group is about, Josh. Initially, I was hung up on the "legal" aspect of it all, but—speaking with my lawyer friend in Denver and reading about the Ben Brown case in Montana—it isn't about whether it is legal. It shouldn't be legal for anyone—that is the point. That's why our group is made up of people exiting this life due to Stage IV cancer. *Our life sentences or death penalties have already been given to us.*

"We are trying to shake people awake to what is going on. To put CEOs and company executives on notice that there is no more protection when their companies use us as profit generators by stealing our wealth and ultimately sacrificing our lives. That is no longer acceptable and will not be tolerated.

"Kesshitai, a unit that expects to die, is our way of trying to correct a wrong we allowed to be created. I'm the one who was inspired by the Kesshitai squads in Fukushima and use that term most. It was Ben Brown, who had no clue about that idea or term, who was the first to get beyond legal or not legal. That is how he represented himself in his court case."

Josh is surprised. "So, someone has done this, and they found him *not-guilty?*"

Hannah shoots back: "No, he was found *guilty* on all charges."

"So, what are we talking about then? He didn't change anything."

Hannah's mind is going in circles, trying to find a way to explain it to Josh. "Have you ever seen those posters that seem to have nothing to them, and then all of sudden you see an animal, a waterfall, or a word?"

"Yeah, so what?"

"It's like that with your mind's eye. Stop focusing on how we are taught to perceive legal versus illegal as moral and immoral. Are wars moral? No, yet they are legal. Is owning a human being as a slave moral? No, but it was legal for hundreds of years in North America. Was what happened to the Jews during World War II in Germany moral? No, but it was legal—and that is why so many otherwise good people went along with it. We are taught to follow laws and to conflate laws with being moral and breaking laws with being immoral.

"If we know a law or what is legal is wrong, we must change it. For decades, all the way up until a few weeks ago, I was trying to change it through "their" system of rules, which are rigged against the people in favor of the wealthy and corporations. Ben Brown was a hundred percent correct. In self-defense of future generations and toward justice for the pain and suffering Vermolite Mining caused his family, he achieved that justice by ignoring "their" system's dysfunctional morality of legal and illegal.

"Josh, I'm so tired right now, and I need rest. I have a meeting with our group tomorrow at noon. I will leave you with one thing: I will send you an email with the study and report supporting my hypothesis.

"About Ashley—I'm sorry for breaking my word by bringing her up again. Ashley's illness and death and her lost pregnancy was due to her heavy exposure to glyphosate caused by Fulcircle. This case study of third-generation exposure to glyphosate causing endocrine disruption and the side effect of birth defects and naturally aborted pregnancies has been peer-reviewed and published. There are so many other chronic diseases connected to it as well. Glyphosate is the key ingredient in Kill-All, the herbicide Ashley's dad used throughout her entire childhood. It has been proven since his death that his type of cancer is directly linked to exposure to glyphosate.

"I hate throwing all of this at you, especially at such a vulnerable time. Still, I genuinely believe that those of us who don't have long to live and have been severely damaged by these companies have a duty to try and create a movement or a shift—a movement against the greed and psychopathic decision-making of the executives at these corporations and industries. If we can concentrate the news cycle on a series of deaths by murder from victims of those who suffer from these heartless executive decisions, it will allow others to connect their illnesses or those of their loved ones to these corporate crimes against humanity.

"This is why it is so important for those of us who have been given this death sentence through the actions and products of these corporations to spearhead the movement. Going to jail for the rest of our lives is no longer an intimidating threat, which is their biggest defense against their victims, outside of corruption. Nobody wants to give up their life for something that might not make any difference. In our group, our futures were decided in board rooms and financial spreadsheets decades ago without our consent.

"I'm sorry once again. Please look for the email with the study in a few minutes. If you want to join our group, come to my house tomorrow around 10:00 a.m. so I can review the actual plan and explain how we will carry it out. Try to get some sleep. I hope to see you in the morning, and if not, I totally understand.

"What I am proposing here is something I would have never considered or believed to be a good idea until the last month or so. It took several different events to come together quickly, allowing me to see the solution. Otherwise, I wouldn't have connected the dots. The key is to have it all done in a short period of time so others can connect the dots as well. Our news cycle and national attention span are extremely short, so it needs to be big and stay in the news cycle. There is more to it, but if you decide to pursue this idea further, I will explain it to you tomorrow.

"I love you, and don't ever forget it."

As they embrace for a goodbye hug, Hannah says to Josh while they are both crying gently, "Riding this emotional rollercoaster together has brought everything to the surface."

CHAPTER FOURTEEN

A GRADUATION—SAWPIT, MONTANA

JUNE, 1972:

Pat Brown asks, "Is Dad going to make it to the ceremony?"

The steam-iron hisses as John-J presses it down on his dress shirt, his voice distracted and focused on something else. "Yeah, he called this morning and said he wouldn't miss it. He's bringing some stuff for the BBQ, and we will all ride together."

Pat Brown chuckles as she peeks around the corner to see her husband struggling to get the wrinkles out of his shirt and jokes, "Do you want me to do it? I did Ben's already this morning."

"No, I got it. I'm so excited to see our boy graduate that I can't concentrate. Dad's even more proud of Ben. He bought a new cooler just for the BBQ. I talked to him earlier—the steaks were marinating, drinks were on the ice, and his clothes were laid out. He just needed to take his pills for the cough."

CONGRATULATIONS—GRADUATING CLASS
OF 1972!

Family and friends walk onto the field at the high school.

Ben Brown is good-looking, tall, well-liked, a varsity-lettered athlete, and loves hunting and fishing. A few months shy of his eighteenth birthday, he is contemplating college. Still, he has let his applications remain unsent, torn between joining the military to avoid being drafted for Vietnam or waiting for the draft to happen. A military recruiter who visited the high school had suggested or lied that those who enlist instead of being drafted are less likely to be sent directly into the jungle.

More often than not, Ben hears stories from friends, returning soldiers, and veterans of past conflicts. They speak about the draft being a form of slavery, where, if drafted, a person's life no longer belongs to them. Instead, it belongs to the war machine, which would use them as it saw fit. Ben knows he wants to spend his life outdoors, not in a classroom or behind a desk. One thing he is sure about is that he does not want to work for Vermolite Mining Company, whether in the mines or at the plant.

As the valedictorian finishes up their inspirational speech about how "We are the future" and how "We are going to reshape the world," Ben leans over to his best friend Arthur Bennett and whispers, "My dad told me they were going to say all these things. 'We are the Future'—because they say it at every graduation. I bet all those guys slaving away for Vermolite who were sitting where we are right now would disagree."

Arthur covers his mouth to muffle his laughter and begins to cough. It was not a clear-your-throat cough but a deep, crackly cough with a real purpose.

Ben gives him a sideways glance. "Damn, that sounds nasty. Keep whatever you got away from me."

A few other graduates, within hearing distance, must have thought the same thing. They all look over and then proceed to scoot their chairs ever so slightly away from the cough.

"Are you and your family coming over right after graduation, or are you doing something at home first?" asks Ben.

"Mikey and Nicole are coming. They tried to get here before everything started, but I don't know if they made it. I guess they had finals yesterday and they're making the trip straight from class. Get this—Mikey is seriously thinking about becoming a lawyer, he's applied to a couple of law schools already and thinks he's got a good shot at getting accepted," Arthur continues with a laugh of approval. That son of bitch said he was going to do it, and it's happening."

Over the speakers, the two boys' conversation is interrupted by the statement: Will all the graduates of the class of 1972 please stand and come to receive your diplomas.

The first of a procession of names is announced: "Sarah Abbott..." She takes two steps up, shakes the principal's hand, and is handed her diploma in her other hand. She throws both arms up in a celebratory gesture.

"Jonathan Abernathy..."

* * * *

Arthur Bennett, Ben Brown, and Jennifer O'Brien have been close friends since elementary school. Rarely would any of them be seen without at least one of the other two.

Later, Jennifer will attend college in Missoula to study biology, although few people in town think that being a scientist is a fitting job for a woman. She will receive her degree with honors and, to the relief of many, meet her future husband, a geological engineer. They will go on to have three children and fulfilling careers. Years down the line, Ben will hear that they are retired and living in Kalispell, Montana, spending much of the year as docents and wandering around Glacier National Park.

Despite missing so many days of school his entire life with chronic asthma and upper respiratory issues, Arthur has managed to graduate with his childhood friends. His options will be limited due to his asthma disqualifying him for service in the military and his poor academic record. College will not even be considered. He will continue to work at The Nugget Theater in the hope that another opportunity will come his way.

* * * *

Eventually, Ben, Arthur, and Jennifer move on to their graduation party at the Brown house. The three best friends are having one last hurrah before they embark on their separate paths.

With a trimmed beard, ironed clothes, and a huge smile on his face, an elderly man calls out to them, "Hot damn, three graduates rarin' to set the world on fire! What plans do you have for the summer before you go out and become productive members of society?" With the last statement, he clears his throat with a sarcastic tone. All three laugh, and Ben answers, pointing his thumb over his shoulder at Jennifer and Arthur, "Thanks, Grandpa, I can't speak for these two, but I'll get in tons of fishing and camping this summer before making any big moves."

"Yep, I'll be fishing and camping, too, when I'm not working at the theater," Arthur adds.

Still sporting a massive grin, Grandpa Jack replies, "Sounds good, boys. I mean—*men*. Arthur, you've got your entire life to worry about work. Get out into the woods as much as possible while you still can before responsibilities become your main priority." He continues, "How about you, young lady—fishing and camping?"

Jennifer laughs confidently, "Yeah, pretty much, but my family and I will visit relatives in Ireland for three weeks before I head off to school in Missoula in the fall. We're all super excited."

Grandpa Jack tells them to enjoy the summer as much as possible: "You've earned it. Congratulations to you all."

Just as Grandpa Jack finishes congratulating the graduates, a loud pickup truck pulls up in front of the house, and Arthur's parents immediately recognize the sound. Arthur's mom calls out, "George! Mikey and Nicole are here! Filled with excitement for her oldest son and her new daughter-in-law, she walks briskly around to the front of the house. Arthur's dad, George, also heads toward the front but seems to show much less enthusiasm."

* * * *

In 1968, the summer before Arthur's freshman year and Mikey's senior year, Vermolite promoted and sponsored an attic insulation project for the entire town to show appreciation to its workers. The project consisted of a new technology of installation of insulation product into the attic to keep a house warmer in the winter and cooler in the summer. It seemed like half the town took advantage of the program of low monthly payments on an already discounted product the company deemed the future of home insulation.

In front of what seemed like half the town one Saturday morning, Mikey and his dad had it out about putting insulation in their home that would expose their entire family to Vermolite Mining Company products. George Bennett was furious. Loud enough for all to hear, Mr. Bennett looked directly into Mikey's eyes: "That company and my work are paying for you to go to college." The volume of his voice jumped up a few decimals as the redness in his face and neck became visibly darker. Veins started popping everywhere as Mr. Bennett tried to contain his anger. "That *company* and *my work* have kept a roof over your head, food on the table, and clothes on your back."

Regaining his composure, his voice shifted to a fatherly tone, his posture softened, veins recessed, and a more normal color returned to his neck and face. "Son, when you speak so poorly of Vermolite, you speak poorly of myself and much of the town who work in their mines or at the plant. We take pride in our work."

Mikey responded, "Is it my time to speak?"

His dad sighed. "Is it something I haven't heard before?"

"Probably not, and I will not stop saying it either. That Company is killing this town. They are having their employees install their product for free on their day off while charging you for it. How in the hell do you see this as a company taking care of its employees? Why do you think there's a company doctor, and anyone visiting a doctor in one of the cities will leave the company not long afterward? What is your blind-faith answer to that? Did you know Nicole's dad, Mr. Hamilton, was just told he has lung cancer that has spread everywhere from a hospital in Missoula? Do you know how your precious company took care of Mr. Hamilton? Told him to either quit or be sued for using an outside-the-company doctor. The Hamilton's were offered $5,000 not to discuss the circumstances that led Mr. Hamilton to seek outside opinions on his worsening condition."

Mikey was screaming at this last point, and everyone helping install insulation at the house couldn't help but hear what was being said. "Does this sound familiar? Grandpa Nick had the same exact health issues but trusted that fucking company doctor!"

Smack! It was the first and only time Mikey had ever been struck by his father outside of a periodic spanking as a young child. "Don't you ever talk about your grandfather or anyone in this family like we are some poor stupid folk!"

Once again, Mr. Bennett, trying to de-escalate the situation, continued in a fatherly tone. "Mikey, you're getting ready to head off to college, and your mom and I couldn't be prouder. But not all of us had that opportunity. You need to learn to appreciate the blessings you've been given and know when to keep your mouth shut."

Arthur, who was only fourteen at the time, remembered thinking that Mikey wasn't going to college to get a good job. He was going to college so he never had to return to Sawpit again.

* * * *

Mrs. Bennett practically runs into Mikey's arms as he steps around the truck. After a few kisses and hugs, she turns towards Nicole, giving her a big smile with tears running down her face, and says, "All our children are back in Sawpit again. Arthur graduated high school—with Mikey and Nicole coming home for a long visit. Does it get any better than this?"

Mr. Bennett makes it to the young couple heading up the front walkway into the house. He cuts Mikey off with a serious look on his face. "Son, it's good to see you."

Mikey, too tired to care, responds, "Dad, it's good to see you too."

Mr. Bennett grins. "Are you sure you can see me through your red eyes?" He looks over at Nicole. "Come here, you!"—as he yanks her in for a hug. "Are you taking care of yourselves? With the all-nighters (mm-hmm), studying, and school activities?" Now, with his arm around Nicole and Mikey, walking up the front path to the door, he asks, "How did the finals go?"

Mikey interrupts, "Can we come in and see the graduate before we get cross-examined? I'm sorry we missed the ceremony. We were so tired that we had to pull over for a few hours to get some sleep. I'm sure it was the same graduation as ours but with different faces. The party is where it matters."

Mr. Bennett laughs and says, "Spoken like a true college kid. Come on, let's find Arthur."

Nicole is chatting with Mrs. Bennett. "I planned to hang out here for a few hours. Then, my mom, my brothers, and I are going to take a hike to catch up. I haven't had time with them since Christmas break." She laughs. "Spring break was quite busy, and we tried to visit as much as possible before the wedding. Then, we rushed off for our three-day honeymoon."

CHAPTER FIFTEEN

ONLINE MEETING AND TIMOTHY

APRIL 18, 2011—4:17 A.M.:

Hannah looks at the clock next to her bed. She has been up and down all night as her pain increases, and she can no longer find a comfortable position in which to sleep.

With her body in steep decline and only recently figuring out a strategy to achieve the goals she has worked towards for the last forty years, she feels an urgency to be clear-headed and concise when speaking with others about her plan.

Hannah Cassidy has always prided herself on her ability to think critically, organize, and use reason when working with others. This idea and plan are her swan song act in life, and she wants—no, she needs—to get it right for it to work.

She needs her head to be clear, and taking opioid pain medications is out of the question despite being encouraged by her doctors for weeks to do so. She endures the physical pain so she can make clear-headed decisions and be coherent when speaking with others.

Hannah gets up and makes herself a cup of ginger tea, since caffeine and coffee have started to wreak havoc on her digestive system. While waiting for her tea to steep, she texts Olga, "Are you up?"

Receiving no reply, feeling anxious, she starts organizing her folders. Each folder contains the names of executives, details about events, event addresses, and the crimes these individuals and companies have committed.

At 5:35 a.m., typing indicator bubbles start appearing on her phone. Suddenly, a flash of anxiety seizes Hannah about how today's meeting is going to unfold. She grabs her cup of tea, waiting to hear the incoming message sound to alert her. She is sipping when the ping happens, and it is Olga: "Drinking my coffee with Robert and talking about today."

"Call me when you get a chance."

"Talk with you soon."

At about the same time, Josh lies in bed, mulling over everything Hannah had said to him the day before. When not thinking about it, he curls up in a ball, screaming into his pillow about Ashley not being here anymore. He can't help but feel sorry for himself and hate himself for it at the same time. The feeling of being alone, not being able to hold down a job because of his verbal and physical outbursts due to his PTSD, not having any sort of health insurance, being abandoned by the US Military, and most of all, his family and hometown.

He doesn't have a clue what his life will look or feel like next month, and he doesn't want to live anymore. The only thing that seems to calm his nerves and gut, allowing him to focus, is thinking about what Hannah discussed yesterday.

Showered and ready for the day, Hannah tries to eat a light breakfast but has almost no appetite. Her home phone rings, and she immediately picks it up: "Hello."

Olga says, "Good morning darling, were you up all night last night as well?"

"I couldn't sleep for longer than a few minutes at a time. Are we really going to go through with this?"

"That's what Robert and I have been talking about this morning. We both know it's the only way, but it's so hard to shut off the thought that says it is wrong."

"I keep going round and round about the same thing. I talked with Josh yesterday, and I felt so horrible unloading all of this onto him with Ashley passing just a few days ago. He is a nice, good young man who has been railroaded into believing he is the opposite. Luckily, he still has his mother, but that is it. Even *that* is done in secret. He has to mail her at a separate PO box to communicate with her. Isn't that horrible?"

"That is so wrong. How does that even work? Wait, before you answer that question—you had *The Talk* with him yesterday, how did it go?

Hannah sighs. "I'm not sure. I wasn't sure how to address it with him. I felt so bad bringing up Ashley and the miscarriage, but it's why we are doing this whole thing. So that there are no more Ashleys, Elizabeths, or Ben Browns. And no more Bobs, Roberts, and my situation—and countless others whose only misdeed is trusting big corporations to have ethics and morals.

"That's right. We keep coming back to that same conclusion. On the new recruit front, we have a man who was a professional at one point but is facing a horrible ending to his life, which has been in a downward spiral since his son had an opioid overdose that ended his life. His son hurt his knee in his teens and was prescribed Paintabs, and he got hooked and eventually took it too far. He overdosed at twenty. It tore the family apart, and his parents divorced within a year or so."

"Oh my gosh, how horrible. Is he part of your group?"

"Yes, he's part of the Manhattan group. He's been coming for a while now, and only since Robert and I approached him to hear his story has he really shared. He has rectal cancer and no insurance. Get this: He caught it somewhat early and was being treated. He was in remission through the divorce, and then he was fired from Case Brothers due to the financial collapse. They used him as a scapegoat and let him go, using his son's death and divorce as reasons he was abusing company policies."

"Typical, those heartless bastards. No severance, no nothing?"

"Nothing. They took his company car and cashed him out of his almost worthless stock options. He had no savings since the divorce, and he is living in a homeless camp filled with people hooked on opioids that almost all of them got started with—you guessed it, Paintabs. In the last few months, he's stopped going to his appointments once he found out that it had metastasized. I will say this: This man hates the entire Morgan family. They're still trying to save their family name, and they're holding a naming ceremony at an art gallery on April 30th. We're not sure which family member will attend the ceremony."

"What are the odds of that?"

"Actually, they're pretty high at this point. More and more reports about Paintabs are coming forward, and lots of the victim's families are making noise. The Morgan family is in hyper public relations mode trying to keep their name on good terms with the public. The one thing that concerns Robert and me is Timothy's stability and whether we can trust him. We haven't told him anything about the group or plan other than there's a meeting today, which he'll join. We told him we'd meet him in the hall around 12:30 before the 1:00 p.m. meeting.

Hannah says, "I left it with Josh to meet at my house at 10:00 a.m. if he wants to participate, and if so, I'll walk him through everything. I introduced Sinclair's name to him yesterday. He doesn't know that Joe lives within five miles of us. I think Josh is fifty-fifty—we'll see. If not, I'm going to need help. I'm not doing so well and getting weaker by the day."

"I'm so sorry, being caught up in planning I forgot to ask you how you're feeling."

"As I said, not so good. I'm not sure if it's the cancer spreading, or my being so focused on Joe Sinclair and the plan, but I have almost no appetite and have lost weight for sure. Tomorrow, I have a follow-up appointment, and we're going to go over my options—which are bad, worse, or horrible—in more detail.

"We're so sorry we're not there or you're not here, Robert's treatments seem to be working for now, and traveling is out of the question. How about your neighbor, Scott? Isn't he the next in line with you on how much he hates Fulcircle and Sinclair?"

"That's true, Scott would be an obvious choice, but there's no way he'd be on board with this plan. I've been feeling him out since that first night I heard about Ben Brown's death. Scott likes the fact that Ben Brown did what he did but has mentioned a couple times how he could not do something like that. Well, I better let you go. Love to both of you, and we'll see each other in a few hours. Today's the day we're all in, or this idea gets shelved."

"We love you too. Today, we have five people on the call, and it will be six if Josh shows up. The three of us—Timothy and Russell, — in San Francisco. Russell is fully on board but believes we need another person to assist him. There is a man from Bolivia who is super sweet, according to Russell. He's seeking an apology from the company for their actions in the Water Wars of 1999 and 2000. The Wasser Corporation subsidiary hired local gangs that burned his farm, killed his livestock, and murdered his wife and two children. He has migrated to the Bay Area and purchased a single share of Wasser stock so that he can ask the board for an apology at their next shareholders' meeting, which is on Saturday April

30th in San Francisco. Russell doubts that Juan is approachable about this plan, but Russell is definitely committed to the cause."

"Wow—just think about getting five top executives on the same day. How about Theresa in Dallas, is she going to be here today?"

"No. She has scans almost all day today, but she *is* on board. We are going to make this happen, and hopefully, it will start a movement that leads to actual reforms. I can't imagine a world where corporations are held accountable for their crimes. Okay, talk to you soon. Bye."

* * * *

APRIL 18, 2011—9:45 A.M.:

With nervous energy, Hannah makes sure Josh has snacks and something warm to drink when he arrives. She is setting up the dining room table with folders about each company and the crimes they have knowingly committed against their employees, customers, and the general public. There are six folders for this meeting and another stack of folders on the coffee table in the front room.

10:00 A.M.:

Hannah looks out her kitchen window for Josh's car to pull up in front of her house, but nothing.

10:20 A.M.:

Hannah hears the squeak of a vehicle coming to a stop outside, a US Postal Service vehicle drops off a package. She slowly walks out through her gate to retrieve it. She takes it out of the protective plastic bag. It is a care package sent from one of Ashley's college roommates with a note that reads:

> I'm devastated after receiving your memorial notice.
> Unfortunately, I'm out of the country on a business
> trip and won't be able to attend. Please let everyone
> know I'm there in spirit.
> Love Always,
> Luanne Martinez

Hannah's eyes well up with tears, not only for Ashley but for all the people who are mourning her while she is here, so sidetracked with planning on how to get justice for her and tens of thousands just like her. It dawns on Hannah at that moment that Josh isn't going to show up. His wife, his entire world, was lost just three days ago.

What was I thinking—unloading all this on him yesterday? How on Earth is he supposed to process anything right now, let alone a questionable, at best, plan to take the lives of other people and their loved ones?

With this new clarity about the bigger picture, not just her own situation, Hannah decides it would be better to keep Josh out of the master plan. She walks back into the house and sees her answering machine flashing. Putting the package down on the coffee table, she hits play. The message is from Josh. The sound of his voice makes it obvious that he has been crying, most likely for some time. "I'm in. Count me in. I'm sorry I wasn't there at ten, but I'll be there soon."

At this point, Hannah slumps down onto the floor and weeps. Much like Josh the day before, the enormity of everything overwhelms her, and she can no longer distract herself from letting go. Memories of her late husband Bob come flooding back, as do the miscarriages she had trying to get pregnant; her childhood with Olga; her workmates from thirty-five years at the library; all the groups she has worked with toward environmental justice, civil rights, and water rights—and most of all, at this moment for Josh.

Josh was a nice athletic young man with a great sense of humor who wanted some life experience and a way to pay for college. He was a young man who met the love of his life and foresaw a lifetime of family outings, camping trips, grandchildren for his parents to play with, and growing old with Ashley. Within a few years, he was turned into a disgraced scapegoat with severe PTSD—unemployable, shunned by his family. And Ashley not only had a miscarriage but found out she had advanced cancer that would take her life in a matter of months. And I promised to take care of him.

What did I do? I unloaded thirty-plus years of research and activism on his head to avenge his wife's death and serve my purpose. He nailed it, and he nailed me: I'm just like the military, and I'm using him. Except mine is much worse, killing another human being and using his grief as the motivation.

Hannah is still slumped on the floor when there is a knock at the door. After waiting, Josh pokes his head in the door and sees Hannah on the floor, sobbing. He rushes over to her and asks with a sense of urgency, "Hannah what's wrong? Are you alright?"

No answer, she continues to lie in a fetal ball, crying. Josh begins to panic, not knowing what to do. He gets a blanket from the couch and covers her while continuing to ask, "What's wrong?" After a few moments of no answer, Josh tells her he is going to call 911.

She finally answers. "No, don't call. I'll be alright. Josh, I'm so sorry about what we talked about yesterday. I was wrong, and it was insensitive of me to drag you into this plan of ours."

Confused, Josh doesn't even mumble a word as Hannah tries to explain. "I'm so completely and utterly sorry for stealing your time to grieve. My latest scans and appointments have lasered my focus on this plan. I genuinely believe that if we can pull it off, we can create just enough of a chink in the armor to allow movement to change how the world operates.

"I still believe that, but you really don't fit our loose rules of being over sixty years old or terminally ill. You're in your thirties and healthy. You have some emotional healing to do, but you have many decades of living left. Will you please forgive me for putting our plans over your emotional health like so many other people have, other than Ashley?"

Josh has brought over tissues for Hannah to blow her nose and wipe the tears from her face as she gathers her composure during her apology. Kneeling next to her, he leans over to hug her and says, "Of course I forgive you. You don't have to apologize for anything."

Now in full embrace, she squeezes him more tightly than ever before. "Thank you, and I love you. Your parents love you, and your grandparents and relatives love you, and your brothers love you—both your military and biological brothers. You are loved, and don't ever forget it, despite how it might feel or seem. As humans, we are very flawed and lose sight of what is important. Promise me it doesn't have to be today or anytime soon, but please promise me you will reach out to your family again."

"I promise to reach out to them. Can you please stand up so I know you're okay?"

Hannah agrees, and while she is being helped to her feet, she notices the clock says 11:35 a.m.

"Thank you, Josh, for everything, but I need you to leave, our meeting is about to start, and I need to prepare."

With an even more confused look, Josh says, "What are you talking about? That's why I'm here."

Hannah, with real anxiety in her voice, insists that he cannot be part of this plan and that he cannot be around when they discuss it. I know what I told you yesterday, but I shouldn't have. It was wrong and a mistake."

Now it is Josh's turn to switch gears. His tone changes from compassionate and understanding to forceful. "Hannah, what you talked about yesterday is the truth we are all living. Don't ever apologize to me for speaking the truth. So much of my life in the last decade, besides Ashley, has been living with lies. Not my lies but the lies our society has grown accustomed to telling to justify all the horrible things we do."

Hannah returns to nurturing grandmother mode and starts heating water, asking Josh if he would like something to eat. He grabs her by the shoulders: "No! I need you to listen to me now. For the last few months, I've been trapped between wanting to save Ashley and feeling sorry for myself. Both of those are wrong. There was nothing I could do to save her, but I would give my life in place of hers every time, if there was a choice. The other thing is feeling sorry for myself as a victim. For the first time in a long time outside the company of Ashley, something distracted my depression of everything. I don't know what life will look like next year—hell, even next week. I don't have any income or any family I can count on. I struggle to try and control my PTSD, and with Ashley gone, nothing gives me a purpose to live any longer."

Hannah interrupts, "Josh, you mustn't think that way."

"Please let me finish," Josh says, cutting her off. As he says this, Hannah sees the clock behind him. It is 11:50 a.m., and she worries that the meeting is about to start. Josh continues, "I don't know your plan or if I am willing to go along with it. But what I do know is that I want to hear about it and help in whatever way I can. That might mean just strategic advice or me fully participating in it. I don't know, we'll see." He glances at his watch and sees it is almost noon.

"So please, let me sit in on this meeting, and what I hear will never be shared with another soul for the rest of my life—other than the people that are part of the group. That's a hundred-percent guarantee and promise. Let's set up your everything and this stack of files you have ready to go. Can we agree to this for now?"

12:00 P.M.:

Hannah scrambles to log onto the online meeting and accidentally knocks over her cup of tea. "*Damn it!*" she exclaims. "I need to be the most prepared, and now I'll probably be the last one online."

"Hannah! I got it."

She continues to move about in pain, mumbling to herself as she tries to clean it up. Josh calls out a bit louder to get her attention, "*Hannah!*" Once she stops and looks up, with a soft look and a calming tone, Josh appears. "I'll take care of the tea. Focus on the meeting. Slow down and clear your thoughts."

Closing her eyes and taking a deep breath, she says, "Okay, I needed that. Thank you for calming me down."

Josh jokes, "I might be half crazy, but I did learn a lot of useful skills in the military. Preparation and clarity about the mission were among those skills. So, they might have ruined my life, but at least I gained a few valuable tools from it. If you ever need someone interrogated, I'm your guy."

Hannah is busy organizing her folders and only half listening, but she hears that last line loud and clear. She gives Josh a fleeting glance, realizing that he has just given her the idea she had been searching for ever since she came up with the concept of Exit Stage IV Kesshitai.

She continues to go online and join the group with Olga and Robert. Once they are dialed in together, they will add Russell. Hannah has a bullet-pointed opening statement ready in the Joe Sinclair folder, but after hearing Josh's joke, she is now reconsidering it.

In the kitchen wringing out a sponge, Josh hears a cheerful woman's voice and then a man's. On a certain level, he feels like he is peaking into Hannah's private life, which seems a bit wrong. He decides to stay where he is and let Hannah bring her device into the kitchen if she wants him to join in. He turns and leans against the sink, looks into the other room, and sees the elderly woman sitting in front of the screen, talking with two people she must have known for a very long time. The conversation seems effortless, and they don't even need to finish their sentences, since the other has already started their reply.

For the first time, Josh sees Hannah as a different human being, not a grandmother mentor or a Yoda figure who knows just what to say at the right time. Hannah is laughing and thoroughly enjoying the company. After a minute or two of catching up, Josh hears the woman on the other side introduce a person named Timothy. The tone of the conversation shifts immediately.

Olga says, "Hannah, this is Timothy, the person I mentioned to you the other day."

"Good afternoon, Timothy. I'm sorry our paths have crossed due to having Stage IV cancer, but nevertheless, it's nice meeting you."

"Likewise."

Hannah is checking Timothy out as best she can through a screen. Although dirty, she can see a man who once took lots of pride in his appearance. It appears it has been days since he had showered or at least put on washed clothes. His face was clean-shaven, but somehow still looked dirty. And even with just one word spoken, she could tell he was a person who had spent many hours speaking with others about serious matters. The crispness and diction of his "Likewise" has already impressed her to the point of thinking—this is a person with personal convictions and strict rules for living."

Olga speaks up. "We have Russell joining us now."

"Hello all, I'm glad to be here today. I think what we're trying to achieve is important, and if done properly can not only send a message to the executives of these Fortune 500-type conglomerates but can also send a rallying cry to all the victims of their abuses.

Robert and Olga: "Here, here, on that statement."

Hannah: "Good to see you, Russell. Timothy, have Olga and Robert given you a little background on the people in our side group?" Timothy nods in agreement. "Okay, that's good; it saves us the time of all of us telling you our stories. As you know, we all have one type of stage IV cancer or another. So, now you're going to be put on the proverbial hot seat for a few minutes. Is that okay with you?"

Timothy: "No problem, both Robert and Olga know my story in detail."

Hannah: "Can you tell us about yourself and your story?"

Timothy: "Well, where to start? I'll try to keep it as brief as possible. I'm sixty-three years old and grew up in a small town in Delaware, called

Longneck. We were raised Lutheran and had a good childhood with two brothers and one sister. My father was an engineer who had contracts for weapons manufacturing during the Cold War, which meant we weren't rich but we were well off.

"I ended up getting my bachelor's degree in Economics at Brown University and an MBA from Yale. Then, after a decade of getting experience with various firms, I landed a dream job at Case Brothers and worked there until the last couple of years." With this last sentence, Timothy shifts in his seat and appears tense.

He continues. "In 2007 I was diagnosed with Stage II colorectal cancer. At that time, I was living alone, divorced since 2005, but with good insurance. Case Brothers was extremely supportive, and everything worked out smoothly until—" (choking up a bit) "the financial meltdown began. All of a sudden, a company I considered family became extremely dysfunctional and fractured. At this point, I had scaled back my clients and was trying to practice mindfulness as much as possible.

"So, I was kind of out of the loop with each of the factions. It was an insane time, and I requested a leave of absence to focus on my health. Little did I know what was about to blow up."

He shifts even more in his seat and the tension seems to take over his entire upper body. "About a year later, I found out through a reporter trying to fact-check an article they were about to publish that I was one of the people Case Brothers was using as a fall guy. They took my leave of absence and used it as an act of guilt when they knew what I was going through with the cancer chemo and radiation treatments. They—"

Hannah interjects: "Timothy, I don't mean to interrupt you, but you don't need to relive things that will bring back so much pain."

Timothy: "I don't know exactly what this group is or what it is planning to do, but my story matters, and I need those in the group to understand where I am and why I'm here."

Olga: "Of course, Timothy, feel free to stop or leave out anything that's too painful. You've told us the story, but maybe you can share the reason and how your marriage ended. From what we can tell, this is the driving force in your life, even more than the mistreatment of Case Brothers."

Timothy: "That's fine; I think they're tied together anyway. Where to begin . . .?

"It started on a ski trip to Telluride, Colorado, in 2000. Our son, Jonathan (named after my father), was a senior in High School and wanted to go to Florida with some friends for spring break. My wife, Bethany, and I didn't like this idea with all the drugs, alcohol, sex, and everything that happens with teenagers and no supervision. We proposed a ski trip instead. Jonathan loved skiing, mainly in Vermont, and had always wanted to ski in the Rockies. It was a win-win for everybody. Bethany and I had been married for twenty-one years by then, and our marriage had grown into a routine so that we had lost our sense of adventure. This trip energized us all. We went all out. We stayed at the Peaks, which is right on the mountain. It was a great time; we seemed to be really enjoying each other as we headed into our last day. All week, Jonathan wanted to do a double-black-diamond run called Kant-Make-M."

Timothy begins to drift off and has a glazed look on his face. The entire event replays in Timothy's mind within seconds and comes through as clearly as the day it happened. Riding up the ski lift on their last day in Telluride, Jonathan asks his mom and dad—for at least the tenth time in five days of skiing—about doing Kant-Make-M. "He had heard why it wasn't a good idea every time he brought it up, but the dreadlocked local mentioned it on the lift on our first day, planting the seed that Jonathan needed to do this run before his trip was over. Jonathan couldn't get it out of his head; he needed to prove to someone he had had a ten-minute ski lift ride with that he could handle a high-level double-black-diamond run in Colorado."

The moment and words ring out loud in Timothy's head: *Maybe, let's try Bushwhacker first, and from there, we can see if we want to actually do Kant-Make-M. We'll give it a try*. It was this one sentence out of the tens of thousands of I-love-yous, the happy marriage, vacations, family holidays, and twenty-plus years of experiencing life together. He can pinpoint the one sentence out of all that time when his marriage and life fell apart.

He shakes his head out of the revelry of his son as a healthy, happy human being and the nightmare of the sentence that starts with *Maybe* . . . that passes through his lips. Timothy continues: "I finally broke down and said *maybe*. Bethany was not happy that I had opened that window. We told Jonathan to go down a groomed trial run right next to the one he wanted to do so badly; it was called Bushwhacker. Over the week, we had stopped at the top of that run and looked down. It was way too steep. Kant-Make-M was just as steep and had enormous moguls. Bigger than anything we had ever seen.

"We told Jonathan we wanted to watch him go down Bushwhacker, which had been groomed that morning, to see what he thought. Our incredible trip became an enormous argument as soon as he left us. He looked good going down the groomed run, but we could see him stop several times because the speed was so fast. We were hoping that he would say it was too much when he got back up to us.

"He didn't; that thrill of speed intensified his determination to do Kant-Make-M. Bethany and I were arguing until we saw him get off the lift and start coming towards us. He was so pumped that he said, 'I thought you were going to follow me down.'

"Bethany told him it was way too steep for her, and there was no way she was doing Kant-Make-M. She suggested we not do it and then skied off, leaving us alone. He was just so damn happy and so damn persistent that we could handle it. Both of us were more experienced and confident skiers than Bethany. I gave in, even though it meant a massive fight with my wife, and I knew better. A father wants to be the figure who his son looks to for approval. I wanted him to have an experience he would remember for the rest of his life. I wanted to show him I trusted his judgment and ability. Is that too much to ask?" Tears are now running down his face.

"I said, 'Let's do it!' Even through his goggles, I could see his eyes light up. We gently skied over to the drop-in point and looked at it. I said, 'Those are some pretty big moguls. Are you sure you can handle them?' He said there was one way to find out, and he dropped in with that youthful, fearless confidence. I stayed at the top watching. As he approached the moguls' first row, he slowed down and took them very cautiously. They were twice as big as he was—and Jonathan was six-foot tall. He got about halfway through and stopped. He turned up the hill and yelled, 'Come on, you can do it. Take it slow.'

"Taking it slow was an understatement; I was scared to death and slowly made it down to him. Laughing, he said that he would go a little harder this time and took off. I yelled to him, 'Not too hard, be careful,' but I doubt he heard it.

"I don't know how many moguls he had gone over, and he was going way too fast, but he made it through. Now it was my turn. Hugging the side of the run and the smaller moguls, I made it down to him. His adrenaline had taken over, and his confidence was as high as the fourteen-thousand-foot peaks that surrounded us.

"I said to him while pulling out my mountain map. 'Okay, you got to do your "Kant-Make-M," and I have to tell you—you're a better skier than your old man. You looked good.' I was scared the entire time down. Jonathan had his little throwaway camera and said, 'Let's take a picture.' We posed, held the camera out, and clicked; the moment was forever captured." As Timothy tells this last portion of the story, he pulls his wallet out of his pocket. "That photo is right here. I carry it everywhere to keep my happy boy with me. That was the last time I saw him healthy and happy. I call it 'the innocence photo.' The last time Jonathan wasn't exposed and addicted to opioids.

"We agreed to take different runs down to the lift. Mine was called Easy-Way-Out and his, Lower Plunge."

"I got to lift-eight and waited and waited. Worried, I asked the chair lift operator if there was a way to page someone. He said he could do it and asked me the name. Once he heard the name and the last place we saw each other, the lift operator contacted ski patrol instead of announcing that Jonathan should meet me over the loudspeaker.

"A ski patrol officer asked, 'Are you Timothy McGee?' I said yes and what's wrong. He told me Jonathan took a spill and was at the local clinic getting checked out. He said, 'Not to worry too much; it was nothing serious—I just happened to be there when it happened. He caught an edge, and his knee got tweaked. It was bothering him by the time we reached the bottom.'

"The clinic was a five-minute walk up a street. When I arrived, Jonathan explained that everything was fine; he had just twisted his leg, and his knee felt funny. A ski patrol guy saw the spill and thought it was best for him to get checked out.

"'Dad, I walked up the street myself; how serious could it be?' I saw the doctor, and they thought he might have a strained ACL or maybe even a slight tear. They gave him a couple of Paintabs for the pain and a knee brace to hold him until he could get home and have it checked out more thoroughly.

"I'll spare you the fight that ensued with Bethany over the next couple of weeks.

"The injury was somewhere between a grade-one strain or possibly a grade-two ACL strain with a slight tear, which didn't require surgery. Our doctor gave us the option of an MRI, but it wouldn't change the treatment and rehab one way or another. So, we opted to not have it done. It took several months to deal with the swelling, range of motion, rehabilitation, and so on. It was confusing to us all that the pain persisted as long as it did. After every rehab appointment, he would complain about the increased pain.

"Eventually, we chose to get the MRI done. And nothing. It showed some remnants of mild injury, but nothing that would suggest pain should be taking place. We were told by the doctors that these pain meds were much less addictive and not to worry because pain is one of those things that is so different from person to person. We asked the doctor if Ibuprofen would work just as well. They told us we could try it, but he would give us an Paintabs prescription just in case it wasn't enough.

"This went on for months. We didn't know; we'd never experienced a drug addict before and didn't know any of the signs. We just saw our son graduating high school and then attending NYU for film and television. He wanted to be a director. He had dreamed of working in movies since he was a kid.

"From there, we only saw him when he needed his laundry done or money for equipment or school projects. In the first semester, his grades were underwhelming, but we figured that being on his own for the first time and around other young people, he was testing his boundaries and figuring everything out. We talked with him during Christmas break, and he promised to get his grades up and take them more seriously in the second half of the year. His grades didn't improve; besides a couple of elective classes, his grades were unacceptable to us.

"He had been an honor roll student through all of his years in school. So we became concerned that there was something else going on and confronted him about the bad grades. He unleashed a hate-filled tirade with rage in his voice towards us, which was totally out of character.

"We began asking his friends about him after he returned to school. Finally, one of his closest friends from high school told us Jonathan was still taking Paintabs, but way more than before. We were shocked and called his doctor right away, and he told us he hadn't given Jonathan a prescription since their last appointment in September. Jonathan got word that we were asking about him behind his back and went into a cocoon of defiance when he came home for the summer. Not acting out, just not letting us into his world.

"So we went back to his friend for more information. At first, he didn't really want to tell us anything, but we wore him down. Evidently, there was a whole underground black market happening, specifically around this painkiller, throughout the city. We asked his friend if he would please let us know if anything more was happening or if he noticed anything worsening. Surprisingly, he agreed without coercion, a warning sign we missed.

"Immediately after talking with the friend, we contacted the doctor and asked if they knew anything like this was happening. He said no, not officially, but talking with other physicians, he added that they were noticing a rise in prescriptions and opioid addiction throughout the city.

"That summer, we monitored Jonathan like a hawk, and if he was getting drugs from someone or somewhere, we couldn't tell. He seemed distant but still Jonathan. Eventually, the cold shoulder act, well, that is what we thought it was, ended. We reviewed his sophomore class options and helped him pick out his classes. He was excited and promised us he would do much better this year. That's when we asked him if he knew anything about the prescription-drug black market. We didn't accuse him of anything. We just said it so that it was a warning to avoid it. He said very calmly and sincerely that he had not heard of anything, and at most, he drank beer at parties. He still wasn't quite himself. We could see there was something off but didn't want to end the summer in an argument.

"Remember, this was August 2001 in New York City. Within a few weeks, 9/11 happened, and he told us that they could hear and smell the twin towers coming down. NYU is only eight blocks away. We were frantic, and nobody could get in touch with anyone. I was on a work trip and out of town and couldn't even contact Bethany; the phone lines were so jammed that nobody could get through. Flights were grounded, and we were all glued to the TV coverage, trying to find out any information.

"There is no need to go through all that with you; we all lived through it."

At this point the entire group was sitting on the edge of their seats listening to this man describe his family's downfall.

Timothy continues with his story: "Luckily, we had talked him into one more year in the resident hall, so he was safe and had not been evacuated for long. In the aftermath, he had a class canceled since the campus was all over the city, and it wasn't deemed safe. Trauma and grief counseling took place with the staff and student body. The University sent home letters explaining how some students might behave or let their studies slide in the coming months due to learning how to deal with the events of 9/11.

"Once again, Jonathan's grades weren't that great, and we talked with him every Sunday night and tried to put eyes on him at least once a month. He didn't look well, and when asked, he would say the amount of stress and anxiety on campus was what we were probably seeing. He had lost weight, and his color looked pasty-white. He was not healthy-looking at all. We suggested that he transfer to a different university that wasn't so impacted by 9/11, but he insisted on staying at NYU with all his friends.

"His high school friend Joel contacted us just before winter break. His university was on a different schedule, and his classes ended the week before Jonathan's. Joel came by our house with his parent's gift and wanted to discuss Jonathan. His accounts or evidence were through second-hand information, but he said Jonathan was really taking high doses of Paintabs. Not only the high doses, but he was crushing it and snorting it like cocaine for an immediate pain-med high that has been compared to heroin. Joel hadn't ever done either kind of trip, but many say it's the best high you'll ever have, so they can't stop chasing it.

"Bethany and I became very concerned. We contacted our church, and they helped us set up an intervention before he came home for the Christmas break. It didn't go well, and we all turned against each other. He took the position that both his physical and mental pain was greater than we could understand. I took the strict approach and brought my professional reputation into the conversation, which gave him ammunition to say that we weren't concerned about him at all—just our own reputations. Bethany tried the compassionate approach, which he then used to pit us against each other.

"For the next few months, Bethany blamed me for his addiction because I had agreed to do Kant-Make-M with him in Telluride. I blamed 9/11 and blamed her for pampering him too much, not holding him accountable, and always coming up with excuses for why he broke his word time after time.

"He returned to school in January 2002, so the Sunday phone calls stopped, and our one-on-one time with him ended." Now Timothy has an expression of agony. "By March 2002, he was not attending classes, but we found that out later. During spring break, on March 14, 2002, Jonathan overdosed, and his body could not be brought back to life. We lost our boy to an Paintabs overdose, a drug that we have since learned was known to be highly addictive, and Adicta Pharmaceuticals did nothing about it. In fact, the sick family of Morgan corrupted the FDA and kept the addictions secret to continue their gravy-train pain medication sales.

"After Jonathan's death, Bethany and I couldn't stop fighting and reliving our trip to Telluride that started this entire nightmare. Our divorce became final in 2005. With her anger towards me and the blaming of our son's addiction, she and her lawyers went for the jugular with the divorce—the house, our savings, alimony, so on and so forth. I was left with nothing but a broken heart and Case Brothers.

"Then, in January 2007, I was diagnosed with Stage II colorectal cancer and started treatments immediately. Bethany claimed it was a punishment from God for being directly connected to Jonathan's death. I couldn't really argue anymore and accepted that this was the reason for my cancer.

"Case Brothers was good with my new schedule and reduced incoming new clientele. I had great insurance, and things went according to plan. I finished my pre-surgery treatments of Folfox and Oxaliplatin along with six weeks of radiation, which were hell on earth. By this time, my surgery was scheduled for late July 2007 to remove the tumor and several inches of my colon, plus resection it together. In the meantime, I had an ileostomy to allow the resection of my colon to heal.

Timothy continues: "In spring 2008, I got a call from a reporter with The Times confirming information that I was, in fact, losing my position with the firm and other executives specifically pointed out that, due to my long history with the firm, my work was trusted and should have been verified before approval.

"The reporter went on to confirm it was my son, Jonathan; his drug addiction, his overdose, my divorce, and cancer that caused me to lose my judgment and ability to handle the stress of the job. That was why I took my leave of absence.

"Here I was, recovering from the closure of my ileostomy and in extreme pain, and the primary pain relief medication was Paintabs. Receiving this call about me losing my job was mind-blowing, to say the least. Within a few days of the article's release, I lost my job without severance or savings. My brothers and sisters reached out, but I was wallowing too much in my misery of both physical and emotional pain. I lost my insurance and went on the New York State Medicaid program with special circumstances since my income from 2007 and the first quarter of 2008 was way too high.

"I became homeless by the end of 2009 and had too much pride to tell my siblings and ask for help. With the surgeries and treatments, a common condition called LARS, low anterior resection syndrome, caused so much pain and adverse side effects I could not keep even the most basic job due to all the breaks and missed days. I will let everyone look it up if you want to understand what that entails. It's horrible, and that's all I will say about it.

"I am almost finished here.

"In 2010, my cancer was stable, but living on the streets, I would lose track of time and miss my appointments. What I found out about six months ago was that my cancer had metastasized into other organs. It is an adenocarcinoma that was a less aggressive form, so I decided to shift my cancer treatment to faith in the Lord of Jesus Christ since the treatments had stopped working.

"I currently live in a relatively sizeable homeless camp full of people addicted to opioids; they call me Minister Tim. I hold nightly sermons on how Jesus loves all of his children, and none of us are free from sin. My congregation is that of Free Grace Salvation. Repentance for our sins and faith in God will lead to everlasting salvation. I am the shepherd of the innocent and a protector against wickedness and evil. My calling in life has become clear to me: to save others from wickedness from families like the Morgans with Adicta Pharmaceuticals and their poisoning of the American population. I am protecting innocent people like Jonathan from becoming addicted and losing their lives to it."

Hannah exclaims, "WOW! I mean just—*wow*. Timothy, thank you for sharing such a personal and heart-wrenching story. I think this speaks for everyone in this group: We are so sorry for the pain and the life tests you've been put through. The other thing it's safe to say, maybe not in the same way, is that we, too, are survivors of trauma caused by the greed of others, and with knowing that, you're not alone. You have a family with us. It's not shared by blood or proximity, but the cancer family is extensive and, unfortunately, grows every year."

Hannah brought her laptop into the kitchen during Timothy's story so Josh could join in listening. Feeling a connection with Timothy based on their shared experience of betrayal, he finally understood that the word *family* could have more than one meaning, even opposite meanings. What Hannah continually said about being part of an extended family was the cancer family, not the bitter connection to the family that had shunned him.

Russell agrees with Hannah: "Thank you, Timothy—Minister Tim—for sharing. It does help all of us understand where your pain comes from. It reminds us all that we are not alone. Our sharing and the ultimate goal as a group is a form of therapy.

"As Hannah mentioned, we're so sorry for the stress and loss you've been through over the last decade. I sincerely hope your new calling brings you the inner peace you seek and deserve. Without butting into your life too much, I would just like to say one more thing before moving on: Please do not blame yourself for going down that ski run with your son. Your cancer is not a punishment. You were being a responsible parent. You didn't send him off alone into a dangerous situation. You went with him as a protector. No parent can be there to catch their children when they fall every minute of every day, especially as they grow into young adults. Thank you again for sharing, and I'm sure we'll talk more in the coming days.

"Hannah, I see another face on your screen. Would you like to introduce your friend?"

"Yes—thanks, Russell, for pointing out Josh. I'm not sure if Josh is up for sharing his story just yet, but he wanted to know a little more about this group. He came over today and helped me get through an emotional morning." Hannah looks at Josh and says, "Everyone, this is Josh, and Josh, this is Olga, Robert, Russell—and we all met Timothy for the first time today.

Josh waves. "Hello, everyone."

The group responds in unison, "Welcome, Josh."

Hannah continues, "Olga and Robert, from my perspective it's a thumbs-up."

Russell says, "I second that motion."

Hannah adds, "I will briefly explain to Timothy and Josh the purpose of this group and then allow Olga and Robert to go into the details of the ultimate plan with Timothy. I will do the same with Josh. The plan will take place in just a few days, on May 1st. Let me apologize for such short notice. This is my idea; it just landed in my lap in the last couple of months. Unfortunately, my cancer is on the move, and I truly believe a quick stealth-like action will have the biggest impact on trying to create the world we are all seeking.

"So here is my elevator speech in two minutes or less: This group, which is not confined to those in attendance today, aims to hold those accountable who believe they are otherwise. With Timothy's story, I can tell you the Morgan family has no intention of being held accountable. In my case, a man with the last name Sinclair, CEO of a major industrial company who poisons and knowingly sells products that cause cancer is who I want to be held accountable. Russell has his industrial billion-dollar company, which has made a fortune on wars and the theft of resources from the poorest people around the world. We have Theresa in another city. Olga and Robert will share with you, Timothy, who they want to be held accountable.

"Let's go ahead and wrap up this meeting unless you have any more questions. Does anyone have any questions that your local group leader cannot answer?"

Timothy raises his hand, and Hannah says, "Go ahead, Timothy."

Timothy asks, "It sounds like Robert and Olga will fill me in on the group's bigger picture, but does this group have an official name? Several heads nod on the screen, indicating they are wondering the same thing.

Hannah responds, "The short answer is no. The extended answer is that I have an unofficial name, and it will be revealed when I finish our press releases, which I will finish before the end of today."

"We are a group in the sense that we all have Stage IV cancer that was brought on by direct or indirect industrial negligence, and we want to see these companies or families held accountable, One could say that we want justice for all the people who have been injured or killed by their negligence. Another, more accurate, description would be that they will no longer enjoy the impunity they receive for their greed and immoral actions in our corrupt legal system.

"As for Timothy, we want the Morgan family to be held accountable. Not just a fine but a tangible sentence that they will feel. Being sentenced to a fine that would make their family fortune go from $65 billion down to $35 billion has no tangible meaning; their lives won't change other than having bad publicity for a few weeks. That is not justice—when their crime has been tens of thousands of severe opioid addictions and overdoses. Thousands of families have been torn apart and are in mourning for the sake of adding zeros to the Morgan-family fortune.

"Back to the name, we are loosely connected with other cancer groups from different cities around the country, and I've heard about some talks with a couple of international cancer groups, as well.

"I don't know if that is satisfactory for everyone, but that is all I have for now. Today, I will send out the first draft of a press release dated May 1, 2011 to all the group heads I know of and will take any suggestions. We want it to be a concise but powerful message that's sent to all major news outlets on May 2nd, when we turn ourselves in. We live in a twenty-four-hour news cycle, and hopefully, within a couple of days, all of it will be connected, and that's where and when the power of our message and mission will be recognized.

"Well, for now, that's it. Olga and Russell, we'll talk in a little bit. We can fill each other in on the explanation that's about to take place.

"I like to end our local meetings by paraphrasing a quote from philosopher of myths: 'When life feels most challenging, we discover a deeper power within ourselves that opens up opportunities we never knew existed. Love to everyone, and have a wonderful night. Goodnight."

2:00 P.M.:

Hannah shuts down and closes her computer. Josh notices that she seems to close her eyes before she speaks or does things like open the laptop or shut it down. He asks her, "Why do you close your eyes before speaking or moving?"

"You've noticed that," she says. "There are many reasons I do it, but mostly, it started just after my husband Bob died. I love to picture him healthy with a smile on his face. It has a calming effect, allowing me to focus on what I will say or do. Otherwise, things can get so jumbled and not make any sense. Also, there is a prayer or mantra that is more of an intense feeling than words that I tap into. It gives me the strength to keep moving forward when all I want to do is curl up into a ball and become invisible."

CHAPTER SIXTEEN

NICOLE HAMILTON BENNETT AND ARTHUR BENNETT

SATURDAY, NOVEMBER 8, 1980—8:30 A.M.

Arthur Bennett, now in his mid-twenties, makes the trip south to Denver to visit his new niece, Amelia, Michael and Nicole's second daughter in two years. They figure Nicole can take a break and work part-time at the organization she was a founding member of, which deals with the devastating destruction of mining towns along the three-thousand miles of the Rocky Mountains that stretch from New Mexico to Alberta, Canada.

* * * *

Although extremely fulfilling, this type of work has forced Nicole to relive her childhood trauma repeatedly, handling cases that drained her emotionally and psychologically, despite years of therapy. After taking a few months' break from work when their daughter Karen was born in 1978, Nicole realized the job was sucking her life dry of any joy. Amelia was another gift that made Nicole's life complete.

Since its inception, Communal Fund of the Rockies (CFR) has taken mining, timber, oil, and natural gas companies to court and won either settlements or convictions of wrongdoing with monetary compensation. These lawsuits began strictly as individuals holding local companies accountable financially for their wrongdoing. As the victories accumulated, the lawsuits became class actions against parent companies. Ultimately, CFR moved on to regional lawsuits and indigenous nations' rights, primarily, the Coal industry on Navajo and Hopi lands, along with BLM Ranchers and water rights that diverted the precious resources away from Indian reservations or the encroachment into other nations' land with their cattle. Also, it won international lawsuits on behalf of the First Peoples of Alberta against the oil production and pipelines that eviscerated sacred lands, poisoned streams, and obstructed traditional passageways.

As a founding member and executive director, Nicole brought to CFR a keen and innate sense of how these companies operate and, more importantly, how they view the people their companies negatively affect. From this vantage point, she became hyper-focused on the small print of legislation, agreements, and notes on court decisions—the areas where cases are won and lost. No one was better than Nicole at finding that one sentence or phrase that made it perfectly clear these companies had violated their charter and the law. She was also skilled at dealing with fellow employees and the board of directors, given her above-board sense of ethics and a transparency learned from growing up in Sawpit immersed in the secrecy of Vermolite Mining Company's atrocities.

In 1980, Nicole notified the CFR board of directors that she would be permanently leaving her executive director position but would want to stay on part-time as a consultant. In her typically conscientious style, she took care of every detail of the transition, from the hiring of her replacement, to sharing the role of executive director for months before her pregnancy came to term.

* * * *

Michael is up early with Karen this fall morning, waiting for his younger brother to arrive for a visit. Karen had been cleaned up, changed into her daytime clothes, fed, and is playing on the floor with her dad when they hear two quick honks. Michael gives Karen a mock-surprised look, and she begins to giggle. He picks her up and walks over to the window to see if it is Arthur.

Arthur sits with the motor running in front of the brick home near Stapleton Airport in Denver, Colorado. Holding Karen in his arms, Michael looks out the window and sees a dust-covered pick-up with various dents that tell tales of adventure. He comes out onto the front porch, lifts his forefinger to his lips, gesturing Arthur to be quiet as he slides out of the driver's seat. Despite his heavy-duty boots, Arthur doesn't make a sound when his feet hit the ground.

The door squeaks loudly as he tries to shut it softly. He stretches and waves to his brother and niece. As his arms come down, Michael hears a very familiar sound—a raspy cough as Arther walks up the driveway to the front door.

Michael opens the door and says quietly, "Welcome to Bennett Manor. We need to be quiet. Nicole is down with Amelia right now. These first few months, the baby never stops wanting to eat, so we— really Nicole—are up and down all night feeding her. Let me bundle up Karen, and grab a coat, and we can go for a walk."

Despite the sun being out, the wind in Denver never seems to stop, bringing stinging cold before the first snow hits the ground. The two brothers slowly walk to a nearby park, getting caught up on each other's lives.

Michael asks, "How're the old man and mom doing?"

Arthur, nods in approval. "Good—they're both doing good. Dad is still at the plant, and Mom has been spending more time with Grandma and Grandpa in Coeur d'Alene since no more kids are at home. Dad worries about her making the two-to-three-hour drive by herself, but she's fine."

"Did they mention when they'd be able to visit their new grand-daughter? We were hoping to make it up for Thanksgiving to introduce everyone to Amelia. Between her being born late and me finally getting to do some actual lawyerin' at work, it makes the timing bad. Maybe Nicole can bring the girls up for a visit in a few months."

"Just starting to do some lawyerin'? What have you been doing all this time?" Arthur says with a snicker as he becomes fixated on his niece, calmly sitting in her stroller.

Michael laughs. "You don't want to know. It's all the grunt work that takes the most time. So, they have those of us who are paid the least to do that type of work. I've been asked to sit at the table with one of the partners in an upcoming case—start doin' some lawyerin'."

Arthur looks at his niece, who is all bundled up with her red cheeks and nose exposed to the chilly air. He smiles a big smile with tears in his eyes. "You did it—you fuckin'. . . oops sorry—" He puts his hands over Karen's ears and whispers, "You actually fuckin' did it."

"What did I do?"

"You got out and became a lawyer. Now, you can have a wife and kids without being at the company's mercy. You said it a long time ago, and you did it."

Concerned, Michael looks at his younger brother. "Okay? Why are you tearing up on me? I know we're close, but I haven't seen you cry since we were kids."

"Michael, you know my cough and the asthma I've had for all these years?"

A drawn-out response: "Yeah?"

In a trembling voice that fades so the last word is barely audible, Arthur says, "I got it."

Michael says, with his heart now securely in his gut and a feeling of dread, despite already knowing what the answer will be, "You got what?"

"*It!* I fucking got *it!*" This time, he did not bother to whisper the swear words in front of his niece. "They spotted it on my lungs on my last visit to the doctor."

"Which doctor, the company guy, or a *real* doctor?"

Almost in an ashamed tone, Arthur says, "Both."

In a quiet, enraged voice, Michael rattles off questions that turn into a tirade: "Did they order any more tests? Are there any treatments you can do? Is the fucking company going to pay for your medical expenses? Does Dad finally acknowledge it's not a coincidence, or does he still play dumb? How's Mom taking this news?" On and on it went.

Overwhelmed by Michael's anger, Arthur stops crying and interrupts, "No, to all your questions. I haven't told anyone but you. I don't know what to do. Of course, I wanted to come visit Nicole and the girls, but I also wanted to ask you guys some questions."

With eyes filled with tears, Michael says firmly, "We'll get through this, Arthur. Nicole and I know so much more now than we did in high school. Getting out of Sawpit allowed us to look into the lung problems Vermolite Mining Company claims not to understand. Studies show a correlation and causation between asbestos and certain upper respiratory health conditions and cancers. The treatments are improving since they know more about these correlations and causes."

Arthur interrupts, "It's everywhere in my chest. All those years of asthma, and nobody has ever looked at my chest with any scans. The company doctors never ordered any tests to see what was going on. If I die, maybe you can sue them and get our family the hell out of that town. If anything is left over, give it to Karen and Amelia."

Michael holds his hands up. "Whoa, slow down, little brother. Nobody is dying yet, and we will do whatever it takes. Rack up as many medical bills as needed to give you the best chance. You're not going to pay a goddamn penny of it, and I will make sure of that.

"The best thing you have on your side is your age and the fact that you haven't smoked or had time to screw up your body yet. That's another one coming out: The tobacco companies have known the whole time that cigarettes cause cancer and are addictive. All these fuckers are evil, and the only language they understand is money or jail."

"That's exactly why I wanted to see you guys before telling anyone else. You don't owe Vermolite Mining Company anything. You can give me honest answers—not some bullshit, weasel-worded answers that answer nothing and everything at the same time. Enough of all this shit. I came down to see you, Nicole, Amelia, and of course," he picks up Karen, hugging her, "this cutie pie right here."

* * * *

1982:

On a sunny summer morning in Sawpit, Montana, words from Saint Joseph's Church can be heard.

> *God, Redeemer of the faithful,*
> *Accord the souls of Thy faithful servants and reprieve*
> *them for their transgressions. Through reverent grace,*
> *may they receive the atonement they need.*
> *Who lives and reigns with God the Father and in union*
> *with the Holy Spirit in a world without end. Amen.*

Mrs. Bennett embraces Ben Brown at the top of the stairs just outside the Saint Joseph Catholic Church. Both are sobbing and asking why this happened to such a young, good person. Mr. Bennett is shaking hands with friends and family who stop to offer their condolences.

Michael and Nicole Bennett remain behind in the church with the coffin. They, too, are shaking hands and hugging friends and family.

A young woman with someone who looks to be her husband approaches Michael and Nicole. The four stand silently for what seems like minutes. Nicole breaks the silence as she reaches out. "Thank you for coming, Jennifer."

"I can't believe it," Jennifer says, "I am so sorry we couldn't do more." She breaks down and sobs in front of everyone.

Her husband has never seen her in this condition before and doesn't know how to react. "There, there," he says, hugging her gently.

Michael grabs Nicole's hand and tells Jennifer, "I'm not sure there is any type or amount of modern medicine that could have helped. It was a lifetime of exposure. I can tell you this for certain, Arthur died content that he'd tried everything possible. I don't know if you two were in touch over the last couple of years, but he could have been a doctor by the end of the lawsuit. That's how much research and experience he gained. He told me to tell you that you and Ben were his best friends and the best friends anyone could ever have. He also gave me letters to give to both you and Ben."

Jennifer was still crying while Nicole dug around in her purse for some tissues. "Michael, Nicole—what happened with the lawsuit? I knew about it, but I didn't really know the details. I didn't realize it was this serious. Gene and I have been moving around so much for our careers that it was difficult to follow. It sounded like you were saying Vermolite Mining Company knows or knew they were poisoning the people of Sawpit?"

Michael is about to flare up, so Nicole cuts him off. "That's the gist of it. Arthur's medical bills were substantial, and he was no longer under the Bennett's medical plan. The lawsuit was about holding the company accountable so that it would open the door for all these industries and mining companies to be liable for the damages they cause their communities and employees."

Michael jumps in. "We settled out of court for the sum of Arthur's medical bills. On the day he told me how sick he was, I promised him that he wasn't going to pay a goddamn penny. Arthur was worried about my parents having to pay those bills and Vermolite firing our dad. So, we settled, and it is over."

Jennifer says, "Gene and I would like to donate to the legal fund and all the time and energy you two put into this case. I was lucky enough not to have my dad working in the mine, but we all grew up together, and all this hits close to the heart." Jennifer and Gene, with a conflict of interest, were trying their best to stay away from the issue while showing their support. Jennifer, a chemical biologist, and Gene, a geological engineer working with fossil fuel extraction, couldn't really speak to insider information on public health issues and the extraction industry.

"That would be lovely and appreciated, Jennifer and Gene. My organization, the Communal Fund of the Rockies, or CFR, deals with the fallout of generations of mining towns. Actually, I had just trained my replacement and given my notice when we first learned of Arthur's diagnosis.

"A few years prior, I started my organization to ensure that more men—like Michael and Arthur's Grandpa Nick and my dad and many other relatives and friends—don't suffer the same fate, giving their lives for a company that doesn't care for them when push comes to shove." Nicole continues, "I'm now an active consultant with CFR and a member of the board, but I still hold onto one client and case, Vermolite Mining Company and Sawpit. For as long as it takes, I will eventually get Carl Shadwick or whoever the general manager is into a deposition room and hold them accountable not only for Arthur and our families, but also for the entire town.

Feeling a bit uncomfortable, Jennifer ends the conversation. "That sounds wonderful, Nicole. Just let me know where to send the check. And Michael, I would love to come by your parents' house to pick up the letter. I am so sorry, and I'm still trying to process everything."

"I have it in my car outside. If you have a few minutes, I'll get it for you. Or if you're coming over to my parents, I'll give it to you then. Thanks for coming; I know Arthur would be grateful and happy you were here."

A few hours later, Dozens of people had come and gone, sharing food, drinks, toasts, and stories of how wonderful Arthur was, and that he will never be forgotten. A few close friends and family members remain. Michael hands Jennifer the letter. "Here you go. I'm not sure what it says, but Arthur made me promise to get it to you if he didn't have the chance."

Jennifer had sent Gene to her parents' place early, since it had been a long and emotional day, and she also had wanted to catch up with friends she hadn't seen in years. Now leaving the Bennett's house, she walks about a half-a-block and sits under a streetlight. She reaches in her pocket, gently takes out the letter, and opens the envelope, knowing that she will preserve this letter for as long as she lives. She reads:

Dear Jennifer,

I can't believe you are receiving this letter before your 30th birthday.

As you know, I have died—or I am dying. I just wanted you to know that you and Ben are as close to me as my flesh and blood. You are the sister my parents never gave me. I will do anything for you and love you until my final breath.

Do you remember when we kissed in 9th grade? Like—really kissed! That was my first kiss, and it has stayed with me ever since, not in lust, but in an important way. I wouldn't have wanted it to be with anyone else on earth. I have no idea if either of us knew what we were doing, but the feeling it gave me of security that someone outside my parents loved me was overwhelming. I have and will never forget that moment.

I am so proud of you for getting your degree, getting married, having kids, and having a career. If any girl were going to do it, it would be you. You are so bright and so confident. I never knew anyone as confident as you. I spent half my time questioning my life and decisions. You seem to be always on track, trying to reach a goal. YOU ARE INCREDIBLE!

I love you and will never forget our love for each other. I hope your life is everything you wanted it to be.

Love Always,
Arthur Bennett

As Jennifer O'Brien Smith sits crying underneath a streetlight reading the letter from Arthur, Ben Brown is sitting in Arthur's old bedroom with a very heavy buzz going from the afternoon and evening events. He is sitting with Michael. A sewing machine, quilts, swaths of cloth, and family pictures on the wall surround the two men. Where Ben is seated, he sees a photo of himself, Arthur, and Jennifer at their high-school graduation party. Every time he looks up, the photo comes into focus, and the question and thought runs through his head: *Did he have cancer when we took that picture, or is there a specific moment we could do over and he would still be here?*

Voices can be heard through the closed door and the walls, but the words can't be made out. "You got to be fucking kidding me!" slurs Ben, "That prick Shadwick said he had never heard of any connection between lung diseases and Vermolite Mine or its products.

"Did you know—that asshole bought me my first hunting rifle when I was like twelve years old? I remember my grandpa and dad being embarrassed by that guy, but he was their boss, so they put up with his fucking bullshit. That guy is so full of shit nobody can believe a word he says. The jury believed that lying sack of shit?"

Michael begrudgingly interrupts because he can never get enough of people bad-mouthing Carl Shadwick or Vermolite Mining Company. "No, it never went before a jury. The whole lawsuit took place outside of a courtroom. That is how these companies continue to get away with murder. I'm not joking, *MURDER!*" he says in almost a yell.

He continues, "If I ever get a chance to take that asshole or Vermolite Mining Company to court again, I will not settle out of a courtroom. Whoever hires me is going to have to agree with this fact. Vermolite has companies all over the place, so there is a chance Nicole's organization might get another case involving them. I'm not sure if she'll allow me to be part of their team in the future. That's the problem. Most people are just trying to settle so their families are cared for, and they don't want to get their case into a courtroom. The companies are always eager to settle out of court, and the money they throw around like it was nothing is disgusting. They have the money to pay their fucking workers and have the money to do business safely, but they don't do it since they're never held legally accountable."

By now, Ben is sobbing into his hands, mumbling, "Those mother fuckers killed my grandpa, my best friend, and who knows how many people of Sawpit? Who knows how long before my dad? I swear to God, if I get the chance, I will take down those mother fuckers."

Both men—speaking out of total emotion and drinking many beers and numerous shots of whiskey while toasting Arthur Bennett through the night—make a promise to each other while sitting in the middle of a sewing room: "Somehow and in some way, we will hold Carl Shadwick and Vermolite Mining Company accountable before our lifetimes are over."

CHAPTER SEVENTEEN

POST-GROUP MEETING

AFTERNOON, APRIL 18, 2011:

"Okay, Josh, do you want to hear more about our plans? I would rather you don't—because of what we discussed earlier. You're not in a good, healthy place in your mind to decide this, especially since it's on such short notice."

Josh feels like he has nothing else to lose at this point and feels that if he doesn't help with this plan, his future will be short-lived, with despair, depression, and probably taking his own life. All the prospects he can see without dealing with his "dark mistress" head-on are grim.

When Josh tries to imagine ten or twenty years in the future, there is only the faintest light. The only thing he sees in the light is trees. Lots of trees. The problem is that to get to the trees, he must travel through what scares him the most: the *dark mistress.*

Last night, after talking with Hannah the day before, Josh had concluded that from this point forward, he needs to take charge and make his own decisions instead of letting everyone else tell him what to do. This doesn't mean being on his own through this journey; it is the exact opposite. He is going to need some major shifts in his life and lots of help from others to get him through the darkness.

He says, "Hannah, I feel silly for saying this since we've only known each other for such a short period. But I love you—deeply—for helping keep Ashley and me calm during what otherwise would have been a meltdown period for me, and what would have made Ashley's last months a living hell. That is a gift I can never repay.

"You haven't shown any judgment towards me and have only been supportive. Outside of Ashley, I haven't felt that in a long time. Please quit trying to protect me and give me the respect I deserve by being honest with me. Not partial truths to meet your agenda, but the whole thing. If I'm to make a decision that will affect the rest of my life, I'm entitled to know the entire mission, not just bits and pieces of it. Can you do that for me? For Ashley?"

Closing her eyes and taking a deep breath, Hannah says, "Sit down, and I'll tell you the entire plan. From A to Z. I've already told you the story of Benjamin Brown from Montana and his lawyer from Colorado. As mentioned yesterday, we are not trying to work within this corrupt system for justice. That's the mistake I've been making for decades. Almost all of us get hung up on the legality of our actions. Sure, we'll put our bodies and lives on the line with civil disobedience because, at most, those are misdemeanors and will most likely receive a slap on the wrist. That's what those who set up and control this system count on.

"This is why our group is made up of Stage IV cancer patients; we don't have long futures ahead of us to sacrifice. This is why this plan will work: There is nothing they can hold over us to keep us from getting the justice we deserve. These companies have determined for us that we are their "collateral damage"—or worth sacrificing—and are figured into the cost of doing business. Our lives and loved ones are sacrifices they were willing to make, since there are no real-life consequences.

"This is also why I had a somewhat shocking revelation of consciousness this morning, which you walked in on. Thank you for comforting me. I've been carrying way too much for too long, and it all just came out when you found me this morning.

"You have a future, and I promised Ashley I would do my best to help you live it with a purpose and quality."

"I get that and respect that you're keeping the promise. The thing is, I also made promises to Ashley, and they won't be kept if I don't help you. Trust me, I've imagined hard and deep what my future would look like for years to come. Ashley was always part of that future—and the only beautiful part. She's now gone, so when I close my eyes, darkness and misery are all I can imagine. All my good times are behind me, not in front of me.

"My future and actions are mine to determine, not for others to make for me. That is what your talk yesterday and the night of tossing and turning cleared up for me. Without a passion for something, I do not see much of a future or a reason for living. We covered this yesterday, and what you're talking about is giving me a purpose and possibly creating something positive in society by avenging Ashley's death. If I'm going to have a long future, it can't be suffering and mourning Ashley's death, the loss of my family, and the reasons they have abandoned me because our National Defense chews its soldiers up and spits them out when they're through with them.

"I've come to this conclusion: If I am ever going to have any closure, I'll need to commit one hell of an act of justice to be able to move on. I know it is not going to be overnight or easy. I promise that if I do join your group and get the justice we're hoping for, I'm not sure how I'll do it, but I'll go to counseling again and try to start the next chapter of my life. Ashley and my family will always be in my heart, but I will need to move on from the heartache. Can you try and understand where I'm coming from?"

Hannah says, "First, I'm sorry if it felt like I was telling you half-truths and using you. That wasn't my intention at all." She stands up and starts heating a teapot, asking Josh if he would like coffee, tea, or water to drink. She is no longer able to hide the discomfort or pain she is experiencing. Josh sees it but knows the answer, so he doesn't ask if she feels alright. "Please let me do that for you. You just need to tell me where everything is, and I'll take care of it."

Hannah wants to say no but is too tired and uncomfortable not to accept his offer. "I'll just sit in my chair; it's my most comfortable place. The tea is on the counter and the mugs are in the cupboard just to the right of the sink. Thanks, I could sleep for twelve-hours-straight right now. Make sure you get something to drink or eat; everything is there for you whenever you want it."

The teapot whistles, and Josh turns off the heat. "How do you take it?" No reply. Josh's gut knots up, and he pokes his head around the corner, expecting to see the worst.

In relief, he sees Hannah is out like a light in her chair. She looks so peaceful, so Josh just lets her sleep. He makes himself a cup of coffee and turns to look at the pictures in Hannah's neat, tidy, comfortable home. After a few minutes, he plops down on the couch and sees folders with labels on them sitting on the coffee table.

Flipping through the folder labels, he sees several familiar names of huge corporations. Each name has multiple countries listed on it, with people's names attached along with the name and city where the CEO or executives live.

Josh looks at Hannah, who is in a deep sleep, then gets up and heads back into the kitchen to the folders Hannah brought for the meeting. He sees three folders on the table:

Adicta Pharmaceuticals: Timothy and Robert— Chairman/ President Raymond Morgan; Museum naming celebration New York City 4/30/11

Wasser: Russell (and possibly Juan)—CEO Roland Durstig; Shareholders Meeting San Francisco 4/30/11

Fulcircle Company: Hannah (possibly Josh)—Retired CEO Joseph Sinclair in Monticello, Indiana 4/30/11

Josh gets curious about this last folder. There are at least fifty pages, if not more, in the folder, and the top page reads as follows:

FULCIRCLE COMPANY
(Internet corporate watch group)

Overview: What you're seeing is a consolidation of the entire food chain, not just seed companies.

INDUSTRY AREAS: Genetically modified (GM) crops, agricultural chemicals, and bovine growth hormone.

MARKET SHARE/IMPORTANCE: Fulcircle Company aims for a future of "Abundant Food and a Healthy Environment," though its approach may differ from others. They are a dominant force in agriculture, controlling a significant portion of the global food supply chain. In 1999, Fulcircle was the largest seller of genetically modified (GM) crops, making up 80% of the global farmland for these crops. They are also the second-largest seed company, with sales of $1.7 billion, and their herbicide, Kill-All, is the best-selling product in its category.

HISTORY: Fulcircle Company is a leading and controversial force in the biotechnology sector of agriculture. With a troubled history of producing hazardous chemicals—including chemical warfare agents like Dioxin, PCBs, food additives, agrochemicals, and pharmaceuticals—it has positioned itself at the forefront of the industry.

In the 1990s, Fulcircle became the first major firm to embrace the "life sciences", divesting from chemical operations and investing nearly $10 billion in seed company acquisitions. It was also the pioneer in marketing first-generation genetically modified (GM) crops, supported by a robust public relations campaign to promote their safety. This strategy backfired, making Fulcircle the focal point of a rising global resistance to GM crops while allowing lesser-known companies to advance unnoticed.

By late 1998, the backlash led to a significant drop in market confidence and share prices. Stability returned with a merger with pharmaceutical giants in April 2000, resulting in the acquisition of Fulcircle's pharmaceutical division. The agrochemical and biotechnology division, still operating under the Fulcircle name, was spun off as a separate entity, with the parent company retaining an 85 percent share, showcasing Fulcircle's ability to adapt in a contentious environment.

Josh is astonished as he flips through page after page of studies, products, poisons, carcinogens, subsidiaries, and more. He sees the studies of birth defects, links to cancers, neurological disorders, and general long-term negative side effects of exposure to Kill-All and other Fulcircle Company products. Ashley's cancer, their miscarriage—he looks over at Hannah sleeping next to the picture of her husband Bob, who died of Parkinson's—are all listed.

"What the fuck—how is this legal?" He exclaims under his breath as he reads on.

The next page, titled Wesley's Lawsuit, is from a court-case file of a seventy-five-year-old Indiana farmer who lost a lawsuit against bioengineer giant, Fulcircle Company. Wesley Boson's lawsuit lasted years and is currently in another appellate court, Josh figures out as he reads one document after another. From what he can tell, Boson, a lifelong soybean farmer, used patented Kill-All-ready seed and was contracted to use Fulcircle Company's schedule of herbicides, pesticides, and synthetic fertilizers, which he did.

As his father did before him, Wesley Boson would try a riskier second crop each year that was legal. Wesley would buy seed directly from his local grain elevator. That grain elevator had mixed the soy crops of many farmers and was selling them in bulk to the farmers. Fulcircle Company has a patent on their soybean seed, whether buying directly from the company or through a third party. Despite these seeds coming from the ground from his field and the fields of other farmers, Fulcircle Company still claims to own the rights to the seed, owning the right to life of those seeds, no matter how many generations removed. Planting seeds is what farming is all about. Wesley was being sued for being a farmer. In the last court decision, Boson lost and had to pay Fulcircle Company over $80,000 in legal fees and damages.

By now, Josh is getting angrier with each sentence he reads. What Hannah and Ashley had told him about Fulcircle Company was true. He stops reading the case documents because he is about to throw his cup against the wall.

He can no longer handle the Wesley's Lawsuit section, but he finally gets to Joe Sinclair's section. He doesn't notice it until he goes to flip to the next page; these are double-sided and stapled together. One cited article, lawsuit, study, and court decision after another with notes on each. About Joe Sinclair's time as CEO. A single product, and there are dozens of them just like it in the children who were born with grotesque birth defects in Vietnam, Cambodia, Laos, and much of Southeast Asia from the use of Dioxin.

Cancers, deformed organs, and US veterans sued Fulcircle Company for $40 billion within years of being exposed and were rewarded $180 million. In 2004, Vietnamese victims filed a civil suit that was settled out of court. Each case was either settled out of court or Fulcircle Company won the decision. Fifty years later, the negative effects of Dioxin are still being exposed by the Vietnamese people and US veterans. Despite receiving hundreds of millions of dollars in the 1960s for their herbicide, Fulcircle refuses to take responsibility. Joe Sinclair is at the forefront of these military deals that catapulted him into CEO within a decade, where he would stay for the next thirty years. The last few pages are thumbnail images of victims of the herbicide Dioxin.

Just about this time, Josh hears a stirring from the front room. Hannah is waking up. He hurriedly puts all the papers back in the folder, tapping it on the table to get everything neat and in order.

He peeks into the room and sees Hannah stretching. He gently asks if she needs anything, which makes her laugh. "Josh, your voice isn't going to hurt me. I feel so much better. How long was I sleeping?"

"It was at least two hours, and I didn't want to wake you. I must admit something: I read some of the Fulcircle Company/Joseph Sinclair folders. I hope you're not mad."

Half-awake, she says, "Oh Josh, I really didn't want to involve you in this at all. It was only for a moment, and it seemed like a perfect fit and a good idea. Before and since then, I've realized it's not fair to you."

"I'm in. I said it to you earlier, and now, reading what's in that folder, I'm positive I'm in. Let's hear your plan."

Hannah sighs, "I'm not sure about this. Let me go to the bathroom first, and I'll come back and tell you the choice of plans. Can you start some water for me? I'd like that tea now."

Hannah slowly and painfully walks back into the kitchen and sees a cup of steaming tea ready for her and Josh sitting at the table with the Fulcircle Company folder in front of him. Her eyes are focused on the tea, and as she raises her view to Josh's face, she can tell he has read enough of the folder to understand the reason for her plan. She has seen this look many times before whenever someone takes the time to read through the history of any of these giant corporations and sees that they are fully aware that Fulcircle is causing tremendous damage to a large sector of the population. This look is beyond rage. Now, that exact same look is on Josh's face.

She thanks him for making the tea as she heads over to get a little honey and milk. Facing away from him, she says, "By the look on your face, you've read enough of the file to understand that this company and Joe Sinclair might talk themselves into believing they're providing the world with a much-needed way of food production, but as you saw, it's much more than that one thing. That is one facet of their company and its products. Even if we focus on the domination of food production and their chemical practices alone, it would be enough to stop them in their tracks.

"We don't have enough time for me to go over everything, and I apologize again for dumping all this information on your lap in such a short period. I have two problems: 1) These companies have been getting away with murder for too long. And I must admit the second one is a bit selfish on my part, but: 2) I'm running out of time to be able to try and do anything about it. I apologize in advance for the lengthy monologue you're about to receive. As you can see now, it's easy to get rolling on all the evil these corporations put into the world and, worst of all, get away with.

"So, how far in the folder did you get?"

"Far enough."

"No, really—how far did you get? It allows me to understand better."

Josh replies angrily, "Far enough. I just started getting through Dioxin and the Joe Sinclair part. I'll repeat: Far enough. I don't need to know any more about the company or Sinclair. They've killed millions of people for profit, and they know exactly what they're doing. I don't need any more information; I don't need any more convincing."

Sitting at the kitchen table with Josh and her cup of tea, Hannah asks, "Have you eaten today?"

"No, but I'm fine. You don't need to feed me."

"I don't know if I could, even if I wanted to. My condition is getting really painful. The White County cancer group made the food I've been bringing you. It's one of the services we provide for our family members. Ashley's situation happened so fast that you never had the opportunity to experience the full benefits of the group we've created. I'm so, so sorry,

Josh. Sorry for everything you've been through these last few months—and really years."

Her hand in a "stop" motion indicates more: "I have containers of food for you in my refrigerator and freezer. You'll see them labeled Josh and Hannah. Just grab a container and heat it, and I'll continue filling you in on the big picture."

Josh is clearly thankful as he hears Hannah being concerned with his well-being, despite her extreme pain. "I know you mentioned yesterday your condition was getting worse, but I didn't realize how much. I know you're sorry—we all are. Don't be alarmed if I break down for no apparent reason. It comes in waves without any warning."

With an expression of pain and sorrow, Hannah says. "You've faced far more than any person should have to handle in such a brief time. Of course, you'll have these episodes of grief."

Josh gets up and heads to the refrigerator. "I'll heat some food for us, and you keep talking. I'm listening to every word."

Hannah continues, "As you read some of the Fulcircle folder and all my rants, you're getting a crash course on how our economic and legal system functions. It isn't pretty or pleasant, no matter which industry or large corporation we discuss. Even the best-intentioned companies work within the rules and laws set by the goliaths of industrialization since they're the ones who own our political parties. I have roughly fifty company folders on the crimes we know about or that are reported on. Hundreds and probably thousands of companies fall into this category of corporate murderers. "The couple you saw at the meeting are old friends. Their company and target is Avidité. Robert is a retired chemical engineer who worked for Avidité for nearly thirty years. Their daughter, Elizabeth, worked for Avidité on the Nonstick line, one of their cash-cow products. God, I remember holding Elizabeth in my arms when she was just a few weeks old. It feels like yesterday.

"Robert and Olga are childhood friends of mine, but Robert is part of the Stage IV family. He has advanced prostate cancer. Their daughter, Elizabeth, was in her early thirties when she died. What she died from was known by Avidité, and they kept it secret from their employees. That's why Olga and Robert are such devoted participants in this group.

"Elizabeth didn't get her job through Robert. She chose a college near their home in Richmond, Virginia. She went to VCU and applied for the job at the local plant without letting her parents know. She wanted to get the job on her own. I remember how proud they were of her. Robert offered her a less monotonous job, but Elizabeth insisted on staying on as part of the manufacturing line she was hired for."

Josh returns to the table with his heated food and a bowl of chicken broth for Hannah. At first, she doesn't want to sip her warm bowl of much-needed nutrients. Josh suspects that if she has only been drinking tea for days, she hasn't been receiving the electrolytes and sodium that are essential for the organs and body to function. He says, "You'd better eat some of that broth."

She lifts a spoonful and blows on it. Her hand shakes slightly as she brings the spoon to her mouth and swallows the warm, salty liquid. "Mmm—I'm not sure which is better, the taste or how it soothes my throat. Thank you, Josh. I wouldn't have made myself anything if you weren't here." She continues with her story while sipping spoonsful of broth: "Elizabeth graduated with honors in under five years and kept her job at Avidité the entire time. She worked part-time and had the flexibility of working days or nights since the line ran from early morning to late at night.. Looking back, her symptoms started presenting in her senior year. By the time she was in her late twenties, she was constantly sick with symptoms that didn't make any sense.

"When the cancer was finally diagnosed, Robert and Olga started digging into the issue to see if anyone else working on the manufacturing lines was getting sick. Case after case began appearing everywhere. Whenever Robert asked a question, he would get a polite runaround, and as Elizabeth's condition started getting worse, both Robert and Olga stopped being polite with their questions. Right now, there is a class-action lawsuit against Avidité which Robert and Olga are part of, suing Avidité for knowingly using a carcinogen in dozens of products. These carcinogens are called "forever chemicals," and they expose workers for decades. "Now we're almost done with the *whys* and we'll move on to *the how*.

"Clearly, you know enough to be able to say you are in. But I need you to grasp even more—enough to help everyone else understand that these acts weren't simply against innocent businesspeople but acts of self-defense. That is what Ben Brown did in Montana, and I believe we can recreate it worldwide if done correctly. The difference is that you will not be turning yourself in. That is a different topic altogether.

"The way we present ourselves to the public after May 1st is where we create change and achieve the justice we are seeking. And then we will be looked upon either as heroes or deranged martyrs.

"Olga, Robert, Russell, Theresa, and I have several press releases ready to go to explain this plan and why it has to be executed in this fashion. These statements are numbered according to release so that we can keep our actions in the news cycle for as long as possible. That's the small group of people I'm in contact with. Each one of us has up to three more contacts from other Stage IV cancer groups. And each has up to three others from all over the country and the world. We agree that more than three other people sets us up to be betrayed. As far as I know, we're the only group with five people.

"We are united in our purpose but independent from each other. The press releases or statements should be able to translate into any language or culture. We agreed upon one thing with the original group, the one you were just introduced to today: May 1st needs to be the day we pull this off. I have no idea how many others there are or if there are any others. What I do know from meeting with online cancer groups is that many people share this opinion. That is why it is going to be successful.

"I'm almost finished with the opening statement, which we will hand to the press on May 2nd, when we turn ourselves in to the authorities. What is going to seem like a random act of violence will become a well-organized revolutionary act of self-defense against corporate mass murder. This is the first act and warning shot to be fired across the bow of large corporations and corrupt governments everywhere. The goal is to give clarity to the victims of these corporate crimes and the strength to demand justice. We will begin by focusing on Joe Sinclair's and Fulcircle Company's actions.

"This new "green revolution" form of food production became mainstream in the 1960s and 70s—a generation ago. We went from thousands of small family farms that sold their products into their regional economy to mega chemical-based agribusiness monocrop farms that sell their products to mega companies that make animal feed or disguise that same poisoned feed as cereal, cookies, noodles, and more. Almost nobody understands the scope and power these companies possess within our system. We are taught to trust our government to keep big businesses honest and in check by using antitrust laws against monopolies or predatory behavior. The opposite is true; the corruption of both of our major political parties ensures that the laws protect big businesses, and through our captured regulatory agencies' use them to provide the illusion of safe products.

"We'll focus on Fulcircle as our target offender. What Fulcircle and other companies have done is to manipulate the DNA of seeds to be resistant to Kill-All, the poison that kills other plants. These manipulated seeds are called Kill-All-Ready seeds. These two practices are the perfect combination for stealing small farmers' land while selling them Fulcircle's poison to do the same thing they were doing before, growing soybeans—or whatever it is they're growing. The process of this theft is based on one primary thing: They have patented the life of the seed and won lawsuits that enable them to own *life itself*. How can they think that, you wonder? Remember, they have written the laws, so they know they have legal justification or standing within our judicial system, which gives the illusion of being a good global citizen."

"Wesley's Lawsuit! I read about it in the folder," Josh interrupts to let her know he understands the concept.

"Okay, good. I'm glad you got that far into it. There is one problem: the entire system is a pyramid scheme for affirming this economy of industrial death. I call it the Pyramid of Affirmation. No matter what company or industry we are talking about, The Pyramid of Affirmation kicks in, and gigantic conglomerate corporations with multi-million-dollar legal teams, lobbyists, revolving doors, legislative organizations, and the like corrupt our legal system—from the creation of the laws, to the judges that control the courts and decisions.

"Even if a jury trial is conducted, the jurors are informed of the corrupt laws, which affects how they view the evidence and case. It is almost impossible for victims to win in these cases, and when they do, corporations drag the case out for years in appeals. For instance, the company responsible for what happened in Alaska: Most people who are supposed to have been paid for damages still haven't received penny-number-one from the company. The longer they can put it off, the less they will have to pay out in today's dollars due to plaintiffs dying or just the inflated value of the US dollar. One hundred thousand dollars had much more spending power in 1990 than today.

"And this doesn't even cover international corporate-governing bodies like the World Trade Organization, a.k.a. WTO. That will have to be saved for another day. Still, I will say one thing: These sovereign, corporate government decisions can override national laws and even the constitutional rights of individual nations.

"I'm so tired right now. Can we pick up on this tomorrow? We'll review and improve my plan if you are part of it."

Josh is torn between wanting to continue and wanting to help Hannah to her bed. She says one last thing in a somewhat needy tone. "You can stay here with me for a few days if you'd like. No, let me rephrase that: I'm asking you to stay with me for the next few days. It will help me out, and all the food is here, so we can care for each other much easier."

"Yeah, no problem. I can stay as long as you want. You just let me know if you need anything."

Relieved, she says, "Thank you—and I will. After my doctor's appointment, we'll pick up where we left off in the morning. The guest bedroom is ready to go, and tomorrow my neighbor Scott is taking me to my doctor's appointment. Maybe you could go home to grab some clothes, a toothbrush, and things. My appointment is early, so it will give us plenty of time to go over everything before I poop out."

"That sounds good. Thanks for everything. And I'm serious—if you need anything, just holler, and I'll come take care of whatever you need. I hope you have a good night's sleep. See you in the morning."

* * * *

APRIL 19, 2011—7:00 A.M.:
"Yes, I'll be ready to meet you out front at 7:45."

"Okay, thanks again, Scott. I'll see you then," Hannah says, hanging up the phone.

Josh comes out of the guest room quietly and gently, feeling a bit uncomfortable about waking up at Hannah's. He has no reason to feel this way, but he does. "Good morning," he says out loud. It is more of a heads-up that he is here than a greeting.

Sipping tea and taking her morning medications, she replies, "Good morning. How did you sleep? I've been told that the guest room bed is extremely comfortable."

Josh pauses a second to think about it and, in a surprised voice, says, "Good. I slept well. I can't remember the last time I slept through the night."

"See, I told you that bed is comfortable. There's food that just needs to be heated, and you just need to turn on the coffee. Everything is set up."

"Okay. You know, I could have taken you to your appointment this morning. I'm here, and I can take you wherever you need to go."

"Thanks for the offer, but it was arranged with Scott a few days ago. My appointment is at eight. We should be back by ten. Don't forget—we'll go over everything today—as I promised last night. So, get some things, because I'll need your help for a few days."

Josh notices once again that Hannah doesn't look good. Her skin color is strange, and her eyes look dull. Out of concern, he asks, "How did *you* sleep?"

"Not very well. With all my different aches and pains, it's tough to sleep longer than a couple of hours at a time. I take mild pain meds and melatonin, but that stopped working a couple of weeks ago."

"Why don't you get a stronger pain reliever if it'll help you rest better?"

Hannah puts on her shoes. "I feel this is what today's appointment will be about."

Hearing that answer, Josh feels there's a pit in his stomach and wants to hug her and tell her he doesn't want her to go anywhere. But he controls himself and leaves it with, "I hope you get whatever you need to feel better." He pours himself a cup of coffee. When he turns around, Hannah is standing there with her arms held out for a hug. Knowing that Hannah is going to find out her expiration date in a few minutes, they hug with every ounce of love they have. They manage not to break down crying, but both are teary-eyed and sad.

"Okay, you—go get your things, and we'll meet back here in a little while. She grabs her jacket and wool hat out of the closet heads toward the front door. Looking back at Josh, she says, "I love you, and I'm very proud of you for being the man you are."

A car pulls up outside, and Hannah leaves. Josh, watching her from the window, sees her slowly walking to Scott, who has the door open for her. She gives him a quick, hello and a hug, and gets in the car.

* * * *

APRIL 19, 2011—8:00 A.M. APPOINTMENT WITH DR. EVANS:

Scott and Hannah are sitting in the oncology waiting room. He says, "Hannah—" she looks up from her magazine, "—how long have you known?"

"Known what?"

"Come on, Hannah, we've known each other too long for this. Since when have you known the treatments have stopped working and the cancer is on the move?"

"For about two or three weeks, but it's been longer that we kind of knew. My last couple of scans have shown a little activity but not enough to throw in the towel. We tried Ibrance. This is it, I'm at the end of the road for options. So, it wouldn't have mattered either way."

Scott is now a little irritated because she could have allowed him to help her with the meetings and Ashley. "I could have helped you out a lot more than making food for you and Josh. You could have been honest with us at the meetings, and you know I could have helped you with Josh and driving around if you needed stronger pain medications."

Hannah tries to explain. "I'm not taking any pain medications other than over-the-counter acetaminophen and ibuprofen combo, which is a nonopioid pain medication. It takes the sharp edges off but not much else. I am involved in something where I need my head to be clear, and the pain is terrible but not so bad I can't function."

Still irritated, he asks, "What is so important that you can't take pain meds or tell me?"

"I can't tell you because you won't agree with it. But let me put it to you this way: All the work we've put in over the years trying to get laws changed or enforced—the petitions, all those hours of writing ordinances and measures will be dwarfed by a single-day action that will be held around the country and maybe around the world."

Hannah sees the nurse coming. Scott was about to start asking questions, so she is relieved to avoid this conversation.

First, they stop at the scale, and alarmed, the nurse asks Hannah, "Have you not been eating? You've lost twelve pounds since we last saw you. That's not good."

Hannah admits she has lost her appetite and can't remember the last time she ate anything substantial. As the nurse straps on the blood pressure cuff and puts the blood oxygen level meter on her finger, she notices Hannah's eyes and skin tone. Her blood pressure is 103/65, and her blood oxygen level is hovering at 90 percent. Now extremely concerned, the nurse goes through the regular check-in questions: "What is your pain level today: one through ten? Have you noticed anything different? Are your medications the same? Is it the same pharmacy?"

Hannah politely answers all the questions and tells the nurse, "Yes, Sandy, I know my liver is unhealthy, and I'm on my way out."

Sandy, who has known Hannah for years, begins to tear up. "Well, Doctor Evans will be in in a moment. And Hannah, if you need anything, just let me know, okay?"

Hannah stands up, hugs her, and says, "Thank you, Sandy. I have everything taken care of, and this might be the last time we see each other. Thank you for everything you've done and for raising such lovely children. I'm glad our paths crossed in this life."

Tears are flowing down Sandy's cheeks, and she doesn't want to let go. "You've done so much for our community—and in the last few years for so many cancer patients. I remember you checking my books out of the library when I was a school girl. We'll all miss you if we don't get another chance to see each other . . ."

At this moment, Dr. Evans walks in, and Sandy immediately releases Hannah and wipes her tears. "Doctor, Hannah is all checked in." She hurries out of the room.

Dr. Evans walks slowly, staring at Hannah, and then takes a seat. She sits in the chair next to him, and he shakes his head slowly. "You look about what I would suspect. Why haven't you returned our phone calls in the last few days?"

"What would be the point. So, you could tell me officially that there's nothing left to do except call hospice in and start being cared for? I knew that already, and I'm trying to squeeze a little more out of this life before being put on so much morphine that I can't think straight."

"I know this isn't your first rodeo, but it's your first time in this saddle. The function of your liver is decreasing, and your skin color and eyes show it. In the last month, we went from your liver functioning in normal ranges to today's results, which don't look good at all. The weight loss has been the case for a while now. I know we went over all this with the scans in your last visit, but I must ask again. Do you have all your paperwork in order? Has hospice has been taken care of, and will a friend stay with you?"

In a childish attempt at being a brat, Hannah, tries to lighten the mood: "Yes, yes, and yes. I got it all taken care of. What type of cancer-group leader would I be if I didn't teach by example? Listen, Richard, I just wanted to thank you for everything and for being such a good friend and an even better oncologist. We gave it a ride, didn't we? Got eight years. After Bob died, I wasn't so sure if I even wanted one more year, and it's been six years since he passed."

Dr. Evans stands up, and Hannah follows his lead. They embrace in a long hug. "As a friend—not your oncologist—is there anything I can do for you? Just ask. As you already know, hospice will walk you and whoever is your person at the house through the medications once again. They'll check in on you twice a day—until they don't . . ."

"Yes, Michelle is the primary nurse I'll be dealing with, and we've talked about everything already. That's why I'm putting it off as long as possible. As a patient and friend, I want to thank you for being one of the good ones. Not all doctors care enough anymore and only go by protocol. Working outside the box gave me the best quality of life over these last years, and I packed in as much as I could to give that time to our community.

"To be honest, I'm split between relief and fear. I didn't think I would be scared, but my philosophy and theories can no longer override my true feelings. We really don't know what happens next, and it's a bit frightening. I can feel Bob's presence at the strangest times. I am not scared of going to a place like hell or anything like that—but more of not waking up, seeing sunlight, and taking a deep breath, that it all will stop. That is the part that seems scary to me.

"Enough of that, I'm so exhausted—and that's where the relief comes in—tired of being tired." Hannah gives one last big squeeze and then lets go.

Dr. Evans, now holding Hannah's hand, says, "Everyone feels and handles it differently. It's nice to think Bob will help you over, and he'll be the first thing you experience. I'll contact hospice to let them know to expect a call from you today. Or would you rather *I* just call and get everything rolling? It would be best if you didn't live the last days of your life in immense pain—that's all. It can get really uncomfortable. As you know, hospice is there to help you manage the pain. We went over all that last appointment. I don't think there is anything left to do. Hopefully, you didn't drive yourself this morning, and you have a ride. Otherwise, I could have Sandy take you home."

"No—thanks, Scott brought me this morning and is in the waiting room. If you can let hospice know, I'll contact them soon. Thanks again for everything."

Dr. Evans opens the door and turns right as he leaves the room. Once she gets to the door, Hannah turns and looks at the office one last time before exiting. She turns left and returns to the waiting room.

Scott has been fuming the entire time Hannah's gone, but as soon as he sees her moving slowly toward him with puffy eyes and a red nose, everything goes away, and all he wants is to take care of his dear old friend.

CHAPTER EIGHTEEN

BATTLE IN SEATTLE AND WTO

DECEMBER 3, 1999:

Journalist: "Can you tell me your name, the name of your group, and why you've joined the coalition opposing the formation and influence of the World Trade Organization?"

Ben Brown: "My name is Benjamin Brown. I'm a Vietnam veteran and a member of the Timber Drivers Local 2 in Montana. I understand who profits the most from war. That's why I'm here to oppose the WTO and global trade."

Journalist: "Do you belong to a specific group or are you here alone?"

Ben Brown: "Both."

Journalist: "Will you identify your group and what goals you're hoping to achieve?"

Ben Brown: "I belong to Veterans for Peace and Timber Drivers Local 2, but I'm not speaking for them right now. Everyone here, whether in an organized group or not, is exercising our First Amendment rights of free speech and redressing our grievances in the court of public opinion. We are communicating with our government and governments around the world. We hope that shutting down these meetings will show the Chamber of Commerce, the business world—and most of all, the Clinton administration that the people do not agree with a corporate-controlled government dictating how business and life are to be conducted."

Journalist: "Can you elaborate on what you mean?"

Ben Brown: "I'm not sure if you've noticed, but we're in the middle of something right now." (He is within a group of people marching with banners and chanting). "It would take hours and even days for me to explain everything we oppose about fascist corporate government controlling the global economy. That's what fascism is—the merging of private and public interests. What comes next is authoritarian policies and perpetual wars that drain the coffers of the US government, and austerity measures follow shortly after that."

Journalist: "What makes you think that is what the WTO represents, and that would be the outcome?"

Ben Brown: "Listen, if you want to meet later today, like this evening, I would be in a much better mindset to answer your questions. Until then, you can consider and research this growing trend in the USA—that corporations have human rights guaranteed by the Constitution. It's a ridiculous idea that has been gaining traction since Supreme Court Justices Black and Harlan were replaced by Chamber of Commerce president Lewis Powell and corporate lawyer now Chief Justice William Rehnquist, who turned our Supreme Court from a civil rights-conscious court into probusiness court. You have until tonight to read up on the Supreme Court decision: *First National Bank of Boston v. Bellotti*. This decision, among a couple of others, has increasingly put our government up for sale to the highest bidder."

Benjamin Brown hands the reporter a piece of paper with his host's family home phone number. "Call, and we can set up a meeting place to discuss this in more detail. It's important; I will ensure you get the time and information you want." As Ben walks away from the reporter, he looks back at her and says, "Call!"

Later that day, the journalist returns to her home office and enters the dungeon. The dungeon is where the newsroom keeps all its records of previous articles. Unless someone is ordered to go there or does an investigative piece, it is almost always empty. After hours of researching the cases Benjamin Brown mentioned, using the dungeon's phone, the journalist calls the number Ben has given her, and the person who answers sounds almost paranoid.

Host: "Hello?"

Journalist: "Hello, my name is Abigale Triest, and I am with K-A-O-S News in Seattle."

Host: "Who? How did you get this number?"

Abigale: "I'm reporter Abigale Triest with KAOS News. I was interviewing your guest Benjamin Brown today, and he asked me to call him later at this number."

Host: "Well, Ben isn't here right now, and he shouldn't have given our number to anyone."

Abigale: "Do you know when to expect him back?"

Host: "Haven't you heard? The city is like a warzone."

Abigale: "No, I've been in the basement of an old building for most of the day. What's going on?"

Host: "The police turned on the people, and everything has gotten really violent with the police and broke up the city. It's like a warzone. I suspect Ben is either in jail, in hospital, or trying to help other people on the streets."

Abigale: "Thanks for the update, and I'm sorry if I alarmed you. If you can, please tell Mr. Brown to contact me at KAOS News. I hope you're safe. Please accept my apologies. Goodbye."

CHAPTER NINETEEN

HANNAH'S PLAN

APRIL 19, 2011—10:00 A.M.:

Josh returns to Hannah's after picking up his clothes, showering, and letting the Hickmans know he will be gone for a few days while caring for Hannah. He also pays them the next month's rent in case his time with Hannah becomes a longer stay than planned.

Josh has exactly $2,235.53 in the bank, with no job and no prospects. Almost all the money that remains was left from Ashley's inheritance. Josh has worked odd jobs for as long as he could keep them, but his outbursts and triggers ultimately would get the better of him. Ashley was an only child, and both her parents passed away within a short period of time. The little inheritance she received was primarily used to pay off her student loans and their move to Indiana. What they thought was a good chunk of money to get started was quickly gobbled up by funeral expenses and medical bills not covered by health insurance.

In the last two weeks of Ashley's life, Ashley, Josh, and Hannah, along with the hospice's palliative care package, helped fill out all the necessary paperwork for the obituary, burial, and funeral service, and all other notifications in case of Ashley's death. As a precautionary move, Hannah and Josh were given the power of health care proxy, which all three agreed was the best way to proceed if Ashley could not make medical decisions. Due to Hannah's own declining health and Josh's severe PTSD, once Ashley was admitted into the hospital after her first chemotherapy visit, Hannah put in an order with Ashley's approval to expedite the death certificate process. The ten copies of Ashley's death certificates were ready within forty-eight hours of her confirmed death.

With all the documents filled out and in order, the dates and signatures for the death certificate were the only things missing. They had agreed to allow Hannah to ensure that everything was handled promptly if that time were to come. Hannah performed her duties and kept her promise of what she believed was most important for Josh by filing Ashley's life insurance claim. (When they had learned that Ashley was pregnant a few months earlier, they each had taken out a $250,000 life insurance policy.)

The moment Hannah received the certificates, everything was mailed, death notifications were sent out, and the funeral and obituary were arranged. The only thing remaining is the repast, which the cancer group led by Scott will handle. That will happen in two days on April 21, 2011.

With the teapot whistling, Josh rushes into the kitchen to take it off the burner. He sees Scott's car pull up as he steeps some tea. He has a fire going, since the mornings are still cold and today is supposed to be overcast. Josh is trying his best to take care of Hannah.

Before entering the military, Josh's mom always bragged to her friends about what a protector and caregiver he was. Loretta Bush would say, "It doesn't surprise me that he joined the military. He is a protector by nature—always there to lend a helping hand or try to be the peacekeeper when people are fighting."

Josh sees Hannah wave off Scott's offer to walk her inside. He opens the front door, waves to Scott, and says, "I'll take it from here."

Scott puts his hands together in a prayer sign and thanks Josh for caring for her. "Call me if you need anything. My number is on the list next to her phone."

Josh gives him a thumbs-up as he meets Hannah halfway up her walkway. "Do you need an arm or any help?"

She waves him off. "I'm not there yet, but it's not too far away."

Trying to stay positive, he says, "I've got a fire going and some tea ready."

Hannah is pleased. "This is precisely what I needed to come home to. Thanks, Josh—for taking care of this old lady."

As she removes layers of clothes, Hannah thinks about the big day ahead. Closing the closet door, she looks at Josh. "Whew, who knew that taking a jacket and hat off could tire a person out? Have you eaten this morning? You need to keep your strength up if you're going to take care of me. That's the first rule we teach caregivers: You can't do people any good if you break down in the process."

"Yeah, I ate. I went home and showered, got my stuff together, and paid the next month's rent in case I'm here for a while. I hope that's okay with you. Your chair and your cup of tea are waiting for you here. I hope the house isn't too warm—I noticed you were chilled most of yesterday."

"It's perfect. We have a big day ahead. So, sit with me. Can you bring me the Fulcircle Company/Joseph Sinclair folder?"

The scent of a fire in the warm air, a cup of tea, and company triggers Hannah to ask Josh for a favor. "Can you go to the bookshelf and grab all those photo albums off the bottom shelf? I hope you'll entertain an old woman by allowing her to stroll down memory lane with you over the next few days. As it all ends, all these great memories and what a blessed life I've lived keep flooding my mind . . ."

Before she is even done asking, Josh is up again grabbing the photo albums and bringing them over to the coffee table. He is amazed at how many books there are on the shelves. With a glance, he looks at their spines and doesn't recognize a single name or author. He stacks the photo albums next to the Fulcircle Company folder, which he places closest to Hannah.

She says, "I suspect today will be a tough, long day for both of us." They sit quietly, looking at photos and telling stories for the next hour or so. Eventually, Hannah claps her hands together. "Enough of memory lane for now. Let me tell you what I have planned. And interrupt me any time you hear a mistake."

The fire is crackling, and Hannah is sitting in her chair. After throwing another log onto the fire, Josh returns to sit by her side. The Fulcircle folder is out and ready to go. Hannah's eyes and skin have a yellow hue. More than ever, she looks frail and like an old woman. Josh is torn between helping her keep what must be an enormous amount of pain at bay and wanting to go over her grand plan. He opts for the latter because that is Hannah's wish.

She begins. "Well, let's get things started. I have an idea that might be a way for you to get justice and use your training as an interrogator at the same time. Josh, you have such a strong, sharp mind, but it's been dulled by trying to win the approval of others. I believe that what I'm about to propose will allow you to set your military demons free while getting Ashley and your unborn child justice. Joe Sinclair is retired and lives in our town. He's a widower and lives alone. He's worth hundreds of millions of dollars for selling poison, bankrupting hard-working small farmers, and corrupting the laws to make his actions legal.

"That's what I've got for you. The plan was to go through the entire file and get you to hate this man. I'm on my way out, and while time is precious, my mind has never been clearer.

"But you don't need to hate this man because, in many ways, you would probably like him as a person. But remember the pain and suffering he's caused you and Ashley with the loss of her family's farm—I can only assume both of her parents died a painful death—your miscarriage, the death of your wife, and now the death of me. All that suffering for what? So, this man and many like him can have enough money to live a hundred lifetimes, maybe more?

"That is all we need to know about Joe Sinclair. He had a choice of basically any direction, and he chose to slowly kill and torture people for a six or seven-figure salary. That's it. That is who Joe Sinclair is, and we will hold him accountable for his crimes against humanity.

"The ultimate redemption for you, and nobody else, is to use your military training as an interrogator to give Joe Sinclair the ability to admit and repent against his crimes before his death. Initially, I planned to get him so drunk that he was barely conscious and then inject him with a syringe of Kill-All—maybe two—or however much it took for him to have a vital organ fail.

"Then the other day, we talked about your time in the military and your training. I promised Ashley that I would take care of you and help you find purpose in life. The second part of that promise left me puzzled until you said, 'If you ever need someone interrogated, I'm your guy.' In that moment, I realized this could be a way for you to confront your demons while seeking justice for your loved ones and countless others. I can't explain how I know this, but I feel deep down that this is the path to shedding the old skin of your past, like a snake, and starting a new life.

"Did you know that in many cultures a snake shedding its old skin symbolizes rebirth or transformation? You've been trapped in a skin of anger, guilt, and letting others define who you are for too long. It's time for a transformative action that will help you shed this burden and start to regain your true identity, which has been taken from you. At your core, you are a loving and caring person. The world needs more individuals who embody love and compassion. This journey will be a process, and you will need support from others after I am gone. However, if I can help you begin this journey, I will have fulfilled my promise to Ashley.

"Enough of that, can you explain the process of waterboarding a person to me in the most basic of terms? But first, I have a question for you. I know it simulates the feeling of drowning; can a person really drown if you wanted them to?"

Josh is shocked at how Hannah is talking about murder. "Yes—to answer your last question. I will explain how it could be done by describing where I learned how to waterboard a detainee."

Hannah says, "Detainee. I like that word; it will be a good word for Joe. Could you make sure you use it when addressing him? It will drive him crazy to know he is not in charge. He has been at the top of the hierarchy much of—if not, *all of*—his life, giving the orders. The idea of him being at the bottom for his final act of life seems fitting. With the motion of her hand, she zips her lip after saying, I'm sorry, I won't interrupt you again."

Josh is now having what he would typically consider a PTSD moment but finds himself controlling his anger. In fact, despite the nerves and anxiousness, he holds his hands up to Hannah, showing her his hands aren't shaking. Hannah thinks, *is this part of the interrogation?*

"Look," he says. "Usually, I would be shaking, and my mind would be reeling with a million different thoughts. You might be right. This might be a way for me to put all this to rest. My mind is calm right now."

Hannah looks at the clock. It is 11:37 a.m. He continues. "For me to explain this technique, it will be your turn to get a crash course in 'reverse-SERE' interrogation. I'm going to go fast and start from the beginning. Just stop me whenever you have a question. Do you understand?" Hannah nods.

"I won't bore you with my basic training and the skills they look for in enlistees to be trained as interrogators. Let's say they saw something in me that brought me into their program. At first, they waterboarded US servicemen to prepare them for the torture they might endure if captured by our enemy. That is where the "reverse" comes from in the term *reverse-SERE*. SERE is an acronym for Survival, Evasion, Resistance, and Escape.

"I'm not sure if it was during Korea or Vietnam, but in those wars, American soldiers were waterboarded. That was when the CIA and the Department of Defense came up with the idea of trying to prepare soldiers for such tactics. This was carried out in a special-forces unit now within the Department of Homeland Security. I remember like it was yesterday, my commanding officer telling us, 'When done right, it is controlled death.'"

Hannah raises a finger to ask a question. Josh stops what he is saying. "Have you ever been waterboarded?"

Josh is silent for a few seconds and eventually answers, "Yes, many times."

"Can you elaborate on your experiences for me?"

"I can, but words can't even begin to express the feeling of being totally out of control and unable to do anything about it. Your life is literally in the hands of another person or people. You're strapped down and unable to resist the water, no matter how much you try. A person needs to breathe, and the moment your body tries to breathe, in goes the water.

"The objective is fear; it begins with detention, and it never ends. The fear leading up to the water torture, and then the fear during the event is beyond description. As soldiers, we are in training. There is a subconscious relief knowing you are not about to die a horrible death, but even then, the level of fear and panic are off the charts. For the detainees who were in prison and dragged out of their cells and waterboarded, it must have been ten times the levels I felt during training sessions. Every aspect of the entire process is to instill fear into the person. The table, straps, music, words said to the detainee, and the waterboarding itself are all to put so much pressure on the person that they'll say just about anything to make it stop.

"After listening to you and reading about all these different corporations and the executives knowingly putting products on the market that kill the consumer, I can say that it is a form of 'When done right, it is controlled death' while extracting as much profit from the consumer first.

"The waterboarding process is fairly simple to set up and perform. . . ." Josh continues for about another hour, explaining to Hannah how the detainee's body is restrained and how it reacts. She absorbs everything he says, including details about setting up the table, the types of straps to use, the preferred kind of rag, time intervals, and more.

The clock now reads 1:11 p.m. Josh asks Hannah, "Do you have any questions?"

"Just two. Can you use any liquid—like, say, Kill-All? And can we pick these materials up today at the hardware store?"

"I don't see why not; liquid is liquid, and all these materials should be at most hardware stores."

Hannah stands up, starts towards the closet, and says, "Let's get going. I'll let you know the plan while we're driving. Please tell me whether you see any flaws." As Hannah grabs her coat, she says, "Here you go. You should wear this cowboy hat—it was Bob's. The other thing, how long would it take you to shave so you have a mustache?"

Looking a bit confused, he says, "About ten to twenty minutes."

"Good, you need to shave anyway." Giving a light tug on his facial hair, she says, "I didn't want to say anything, but your face is much nicer than a beard."

A few minutes later, Josh comes out with a 1970s handlebar mustache.

"Whoa! I was not expecting that, but it's perfect. You're wearing a cowboy hat and mustache because I will be the one to turn myself in, not you. You have a long life ahead, and my death sentence has already been given to me. I doubt I will even make it to a trial. That's why it's so important for Stage IV cancer patients to be the people who perform these acts.

"I'll explain the rest of the plan on the way to the store." By the time they get to Highway 24, Hannah's color has turned from a light-yellow hue to a darker yellow and she can barely keep her eyes open. As they pull into the hardware store parking lot, Hannah comes out of her daze and says, "Not this one, we need to go to Logansport. First, let's stop at my bank, it's on the next block up, and I can get some cash."

Josh says, "Listen, I know what we need to get, so let's get the money and then I'll take you back home. You can get some rest, and we'll talk a bit more about the plan when I get back. How does that sound?"

With a grimace on her face and her pain increasing by the hour, she needs to get Josh up to speed on the plan before she can call hospice and risk losing her clarity. She agrees that it's the best idea. "I would only slow things down. Make sure you use cash and keep that cowboy hat on and low. Don't look the cashier or any other employee directly in the eye."

With adrenaline pumping, she musters up enough energy to walk to the ATM and withdraw the maximum, $300. Josh offers to withdraw the cash, but Hannah wants to do it herself. He walks by her side the entire time, and Hannah tells him to remind her about getting the rest of the money when he drops her off.

Hannah has experienced a dimensional shift in the last twenty-four hours, and she is viewing herself outside her body. This is not an out-of-body experience but a surreal perception of what is actually happening. She sees her hands and fingers press the buttons on the ATM. It is pure muscle memory because she isn't thinking about it, but she views her hand as separate from herself. In her head, she thinks this is her last time using an ATM.

Once they return to Hannah's home, the walk to the house gets slower every time they venture away from it. Josh reminds her as they open the front door, "You were going to give me some more cash?"

"Of course. See—I had already forgotten about the money because I'm so focused on everything else. Come with me. I always have cash in this box in my bottom drawer if you need any in the coming days." Hannah has always kept a petty-cash box in her bottom drawer. Recently, she has cashed out one of her bonds, and now, in tightly rolled up one-hundred-dollar bills, the box contains a bit more than $50,000. This money is intended for Josh and no one else. When the time comes, it will be explained in the note of instructions she has left for him to be read after she is gone.

Josh follows her into her room, and she gives him another $500 and asks, "Will that be enough?"

"More than enough, and I'll make sure you get your change back. I'm going to take my car instead."

"No, take the truck, so everything is easily packed. And you keep whatever's left over for more supplies, if need be." Hannah doesn't want Josh or his own vehicle to be recognized by anyone.

Josh opens the front door to leave, and Hannah yells, "*Wait!* Take your jacket off, go into the closet where I got the cowboy hat, and grab Bob's jacket. I've kept those things all these years, not knowing why. I guess this was the reason. We've got to take precautions with you because you're an honorary Kesshitai Exit Stage IV group member. You have a long life ahead of you, and we need to make sure it's not spent in a prison cell. Good luck, and I'll be here—nicely rested by the time you return."

Logansport is roughly a forty-minute drive from Hannah's house. Josh needs some music to keep his mind distracted and his mood good. He looks in Hannah's glovebox for CDs and hopes her CD player still works.

Nothing, no CDs anywhere. He starts searching the truck. Jackpot! Under the passenger seat—Johnny Cash, Waylon Jennings, Merle Haggard, Dwight Yoakam, and more are in a container, along with Frank Sinatra, Marty Robbins, Dolly Parton, and Tom Jones.

He pops in a Johnny Cash CD, and the player works perfectly, instantly transporting Josh back to his childhood. He recalls the sound of an old, squeaky truck with Johnny Cash playing on the radio. He remembers seeing his dad's hands gripping the steering wheel, with his brothers nestling beside him in the cab on chilly days. Those hands fascinated him; without them, his family wouldn't have had a house to live in or food to eat. All the coal those hands had dug from the mountain made their life possible.

During the summer months, everyone piled into the truck bed, and his dad would turn up the radio, letting the music flow through the open sliding window for his sons to enjoy. With the sun shining, the wind blowing in their faces, their hair dancing in the breeze, the music playing, and their dad behind the wheel—life felt utterly free and perfect.

As Josh approaches the hardware store, he puts on the cowboy hat and tips it low. He parks away from the entrance, in almost the furthest spot from the store.

As the two automatic doors slide open, it dawns on him about the tools he will need. He thinks to himself, can't worry about that now. Today is about getting the materials. Casually cruising the aisles, he picks up one material item after another. He finds the tool issue very distracting as he sees all the things he will need within grabbing distance.

Thirty minutes later, he is standing in line thinking about how he is going to pull this plan off by himself when he hears, "Your total today is $478.37, says the cashier. "Do you have a store or rewards card?"

"Cash—I'll be paying with cash." The cashier does her job and goes into the sales pitch to lure him to sign up for a store credit card, which will give him 10 percent off the first purchase.

Josh's corporate-control senses are on high alert for the first time, and hearing the pitch clearly now, he ponders that this leads almost everyone straight to the hook. *We bite at the bait of 10 percent off. Bam! We are now in their house of mirrors system. That is how they got Ashley's dad and their farm. That's why my parents have been paying off our home for the last thirty-five years on a thirty-year loan—those motherfuckers.*

He pays with mixed bills, mostly twenties, and apologizes to the cashier, saying he had just sold his car, and the guy had paid him with a bunch of twenties and tens—and even gave him the last few dollars in change. He speaks with an accent different from his native West Virginia drawl. As the clerk rings him up, he notices that everything has scan codes, and he makes a mental note to remove them and wipe down all the items for fingerprints.

On his way out of the store, Josh hears a man's voice: "Joey, hey Joey," and feels someone grabbing his shoulder. He turns around, and the person sees a middle-aged man with a handlebar mustache. Embarrassed, the man says, "Sorry, pal. I thought you were somebody else. Have a good day."

With his heart racing despite having done nothing wrong, Josh replies in his new midwestern accent, "No problem. You too."

Under normal circumstances, this would have triggered Josh since it was a stranger touching him. One of his brother's names is Joseph, and all his friends call him Joey. Josh was rattled, but he didn't lose control. He is now on high alert but controls his nerves and calmly walks to the truck, unloads his stuff, and returns the cart, doing everything at a smooth, steady pace. As he climbs into the truck, he decides it will be Willie Nelson for the drive back.

It's now just after 4:00 p.m. as he pulls up to Hannah's place. Although he has never seen the inside of it, Josh decides to go in and unload everything into what he assumes is a separate garage-workshop. When he opens the sliding door, he says, *Holy shit!*"

A voice behind him says, "I know, right!" Josh jumps out of his skin because the voice is a man's.

Josh repeats, "Holy shit—you scared me. How's it going, Scott?"

Now, it's Scott's turn to be surprised. "Wow, you look way different with the whole look you have going on. I'd never have guessed that to be you. That's why I came over when I saw Hannah's truck with someone who looked like Bob driving it wearing his cowboy hat and jacket."

Josh says, "I've only seen pictures of Bob. Since I'll be staying with Hannah—last night was my first night—she told me to go ahead and use Bob's jacket and hat."

"When you come from town, you drive right past my house, and I just happened to be outside when you drove by. I wanted to come to check in on Hannah anyway. How is she doing? And really, how are you doing? Are you hanging in there?"

Now, brought back to reality, Scott can see a flash of pain on Josh's face. "I'm hanging in there, *barely*—but without Hannah I would have lost my shit. That's why I agreed to stay and look after her. It gives me a purpose and allows my mind to focus on other things. My mom always called me her little caregiver. Out of all us boys, I was the one that helped her the most, taking care of things and my brothers—making sure they stayed out of trouble."

"That's nice. Hannah is a special person, and you would have enjoyed Bob; he had a great sense of humor—and he was a good husband and man. What is all this stuff?"

Josh changes the subject back to Hannah. "Did you look in on her yet?"

"No, I just came over. Would you like me to poke my head in and say hello? First, I can help you unload everything."

Once again, Josh changes the subject to Hannah. "I got it handled here. She'd like to see your face. We pulled out a bunch of photo albums this morning."

"Are you sure it wouldn't be a problem?"

"No, I got it. This'll only take me a few minutes. I'll meet you guys inside."

"Okay, see you in a few minutes. Thanks again for caring for her; she means so much to me and to many, many people in this county.

As Scott walks toward the front door, Josh suddenly remembers all the folders on the table, and by the time he can say anything, Scott has his head inside the door.

Josh thinks, well, it's too late to do anything now. He looks back at the garage and says *holy shit* once again.

Bob not only drove trucks for a living but also worked on them. This looks like a professional garage for semis. There will be plenty of space and tools for Josh to work with. He backs the truck in and closes the doors to speed things up. He hears laughter as he walks up to the front door. When he walks in, Hannah is standing in the kitchen with Scott.

Josh quickly scans the house and sees that all the folders except the Fulcircle Company/Joseph Sinclair file have been put away. Then he asks, "Have you been up since I left?"

No, I sleep as well as I can these days, until I heard the truck pull into the driveway. I got up, went to the bathroom, and came into the kitchen to heat water when Scott showed up."

Both Scott and Josh can see the pain and discomfort Hannah is trying to hide. Scott asks, "Have you called yet?"

"Not yet, but I'm getting close. I want to keep seeing the world through non-drugged-out eyes for as long as possible."

Scott says that seeing the world through yellow, jaundiced eyes and in severe pain cannot be a good feeling either. Being the newcomer and by far the youngest, Josh stays out of this conversation. Hannah laughs it off: "Scott, you know me. Pain is part of life. I'll put it off as long as possible, but I promise they'll have been called by tomorrow. You could come over in the morning, and we can go through the photo albums with Josh. I'm sure the nurse will be here or on her way. Dr. Evans called to give them a heads-up."

Josh doesn't know who "they" are, but he can take a guess. Scott walks over to Hannah, hugs her, and says, "*A hui hou*. We'll see each other in the morning, and I love you."

She repeats, "A hui hou, and I love you too. See you in the morning." Hannah and Scott know, and Josh hasn't figured it out yet. She is in the last days of her life. Any time they leave one another, it might be the last time.

As Scott heads to the door, Josh thinks he sees him glance at the Fulcircle Company/Joseph Sinclair folder. He could have been looking at the stack of photo albums. Josh isn't sure, but he is getting a bit paranoid about everything.

After Scott leaves, curious, Josh asks, "What was that thing you both said?"

"A hui hou?"

"Yeah, what does it mean?"

"It means "until we meet again" in Hawaiian. Scott, Bob, Kathy (Scott's ex-wife), and I took a trip to Hawai'i together. Scott and I have known each other for many years, and our friendship has stood the test of time. You'll see this when we look at the photo albums."

Hannah walks slowly into the front room and asks Josh to stoke the embers and throw another log onto the fire. She picks up the Fulcircle folder, then sits very uncomfortably in her chair, and says, "Did you get everything? I only have a little time to go over everything with you, and you'll have to figure out what is a good idea versus a bad idea on your own. You can always contact Olga and Robert through Skype, and their phone numbers are written down on my list of contacts next to the phone. We've been talking almost daily for the last week or so. I was hoping it would last until at least May 1st, but it doesn't seem like that will happen."

"I promise you that your plan for Joe Sinclair will be completed," Josh says. "The more I think about it, the more upset I get, and I see what you explained to me as the truth. He decided on a big payday through his power to poison people, sue small farmers, and corrupt our government. All those things are the actions of a bully. I hate bullies."

Hannah says firmly, "Yes! That's exactly what Joe is—a bully. He and I also go back a long way, even before he retired in Monticello. I won't go into it, but I belonged to a group that attempted to sue Fulcircle many times. We would meet him in Missouri when he was the active CEO. Those meetings went as well as you might expect. They are all that way, it seems, CEOs of big corporations. I'm not sure if being a sociopath is a prerequisite or if they are just great liars who convince everyone—even themselves—that they are providing the world with a needed service or product.

"Anyway, were there any problems getting the materials? I see you found Bob's garage. I forgot to tell you about it before, but you'll have any tools you might need in the garage. Bob just loved driving his truck. He was a certified heavy equipment/truck mechanic, but he preferred being on the road and having relationships throughout the tristate area of Southwest Indiana, Illinois, and Kentucky.

"Well, are you ready? Because I'm running out of gas . . ."

"Okay, let's get to it."

Hannah does her thing, closing her eyes and taking a deep breath before she starts. "I'll go slow despite being in a hurry. There's a ton of information: First, there is a notebook in this folder. You should write down notes or highlight them. I've covered everything, but please jump in and tell me if I missed anything."

"You got it."

Hannah begins with Joe having a Saturday golf day with the same three friends for the last fifteen years. "It can be on any number of courses, but their tee times are almost always between 10:00 a.m. and 10:30 at this time of year. The nights are too unpredictable, with how cold they get. So, they make sure they get there late enough for frost delays. Anyway, they all stink at golf, but they enjoy betting, drinking, and smoking cigars with each other. It's actually sweet that they've stayed friends all these years.

"After they play, they'll have a light lunch or early dinner with a couple more drinks. I swear they all would fail a drunk driver's breath test if they were ever to get pulled over. Joe returns home between five and six every Saturday. I know all this because we used to stage protests outside his house. In the last couple of weeks, I've called to have him paged at one of his three main golf courses, and like clockwork, they still have the same schedule. I hang up when I hear him pick up and say hello.

"Are you with me so far?"

Josh nods and points to the folder, showing Hannah that he has highlighted her timeline.

"Okay, great. The next part is the part that should take the stress of being seen away. Sinclair bought the neighboring properties on all four sides of his own. He writes them off as nature preserves and pays almost zero property taxes. One of the bonuses of being rich is using your money to accumulate land and wealth and get tax breaks no working-class person could ever get.

"Here is the other part: Did you see his address under his name? You live really close to him, and I'm sure your landlords know him. Joe can't help himself. He is the homeowner's association chair, and if he isn't jamming his opinions and what he wants down other people's throats, he's not happy.

"He clearly has a type-A personality, which means he needs everything to be in order and always wants to be in control. If he isn't, he struggles to cope. Interestingly, he often likes to break the very rules he imposes on others. Frequently, you'll find him playing Frank Sinatra on his outdoor speakers while he practices on his putting green, usually in a drunken state. I'm not sure if that was meant for us during our protests or just something he enjoys. Regardless, it's commonplace for him to have the music playing.

"The putting green is located in the back of the house, and once you're on the property, it's clear he values his privacy. His setup creates a perfect area for interrogation, as there are no neighbors nearby who can see his putting green or swimming pool from any direction.

"And just let me know if this seems like a bad plan. He does not have a security system anywhere on his property, but he does have many guns. They are in a safe in his den.

"So, here's the plan. (I always needed a helper since I am so small.)"

Hannah continues with her plan with Josh altering it a bit in places, including wiping down all materials for fingerprints and removing scan numbers off of said materials: duct tape, extra strength twenty-four-inch zip ties, a modified plastic table with holes drilled out for forehead/wrists/ankles/elbows/knees, rags, five-gallon paint strainer bag, Kill-All, etc.—and for good measure, Josh's handgun with silencer to keep the detainee quiet. After Josh was dishonorably discharged and came home for a few weeks, Josh's dad asked him to leave town and all connections with the family. His brother gave him the handgun with a suppressor as a going-away present since Josh was no longer able to purchase firearms because of his PTSD diagnosis.

At the same time, Sinclair is allowed to repent for his greed and murderous decisions over his lifetime. Hannah continues that this repentance is strictly for the detainee to come clean, and the outcome will be the same no matter what is said or not said. When the interrogation is over, this note will be left behind taped to the cover of the untouched folder titled Fulcircle Company/Joseph Sinclair:

> The People of Earth are exercising our democratic right
> to self-determination and breaking away from our cor-
> rupted political, judicial, legal, and economic system
> that protects and promotes corporate mass murder.
> We no longer give our consent for our environment

to be mined and sacrificed for profit; our bodies and minds to be robbed of their wealth; products to be experimented on the masses without the precautionary principle being the highest priority; the accumulation of wealth either earned or unearned to have undue influence over public policy; and laws to be explicitly created to protect those who have wealth and power to oppress, suppress, and repress the people who perform the duties that allow society to function.

We hold these truths to be self-evident: That all men are created equal; that they are endowed by their Creator with certain unalienable rights; that among these rights are life, liberty, and the pursuit of happiness—and to secure these rights governments are instituted among men deriving their just powers from the consent of the governed—and that whenever any form of government becomes destructive toward these ends, it is the right of the People to alter or to abolish it and to institute new government, laying its foundation on such principles and organizing its powers in such form as to that which shall seem most likely to affect their safety and happiness.

CHAPTER TWENTY

HANNAH'S PLAN—CONTINUED

APRIL 19, 2011—6:55 P.M.:

"I'm so tired, Josh—I need to get some sleep. Can you help me stand up? I've been sitting for too long."

Josh extends his hand as he stands up. "Should you have called hospice?"

Hannah cannot hold the pain in any longer and lets out a moan that comes from a very deep place as she rises to her feet. Almost instantly, she bends forward and to the right. She stays in that position. "Oh my, this is not good. Let's get me into bed, and I'll call them."

"Do you need me to carry you," he asks.

She answers with a painful laugh. "God, no. I feel like I might explode if I was squeezed like that. Just get me to my bed, and I can handle it from there."

Josh is torn between being irritated and supportive. "Don't forget, Hannah, I just went through all this with Ashley. I remember everything."

"My dear Josh, I'm eighty-five-years-old, and our bodies are the same but very different from when we were in our thirties. And I've got fifty more years of pride built in. I suspect by this time tomorrow it won't matter, and I'll be on enough morphine to dull it, but for now, just get me to my bed, and I will manage the rest."

A very painful forty-foot walk to Hannah's bed takes some time, and both the caregiver and the receiver are winded by the time they reach it. "I got it from here and I'll call you when I'm ready. Bring the phone and that paperclipped packet for hospice with you."

Now worried that she will fall, Josh leaves the room and closes the door. He doesn't move once the door is shut and just listens. He hears a series of moans and groans as she navigates her bedroom and bathroom, and eventually, a sigh of relief indicating that she is back on the bed.

"Okay, I'm ready," she says loudly.

"I'll be right in." Josh has the phone, the packet, and a small glass of water. He gives two light knocks and says, "I'm coming in."

Everything in the room looks the same, except she already has two small glasses beside her bed. Josh does a pirouette, looking for a place to put his glass; Hannah tells him to put it on the dresser and bring her the packet and phone. "I was hoping to put this off for another day or two, but I'm not going to make it."

Josh is almost sure she is talking about the morphine, but at this point he doesn't know what to expect. He hands her the packet and phone. Feeling useless standing there, he says, "I'm going to give you your privacy," and starts heading out of the room.

While dialing the phone, she waves him back. With her hand over the mouthpiece, she says, "Please stay with me. They're most likely going to want to talk to you." Josh does what he's told. Somebody on the other end of the line answers. Hannah thinks, *this is it—here we go.*

Hospice: "City of Bridges Hospice Call Center, how may I direct your call?"

Hannah: My name is Hannah Cassidy, and my doctor Richard Evans's office called you earlier today.

Hospice: (Typing is heard through the phone.) "Oh yes. We were expecting a call this morning. Is this an emergency?"

Hannah: "It's not an emergency in the way you are speaking, but for me, my pain levels have reached a point that I cannot ignore any longer."

Hospice: I see you have spoken with our head nurse and coordinator, Michelle. She has gone home for the day. We do have James, the night nurse. Would you like to speak with him?"

Hannah: "Yes, that would be lovely. Thank you."

Hospice: "We are here twenty-four hours a day, so if you have any questions or concerns, just give us a call. I'm connecting you to James, one of our best nurses. Good night."

The phone is ringing. Hannah tells Josh they are connecting her with the night nurse, James. Josh writes down James's name with the side note "first night nurse" next to it.

James: "City of Bridges Hospice Center. This is James. Is this Hannah Cassidy?"

Hannah: "Good evening, James. Yes, this is Hannah Cassidy."

James: "Well, it looks like you came in a few days ago, spoke with Michelle, and have everything in order. It also looks like Dr. Evans called this morning, and we were expecting a call from you much earlier today. But first, we must get the usual identification out of the way. Can you state your full name and date of birth?" Hannah answers all his questions.

James: "What are your pain levels now, zero being no pain and ten being unbearable?" (Hannah doesn't want Josh to hear a numerical answer since he knows exactly what it means, having gone through this with Ashley four days ago.)

Hannah: "It's fairly sharp and consistent."

James: "Where is your pain, and on that same scale, at what number would you put yourself?"

Hannah: "I will put it to you this way, it is everywhere and bad enough for me to call you. Is there a way you could come out tonight?"

James: "Oh, of course. We have all the information and your wishes. Has anything changed? Do you have a loved one who can manage your pain responsibly and ensure you get moved every couple of hours?"

Hannah: "Yes, he will meet you at the door. His name is Josh; it should be in the records. And yes, he knows my advanced directive and wishes."

James: "Uh, yes. I see his name right here. Have you noticed any significant changes in your weight since we last met? Are you still eating?"

Hannah: "I've lost some weight, but I'm not sure exactly how much since we last met, maybe five-to-seven pounds. I've lost my appetite for a few days now. I've been drinking lots of tea. It feels good in my throat, and I cannot seem to stay warm no matter how many layers of clothing I wear. I've been very active up until today, so I'm choosing to call you now."

James: "Okay, I have everything needed for now. I'll be over with supplies within the hour and walk you and Josh through the entire process again."

Hannah: "Good. Just so you know, Michelle has given me the bed covers, and they are on. I have to say that they are uncomfortable to sleep on, but I understand why they are needed. We'll see you soon."

APRIL 20, 2011—8:00 A.M.:

Just as James did the previous night, there is a gentle knock on the door at 8:00 a.m. Josh answers the door expecting a hospice nurse, but it was Scott.

"Good morning, Scott. I was expecting someone else."

Both men speak in a low whisper. "I know. I saw James's truck outside last night. How bad is she? She didn't look good yesterday, and we really didn't have a chance to talk about it on the way home from Dr. Evans' appointment. I was so angry, but then I thought about who I was angry with and let it go. But she could have told me sooner—so I could have helped more."

Josh walks into the kitchen and offers Scott coffee or tea. "Tea would be great with just a little bit of honey and milk."

"Just like Hannah takes it. No problem."

"Is it alright if I poke my head in on her and say good morning if she's up?"

While making the cup of tea, Josh says, "I gave her a dose about four hours ago. She might be awake. Luckily, she was fine with the lowest dose, and her mind won't be too bad."

Scott insists, "Give me a call if you need any help. Tomorrow is a big day for you, what with Ashley's funeral. But you don't have to worry about anything—everything is handled."

Trying his best not to think about the funeral, Josh says in a sad, bordering on angry tone. "Thank you all for everything. I wouldn't be able to handle it myself." His eyes fill with tears, and despite his best attempt at keeping them back, they begin to stream down his face. "Ashley was my entire life—and life has no meaning without her. I can't promise anything about tomorrow. I've barely met her childhood friends and haven't seen her college friends in years. Please don't ask me to say anything. Being here with Hannah is the only thing keeping me sane at the moment; it gives me a purpose."

Scott's heart breaks while listening to Josh try to hold back his emotions. "Of course, you don't have to do anything tomorrow if you don't want to. People will want to give you their condolences, and it's normal for you to be emotional. Outside of what you want to say to Ashley privately and sitting through the ceremony, you won't have to do anything."

"I'll just poke my head in to see if she's awake. Hannah, are you awake?"

With a little groan, Hannah tries to push herself up in bed and answers in a sleepy voice. "Come on in, Scott. It's nice waking up and hearing your voice."

Relieved that she is coherent and wants to socialize, Scott enters the room while Josh makes tea. "Are you eating, or are we past that stage of things?"

Hannah laughs. "We? I'm just joking. Yes, I haven't been able to eat solid foods for a few days now. It hurts too much. I think this will be a quick one—painful and quick. It's strange being on this side of things and seeing it through a different lens. I can now see how much the caregiver hovers. It's too much. Let them know I said that after I'm gone, won't you?"

"I'll let hospice and our group know to minimize the caregiving—just come in and get out," he says in his best sarcastic voice.

"Yep, that's what I want you to tell them," says Hannah, playing along with him. Then she quietly asks, "How is Josh doing this morning?"

"He seems fine but a little on edge about Ashley's funeral tomorrow."

"That's my only prayer right now—that I'm well enough to get there and be by his side. It was a promise I made to him. I'm unsure if he knows, but I promised Ashley I would care for him. I know his PTSD must be wracking his brain at this point. I need to be there to hold his hand and distract him—well, not *distract* him but allow him to focus on something else."

"Hannah, you can't stop taking care of others literally until your last minutes in this life, can you? Take care of yourself for a change."

"Taking care of others is how we take care of ourselves. You know that better than anyone."

"True, but still, at some point you need to put yourself before others."

"It's a little late for that. I promise—if we can get through tomorrow—it won't be long, and I will put myself before others.

"Now help this old dying woman to get out of bed and to the bathroom. Luckily, I haven't lost that function yet. I had Josh put some clothes for me in there on a hanger for the morning. Positive thinking on our part. Then, we'll look through those photo albums for as long as possible before I need a nap."

"Now you're talking. I also brought over some photo albums with all of us in them. Let's get up and go to the bathroom. I'll wait outside the door, and you can let me know if you need any help. If you're good, I'll tell Josh to set up tea and photo albums on the coffee table next to your chair."

Scott gets Hannah to the bathroom, and she gives him the okay that she is alright. As Scott leaves the room, he runs into a woman. "Good morning. I'm Julia, the morning nurse assigned to Mrs. Cassidy. James was here last night and he'll be the primary night nurse. As things move along, we'll be checking in more often with a few new faces. But for now, it's just an a.m. and p.m. check."

"Nice to meet you, Julia. I'm Scott, Hannah's next-door neighbor and very old friend. Josh, whom you've already met, will be the contact person here at the house. But I'll be over as much as needed. We're about to have some tea and look through old photo albums."

Julia points towards Hannah's room and says, "Sounds like a wonderful morning planned, but I need to get to work."

"Of course, sorry about that. Hannah said she's fine and is changing in her bathroom. I was going to send in Josh, but we'll leave it with you. Thanks so much for taking care of our dear friend."

A few minutes pass while Scott and Josh look at some of the old photos in Hannah's album. As Julia escorts Hannah out of her room, Josh says, "Look how young she was here, pointing at one of the pictures.

Julia says, "So far, so good. I would keep her liquid intake down since it's becoming increasingly difficult to process everything. As you know, anytime Hannah receives a dose, write down the amount and the time in the journal. I see that she got through the night with low doses."

Then she walks Hannah over to her chair, which is covered in blankets for her and says, "You guys seem to have everything handled here. Keep the house nice and warm. Hannah will find it harder to stay warm as things progress."

All three nod yes like schoolchildren, and Hannah is the first to break the silence. "Thank you, Julia. I'm in great hands here. What time should we expect James?"

"Between four and five. You're going to need to nap much more often to get through the day. It makes everything so much easier for everyone, especially yourself."

Josh stands up and reaches out to shake Julia's hand. She thinks it's an odd gesture but smiles and reciprocates. As soon as the door closes and Julia is walking down the pathway, Scott says to Hannah, "Is there anything you want? We're getting to the last-time stage."

Hannah smiles. "No. I think we passed that stage already a couple of days ago. Let's look at some pictures of a life well-lived. Come on.

APRIL 20, 2011—4:35 P.M.:

James is walking up the pathway with a transfer wheelchair. Josh meets him at the door, and James says softly as he works his way through the door, "How's she doing?"

Josh, trying to help but probably making the process harder, finally gets out of the way. "She's hanging in there. She's been down for about three hours now. Everything is in the logbook."

"Hannah told me that tomorrow is an important day for both of you and asked me to bring the wheelchair so she can be there. I'm sorry you have to go through all this so close together." Josh nods a thank-you. "Well, let me get to it, and we'll see how she's holding up. Just a reminder: When the pain increases, call our office. Someone is on call twenty-four hours in case you need to increase the dose."

APRIL 21, 2011—THE DAY OF ASHLEY'S FUNERAL:

At 7:45 a.m. Hannah is still sleeping. Josh doesn't want to check in on her just in case she isn't alive. Scott had called earlier in the morning and talked Josh through the funeral process. The repast will be at the community center. Everything has been taken care of, and Josh doesn't have to do anything. Scott has also told Josh that the community center might not hold everyone who has responded.

Josh has been so disconnected from the process that he thought it would be a very small service. "How many people are coming," he asks.

Scott answers with a nonanswer: "It's hard to tell, but many of Ashley's family members are coming from Iowa".

"How many?"

"It's hard to say with some people saying they'll come and others who just show up."

"How many?"

"Over a hundred," Scott finally answers.

Instantly, Josh's gut turns into a knot, his head starts racing, and he begins to mumble. "They're going to want me to speak or do something—I'm the reason all these people haven't seen Ashley for so long. They're going to blame me for her death."

Both Ashley and Hannah had warned Scott about Josh's insecurities and PTSD after one of the two meetings Ashley attended. "It's not going to be like that at all, Josh," Scott says. "We've taken care of everything. At any moment you feel like speaking, give me a signal, and you can say whatever you need or want. Nobody is expecting anything from you. Today is about Ashley. Look, *Hannah* didn't even say anything at Bob's service."

"She didn't?"

"They had been together for fifty-eight years, and the last two years were tough on everyone. She couldn't bring herself to talk without breaking down."

Hannah had been listening from her bedroom door and butted in at that moment. "That's right, Josh, nobody will want anything from you other than to give their condolences. What I will need from you is for you to take me home when needed."

Scott interrupts, "We have all that taken care of already. There's no need for Josh to worry about that today."

"No," Hannah says firmly. "Josh will be the one to bring me home unless he chooses otherwise."

Taken aback by Hannah's intensity, Scott figures this is important and should be left alone. "Okay, Josh will bring you back."

"First thing this morning, Josh, you need to get rid of that mustache and shower," says Hannah. In case you didn't bring your suit, it's at your place, hanging in a dry-cleaning bag in the closet. Julia will be here at any moment, and I've got to prepare for the day. It's a big day for all of us, and Ashley needs to be at the forefront of our thoughts."

1:40 P.M.—DRIVING HOME FROM THE COMMUNITY CENTER:

Hannah says, "That wasn't as bad as you thought it would be, was it now."

"Not really. I honestly thought they all would hate me. Do you think I should have said anything more than thanking everyone for coming?"

"Your words were perfect, and many of them were extremely relieved that you were her partner and the person she chose to share her life with."

"Is that what you felt? I've been so numb all day, I couldn't really tell. It was the first time I've met many of the people who came today. When we got married, we were in North Carolina and her parents were gone. A couple of her aunts and uncles came and one set of cousins. The rest were her college friends."

Hannah's eyes are closed while Josh continues talking. Then she stops him. "I want to say one last thing to you today because it's on my mind. You are a good man. Life is not fair, and you've been dealt a pretty shitty hand way too early in your life. But I've come to know this one truth about life: We need to do the best we can with the sense we are given in life and try to positively influence the people and lives we touch throughout it.

"Eighty-five years of living, loss, suffering, an education that has never stopped, and all the love I have given and received. The older I got, the more I kept waiting for the day that everything would make more sense, but here we are in my last days, and I know less about the meaning of life now than I did when I was an all-knowing teenager.

"I'm going to share something with you right now. For the last few days, I have felt Bob's presence and energy around me. Last night, when you gave me the last dose, I thought you were Bob's grandmother, Sadie, coming in to take care of me. She was a sweet woman and Bob's favorite person, apart from his mother. I don't think it will be long now. I'm a little afraid, but feeling Bob and Sadie around me makes me more comfortable."

As they pull up to Hannah's and Josh turns off the ignition, his mind instantly returns to when he and Ashley pulled up to this exact spot for dinner just a few weeks ago. He breaks down with an uncontrollable cry. He is no longer trying to look or feel strong. Even in the driveway, when learning of Hannah's cancer advancing, he held onto his ego. In this moment, there is no ego. No yelling, swearing, blame, guilt, or anything. There is only crying without thought.

Hannah, as a trained grief counselor, understands this is exactly what she has been trying to gently lead Josh toward—an emotional surrender. He has come close a few times but has never had a complete emotional release. This is one more box checked off in Hannah's promise to Ashley. She just rubs his back and allows him to get it out.

Once Josh stops, he begins looking for something to wipe his face with and Hannah hands him a tissue. "Take as long as you need."

"I'm fine. It just hit me that Ashley and I pulled up to this exact spot when we came for dinner."

Another cry lets loose, and Hannah softly rubs his back once again. He looks up, and Hannah has another tissue ready for him. She tells him he has finally let the wall down or the door open and to expect moments just like this to happen in the next few days. For her, it took months for the unsolicited cries to dissipate. She, too, was a personality inflicted with a habit of controlling her emotions, so this was one of the most healing times of her life.

Josh is now ready. "Let's go in." He gets out and pulls out the wheel-chair and brings it around for her.

She asks if they could just sit out in the sun for a while. "The sun just feels so good on my face—its warmth and everything it represents. I just want to soak as much of it in as I can before I get too tired."

"Whatever you want, I get the feeling we'll both have long naps today." He rolls her to the new spring grass that now covers her yard. Although the lawn is still short, Josh asks, "Would you like me to take your shoes off and put your feet on the grass?"

"I would absolutely love it."

Josh takes his shoes and socks off and brings a kitchen chair out to sit in the sun with his dying friend. Sitting in their chairs, they wiggle their toes and sit quietly, allowing the sun to heat their faces and fill their souls.

Hannah looks at her feet and says, "Look at that."

Josh is unsure what to look at and follows her gaze down to her feet. "Whoa, is that normal for you?" Hannah's feet have started mottling. Her skin has a bluish hue, and her veins are dark purple.

She replies, "Yes, that's normal for my current condition." Hannah knows she doesn't have long to live since her body is drawing her blood in for her vital organs, and her heart isn't strong enough to move her blood out to her extremities, but she keeps this information to herself.

After thirty minutes or so, Hannah says, "That was glorious. But it's time for me to go in. As much as I don't want to, it's time."

Josh stands up to start wheeling her to the house, and she asks in an almost childlike voice: "Can we walk into the house? I get the feeling this will be my last chance to walk through my door and into my room. From this point forward, I will be on wheels and pushed by someone else."

"Of course. Whatever you want, just tell me."

"Unfortunately, you can't give me what I want most—just a little more time in an able body."

Josh bends over, and Hannah puts her arm around his neck. "On a count of three—okay? One, two, three." They both stand up slowly, and Hannah's pain is immense—so much so, that she cannot stand totally upright; once again it hurts too much in her right abdomen. Yet, she insists on walking through the door and into her bedroom.

It is a slow walk to the bedroom, and they finally reach her bed. Hannah, out of breath, asks Josh to help her get her legs up on the bed and into a comfortable position. He agrees and asks about her next dose of morphine. It is much easier for you to take it sitting up. She agrees and also asks him to double the dose.

"I need to get the doctor's approval first." He looks at the clock and sees it's 2:45 p.m.

Hannah's pain is so intense that she gets a bit short with Josh and tells him, "I've done this with dozens of people, and that is what they are going to tell you. Let's just get me comfortable, and then you can call it in and write it in the logbook."

Despite disagreeing, he does what she asks. He retrieves the bottle and syringe from the bathroom. "This seems way more than before, so it will take at least two or three times to rub it into your gums."

Now, in a role reversal, Hannah becomes the child, and Josh is the parent; she opens her mouth to allow him to push down on the plunger, and she begins to rub the medicine into her capillaries. It takes three plunges and many minutes to get all of the morphine rubbed in, and by the time Hannah finishes the third, she tells Josh, "I love you and don't ever forget you are a good man. Ashley saw it, both your mom and I see it, and many of the people you met today see it. You're on your way to finding that man again. We all want you to live a good, long life with purpose. Promise me, you'll continue to find yourself again and live a good, purposeful life.

Tears run down his face as he raises Hannah's legs on the bed and puts her into a comfortable position. He says, "I promise."

The morphine beginning to take effect causes Hannah's speech to slur. "I mean it. Find yourself again and live a good life. I love you, Josh."

Josh takes a moment to gain his composure as his tears fall onto her blanket. "I swear—I promise."

Almost completely unconscious and the morphine dulling or maybe opening her mind to new dimensions, Hannah says, "I love you, Bob."

As Josh leaves the room, he looks back at his friend Hannah, now curled into a fetal position covered in blankets, and says, "I love you too." Emotionally drained from the entire day, Josh heads into the guest room and passes out on the bed.

5:55 P.M.:

James is shaking Josh awake. *"Josh—Josh. I need you to wake up."*

Waking from a deep sleep, not really knowing where he is or what day it is, he answers, "Yeah, I'm awake."

"No—I need you to wake up."

Everything comes into focus, and his mind realizes he is at Hannah's and James is talking to him. He becomes alert immediately. "What's wrong? What do you need me to do?"

"Slow down. There's nothing wrong. Just get yourself together— you've had one helluva long day."

Rubbing his face, Josh says, "Okay, okay, I'm awake. What's going on?"

"Hannah is gone. She's passed over."

"Wait—*what?* She couldn't have—I just put her to bed." He looks at the clock and sees he's been asleep for three hours.

"Oh shit! Did I kill her? I doubled her dose and didn't call it in first for approval. Would that have done it? I totally forgot to call it in or write it in the logbook." Josh panics, and his first reaction is that it is somehow his fault.

James talks him down from the ledge. "That was totally normal. Was her pain increasing?"

"Yeah, like a whole lot. She didn't take any morphine before the funeral because she didn't want to be drugged out. By the time we got back, her pain was really bad. She told me to double the dose and then call it in. She said that she had done dozens of caregiver duties for hospice patients, so she knew that it was what hospice would tell me to do. But she wanted me to help her get out of pain first."

"Everything Hannah told you is true. You did nothing wrong, except for not writing it down in the logbook, which we'll take care of now." James is completely focused on reassuring Josh. He emphasizes that this is a critically important task, and very few people are trained to do it, beyond having a genuine love for the person they're caring for.

"There is a lot of flexibility when it comes to the logbook, since untrained caregivers might occasionally forget to record something. Everything you just told me checks out with the amount of morphine left in the bottle. I'm going to ask a few things, and you tell me what you remember as best you can."

"Okay—First: What time did you administer the morphine?"

"I remember looking at the clock at 2:45, when she told me to take care of the pain first, so she finished her last dose at probably around 3:00 p.m."

"Okay, good. And did you double the dose?"

Josh's military training and mind are creeping in and wanting to take over. Everything needs to be written down by the book despite how it really took place. "Yeah. Should I admit that or should I write it down multiple times?"

James is hitting all the correct buttons as he walks through the process with him. "Not at all. Like I said, what you did is exactly what the doctor would have told you to do. We touched on it briefly in your thirty-minute crash-course hospice caregiver instructions: Any time the pain increases, the caregiver administering the morphine can make a judgment call on increasing the dose or not. Hannah was at the lowest dosage level, so doubling it was exactly the correct thing to do. You did a great job. You did it perfectly. Well, almost perfectly, but we've just corrected that mistake."

Calmed down and now thinking clearly, Josh asks, "Can I go in and sit with her?"

"That was my next suggestion—go spend time with her. Her body is no longer alive, but she's still here with us". I also have a question, and the answer's totally up to you: Can I call Scott? I know they've been close friends for a long time. I've gotten to know them both personally over the last few years as they've helped others through their cancer journey, many of which end right here with Home Hospice Care."

"Today was my wife's funeral," Josh says calmly. "I've never done the home care before, but we did hospice care in the hospital. Of course you can call Scott. Can you give me a few minutes alone with her first?"

"No problem, and either I'll call or you can, when you are ready. Scott can call the main line at hospice, and we'll call the mortuary , and they will send someone to pick her up. There's no hurry. I noted her time of death—I was in the room with her when she passed. Everything else is taken care of, and you'll receive phone calls and mail here over the next few days and maybe weeks."

Josh tells James, "I'm going in now, just give me a few minutes before calling Scott—okay?"

James replies, "I still have a few forms to fill out, which'll take at least a half-hour."

"Thanks." Walking slowly, as if sneaking up on somebody, Josh enters the bedroom to see Hannah curled up just as he left her a few hours prior. The tears start flowing once he sees her body, but he tries to remember what James said: Hannah is still here with us.

He sits next to Hannah's body on the bed and begins to whisper what he wants to say to her as she transitions over. "I heard you and felt your love. You're right. Ashley and my mom love me and understand who I am. Deep down, everyone in my family understands. Going through everything these last few months, especially last month, has given me the strength to forgive them for abandoning me. I get it. My dad was right. I can live outside of our hometown, but my family doesn't know any other place or way of life. I'm not dead to him or my brothers, not in their hearts. In my next letter to my mom, I will ask her to let them all know that I love them no matter what, and I will continue to communicate with her at her secret PO box.

"If you cross paths with Ashley, please tell her I will be all right. You've been my greatest teacher, and she is my greatest inspiration to take advantage of the life given to me.

"Joe Sinclair will be taken care of as planned. After that, I'm not sure what life has in store for me. I'm praying this will be the answer to my dark mistress and all my anger. I get the feeling you're right. This one act will allow me to shed that skin and start again. Thank you for every-thing. Thank you for being our mentor. Thank you for being our friend. Thank you for being you. I love you and owe my life to you."

Josh leaves the room and tells James to call Scott to let him know. "But first, can I ask you a question?"

"Of course."

"Was it peaceful? You said you were in the room with her. Was it peaceful? Ashley had so much pain, and the last couple of nights had that horrible, death rattle."

"Peacefulness is tough to describe when someone dies. I'll say it this way: I think Hannah staying so active and dealing with the pain for so long without the pain medications allowed her a more peaceful death than most. Her body was tired and working so hard just to keep her moving when most of us would have been bedridden for at least a week prior.

"Josh, one last thing before I make the call. Hannah named you, along with her friends Olga and Scott, to handle her affairs after her death. Olga will handle much of everything, but you and Scott must take care of her local things, since Olga is in New York. Nobody can ever say Hannah didn't have things under control. I'm sure she could have missed some details here and there—but very few.

"I'm finished here. Do you want me to stay, or can I go and file the paperwork? You have my number if you have any questions that need answering tonight. The folder on the table has instructions for how this will work tonight and for all the other things Hannah has already prepared. Michelle will be in the office all day tomorrow, and she might give you a call or stop by.

"I'm sorry for your losses. Would you like me to set up a grief-counseling meeting for you? It doesn't cost anything, and people find it helpful."

Surprisingly calm, Josh replies, "Yeah, it would be a good idea. I would appreciate it if you could set up something like that."

Scott answers the phone. "Is everything all right, Josh?"

"It's James, Scott. Hannah has passed. Josh has sat with her, and we wanted to give you time to come over before making the call."

Scott says, "Sorry, James. When I saw Hannah Cassidy on the caller ID, I figured it was Josh."

James hears crying on the phone. He waits a few seconds to let Scott get through the initial realization that his best friend is gone. Fighting through the emotion, Scott says, "Thanks for calling. I'll be over in a couple of minutes."

8:00 P.M.:

Scott and Josh gave a ceremonial sponge bath to Hannah's face, feet, forearms, and hands. Hannah was already bathed that morning and wore a nice black dress for Ashley's funeral.

Both say their private prayers as they perform their ceremony. Josh asks, "Would she like her nails done?"

Scott answers, laugh-crying. "Let's look in the notes. I'm sure she has a dress and everything planned out." Hannah had all the instructions for what she wanted and left it up to Scott and Josh to decide if she missed anything. "All we need to do now is call hospice." Scott knew this day would come, but he hoped someone else would have to make this call because Hannah had outlived him.

"There is one last thing we need to do: smudge Hannah and the house."

"Smudge—what's that?" Josh asks.

"We're cleansing Hannah's body and soul of any negative energy in the house. We need to open the windows to allow that energy to escape and be blown into the wind. This way, her transition will be a much smoother and more positive one, and it will free the house from any negative energy.

"I'll walk you through the process. As I cleanse the home and person, I have a prayer or mantra of thanks and safe travels. Just think positively of Hannah and pray for an easy transition.

"This isn't a new practice; it's very old and is used worldwide. If your thoughts and intentions are positive, there is no way to do it wrong. I brought my sage ties and the abalone shell we got during our trip to Mendocino, California, about twenty years ago. These particular sage ties were made with Hannah, so I know she will appreciate them. The ties consist of white sage, cedar, sweetgrass, and tobacco—all wrapped together. We'll conduct this as a silent cleanse, with the exception of me guiding you through the process.

"First, we get our supplies out and on a table. I brought mine rolled in an elk-leather wrap. Whenever hunting, I try to use as much of the animal as possible. We have already opened the windows.

"Second, we need to focus on Hannah with positive energy and thoughts. Once this is achieved, we'll light our sage tie and get it red-hot and smoking. We'll first smudge ourselves and cleanse any negative energy before moving throughout the house. Here, I'll show you."

Scott holds the sage tie at the level of his heart and makes a sweeping motion over his head a few times. He then performs the same motion for the rest of his body. He tells Josh that he is focusing on his prayer while doing these actions.

Josh follows the instructions and offers his prayer: "Thank you for caring for Ashley. Thank you for caring for me. Thank you for making the world a better place. Thank you for saving my soul and for giving me a second chance at life. All my energy goes to you and your transition. I hope it is everything you hoped it would be. Hannah Cassidy, you will be forever in my prayers."

Scott continues: "Third, what we just did to ourselves, we will both cleanse Hannah's body using the same order and method. Finally, we'll enter each room and do the same thing. Once we're finished, we'll make the call for the mortuary to come pick her up."

As they're sitting waiting Josh asks, "Can you do a smudge in a hospital room?"

"Yes, until they smell it and tell you to put it out. It wasn't this exact smell, but Hannah did something in Ashley's room after she passed. It was probably an essential oil cleanse since she wanted it to be positive, and breaking hospital rules and being reprimanded would have defeated the purpose."

Josh volunteers to call Olga and Robert in the morning to let them know. "Do you think they would want to know now?"

Scott prefers it to be tonight. "I'm not sure how long Hannah will stay around, but we want them to have a chance to say goodbye to her directly." A bit confused, Josh asks if he thinks they will fly to Indiana tonight.

"No, nothing like that, but being in this cancer game as long as we have, there is this feeling we all have that the soul or spirit of the person hangs around before totally passing over to what comes next. Hannah has friends worldwide, and she is near them when we talk. I know Olga is her oldest friend. They've known each other for more than seventy-five years. All through their childhood until both graduated from CCNY. Then Hannah continued her librarian studies at Indiana University, where she met Bob.

"We'll call now and let her know. She's also the executor of Hannah's affairs. And I'll tell her that hospice has already filed the paperwork."

CHAPTER TWENTY-ONE

NO MORE WAR

2002—HELENA, MONTANA:

NO BLOOD FOR OIL! —a sign proclaims with vivid red drops of blood cascading from the bold letters. Two protesters are raising this sign as they march toward the State Capitol in Helena, Montana.

A man brings up the flank of this group carrying his own royal-blue sign with white lettering. It features a pair of doves hovering over the statement, WAR IS NOT THE ANSWER. Ben Brown, a Vietnam veteran, avid hunter, fly fisherman, and outdoorsman, is the local chapter cochair for the national organization Veterans for Peace.

Veterans for Peace's Statement of Purpose reads as follows—

> We, as military veterans, do hereby affirm our greater responsibility to serve the cause of world peace. To this end, we will work with others both nationally and internationally:
>
> 1. To increase public awareness of the causes and costs of war,
>
> 2. To restrain our governments from intervening, overtly and covertly, in the internal affairs of other nations,
>
> 3. To resist racism and repression in our home communities,

4. To oppose the militarization of law enforcement,

5. To end the arms race and to reduce and eventually eliminate nuclear weapons,

6. To seek justice for veterans and victims of war,

7. To abolish war as an instrument of national policy.

To achieve these goals, members of Veterans for Peace pledge to use non-violent means and to maintain an organization that is both democratic and open, with the understanding that all members are trusted to act in the best interests of the group for the larger purpose of world peace.

When speaking with news reporters about US interventions in foreign nations, Benjamin Brown begins by stating, "I cannot speak for the VFP as an organization, but can speak of my interpretation of the organization's mission."

He discusses the primary beneficiaries of war, which are rarely, if ever, the people of the USA directly.

His go-to answer is about Major General Smedley Butler refusing to be a mercenary, using air quotes for "US interests," in a planned coup of then-President Franklin D. Roosevelt. It was known as the Business Plot.

"The Business Plot was a scheme devised by industrialists, primarily bankers, in the early 1930s who admired and were financially invested in the fascist governments of Germany and Italy. These millionaires opposed President Roosevelt and his New Deal policies because they realized their accumulated wealth would be essential to implementing Roosevelt's ambitious plans. It was rumored they had pledged over $300 million toward the plot. The conspirators were several members of the American Liberty League, which consisted of prominent industrialists of the time. They planned to organize a military force of five-hundred-thousand trained men, who they intended for General Smedley Butler to lead to overthrow the federal government of the United States. President

George W. Bush's grandfather, Prescott Bush, was one of those scheming bankers who later became a US Senator.

"I'm paraphrasing the Major General Butler here: The profit goals of a standard business are around six to ten percent. But war-time profits—ah! That's another matter—twenty, sixty, one hundred, three hundred—the sky's the limit. Uncle Sam has the money. Let's take it. But we must remember it isn't put that crudely in wartime. We are told to be patriots and sacrifice for our country while profits skyrocket and are safely pocketed for the wealthy, whose contributions are investments repaid handsomely. The poor are required to invest their lives, limbs, and mental health to create this windfall of wealth."

Reporter: "How do you reconcile the opposition to war when terrorist acts like September 11 take place? Don't you think someone needs to be held accountable?"

Ben Brown: "First, once again, I'm not speaking for VFP but my interpretation of its goals. Now we got that out of the way. That's an interesting way of framing the questions. In many parts of the world, the horrific events of September 11, 2001, were about accountability."

Reporter: "How do you mean? Three thousand innocent people were murdered or jumped to their deaths from the windows of the World Trade Center buildings."

Ben Brown: "All those deaths are wrong and should not have happened. Anyone who knows Veterans for Peace understands what we stand for. In essence, anyone who doesn't receive due process and loses their life in an act of violence needs to have accountability and justice."

Reporter: "Then why is your organization participating in the protests if accountability and justice are what you stand for?"

Ben Brown: "Good question. And I can't emphasize this enough: I cannot speak for VFP as a whole, just as an active member. As citizens of the United States of America and the most powerful military empire the world has ever known—when and where does our war machine get held accountable, and how do the families of those innocent people called 'collateral damage' find justice? Which includes US Veterans. We can go through a litany of examples, but that would detract from the issue.

"The cycle of destruction and death for the acquisition of resources must end somewhere and at some point. We want the largest military empire to be the one that changes the trajectory. Break the cycle, and we can create a different world that is more cooperative and peaceful. Every region of the world has its value and wealth. We live in a truly global economy with the World Trade Organization, International Monetary Fund, and World Bank. We all have essential resources that are needed for this attempt at a global economy to work. The problem that remains is that it still functions through violence."

Reporter: "Can you elaborate on what you called 'a litany of examples of the USA War Machine'?"

Ben Brown: "That's a loaded question. It would take volumes of academic research and studies to answer it. We are here to talk about our president, George W. Bush, pushing for the US and its military to illegally invade another nation that had little to nothing to do with September 11, 2001. Even worse—from what I'm hearing in Afghanistan, private mercenaries are being hired for much more money than our military personnel are compensated. These mercenaries have no oath to a constitution, no rules of military conduct.

"From what we've been told, fifteen of the nineteen 9/11 hijackers were from Saudi Arabia. The convenient relationship between the US fossil fuel industry and the Saudi royal family is vital for 'US Interests' [in air quotes once again].

"We need to reflect on the domestic issues that consistently rank among people's top concerns. This reflection aims to help individuals understand the link between domestic and foreign policy, as well as how war and militarism adversely affect both. This organizing strategy is directly aligned with the broader mission of ending war.

Reporter: "Can you expand on how our domestic policies influence our international policies? Where is the connection?"

"Addressing veterans' issues is imperative. We must confront suicides, addiction, homelessness, unemployment, mass incarceration, PTSD, and the VA healthcare system—each one directly linked to the realities of war and militarism. It is our duty to take decisive action on these critical matters.

"Everything is interconnected. Our domestic actions influence how we are perceived internationally, affecting our ability to impact global events, including conflicts. The international community has observed our criticisms of others while we still face challenges regarding equality for our own citizens, particularly the poor and people of color. By addressing these issues at home, we can strengthen our global position and contribute to a more equitable and peaceful world.

"The mission remains vital. The impacts of war are felt at home through poverty, racial inequality, and the deterioration of our cities and infrastructure, as well as limited access to healthcare and quality education. Recognizing the interconnectedness of these issues is essential. By standing in solidarity with those advocating for justice in their communities, we can strengthen the movement for peace and increase the likelihood of ending war worldwide.

CHAPTER TWENTY-TWO

HANNAH'S FUNERAL AND OLGA

WHITE COUNTY, INDIANA APRIL 25, 2011:

A couple of days have passed since Hannah's last breath was taken. With the sun setting, the light in the kitchen changes slightly from a blue hue to salmon pink as Josh and Scott wait for their guests to arrive. The light also illuminates several photos on a shelf that Bob had built. The images are of Hannah's parents, sisters, nieces, and nephews—and the biggest one is of Hannah and Olga at Coney Island around the age of ten.

The two men are discussing whether they should have picked Olga up at the airport or not when they hear a car pull up to the front of the house.

Josh says, ". . . and she insisted, what was I supposed to say to a woman fifty-plus years older than me?" Josh and Scott are emptying out the cupboards for Hannah's nieces and nephews to scavenge through to either keep, donate, or sell.

Scott advises, "If physically able and competent, it's just best to let people in their eighties decide on what they're going to do. As much as Hannah was organized, she wasn't a control person. The only way to sum up Hannah's personality is: fiercely independent and loyal. Once you get on team Hannah, she will move mountains for you. She wasn't always correct, but the odds of her being correct versus incorrect in the decades we've known each other has to be nine-to-one. I know it hasn't even been forty-eight hours, but I don't think there will be a day that I don't have a 'Hannah memory.'"

Josh sees an older women exiting a car in front of Hannah's house. Olga is now walking up to the house, and Josh opens the front door and greets her. He begins to say, "Evenin' ma'am" when Olga gives him a big hug and says, "Thank you."

Taken aback by both the hug and especially the thank you, Josh doesn't know what to say, so he squeezes her tighter. Once she opens her eyes, she looks over and sees an old face that she recognizes. Letting go of Josh, she goes in for a hug with Scott. Just before they embrace, she makes the joke, "right or left side?"

Scott gives *Halekakula* a couple of pats and says "right."

Olga goes in for a big hug on his left side and says the same thing, "Thank you."

Scott, having met Olga several times over the years, and in his late sixties, knows what to say. "We're all family, and that is what family does: take care of each other. Are you staying in town? I have an extra room if you'd rather save a few bucks and be closer to everything."

She butts her head with her palm and says, "I didn't even think about asking you. I was just in a hurry to get here. I'll tell you what, let me stay the night in town, and I'll let you know tomorrow. Thanks for the generous offer. *Josh*—let me get a good look at you!" she says in a booming voice.

A bit embarrassed, Josh puts his arms up and does a twirl, which makes her laugh. He hears the New York accent when she says, "Now I see why Hannah liked you so much."

"I guess . . ."

"I assume you boys have a copy of Hannah's will and last wishes here. Let's get to it. My copy is in my suitcase and it's highlighted with everything I need to take care of. If I had to guess, Hannah has taken care of almost all the stuff you're on the hook for, am I right?" They say yes.

Josh now understands why this woman has been Hannah's best friend since childhood and they never lost touch. Although in her mid-eighties, she is a bundle of energy. He can't even imagine what she must have been like in her teens and twenties.

Scott says, "Pretty much, we're to pack up everything and make a list for relatives—mainly her sisters, nieces, and nephews. More and more people are joining this Facebook thing. I've friended several of Bob and Hannah's relatives who I've met over the years. I'm not sure if Facebook or any of these other social networks are particularly good for society— but for old-timers it's a great way to stay connected to people."

Olga says, "You won't catch me on Facebook or any of them. The only thing I know how to do and care to do is Skype. I like seeing people's faces when we're *tawking*. Anyway, that's it. What else did she have you guys doing?"

Josh is relieved that Scott is doing all the talking. "Well, once things are claimed, we'll either donate or sell the remaining things. That's what she wanted. Once that's taken care of, we'll hand the controls over to Dawn Baker, who will take care of the rest and put the house on the market."

Olga replies, "Okay, that's how I understood everything as well. Josh, this was a last-second edition. Hannah wanted you to stay at the house until it sells. She contacted your landlords, the Hickman's, and let them know. She wanted you to be able to save money and have Scott as your neighbor for the coming months. Now, I know this will sound like babysitting, but she wanted Scott to check on you every day at 4:00 p.m. and for you to check in with Scott if you aren't going to be here—just for the first couple of weeks. I don't know why she wanted this, but she was very insistent that Scott call or stop by at 4:00 p.m. every day. Also, she left you a note in the box in her bottom drawer. She said you would know exactly where to find it. I have no idea what it says in the note. She didn't even give a hint."

Josh places the folders and estate binder, which have the will and legal papers with Hannah's instructions, on the kitchen table. Olga hasn't sat down since she arrived. Josh offers her a chair and asks if she would like a cup of tea. "Tea—no thanks, I never touch the stuff. I'm a cawfee gal, and I always have been. I'll take a cup if you've made it—otherwise, don't bahthuh."

"Making you a cup won't take a minute."

"Never mind, by the time we rifle through this binder, I'll be on my way, and I'll be back tomorrow morning at around nine. Scott, I know your cancer group, along with Hannah herself, has taken care of everything to do with the funeral, and we're meeting back here afterward."

Scott says, "The plans have changed. We're expecting at least one hundred-fifty to two hundred people to show up for the funeral, and we're not sure how many will stay. We booked the community center and asked everyone to bring pictures and lots of stories to share about their time with Hannah. Also, the service has been changed to ten instead of eleven because we get the feeling that the repast is going to go on for a long while."

"Okay, all that sounds good. I just want to give you the rough copy of my eulogy to let you know that I will be standing up there for a good chunk of time. Hannah and I had so much fun as kids, and that went on for nearly seventy-five years. We always kept in touch, usually through letters when Elizabeth and Bobby Jr. were young, but we talked on the phone on the first Sunday of almost every month for decades." Olga sees the picture on the shelf and says, "Oh boy, did she ever tell you the story behind that picture?"

Scott says maybe, but he doesn't remember, and Josh shakes his head.

Olga goes on, "We were at Coney Island and were within a half hour of having one of our biggest fights as kids. You could never tell in that photo. I don't know how old we are there, maybe twelve or so. But anyway, Hannah always had a weak stomach when it came to the rides, but she was always game for trying everything at least once.

"We were having a blast, and then we went on what should have been an easy ride, the one that has you in a swing on a long chain, and it just goes around like a merry-go-round. That was it, so Hannah lost her lunch during the ride. Luckily, she was on the outside swing; I felt bad for whoever was behind her. We ate everything from ice cream, hot dogs, roasted peanuts, and cotton candy. Remember that this was the mid-thirties, so the entire day might have cost 25 cents. Her family was poor, but they had enough, and Hannah was working jobs. I think she started babysitting when she was nine or ten years old.

"Back to the story: We got off the ride, and I couldn't stop laughing at how much she threw up. I asked her if she wanted to go again, and that's when we got into the big fight. We didn't speak a single word during the entire subway ride home.

"Isn't that the best picture? I have the same one framed at our house. She made them for our fiftieth birthdays—since we were born only a few weeks apart.

"Okay boys, it looks like you handled everything here, and I still need to check in at the hotel. I'll see *you*," pointing at Josh, "tomorrow morning, I'll come over early, and we can go together."."

Once Olga pulls away from the front of the house, Scott looks at Josh and says, "She's always like that—she's a hoot. When she used to visit, she and Hannah would pick up like no time had ever gone by. That was the first time I heard the story of Coney Island and the swing ride. It was probably a story Hannah didn't like to remember."

Scott stretches his arms out and tells Josh, "I'm calling it a day here. I'll finish the last few things at my place. Olga's right—there are people and jobs to organize before the funeral, and it's hard to believe it's tomorrow morning. I'm glad Olga's here; she's going to make this a party instead of something sad."

APRIL 26, 2011—6:00 A.M., THE MORNING OF HANNAH'S FUNERAL:

Olga's wake-up call rouses her from a melatonin-induced sleep. She picks up the phone, and a cheery voice on the other end says, "This is your requested 6:00 a.m. wake-up, Mrs. Wontrobski."

"Thank you, I'm awake. Before you hang up, do you know if there's cawfee made yet? Today is going to be a long day and I'm going to need it to be strong."

"Yes, ma'am, it was just made and put out. The breakfast bar is being set up right now."

Olga thanks the person on the other side of the line again. "I'll be over in a few minutes."

She does her eighty-something-year-old in-bed morning stretches and yoga for a few minutes while trying to figure out how to breach the subject of May 1st to Josh without sounding like she has a manipulative agenda. She muses, *you're just going to have to bite the bullet and bring it up.*

As she walks back to her room from the lobby with a coffee cup and a bagel with cream cheese in hand, it really sinks in: *Today is Hannah's funeral.* Her pace quickens, and she barely gets the door shut before she begins to weep. She puts the food on the dresser and braces herself with both hands.

She weeps, "Oh, Hannah, I can't remember life without you in it. I don't want to do it without you. I'll get through today, but once I fly back to New York, it'll be the last time I ever come to your home. I will never speak to you on the phone again, and there will be no more silly texts, no more reminiscing about our childhood, and no more laughing ourselves silly. I miss you already . . ."

6:30 A.M. AT HANNAH'S HOUSE:

Josh finally gets up after tossing and turning all night. He goes out into the kitchen to get a glass of water and make a pot of coffee for two. As he is scooping the grounds into the filter he glances over to Hannah's bedroom door. He hasn't been in there since it was smudged. He looks down into the coffee filter and puts another scoop of grounds in; it will be a long day. Pressing start, he hears the water heat up, and he slowly walks toward Hannah's bedroom door. He reaches out and grabs the doorknob. It's cold, and he instinctively pulls his hand back.

Of course, it's cold, he tells himself. *It's six in the morning. Just go in and get the box and come out.* He opens the door slowly and tiptoes over to the dresser, opens the bottom drawer, and grabs the box. He quietly closes the drawer, tiptoes out of the room, and closes the door without a sound.

As he leaves the room, he realizes he is not sneaking or doing anything wrong. He straightens up, confidently walks back into the kitchen, and puts the box on the table. The coffee is not finished brewing, so he starts a fire to warm the place before opening the box and reading the letter.

The kindling burns brightly, and the warmth of the fire feels comforting. He pours himself a cup, grabs the box and a blanket, and settles in front of the flames. The scent of cedar fills the air as the firewood catches. After a big sip from his mug, he places it on the bricks and reaches for the box. He sees the glow of the flames on his hands and is reminded of Hannah, his father's hands on the steering wheel, and Ashley's hands reaching for him. Blinking away the memories, he looks to the window, where morning light begins to fill the sky. He whispers, "Ashley, help me find the strength to read this letter and keep wanting to live."

Okay, there's no turning back. He opens the box, and there is a letter on top of at least a half dozen rolled-up what appear to be hundred-dollar bills.

He puts everything down and takes another big drink out of the mug, and the warm feeling as he swallows gives him comfort as does the warmth of the fire. Now staring at the letter and having no idea what it is going to say—he thinks, *let's do this*—trying to muster up the courage to read what was probably the last thing his dying friend ever wrote. As he grasps the papers, he pictures Hannah alive and writing these letters at the kitchen table. He unfolds the papers and begins to read aloud:

–1–

Dear Josh,

My sweet-hearted, misunderstood boy—if you read this letter, I am gone and didn't make it to May 1st.

First, I want to express my deep gratitude for our friendship and the care you've shown me during my most vulnerable moments. It truly means the world to me. Please do not consider the money I left for you as payment for anything. Until your life insurance check arrives, you will need funds to support yourself. Olga is aware of the check and will be in touch with you soon to discuss the part of the plan we never had a chance to talk about—what happens next.

Whether you choose to go through with our plan or not, I hope you will take this opportunity to fulfill my and Ashley's last wish for you: to leave your past behind where it belongs and to embrace a life filled with joy, happiness, and purpose.

Life happens to all of us. Sometimes we experience wonderful surprises, while other times we face terrible challenges. Fairness does not play a role in this. It is neither a punishment nor a reward—it is simply life. It is up to us to choose how we perceive our experiences. Both Ashley and I had one last wish for you: to sing "The Sound of Music" for us, whether you're wearing lederhosen or not. Remember our first dinner together?

Take deep breaths whenever the air is clean. Feel the energy of the sun, which has traveled 90 million miles to warm your face. Listen to the bees and birds welcoming the new day. Most of all, think of this old woman and your beautiful wife as you smell the flowers when they are in bloom. Live life for all of us.

Thank you, and I love you.

A hui hou,

Hannah

–2–

Please read the following pages and share the titled ones for Scott and Olga with them individually.

As mentioned on page one, I'm not sure if you will follow through with the plan we discussed. I have asked Scott to check in with you for a couple of weeks. One: I would like both of you to get to know and be able to help each other in the coming weeks.

Two: If you are to go through with our plan, Scott has no idea about it and his checking in on you at 4:00 p.m. every day will give you an alibi. Have your car parked in front of the house for Scott and everyone to see. Keep the truck in Bob's workshop and only use it on Joe's Saturday golf day. I have left the receipt from us getting cash from the ATM on the seat. If anyone were to ask—and I doubt anyone would, but if they were to ask—that was the last day it was driven. Be sure all materials and any proof of visiting Joe Sinclair's are taken out and cleaned up. Once you read this page and fully understand what it is saying, destroy it. Cut it up, burn it, tear it into pieces, and use it in the compost pile. Do whatever you need to do.

Joe Sinclair chose to sue and exploit small family farms, driving them to bankruptcy and poisoning the soil, water, and air. He has corrupted our government and profited from death and destruction, rather than using his privilege to help people and improve our environment. He has lived a long life while cutting short the lives of so many others.

We plan to hold him and others like him accountable for the trauma and pain they have inflicted on Ashley—resulting in the loss of her parents' farm, their lives, your unborn child, Ashley's life, and now my own. This is about seeking justice, not revenge, in a corrupt system designed to protect individuals like Joe Sinclair. There is little justice for the everyday person in this system.

Josh reads through page two several times to ensure nothing is missed. He crumbles it up and throws it into the fire, sipping his coffee while watching the paper heat up, smolder, and eventually catch on fire. Once the paper is finished burning, he reads the last two pages: one for Olga and the other for Scott.

He stands up, stretches, and says, "A hui hou, Hannah. And we will get justice the only way we can." He turns the bathroom heater on, grabs the second cup of brewed coffee, and takes a shower.

7:40 AM:

It's a warm, sunny morning with nothing but good weather in the forecast. Josh is walking around the property, looking at all the trees leafing out and the little buds on plants that are starting to develop when Olga pulls up.

He hears her voice, "Mornin' Josh. I brought some strong cawfee to keep us going through the day. How did you sleep last night?"

Josh shields his eyes from the low morning sun and replies, "Mornin'. I've already had two cups, but as to how I slept last night, I'll take that strong cup you got for me."

As Olga hands Josh a cup of coffee, she sighs, "I love this property. I've been coming here for at least fifty years. When Hannah first took a position in Indiana, I assumed it was in Indianapolis or at the university in Bloomington, Notre Dame, or Purdue University—where she would be challenged and could continue pursuing her goal of becoming an academic librarian. But when she told me it was in a small town in Indiana, I couldn't believe it. I had already been out of school for two years and was working in New York City as a registered nurse."

Curious, Josh asks if White County has changed much.

"Oh yeah, but back then there were only two high schools in all of White County, and things were so much more personal. On so many fronts, it was worse for single women trying to get a fair shake, but all around, I think it's worse now for almost everyone. Back then, everyone was from low-income farming families, and everyone just understood that's what life was like. But there was a common thread in the community that they were all together. Today, that feeling of camaraderie has almost been wiped out everywhere in the United States.

"It looked similar, but all the local business owners were locals with unique shops, and now they've been replaced by chain and franchise companies taking over. It's the same everywhere. What I notice the most is the absence or shrinking number of young families and kids graduating high school and staying. Since I'm a city girl, I can't explain it from the point of view of experience, but just how Hannah would talk about it."

Josh asks how Hannah explained it. "Well, in short, the shift from agriculture to agribusiness is what happened. Until the end of the seventies, kids grew up on farms that had loads of daily chores of feeding livestock, collecting eggs, letting animals out, milking cows, and things like that because small farms not only were the source of income but were the primary source of the food eaten. Every farm had multiple income generators at different times of the year. It could have been hay, corn, cattle, dairy, or other things. It was a lifestyle passed down from generation to generation. Everybody had chickens for eggs and possibly a hog or two they would slaughter and take to Beutler Butcher Shop. Beutler Butcher still existed in Lafayette a decade ago, but who knows if they are still there? It was a couple of brothers who learned it from their family and taught their kids the business and trade. As family farms went by the wayside, only one shop continued the family business. It's the same in New York City. All the neighborhoods that Hannah and I grew up walking around in are being replaced. The trades and businesses have been outsourced and imported"

Realizing that she is dominating the conversation, Olga asks Josh, "You're from West Virginia—mining country, right? Has it changed much?"

"Not really. At least for the workers in the mine, it's the same—but more machines and fewer miners. Our town is dying the same death of dependency on the mine, and as equipment gets better, the less work there is for miners. And when I left after high school in 1999, they had started blowing the tops off the mountains to get to the coal, and that has increased all over the state. So, I guess it has changed, but one thing remains the same, working people struggle to earn a living. But I haven't been back in a long time, so I can't say what it looks like now."

Olga, knowing enough of Josh's back story and looking for a way in to give him a pitch at Hannah's request, asks, "Why haven't you been back?"

"It's a long story I'd rather not talk about. Let's just say I didn't leave on good terms."

"Point taken—and there's no need to explain anything. As for now, there are the haves and have-nots in almost every community in the country. Most of the haves are corporations or the executives that represent those corporations—buying up land to extract whatever resource it might hold or just accumulate more land. It's a twenty-first-century form of feudalism. People with money have all types of dreams they can pursue. Some want to own a tropical island—others want thousands of acres in Montana. In New York City it's owning a building with your name on it, and some people dream of being the big shot everyone has to answer to. You know, being the big fish in a small pond.

"That's what you got here with Joe Sinclair. The problem with Mr. Sinclair is he truly believes he is a good man and the smartest guy in the room everywhere he goes. That's why he retired in a small community whose entire economy depends on the products his company sells, and where the universities teach Fulcircle Company's way of agriculture—when the truth of the matter is, for a very small window of time their version of agribusiness or industrial agriculture is viable. Then it begins to break down, and that's where we are today. At the beginning of the breakdown.

"At first, when the poisons weren't so widespread, it was isolated incidents, but greed has a funny way of exposing the truth. They—Fulcircle, or you name the biotech company—couldn't be happy with hundreds of millions in earnings each year, they need it to be more. It was during Joe's stint as CEO that they went from a big corporation to a behemoth corporation with global reach. I'm no Marxist, but he hits the nail on the head when he talks about the DNA of capitalism leading to the concentration of capital. The corporations that have access to the most capital will buy out their competitors until there are only a few left standing. That is where we are today. You mark my words, Fulcircle will either get bought or will buy another major seed company in the next decade or so. That is the DNA of capitalism without strict regulations. Since large corporations and industries own and control governments all over the world, few regulations are enforceable by law. And even then, if someone has the means and fortitude to challenge these corporate criminals and actually win, it will be a fine that is a fraction of the profits generated by the violations in question."

Once again, Josh is listening to an elder tell him where they made the mistake and explain how the current system is out of control.

Olga catches herself. "I'm sorry about talking about this so much," (consciously or subconsciously, Olga is making her pitch to Josh), "once we lost our Elizabeth, both Robert and I learned to a certain extent about the corruption and cover-up of the corporate world, but when we scratched the surface a little bit deeper, it uncovered so much more than we could have ever imagined. People we considered friends had been lying to Robert for thirty years and had let our Elizabeth work on a manufacturing line with C8 when they knew there was a good chance that she could get sick. It's bad enough to think that they would allow that practice toward any employee, but toward the child of a longtime friend and employee somehow seems much worse.

"Maybe it's because she was *our* daughter—I don't know."

In years past, tears and pure emotion would have taken over when Olga spoke about it. Today, there was calm, and more importantly, there was complete focus in her words. "Hannah knew our targeted executive, and we knew hers, just like we knew Minister Tim's. That's it, that is all we know for sure about this plan. However, we do know of at least three, if not more, other cancer groups that have joined in on the plan around the country. Also, we know of one person and group in India. Hannah and I started this idea, but we're not sure how widespread it has gotten.

"Robert and I are part of a class-action lawsuit against Avidité, and the law firm heading it up is a corporate law firm, which tells us there is a shift coming to start holding polluting and human rights-violating corporations accountable. They are just concluding one of the largest biological data studies about the effects of C8 and its interaction with human health. We are out of the loop within Avidité, but some of Robert's former partners have told him the company doesn't plan on adhering to the agreement they made a decade or so ago. When we heard that news, it was about the same time Hannah mentioned the story of Ben Brown and this idea to us."

Hannah's house has a large yard filled with perennial plants, shrubs, and trees just coming to life. Josh and Olga walk around, observing the plants as they speak. Finally, they make it to the back of the house, slowly wander up to the back patio chairs, and sit. Like two sun dials, they each grab a chair and face it toward the sun. They sit in silence for a few minutes, soaking in the heat of the sun together.

"This is nice," Josh says.

Olga, who just finished thirty minutes of a monologue about how the greed of large corporations is ruining civilization and the planet, is a bit confused by the comment, but she sighs and agrees with him. "It is nice, and Hannah would have loved to have seen her yard come to life."

"She did," he replies. "It was just a few days ago after my wife's funeral. Hannah and I were sitting in her front yard, feeling the sun on our faces and the grass under our feet. That day will be the saddest day of my life. Hannah passed just a few hours later. I think she knew."

"Knew what?" asks Olga.

"She knew she wasn't going to live through the night. Despite her being in so much pain, we walked in through her front door and into her room. She said that from this point forward, she would be wheeled through those thresholds. She was right. When they put her onto the gurney, she was wheeled out of her room and the front door. One of the wheels had a wobble in it. My eyes were fixed on the wheels going through the doorways. That's when I said my final goodbye to her. Now I speak to her directly."

They sat in disbelief, staring off into the distance, when a voice interrupted them. "Here you two are," says Scott. "It's time to go."

Olga puts her hand on Josh's knee. "Thank you for caring for my best friend in her final days. She was lucky to have you in her life."

APRIL 26, 2011—3:00 P.M., HANNAH'S FUNERAL:

Olga stands at the podium in front of at least two-hundred and probably closer to three-hundred people. Sniffling, crying, and laughing are heard throughout the room as Hannah-stories are told.

"Hearing all these stories about Hannah fills my heart with love and gratitude. My relationship with Hannah dates back to the mid-1930s, and she has always had a remarkable ability to make friends and enjoy life. I have countless wonderful memories with her, but for the sake of everyone's time, I've chosen to share just two. The first story is about the

59th Street Bridge, and the second is from our time together at CCNY in Hamilton Heights." Olga begins by telling the story of meeting Hannah in the third grade at P.S. 110 on the lower East Side of Manhattan.

APRIL 27, 2011—THE FOLLOWING MORNING:

After a few minutes of knocking, Olga finally opens the door and walks into the house. She says loudly, "Josh, are you here?" She doesn't realize that Josh is in a deep sleep. He was up until at least 4:00 a.m. in Bob's workshop making alterations to the materials he bought a few days earlier at the hardware store. "Josh, are you here?"

Sound asleep in the guest room, Josh suddenly awakens from a dream he doesn't want to leave. It was a mix of several memories, featuring all the people he loved most in his life. Surprisingly, Hannah was one of the main figures that kept recurring. Was this because she had been part of his life recently, or did it stem from their deep connection that offered him a second chance at life?

When Josh finally opens his eyes, he and Ashley had been driving home from her first prenatal appointment. They were the happiest they had ever been as a couple, and they couldn't stop discussing the life they were going to build for their child.

Ultimately, this appointment had initiated the nightmare that resulted in Ashley's death. The blood panels taken indicated the need for further testing. First the miscarriage, and then the Stage IV ovarian cancer. For Josh, his dream was interrupted at the perfect time to remember Ashley's smile, laugh, and dream of a long future together.

"Yeah, yeah—I am in here and I'll be right out." Coming out of the room, Josh looks like he has an extreme hangover.

Olga remarks, "It looks like you came back and had a few toasts by yourself."

"Naw, nothing like that. I came home to work on the bench for Joe Sinclair. I was up until—" Josh pauses, trying to think. "Hell, I don't know what time it was, but the sunrise hadn't happened yet."

Olga had gone over in her head a dozen different ways to bring up this topic with Josh on this very day, as per instructions from Hannah, with all the pitfall subjects to avoid. Josh had just made her day that much easier.

Handing him a cup of coffee and a pastry she says, "You're still going to go through with the plan? I don't know exactly what the plan for Joe is, and we need to keep it that way. All I know is Joe Sinclair was Hannah's executive-to-hold-accountable. He's a real piece of work. Hannah and Joe had a long history of locking horns, and he always came out on top since Fulcircle either owns or controls the Indiana Farm Bureau, the Agriculture Alumni Seed Improvement Association, the National Swine Registry, and just about every seed company in the state along with having control over our governmental agencies. And more importantly, Fulcircle owns the science our government accepts and promotes since it comes from their labs and studies."

Josh sips his coffee after dumping it into a mug filled a quarter of the way up with half and half. "Oh yeah, I'm going through with the plan. I truly believe if we can get even three executives by Sunday—with those letters, it will send shock waves through the business world."

Olga agrees but cautions, "What will happen initially is that the media will spin it as the executives were victims of violent crimes. But as we give our timed press releases over the next couple of weeks, more people will see the reason why it had to be done this way."

Josh continues, "Once they connect those dots, most people will see us as achieving justice, not as criminals. We need to make people aware that they could be, or already are, victims of corporate crimes. It's essential for them to ask: for what? So a few individuals can receive large paychecks while the rest of us struggle to get by? These are the important connections and questions we need to encourage ordinary people to consider, especially in relation to May 1, 2011."

Olga adds, "And it's even more nefarious than that if we want to really dig down into the issue. This is about power and control—more than about money. The six- and seven-figure salaries are to buy off the middle guy to do the dirty work. They get their orders from true-blue capitalists, people who have billions and billions of assets and strategic investments. I call them *the untouchables,* the truly unaccountable people behind the scenes. The executives and board of directors members, high-priced lawyers, lobbyists, scientists, legislative councils, and just going down the line—are who we are targeting because we don't know who the untouchables are, that is why they are untouchable.

"So we target the ones that make the legal decisions in an economy of death and destruction. These carnival barkers get the public on the treadmill and in debt. And the public becomes enslaved to the system and will defend it because it is all they know. Weirdly, this is an economically organized anarchy conspiracy. It is done by a vague understanding between all these interlocking boards of directors and industries colluding together in the single, shared interest of profits being the only thing connecting them. We, my generation, were part of the machine for many years because that is what we were taught a 'successful life' meant. You must understand—when we were kids during the Depression, resources seemed unlimited, and we came into adulthood with this mindset. We were like little kids getting to play with dangerous toys for the first time, not realizing the damage we were doing to our environment and, ultimately, to ourselves.

"Avidité encapsulated our entire generation with their slogan: Better Living through Chemistry and Science. We all believed it to be true and hardly anyone worth listening to was asking questions as to whether we should be screwing around with it at all."

As Olga talks, Josh has flashbacks of information on these companies in Hannah's files: the internal studies of the known cancers, diseases, environmental damage, pictures of victims, and the billions in profits that were made through their deception. *Carnival barkers*, he thinks, *is a perfect way to describe these snake-oil salesmen.*

At this point, Josh is only half-listening and trying to figure out if he is numb or if he is just not feeling any stress or anxiety. A month ago, all of this would have sent him into an out-of-control rage against himself emotionally and physically with inanimate objects in his vicinity that only time and/or Ashley would be able to bring him down from. But right now, it was like going into these black prisons to interrogate. He is conscious of everything and thinks to himself that the mind must get overloaded somehow to filter out all of the noise and slow down the important information. He finds himself calm, clear-headed, and in complete harmony with the mission that lies in front of him, which amazes and frightens him at the same time.

As Olga concludes her lengthy speech, Josh nods in agreement. The more he reads and hears others discuss the intertwined nature of our government and economic systems, the more he connects these ideas with his own experiences in the military. He increasingly recognizes the relationship between fossil fuels, rare metals and minerals, military weapons, and the true objectives of military operations. This relationship is not about democracy or the self-determination of the people. In fact, it is quite the opposite. The US military is often used to establish governments that enable US corporations or interests to exert control over those nations. Most of the time, this is done covertly.

What occurred in Iraq had nothing to do with bringing democracy to people who desired it. If that had been the case, there would have been no need for waterboarding or for his fellow soldiers to conduct nightly raids on ordinary people's homes. Additionally, the US military would not have had to establish military bases and spend trillions of dollars if promoting democracy had been the true purpose of the invasion. When people see a good idea, they don't need to be forced to accept it. They will naturally adopt it and try to emulate it.

"Of course," he says, "I am a man of my word. Would you like to see the setup in Bob's workshop?"

Olga is caught halfway into a sip and brings her hand up to her mouth to cut it off. She swallows. "No. I can't know anything about your plan and you cannot know anything about ours."

Josh says, "Avidité, right? Yeah, I read that file along with the dozens of other ones Hannah had made on these individual companies and executives. That's why I'm one-hundred percent in. I know this isn't just a personal vendetta against Joe Sinclair—this is a well-thought-out plan of attack against very public figures in the business world."

"Exactly," she says. "That's why we each have our own assigned executives, because at a certain level it is a personal vendetta. But we also know we weren't the only ones who suffered from their decisions. That's the point: We need people to start thinking or asking themselves, will I or my loved ones be the next victim of their corporate murder? It's about self-defense against future assaults."

"Well listen, I leave tomorrow night for New York and have a busy day finishing up Hannah's affairs here all day before my flight. You go take a shower and then I'd like to talk to you about something that is complex but could be helpful toward your moving forward. Hannah suggested it in our last conversation. Go take your shower and get dressed. We'll go for a drive and maybe pick up some lunch for a picnic at a park, so we can talk. Does that sound alright?"

"That's fine, I'll be less than fifteen minutes."

LATER THAT MORNING—VERMONT AND DAVID EDWARDS:

After a quick stop at the Steaming Bean, they pick up some drinks, a couple of sandwiches, and two pieces of carrot cake, Hannah's favorite dessert from the cafe.

Olga asks Josh, "Have you heard of Bluewater Beach? It's off the Tippecanoe River, not that far out of town."

"When Ashley and I first moved here, we were trying to find a place near the water but couldn't find one. But I don't think I have ever been to that beach."

Olga drives with the familiarity of someone who knows Monticello (White County) Indiana, well—navigating the roads effortlessly as she pulls into the parking lot of Bluewater Beach Park. It's spring; the waters are cold, the grass is beginning to grow, and the trees are coming alive. As she sets the parking brake and removes the keys from the ignition, Olga thinks, *this is perfect. The park is empty, the sun is shining, and there's plenty for us to discuss.*

"Well, let's get to it," she says, grabbing their sandwiches and drinks.

They see a picnic table under a hickory tree. Josh picks up a handful of stones as they approach the table, and Olga asks him what he is doing. "You'll see," he replies, and once they reach their destination, he puts the stones on the table.

Olga says, "Dig in anytime you're ready. I'm going to wait a little bit."

"Thanks, I'll probably wait a little while, myself, I generally don't get hungry until early afternoon." Wanting to break the ice, Josh adds, "I'm going to execute Hannah's plan on Saturday night. Her overall plan had several holes in it because we didn't have a chance to talk much about it. I'll make the adjustments, myself."

Nodding, Olga is nevertheless somewhat taken aback by Josh's straightforwardness. "Okay, let's get started. Good, I'm glad you're taking this seriously, and I'm sure you've heard this from Hannah many times—these goddamn executives who make these decisions aren't innocent. They're playing with hundreds of thousands and even millions of people's lives directly because they want approval and acceptance into this disgusting pseudo-aristocrat club."

Olga sadly admits, "We—Robert and I—didn't want to be in that club, but we were attracted to the big houses, stock options, vacation homes, big trips, and rubbing elbows with corporate bigwigs. In short, we were hypocrites. We either came up with justifications or buried them deep down, and it was never discussed. We have to live with it every day that our little girl did nothing wrong other than wanting to pay for her own higher education by working for Avidité, just like her dad."

Josh doesn't want to be callous regarding Elizabeth's death but has been thinking about it since Olga first mentioned it earlier. He says, "I have a question for you. What did you call the economic system earlier? Economic anarchy or something?"

Olga thinks, *have I been talking that much to have said that to him?* "Yes, it's an economically organized anarchy conspiracy."

"Yeah, that's it. That's kind of the way this plan and group is set up, isn't it? Not necessarily the economic part but a plan loosely put into motion and shared with separate groups all over the place with one not knowing about the others. I remember Hannah saying something about it. She thought that the letters, or whatever they are called, all being the same would make this look like a well-organized movement."

Laughing, "Yes, that was her idea, since she was a lover of the written word. That's when both Robert and I really got on board with the concept. Listen, Josh, I would like to discuss something with you that isn't part of the group but is a last-minute addition to the plan. Would that be alright with you?"

Feeling nervous, he grabs his sandwich and looks at Olga, holding it up for approval with a questioning glance. She encourages him. "Go right ahead."

As he unwraps it, he says, "I thought yesterday went really well. It was the first time I ate anything solid since Ashley's funeral and Hannah's death." He bows his head and starts to cry. "Sorry, sorry—I can't help it. Whenever I think of Ashley, it just starts. But the good thing is, these episodes are getting shorter."

Olga reaches over the table and grabs one of Josh's hands. "You have nothing to apologize for, and if you weren't breaking down every few minutes, I would be worried about you. It took me years before I could control it when thinking of our Elizabeth."

Now sniffling and regaining his composure, he says, "It was Hannah who forced me to eat after Ashley's death, and that was the day she told me about the idea and plan." He blows his nose in one of the napkins.

While walking over to the garbage can, he says. "I thought yesterday was incredible. I knew Hannah had lots of friends, but I had no idea how much she and Bob did for White County."

With a hand on her heart, Olga replies, "Hannah was an incredible human being. That was only the tip of the iceberg of what she was involved in over the years. It was a nice service and so many nice people . . ."

Josh opens up his sandwich and grabs one of the stones to set on his napkin.

Olga points her finger and says, "Ah, the stones—good thinking. You just keep eating, and I'll tell you my idea. Let me finish the entire thing before you say anything because you'll have lots of questions." While chewing, Josh gives a thumbs-up. "Okay, where to begin? I'm going to leave out all the background because either you're going to trust us or you're not.

"As part of the repentance for our hypocrisy along with concern for others, Robert and I help domestic violence victims and migrants get new identities in New York, Maine, Vermont, New Hampshire, and a couple of other states. They get valid IDs and, when run, will have clean records. The only time you'll get nailed is if you are fingerprinted. We've been doing it for many years. The only problem we are running into right now is that digital fingerprints are being implemented everywhere. So, when the time comes to renew a license, it might get flagged. We're trying to figure out a way around this glitch, but at least we can make that license good for a decade or so.

"This is the first part of the plan. In my last conversation with Hannah, we discussed taking care of you. It was an extensive discussion, and when Hannah makes a promise, she follows through. She promised Ashley that she would help you create a new life, allowing you to start over without any baggage that others would need to know about.

"There are multiple reasons for this plan, and you can choose to accept them or disregard them—it's entirely up to you. I suspect that how smoothly things go on Saturday night may influence this decision. As I mentioned earlier, I don't know anything about your plans or your history, except that Joe Sinclair is 'your executive,' and Hannah did mention that you suffered from PTSD due to your time in the military. I don't know any specific details, as nothing beyond that one fact has been shared.

"We own a five-acre property just outside Hardwick, Vermont, which includes two small houses. We purchased this property in the 1980s with the intention of using it as a summer house. A granny unit was built on the property when we relocated one of our domestic violence clients to Vermont. She is a wonderful person and has a son who is about ten years old. To the community in Hardwick, she serves as our property manager and has established a permaculture farm. She has been living there for about four years. While she does not pay rent, she earns enough to live comfortably. Additionally, she ensures that our house, which is similar in size to the granny unit, is winterized and safe during the times we are not there."

Listening and eating, Josh holds up a finger, wanting to say something. Olga waves him off. "No, let me finish, and then we can talk. Robert and I have agreed to sell David Edwards the property with the one condition that Jeannette Sands and her boy, Jonathan, stay on as property managers. Josh, you will become David Edwards and you will own the property. You can either try and work with her on the farm or have your own life in town. It's a small town and we know just about everyone. What we will do is let our friends know you've purchased the property and give them whatever backstory you want David Edwards to have going forward.

"Remember, this backstory needs to be believable. It should be a story that you can relate to and understand without revealing your identity as Josh Bush, which no one up there is likely to care about or suspect. I'm not sure if you remember, but you have a life insurance check on the way. Who knows if they will send the full amount, but if they do, it will be a lump sum of $250,000. Hannah had Ashley's death certificate expedited, so the paperwork was sent off within a day or so of her passing."

Olga's heart is breaking as she tries to get this information out while staring at Josh, tears pouring down his face. "Hannah should have left you some money in the box with her letter. How much, I don't know, but my guess is going to be in the $25,000 to $50,000 range. She also wants you to stay at her house until that check comes in and clears. Once that check is cleared, Scott and I will put the house on the market, and the money will be divided up for her nieces and nephews."

Josh is wiping away tears and nodding that he is following everything Olga is saying. She continues. "That is also when Josh Bush needs to get

everything in order to disappear. A shedding of the skin, you might say."
At this comment, Josh remembers Hannah talking about a new life for
himself and how the snake shedding its skin symbolizes a rebirth or transition. It is all starting to make sense to him now.

Olga goes on, "Once again, you'll need to come up with a believable
story for your friends, Scott, and the cancer support group about your
trip to Mexico, Costa Rica, or another location where you can live off
the insurance money for an extended period. I suggest you get rid of anything that indicates your marriage. This is the hardest part for everyone.
If you must keep a picture of Ashley, you can say she was a long-lost love
from your youth who got away."

Having had this talk before, Olga knows he will need a moment to
let this information really sink in. She stands up and says, "I'll give you a
minute," and walks away without waiting for a response.

Josh sits alone at the picnic table, reflecting on everything. He thinks
about Joe Sinclair, the life insurance money, the convincing story of his
escape, Josh Bush's death, and David Edwards' birth. Most importantly,
he considers how he would have to compartmentalize all of his past relationships for his own benefit. At the moment, it seems too monumental
a task, but he knows deep down inside—because Hannah knew deep
down inside—that this is his path to a new chance at life with a purpose.

After a few minutes, Olga returns. "I know there isn't enough time
to think everything through carefully and be okay with it, but we need
to keep moving forward if we're going to get all the information you'll
need to make an educated decision." She takes over the conversation once
again. "With David Edwards as the name on the deed of the property, your
identification will likely never be questioned again—except for fingerprints. As mentioned earlier, your backstory needs to be believable. You
can't claim to be a retired professional in a field you know nothing about.
It's best to keep your background simple and vague. Consider using real-
life stories that align with David Edwards' interests and experiences.

"Attending counseling is essential for this to work, as it was a require-
ment for Hannah. One-on-one sessions are private, and that information
cannot be shared with anyone unless there is a belief that you pose a threat
to yourself or others. Even in those meetings, Josh Bush does not exist—
you are David Edwards. Jeannette will know you as a relocatee with us
and will not inquire about Josh Bush. She will only be aware of David

Edwards and the story we provide her. For you, she will be Jeannette, a mother with a young son.

"As your get-out-of-town date approaches, we'll provide you with more information about her personality. She is a lovely woman who is thriving in Hardwick. Additionally, you should be aware of your annual property taxes, which are approximately $3,000 per year. We will document everything in a format that resembles an interview we conducted before selling you the property. Please keep this information in your packet with the legal paperwork related to the sale and review it regularly during your first year."

For the rest of the afternoon, Olga continues briefing Josh about the process of creating a new identity and what it would mean, while answering all of his questions.

The sun is dropping behind the tree line, as the temperature is as well. Olga says, "That sums up the situation for you. You have a lot of information to process and a significant decision ahead of you. What you are being asked to do is monumental, and I know you need to think deeply about it and reflect on what it all means, as well as whether this is the right path for you. This decision is yours alone. All Robert and I are doing is offering you an option and opening a door that otherwise wouldn't exist.

"That's the pitch and our offer. If you decide to go through with the plan, know that this was last request Hannah made to Robert and me, and we agreed to it. And just like Hannah, we follow through with our promises. Everything we just talked about is real. The proposal is genuine and without any strings attached. David Edwards will become the new owner of a five-acre farm in Hardwick, Vermont, which includes a live-in property manager. Josh Bush will disappear. First, you will need a credible plan for a long visit to a place where no one knows you. Send letters or postcards from there, letting them know you're exploring and finding yourself after a transformative year. That will be your last contact as Josh Bush.

"Enough of that for now." She looks at her watch. "Holy cow, we need to get you back for the Scott check in. Would you let me take you out for dinner tonight? We probably won't have a chance to see each other tomorrow. My meetings with the realtor start early, and then I have several other tasks to handle concerning Hannah's affairs. Also, we have a new laptop for you registered in Vermont in David Edwards' name. I hope you're a Mac person—it's an Apple Macbook Pro 13.3 laptop.

"Remember, Hannah wanted you to stay at her place until that check arrives and clears. One last thing: Be careful with Joe Sinclair, and please don't discuss anything with anyone. After you're done with him, leave the note and folder in the plastic bag behind. That's all you need to do. Clean up after yourself and leave nothing that can be traced back to you.

"Hannah has complete faith that you can manage this. Whatever your plan is, our government has trained you to execute it correctly. You will be the only one who doesn't turn themself in, because you have a second chance to create a meaningful life."

HANNAH'S HOUSE—4:00 P.M.:

Josh hears the phone ringing as Olga drops him off from their afternoon talk at the river. He yells as he jogs into the house, "I'll see you at the Ice House at six."

Olga observes a young man who has a history of severe PTSD. Despite having recently lost both his wife and mentor within just a few days, he is running with a bounce in his step. *Goddamn, Hannah, you were right again,* she thinks. *Let's hope you're right about everything else regarding that boy.*

By the time Josh gets to the phone, the answering machine has been triggered. He is so focused on answering it that he doesn't even hear Hannah's voice on the recorder.

"Hello! I am here—hello."

Scott says, "Sorry, I should have given you a couple of minutes to say goodbye to Olga. I saw you guys driving by my house."

Catching his breath, Josh says, "We went to Bluewater Beach for lunch and talked. We're going to the Ice House for dinner tonight for her last night in town. Would you like to join us? I'm sure she would enjoy the extra company, and you both could catch up a bit more."

"That's a nice offer, but I'm really exhausted from the last couple of weeks, and I'm currently on my chemo pump. Besides nausea, there are so many side effects related to eating that it wouldn't be much fun for anyone. How are you doing? You sound good."

Josh takes a deep breath. "Having Olga in town and being busy keeps my breakdowns—crying, that is—to a minimum. So far, I'm doing alright."

There is a slight pause on the line. Josh can hear a couple of big gulps and then Scott inhales. "That sounds good. I'm glad you're staying busy, but be careful, because you need to take care of yourself not only physically but emotionally as well."

"I know. You probably won't see much movement over here tomorrow and for the next few days. I have all this food left over, and my plan is to sleep as much as possible. But I'll make sure to answer the phone for your check-in calls."

"That sounds good. We canceled tonight's cancer group meeting because the funeral was just yesterday." Scott's voice is fading with every word. He catches himself and concentrates on speaking louder. "We need to regroup and figure out how to move forward without Hannah. It's a bit of relief for me because I won't be leaving my house except for emergencies over the next four-to-five days. I do have to go tomorrow to have my pump removed, and I'm concerned about how bad the nausea will be throughout the weekend. This is the part that really grinds a person down to nothing, going through all the treatments and still feeling horrible with no end in sight.

"Anyway, I hope you get the sleep you need. Let's check in tomorrow at the same time. Please give Olga a hug for me and have a good night."

"Yeah, you too. Get some sleep, and hopefully, this time around the nausea won't be so bad. I'll be sure to give Olga a hug for you. Goodnight." Josh hangs up the phone, and the answering machine gives out a loud beep.

CHAPTER TWENTY-THREE

OPENING STATEMENTS AND LINDA ROBERTS

OCTOBER 2010—SAWPIT, MONTANA:

A few weeks have passed since Ben, Bula, and Yabo were in Michael's rear-view mirror as he left the remote property just outside the small town of Eureka, Montana. During those following weeks, Ben and Michael have discussed the same objective repeatedly. With each phone call, Michael has seen a bit more clearly how Ben's plan was perfect.

The only surprise for the defense was the introduction of Linda Roberts into the picture. In reality, she wasn't part of the defense, and yet she was a piece of the puzzle that Michael couldn't figure out and couldn't bring himself to ask: Why did Ben Brown—good-looking, intelligent, responsible, kind, great with kids and animals—remain single his entire life?

After the dust settled, Michael concluded that *time and patience* were the reasons. At Arthur's funeral, Ben Brown hadn't yet established his plan, but he knew the purpose of the remainder of his life: helping others and holding Carl Shadwick and Vermolite Mining Company accountable.

* * * *

THURSDAY, OCTOBER 28, 2010—THE TRIAL:

After an hour-long opening statement against Benjamin Brown with photos, prosecuting attorney Champ Sanders concludes that: "the State has the blood, the tarps, the weapon, the victim's tortured body, and the confession of Benjamin Brown taken upon his voluntary surrender to

Sheriff Patterson, and this evidence proves without a reasonable doubt the guilt of Mr. Brown. Thank you."

Judge Anderson states, "Thank you, District Attorney Sanders. Mr. Bennett, as the defense on behalf of Mr. Brown, are you ready to proceed with your opening statement?"

"Yes, your honor. Thank you." Michael walks around the defense table, his heart pounding so hard he thinks that the packed courtroom can see it through his suit.

"Good morning, men and women of the jury. What you just heard from Mr. Sanders and the prosecuting attorneys was very compelling, and it seems like an open-and-shut case. My client, Benjamin Brown, volunteered to come into Sheriff Patterson's office and confess what he had done. The evidence the prosecution has presented was found where Mr. Brown told them it would be.

"You might ask yourself, why are you here wasting your time and taxpayer's dollars? The reason you are here is for the truth. What Mr. Sanders left out of his opening statement were the circumstances. It is easy to present evidence of your case without context, but there can be no truth or understanding without the context of a situation.

"Benjamin Brown is not a violent man—not at all. In fact, for decades Mr. Brown has been a trained counselor for both domestic violence and for veterans affected by PTSD. Mr. Brown is also an active member of Veterans for Peace. He cares about others and their well-being to the point that he started his 501(c)(3) nonprofit organization, Brown Expeditions, to help people suffering from domestic violence and the horrors of war.

"The defense will prove that Mr. Brown was acting in self-defense to protect himself and the entire county and region from something much larger than a single person—future murders."

A collective gasp, leading to rustle and talk, fills the courtroom. Judge Anderson taps her gavel: "Will those seated in the courtroom remain quiet until the session is complete and recessed? Go ahead, Mr. Bennett."

The courtroom quiets down, and for effect, Michael waits an extra few seconds to allow complete silence to overcome the entire room.

"Not only will we prove Benjamin Brown was acting in self-defense, but we will prove companies and executives such as Carl Shadwick and Vermolite Mining Company are existential threats to any community in which they do business—a business that poisons entire populations knowingly without allowing the community to understand the risk. Executives and companies like this should not be allowed to exist. Today, as I speak to you in this courtroom, Vermolite Mining Company has affiliated companies worldwide. Who knows what damage and toxins they are exposing many other communities to?

"Vermolite Mining Company was a company that had access to decades of scientific studies revealing the damage their products and business were doing to Mr. Brown and his entire family, who have all suffered from the same disease caused by the exposure to asbestos. We know that Mr. Brown's grandparents, his father, and most likely his younger sister were all victims of the disease mesothelioma. We don't know how many of his cousins, aunts, and uncles were killed as well by Vermolite Mining Company.

"Why? Mine Manager Carl Shadwick and Vermolite Mining hid scientific evidence from the people. In fact, Vermolite Mining Company forced their workers to go to company doctors and made them sign agreements that prevented them from seeking outside medical help for basic health-related issues. When a worker became seriously ill from the toxins produced at Vermolite Mining Company's mine, settlements were made outside of a courtroom, requiring that those who received compensation would not discuss settlement details with anyone other than Vermolite Mining Company. These are called non-disclosure agreements, or confidentiality agreements.

"You might be asking yourself, how do I know this is true? I know it is true because my family and my ex-wife's family had to sign such agreements. I suspect that many of you here today have also signed such agreements.

"Let's make no mistake: Vermolite Mining Company isn't unique. Companies like Avidité and Fulcircle Company are being sued for something similar as you sit in this courtroom today.

"I will conclude with this thought: Has justice been served when a person and company knowingly hide scientific evidence that causes the death of hundreds and possibly thousands of people in a community, and the people who made those decisions and the company remain free to live their lives with millions of dollars in the bank?

"What the defense will do is to show that Benjamin Brown isn't a crazed lunatic murderer but a citizen who has experienced how the legal system has been circumvented by the corporate world time and time again. The only way Mr. Brown thought justice could be served was by begrudgingly taking the law into his own hands. Benjamin Brown didn't make this decision on a whim. He believed in the rule of law but saw how the law was being abused by loopholes caused by desperation. What do I mean by desperation? The desperation of being so dependent on the company that is making you sick, increasing your medical debt, causing you lost wages from missing shifts, and much more. Families sign agreements with these corporate murderers and stay quiet to be able to pay their bills, and keep food on the table and the heat on.

"Benjamin Brown is a patriot who helps veterans. He, himself, is a decorated veteran who understands the psychological pain that morphs into physical pain through self-medicating and a culture that glorifies violence. As a child and young man, Benjamin Brown watched his family members die of the same disease one by one, and now he too is suffering from mesothelioma and doesn't have long to live.

"I'm not sure how many of you know, but alleged murderers rarely take the stand for questioning. Benjamin Brown will take the stand with more than three dozen character witnesses to explain the circumstances that have brought us together today before the honorable Judge Anderson in this courtroom. Thank you."

* * * *

During the weeks that turned into months after the unprecedented verdict of first-degree murder with time served, Ben and Michael spoke on the phone several times a week. Up until the day Benjamin Brown died the following spring, Michael and Ben forged a tight friendship.

Ben insisted on paying Michael for his services and for believing in his plan. Going against virtually everything a student learns in law school, Michael followed Ben's plan to a tee, which worked exactly how he said it would.

An unintended consequence of this friendship was Ben counseling Michael through his own PTSD due to growing up in Sawpit, and getting him on a path to a healthier and more fulfilling life. Before Michael stopped drinking, the two men had had a conversation about Linda

Roberts one night when they both had consumed way too much whiskey and poured their hearts out to each other. Ben didn't know that Michael had been in touch with her since the trial began.

During the trial, Linda had approached Michael and asked him to stay in touch. She told him her backstory of a love affair with Ben and wanted to know if there was a reason for Ben's inability to follow through with their relationship. Linda Roberts, now a grandmother of three and married to her loving husband for twenty-four years, still thought of Ben Brown as the love of her life and the one that got away.

Michael shared with Linda what he could remember from the drunken conversation: Ben Brown knew his purpose in life was to hold Vermolite Mining Company accountable, which most likely meant he would have to take the law into his own hands. His love for Linda was too great to pull her into what most certainly would be a legal mess. Also, and more importantly, Ben most likely knew that he would eventually succumb to the same disease that ravaged his family and didn't want to bring a child into the world to experience the helplessness of watching parents and loved ones die a horrible death.

Linda deserved to be loved unconditionally, have children, and enjoy a life knowing her husband wasn't going to spend years locked up in prison or slowly dying in front of her and their children. And Ben knew he could not go through with his plan if he had a family. It was the final sacrifice he made for Lincoln County, Montana. Next to his family, he loved this region more than anything else in the world. And for justice to be served, he could not be linked to anyone or anything that could take precedence over his quest for justice.

NO MORE TALK—
EXIT STAGE IV ACTION!

SATURDAY, APRIL 30, 2011—2:30 P.M.:

Josh is just returning from setting up his work area in Joe Sinclair's garage for this evening's festivities. Being cautious, he drives back via a different route to ensure that he doesn't pass in front of Scott's house in Bob's truck. For this mission to be successful, Josh needs Joe Sinclair to be dead, with no witnesses and no evidence traceable back to him. Today, Josh must rely on the discipline that made him a good athlete and soldier.

The sun is out, and spring is in full bloom, which means Joe's golf game and three-martini clubhouse, early-bird dinner with the boys will surely be on, giving Josh more than enough time to have everything ready.

The morning air is filled with Waylon Jennings, Merle Haggard, David Allen Coe, Dolly Parton, Hank Williams, and son Hank Jr. playing softly while the work area is staged. The music brings back good memories of his childhood and simpler times of friendships, hunting, truck beds on weekend nights, drinking beer, football, and most of all—his dad. It was back when Josh trusted people, and someone's word and handshake meant something.

All morning, Josh has Hannah's intelligence on Joe's Saturday afternoon schedule on his mind. He's trying really hard not to question her intel. What in the hell did an eighty-something-year-old librarian know about gathering intelligence on such an operation? Whenever these thoughts came, Josh would hear the music of his favorite country singers, and he would think, *you might be a real asshole, Joe Sinclair, but you sure do have a nice sound system.* He would then join in and sing with Uncle Merle or Aunt Dolly.

So far, Hannah's information has been perfect about Joe's schedule and house and about the neighborhood. Joe's garage is now ready to go, with the table and supplies covered in the corner. The Frank Sinatra CD is prepared to play. The only thing left is how much morphine it will take and how long before it kicks in. The big question mark is—what size is Joe Sinclair? Josh had asked Olga at their dinner, but she hadn't seen him in years, so she guessed: roughly the same size as Josh, medium build, and about six feet tall.

Two thoughts have been consuming Josh's waking hours over the last couple of days: Joe and cancer:

1) Getting Joe to swallow the morphine injected into his mouth, the correct dosage, how much alcohol was consumed, and how long it will take for him to come to.

2) Thinking of Scott, Hannah, and all those who have drawn-out cancer journeys. All the pain and misery they suffer in hopes of getting a few more years of life.

Until talking with Scott during that first four-o'clock check-up call, Josh never thought about how much pain Hannah must have been in and how it was a fucked-up blessing that Ashley's cancer journey was so short.

These second thoughts always bring on an emotional release of either crying, fierce anger, or emptiness that feels like it is going to consume him. This wasn't the plan. Ashley wasn't supposed to be gone so young. They had kids to raise and lives to live. Now, it is just gone, with little warning and only speculative reasons for why it happened this way. It's not good enough, not now and not ever. He will never understand and receive the answer to the why-this-happened question.

Once the crying when he thinks of Ashley stops, his thoughts go to Scott and the rest of the cancer group. They are living what is most likely their last days in misery, trying to figure out a way to become cancer-free, conceding the quality of life along the way to extend life long enough to find the correct combination of medications and balance. At the same time, a relentless search for relief from the pain, side effects, and fatigue caused by all the drugs and living with a growing parasite consumes much of their time.

It's got to be hope—that one thing that keeps everyone going, he thinks.

Then, an image of the exact opposite of hope pops into his mind: Joe Sinclair. He stole the life of one of the kindest, most hopeful human beings he has ever known. The memory of Ashley comes flooding back, which starts the cycle all over again at any given moment, and his big worry for tonight is keeping his cool, especially when he first sets eyes on Sinclair. What if Joe puts up a fight? Can he control his emotions and execute the mission instead of tearing him apart piece by piece?

Josh finishes the setup and parks the pickup back home at Hannah's. As he closes the door to Bob's workshop, adrenaline has his mind racing. He double-checks his list to see if everything is in place and ready to go.

Unlike many of his US Military or MOS-35m brothers who shared his profession as an interrogator in Iraq, Josh had never totally bought into the idea that we, the USA, were the good guys and those opposing our occupation were the bad guys. The unspoken truth was that many soldiers didn't believe in the propaganda that anyone the USA opposes is bad. But at the same time, many did it because it was drilled into their heads during basic training.

Still, this would not even be whispered to another soldier for fear it would eventually spread to the wrong ears, and they would be reprimanded. Many took their duties lightly, like punching in at a nine-to-five job. Not Josh; he saw every detainee about to be interrogated as a person first, and this compassion made the information he collected much more reliable. Studies have been conducted and have proven this approach to be much more beneficial. That wasn't necessarily why Josh held this belief, but it was a beneficial unintended consequence of not handing over his entire soul to the military.

Not all, but many others, got off on having the authority and power over the detainees. From Josh's point of view, this bravado or lack of compassion toward other human beings was a defense mechanism to allow interrogators to be indifferent to carrying out such horrible actions. Josh knew his orders, the critical information they were looking for, and how to read detainees' ability to withstand pain, and he wrote down everything in his journal or unofficial log books. During basic training, this ability to analyze and troubleshoot in real-time gained the officers' attention. Now he has been doing the same thing since Hannah introduced the plan.

During his time with the JAG and counselors, Josh repeatedly brought this up. Everyone would advise him not to mention these ideas during his court appearance. He was going before a military court, and such opinions would look more like treason than principles or convictions. They all said, "Just stick to the orders coming from a non-military authority, and your oath is not to a private company (Darkwater) but to the government of the United States of America and to upholding and defending its Constitution."

Josh is having those same contradicting ideas in his mind now. He continually asks for Ashley's forgiveness. He knows this isn't for her because this isn't what she would want him to do. But Ashley is gone and doesn't have to live with all the heartache and helplessness against these monsters.

These monsters cause all of this unnecessary suffering, destruction, and death so they can have more money than they could spend in multiple lifetimes. All their decisions and practices have a ripple effect on their victims' families and friends. Josh is avenging all the people who never received justice. It is for the suffering that these executives never recognized, and it is an act of desperation to shake the world out of the hypnosis that this is the only way life can be.

What Josh is praying for with this one last act is release from all the guilt he has accumulated and the images of tortured detainees that flood his mind whenever he has a quiet moment to contemplate life.

3:45 P.M.:
As he enters Hannah's house and guest bedroom, the clothes he laid out earlier on the bed, along with all the supplies he will have in his backpack or in a pocket, are still there waiting for him—waiting for him to either step towards a better life or to fall into a precipice of despair. Four o'clock—and Scott's phone call can't come soon enough. He pulls out Joe Sinclair's folder and reads through it while he waits. When he starts questioning himself, he reads further through the folder and knows this is the correct thing to do.

3:55 P.M.:
Josh is dressed and sitting with a second glass of water, staring at the phone, knowing this will be his last drink for the rest of the day.

4:05 PM:
With an empty glass on the table and one hand on the phone, Josh is

debating whether or not to call Scott. "Screw it," he says in an anxious voice and calls Scott's home phone and leaves a message. Now worried, he calls Scott's cell phone, praying he will answer. It goes to voicemail. Josh's mind, focusing on Joe Sinclair, is now debating whether to go to Scott's house. He has a tight window once that garage door opens; the latest he can leave is 4:20 p.m.

He needs to get into everyday clothes and get over to Scott's immediately if this plan is to be executed properly. Shaking his head while changing clothes, he says, "God damn it," with a twisted-up look as the internal debate gets inflamed. He is halfway out of his pants and has no shirt on when the phone begins to ring. He hops toward the phone and picks up as the answering machine kicks on. He hits stop, but the message keeps playing. "Scott, are you there?" He hits stop again, but the machine beeps and Scott is saying hello in a sickly voice. Finally, he gets the answering machine to shut off and says, "Hey Scott, I was just on my way over to make sure you were alright."

"I'm fine, sort of. The nausea is really bad, this time around, and I'm just getting out of the bathroom. I can't keep anything down, and I might need to go to the emergency room tonight or maybe show up at the hospital tomorrow."

Josh is trying to control his breathing. "Is it really that bad?"

"Yeah, I have sores in my mouth, and it feels like they're also in my throat. It's not the first time this has happened. It's been worse. But each time it happens it seems like my tolerance becomes less, not more."

Josh lies, "I just took some pills that allow me to sleep, but I can probably get you to the emergency room if you need to go." He has no intention of fulfilling this offer and feels horrible about it.

"Nah, if I go to the emergency room, I'll be there for at least a week. They need to really boost my immune system to heal the wounds and keep my mouth sterile at the same time. I had to do it once before and I wouldn't want to drag anyone else into that mess. I'll wait a few more hours and see if I can get some sleep. Otherwise, I'll drive myself over. Thanks for the offer, though.

"These calls are supposed to be checking in on you and how you're doing, not the other way around. Everyone in the group is available to you if you need anything. Just remember that there's no shame in needing help during these times of grief."

Knowing that he needs to get off the phone and on the road, Josh says, "I'm doing way better than I thought. I still have *moments* every day, but these sleeping pills help me get at least a couple of hours of rest. Speaking of which—they're just starting to kick in now. Are you sure you don't need my help with anything?"

"Get some sleep, and we'll talk tomorrow. I have nothing left to come up since it's all been flushed in the last couple of hours. Now is the joyful time of trying to keep these sores from getting worse."

"How about I come over in the morning to check on *you* for a change? Good luck with everything, and I hope the rest of your night improves."

"Thanks. That sounds like a plan. I'm not sure what you'll find, but whatever I look like, trust me, it's been worse. See you then."

Josh glances at the clock. It is 4:22. He yells "FUCK," and continues to hurry into his project-Sinclair clothes and get back to the staged area. This is not how he wanted to start this evening.

* * * *

APRIL 30, 2011, NEW YORK CITY:

Minister Tim has received the money and ticket for the event from Olga and Robert the night before. As per their instructions, with the money he goes to get a haircut and shave and then a day-pass at a spa for a good long shower, scrub down, and steam. The tuxedo will be ready at 2:00 p.m. to wear for an old, well-respected museum's black-and-white dress-code naming ceremony. Robert's tailor has taken Minister Tim's measurements a few days prior. The tailor asks about the occasion, Robert tells him it is a Avidité-sponsored dinner and silent auction, which for Robert and Olga is true. However, for Minister Tim, it is a different kind of black-and-white function—a Kesshitai Stage IV action.

From the "Robber Baron era" of the late-nineteenth century, through the twentieth century, philanthropic families have created space for art to flourish and for new young artists to have a place for exposure. Although the Morgans think of themselves as old money, they are actually very new money. The Morgan family has mastered the twenty-first-century version of philanthropy to keep their name relevant and in a positive light within high society circles. This way, they get their name and picture in the *Times* and every other major publication on the East Coast, and a handful of televised coverage that will help reinforce what an upstanding family the Morgans are for society. This is also designed to drown out growing nationwide concerns over the opioid-overdose epidemic and the increasing gap between the haves and have-nots. The more things change, the more they stay the same. A new Robber Baron era has been created.

After picking up his tuxedo, Minister Tim returns to the spa to store the suit in a locker until tonight's purge. He is now clean-shaven, with new clothes and brushed hair. Minister Tim sees himself in a mirror as he leaves the locker room. At first glance, he likes his appearance and feels more like himself than in years. Then, while gazing and daydreaming that his life is the same as it was just a decade earlier—*wham!* Without warning, a deep-down cramp doubles him over as if it were a reminder of the current reality that he is a host for a colorectal cancer that is jumping from one organ to the next and increasing in size daily. While doubled over in pain, memories—of his years at Delaware, Brown, and Yale universities; with his wife, Bethany; in his job at Case Brothers; and finally, dealing with his son, Jonathan—come flooding back. Several men changing in the locker room hear his rattling coughs into a handkerchief and give him a sideways glance to see if he is alright and to figure out if they need to create some distance.

What they see is chunks of something along with blood. "I'm sorry, sir," says the locker room attendant. "Can I help you in any way? Would you like me to call an ambulance or some assistance?"

Doubled over with cramps, Minister Tim waves his hand and thanks the attendant for his concern. "This will pass in a moment; I'm a very sick man with cancer and don't have long to live." He then announces to anyone in earshot of him, "I'm sorry for any inconvenience or discomfort I might have caused you. I'm not contagious and pose no threat to your health."

After a few moments, the cramps subside, but they are happening more frequently than just a couple of months ago. Disposing of his handkerchief in the garbage, he returns to the locker, grabs a new one, and remembers to take the untraceable burner cell phone out of the locker before going home to his tent city a few blocks away.

As Minister Tim walks into camp, he hears whispers from Farmer Chris, Caveman, 3 Dog Kev, Little Deb, and every tent he walks by until he reaches his pulpit, which the tent city calls "The Lounge." He rings the bell to call in whoever might want to listen to his sermon. A few people show up, and he asks them to go through the camp to gather as many people as possible. As his congregation grows, the whispers continue about Minister Tim's new cleaned-up look. Once the numbers swell to a tipping point, his message will be retold throughout the camp:

"Welcome to this unusual time for a sermon, my brothers and sisters. I have been given a gift from God to help rid our world tonight of some wickedness. This gift isn't clean clothes, haircuts, or warm showers. These outwardly material things allow me to lure a ravenous wolf who has portrayed himself as a shepherd of the lamb. I will trick the wolves tonight, and we will become the predators instead of the prey.

"In truth, the man I will bring back to you tonight is the false prophet of ridding ourselves of pain. In reality, he brought addiction, more severe pain, and ostracization from our families and communities."

For a few more minutes, Minister Tim continues about righteousness, cleansing our sins by ridding the world of wickedness brought to us through Satan's ability to poison our minds, and more. Then he concludes: "When I return later this evening wearing a tuxedo, accompanied by a member of the Morgan family, our destinies can and will be fulfilled. We must unite as a community and rid this wolf and its wickedness from this earthly life. I will take sole responsibility for your commitment to our congregation and community for any sin our God says has been committed. I will also take sole responsibility for the false laws of men and government.

"God loves all of his children, and I will forever love all who will step forward and help me rid the world of the wicked wolf that caused me to question my faith—that stole my ability to earn a living—that stole my marriage, my church, and through the most unforgivable act of all, stole my son Jonathan."

Minister Tim exits the stage and walks among the people within The Lounge. It consists of a moldy old sofa, a Lazy Boy chair, and room for about fifty if they jam themselves in and sit on the floor—along with a podium for meetings and Minister Tim's prayer services. The true centerpiece of The Lounge that makes it special is the coveted sole electrical outlet the tent city people have rigged from their only street light, which has been burnt out for longer than many can remember. There are keepers of the outlet with every type of charger imaginable by which citizens of the tent city can charge their devices. These keepers have every minute of every day scheduled, and the charging never stops.

Minister Tim gives orders to members of his congregation to find a sturdy patio chair and rope, and some dedicated members appear to be willing to give up some of their Paintabs to fulfill God's will. "God has spoken to me and has given me the job of punishment for those who knowingly hurt others. His message has told me to use the very poisons used on his innocent lambs. And all those who assist me with loyalty to his message shall be rewarded."

CHAPTER TWENTY-FIVE

JUSTICE

APRIL 30, 2011—4:43 P.M., WHITE COUNTY, INDIANA:

Back into his work clothes, Josh parks Bob's truck on a side road about a half-mile from Joe's house. He has put a push broom in the truck bed to clear away any tire tracks when he is finished. He is nervous about approaching Joe's house without knowing whether Joe has already come home. He is carrying a backpack stocked with a syringe, a bottle of morphine, a rag, tape, and the handgun his brother gave him the last time they saw each other. Everything else is already set up and under the tarp in the garage. At this point, he walks the half-mile casually and hopes the odds of running into or seeing someone play out in his favor.

So far, so good. Josh is now behind a hedge that hides Joe's fence line, trying to figure out whether Joe has come home yet or not. The garage is closed and no music is playing. Whispering to himself, Josh is debating whether to make a run for it or work his way slowly undercover. Then he shifts his mind into action-mode to go through with the plan and says, "Fuck it, let's go!"

He begins to run towards the garage's side entrance, steps into a hole, twists his ankle, and goes down. "Motherfucker," he says through gritted teeth, lying in the middle of Joe's lawn. He gets back to his feet and realizes that there is something definitely wrong, but it is something he needs to shut down and block out.

He has at least fifty yards to cross to get to the garage, and by the time he reaches it, he has no limp and feels no pain. Peeking in the window, he sees no car, but now he can hear one coming down the road. He enters the garage and gets into position.

Once inside the garage, his mind begins to slow down, and everything becomes clear as he pulls the syringe and morphine out of his backpack. The syringe for Hannah was oral, but in a last-minute decision, Josh has chosen to use a basic insulin syringe with a pink-colored 0.2 mg dose loaded and ready to be injected.

He thinks, *what the fuck am I so worried about? This is an eighty-year-old man. If I can't subdue an eighty-year-old, please let me die now.*

With the stereo remote in his hand, he waits for the car to pull into the driveway and the garage door to open. His adrenaline is now peaking, but his hands are as steady as his mind.

Nothing. Nothing happens. The car wasn't Joe's.

With the rollercoaster of hormones and chemicals pumping through his body comes a big crash, and he instantly becomes drained. In this weakened state, he can now feel his ankle begin to swell. The PTSD of his military experience wants to take over his mind, and he knows that if he doesn't get this under control quickly, tonight is going to be a disaster.

Now, all his years of training to control physical pain as an athlete and soldier kick in. Josh begins the 4-7-8 breathing method. Breathe slowly for four seconds, hold it in for seven seconds, and very slowly exhale for eight seconds. He learned this trick from one of his dad's hunting buddies who once broke his ankle when they were in the middle of nowhere. He said he learned it while in Vietnam after he had been hit and was waiting for dust-off to come and collect him in the middle of bumfuck nowhere. The medic told him about the method, and how, if a person can concentrate on a specific part of their body while performing it, they can slow blood flow to the injured area. Chuck, his dad's Vietnam friend, said, "Hell, at the time it sounded like horseshit, but better to focus on something positive than to go into a panic, which would cause the blood to pump out even faster. Sure as shit, about a minute or two into it, the pain went away, and the blood was just a trickle." Chuck figured that either all his blood was gone and the pain went away because he was dying, or this fucking breathing thing actually works.

So, Josh conjures up Chuck and concentrates on the time intervals of breathing, holding, and exhaling. Eventually, after a few repetitions, Ashley fills his mind and memory with all the good and important times of their life together. His heart-rate drops, his mind settles, and he can no longer feel his ankle. He is almost in an out-of-body experience when the garage light turns on and the electric opener kicks in. *Click*—the motor is engaged, and the chain links perfectly with the gears that open the garage door.

Josh calmly picks up the stereo control and hits play while he retreats to the back corner on the driver's side, where he'll be behind Joe when he exits the car. As the car backs into the garage, Josh can see a drunken look on Joe's face as he hears "Old Blue Eyes" singing. Sitting in his corner, he waits for him to reach up and press the button to shut the garage door.

Frank Sinatra is serenading Joe from the garage speakers, except he believes it is coming from the car radio. In his drunken state, he fumbles with the radio knob for the first two verses. Singing along, he opens the car door and reaches up to click the garage door control. The motor kicks back on, and the door begins to close. The door finally reaches the ground, and the motor shuts off. Now Joe is standing as erect as a drunken old man can, and Josh notices that he might be five-foot-nine and weigh maybe one-fifty at best. In a fraction of a second, he decides the morphine isn't going to be needed but should be available and ready in his sleeve pocket.

Joe is still drunkenly singing along with Frank. Josh comes up from behind as Joe closes the car door and jams a rag into his victim's mouth while wrapping his arm around his neck. He shifts his grip to Joe's wrists, which he secures behind him with duct tape and a zip tie. This allows him to walk Joe backward and sit him down. Then, to free up his own hands, Josh wraps duct tape around Joe's mouth and head.

The song continues to play, and Josh thinks—*either Joe is so drunk he is cooperating, or he is one brave motherfucker.* As the next track comes on the loudspeaker, Joe Sinclair hasn't offered any sound or physical resistance to his abduction. He is sitting on the garage floor with his head staggering back and forth while watching Josh uncover and prepare the table, zip ties, rags, and two-gallon containers of Kill-All weed killer. Once the interrogation table is set up, Josh checks its hinges to ensure that it moves from inverted to inclined positions. The five-gallon paint strainers are taped to the head side of the table. This routine is part of the interrogation and is meant to instill fear into the detainee.

Joe sits quietly on the ground, watching Josh do his work. After the second track, Josh grabs the remote, turns down the volume, walks over to Joe, and says, "You're a lot older than I thought you would be. If I take the rag and tape off, will you be quiet? If yes, we can talk like civilized men." Joe nods his head in affirmation.

Josh checks the zip tie and tape on Joe's wrists to make sure they are still tight. He begins to remove the tape from his mouth slowly, and there is no struggle or screaming. Joe allows Josh to take the rag out of his mouth without making a noise. Josh asks him, "Do you want to know why I have all this set up and your hands tied behind your back?"

"Actually, I don't give a shit why or what you're doing. It doesn't change anything. Twenty or thirty years ago, I would have cared. You're going to do whatever it is you're going to do."

Surprised by this answer, Josh is now intrigued by Joe Sinclair in addition to hating him. Josh feels pity for him while curious about why he isn't scared. Now feeling bad, Josh grabs a folding chair, stands Joe up, and backs him into the chair to sit down. Everything has shifted. No struggle, fear, or pleading means no satisfaction or revenge.

"So you aren't interested in why I am here and have you tied up with a table full of straps?"

"Nope. I'm too old to care. Nobody left in my life I care enough about to miss. My daughters and grandchildren—but they know how much I love them, and to be honest, I'm too damn old and I tire out too quickly to keep up with my family anymore. I don't like being the burden that holds up a good time for everyone else.

"I will miss my Saturdays. It's down to a twosome—good old George and me, that's it. We mostly drink and talk about when we were younger and could do things. Our golf times are just a way to schedule a drink outing without being too pathetic."

"Bullshit. Aren't you on the neighborhood housing committee? Don't you have an organization with your name on it and tons of business investments?"

Joe sighs. "Yeah, but those are only titles now. I don't do much other than lend my name to things to keep income for my kids and grandkids."

"Do you know the name, *Hannah Cassidy*?"

"Yeah, I know that old broad. How is she doing?"

"She's dead! She died just a few days ago. Hundreds of people came to her funeral. Do you think hundreds of people will come to yours?"

"Probably not. I'm sorry to hear about Hannah. We butted heads over the years, and I always enjoyed her quick wit. She knew her shit and wasn't going to accept no for an answer."

"Most likely, her death was from *this* fucking shit." Josh kicks the can of Kill-All. "Decades of being exposed to the overspray floating across from the farms toward the school —all the little kids, and the entire fucking town."

Joe mumbles, "I doubt it. She died because she was old. That's the truth, kid."

Now enraged, Josh screams into his face, "How about my fucking wife and unborn child? My wife was in her early thirties and excited about being pregnant for the first time. We had our whole life in front of us. Her mom and dad died from non-Hodgkin's lymphoma when my wife was in her twenties. That was only after Fulcircle Company bankrupted their third-generation farm with their goddamn poison-resistant seeds that allowed their poison herbicides, fertilizers, and pesticides to become necessary to grow anything in the dead dirt you created. Do you want to know how long ago my wife died from your over-the-fucking-counter poisons you coerced her father into spraying onto his fields?"

Joe nods his head and starts to say, "No, not really. I—"

Josh holds up his finger, interrupting Joe while looking at his watch. "Three hundred and twenty-seven hours ago she took her last breath. *DID YOU FUCKING HEAR ME? HER LAST BREATH!*"

Josh now pulls out his handgun. "Go ahead and tell me how natural it was for my wife's family to go bankrupt and die because of your fucking company of death—how natural it was for my wife to die in her early thirties? *Say it, motherfucker!*" He pulls the hammer back.

Joe still shows no emotion or fear. "No. I won't tell you that. But I will tell you something else. Hannah and all the activists, scientists, and farmers were correct. Kill-All does cause diseases, and we have known that for a long time."

"Then why haven't you stopped making it?"

"Do you really think it's my company? It is over a hundred years old, and yes, much of our product line has to do with death, which makes life easier through chemistry. To answer your question, too many people are making too much money, and they want to continue. That's why."

"You were in charge when the company went into overdrive, selling farmers the idea that this was the way of the future. To prove it to them, you and your industry corrupted our government to say it was safe and effective."

Joe changes the subject: "Do you know what I wanted to be as a child?"

"No, enlighten me."

"I wanted to be a pediatrician. I wanted to help children be healthy and strong. That's it."

"How did you go from that to being a fucking monster who controls behemoth corporations that destroy communities while making the wealthy even more powerful?"

"I wish I could give you the exact moment it happened, but when you're young, proving to your parents that you can care for yourself is crucial, especially in my generation, which grew up during the Depression. Then came serving in the military and finding out I have a good aptitude for dealing with people and business. Getting all these old farts approval felt so good and made me feel important. I lived in their bubble and believed everything they told me—hook, line, and sinker. I didn't think twice about the big picture other than from the company's point of view. That was my job. All these hippies and deadbeats wanted to see America fall behind the rest of the industrialized world, but not on my watch. We didn't stop the nazis and communism only to let the American way of life slip away because some fish-spawning areas were disrupted."

"But you knew it was way more than some fish or bird habitat being ruined."

"Honestly, I didn't know it at the time. All I knew was that we had top scientists from top programs around the country telling me otherwise. I knew my wife was pregnant with our second child, and a company was paying me six figures to keep the profits coming in. And I was good at it. That is what I knew. Thinking decades down the road didn't factor into the equation. That is the truth of the matter."

"Just a minute ago, you told me Hannah and all the environmentalists were correct. When did that become the truth for you?"

"Honestly, I knew they were correct when I saw farmers losing their farms in the 1980s. That's when I started looking into the science from outside studies. Also, by this time, my alcohol addiction was well beyond business drinks at lunch. It was me self-medicating because, on the outside, I was a successful businessman with a family and a major supporter of charitable organizations. But on the inside, everything we had built up was a fraud. We were killing our great-grandchildren to live a life of luxury today. So, if you're going to kill me, just get it over with. I probably deserve it."

Josh shakes his head and waves his finger at Joe. "You sly son of a bitch, you almost had me. Hannah had you pegged perfectly, and I was beginning to question everything. You've been doing what she warned me about since the second I grabbed you from behind. That was a heart-wrenching story, and I hope even ten percent of that bullshit is true. Now let me tell you a different story about life you entitled pricks cannot even fathom.

"This story goes back generations of poor people working their asses off for a big company so it could supply other big companies with the energy to have their factories—to magically have endless energy for lit parking garages in fifty-story buildings in cities across America. Those companies and factories exploit their workers with poor working conditions and wages. One big company after another with a few executive fucks, like yourself, treating workers like shit and convincing them they were lucky to have a job at all."

Joe interrupts, "And with that energy and those factories, we create jobs?"

Josh brings the muzzle of his gun to Joe's forehead. "There you go again with that ass-backward way of looking at the world. The lens of the oppressor should be considered a disease." Now he is screaming. "*Listen, Joey, people buying things creates jobs, not wealthy fucks who corrupt our systems of living. There would be no factories if millions of people didn't purchase the products. You are simply meeting a demand created by marketing campaigns, otherwise known as propaganda.*"

Joe begins to interrupt again, and Josh moves the muzzle of his gun from his forehead to his mouth. "Maybe this will shut you up.

"But this story is about the life where miners die doing their jobs, and yet the company never wants to pay for the risk they and their families are taking. We hear about the financial risks of the soft-hands, white-collar pussies that, for whatever fucked-up reason, give them more standing in our society. But rarely, except for the occasional compassionate news coverage of a mining tragedy or something, are our stories told to all the people living in the cities. We have no standing in your fucked-up world."

Josh removes the gun from Joe's mouth and starts pacing back and forth while he continues to talk. "In my story, I've had uncles and cousins die of black lung, cave-ins, and two or three families living under one roof because nobody will give coal miners a living wage or life insurance. At the same time, the company doesn't want to honor its pension agreements.

"I, too, served my country, but it wasn't against nazis or communism. It was for US and NATO corporations to get access to needed resources in the Middle East. Just like you, we were told by the top military minds that Saddam Hussein had weapons of mass destruction and he was part of the attacks of 9/11. Like you, I had an aptitude for reading people, and the military put me in a perfect position to help their mission. I was being a good soldier, just like you were for your mega-corporations, soaking up all the praise and feeling important while serving my country.

"But you know what—it was a lie. Do you want to know what I was trained to do?"

"Probably not, but what the hell—what is your unique talent?

"I was a special forces interrogator.

"How about that? Good for you for serving your country honorably."

"Triggered by the word *honorably*, Josh snaps, "Hannah warned me you were a great manipulator and a control freak. Boy, was she right, but that bullshit ends here tonight, right here, right now. You're a coward, Joe Sinclair, a scared little boy who bullied everyone around you so they wouldn't find out how frightened you were. I guarantee you were a terrified child and you are now a scared old man. That is why you migrated to positions of power. It wasn't to feed your family and get patted on the head by your daddy figures. It was because you knew deep down everything terrifies you. One way of ensuring not being a victim was to be the predator. In reality, Joe, do you know what I just described?"

Joe's face is now a different shade of drunken red, more resembling the red of rage. "*You fucking hillbillies are all the same losers at life and like to play the victim. If you don't want to mine coal, get an education that teaches you to do something else with your life.*"

Josh continues, "You must be the most ignorant man I've talked to in a long time. For someone with so many degrees and letters after their name, you got to be one of the dumbest I've ever met. When the only people you can depend on and you loved more than life itself need you to start working and chipping in to keep the lights on, your house warm enough, and food on the table at the age of ten years old, tell me mister PhD, when does that child have a chance at dreaming of something bigger? When will the time come for them to be able to get an education they can't afford and to live in a culture and society they do not understand or fit into?

"For me, it was football or the military. An injury that took a split-second ended my football dreams, and I knew working in the mines or for the company was not a life I wanted. So, I abandoned my parents, brothers, cousins, aunts, and uncles to try and get a better life. You know what was waiting for me? Pieces of shit just like yourself—too soft, weak, and scared to actually work for a living. Instead, they order others to do their work for them and then take all the profits for themselves.

"The more I learn and think about civilization, the more it becomes clear to me that this entire system is developed and rigged so that your type of people live a life of comfort while most other people live lives of struggle and suffering."

Now laughing, Joe says, "I don't know your name, but you keep *thinking and learning*. You think, one day you'll figure a way out of the miserable life you've created for yourself by trusting others, having principles of morality, and believing that love is the most essential energy force in the universe. But the good news is that the universe isn't moral. It just *is*. Life is about surviving by taking the lives of others. The quicker you learn that lesson, the better off you'll be.

"And regarding your little stunt here, I've been in control the entire time. The second I saw the covered contraption in the corner and the music playing, I was in control. When I was a younger and a stronger man, I would have taken you out the second you were within striking distance. Right now, I've controlled all your actions by being passive. You see, control doesn't always mean giving orders, often it means knowing when to be quiet and allow others to believe they are dictating the situation. I've passively dictated everything since I allowed you to grab me, son."

"*SON!?* Don't you ever call me *son*, you piece of shit!" Josh jams the rag back in Joe's mouth and tapes it in place. "When I saw how pathetic, small, and frail you were, I came up to you the way I did. If it weren't for my trust in others, my principles, and my love for my wife and Hannah, I would have shot you in the back of the head before you even turned your car off.

"That's the difference between the small few sick fucks who control things and the rest of the world. That is the difference between you and me. If you have no morals, don't love but only have relationships, and don't trust anyone else, tell me, smart guy, who is the one living a life of misery, drowning it and your mind away in alcohol and who knows what else?" Josh cups his ear, pretending to want to hear Joe's answer. "Oh, that's right, I'm in control, and you'll never say another word to anyone again unless I allow you to speak.

"We're trained through TV, radio, advertising, the internet—that your fucked up way of living is successful, but in reality, it is just parasitic, like cancer. You are a cancer that has spread everywhere worldwide. You are just like the tens of thousands of CEOs and executives who, just like you, have an empty life because you've suppressed the ability to have compassion and love for others. Why? Because you're afraid, and that fear will not allow you to be vulnerable to others. You always have your guard up and your heart encapsulated in armor so nobody can get to it.

"Back to my training and what you're about to endure. I guarantee you that you will suffer plenty in this life, no matter how little time it will take. You're last living thoughts will be consumed by what I am doing to you, and those thoughts will not be about your wife, daughters, grandkids, vacations, or any of that shit. I won't allow it. It will focus on not drowning, whether your mind wants to fight it or not. Your primitive brain will kick in no matter what and will try and cough out the Kill-All I'll be pouring over your face and into your system. Some will reach your stomach, and some will enter your lungs. If I have mercy, I can make it so it goes quickly for you, and you'll drown in the product that made you millions and your company tens of billions.

"I'm the one in charge of all detainees. Hannah wanted me to tell you that you had no control over the last act of your life. That your swan song was going to be filled with lots of pain and panic for all the suffering you have caused millions of people, if not more. Do you remember the waterboarding that the American public was denied access to until those pictures came out? That was my service for my country until business fucks such as yourself saw another way of bankrupting the American public by outsourcing the acts of war without any official declaration from Congress.

"Tell me, you served in Korea. Do you remember Congress declaring war against Korea?" Joe mumbles no through the rag jammed in his mouth. "That's right, but we went into that divided country and did unspeakable things that the American public doesn't know about. We did the same thing in Afghanistan, Pakistan, and Iraq when I served my tours."

Josh has held his PTSD in check until now, and it is starting to kick in. "My fucking service was to strap insurgents or just some unlucky guy walking down the street to tables and perform what international law considers torture on these poor fucks. You know what I see in front of me, Joe?"

Joe, sobering up, indicates he wants to talk, and Josh pulls the rag out of his mouth. "No, I don't know what you see with your fucked up, damaged mind?"

"I see the same pieces of shit, soft-handed, white-collar businessmen who make millions while people like my family and Ashley's family work their asses off putting our lives at risk so you mother fuckers can have multiple vacation homes, start charitable organizations, and have fancy parties to make yourselves feel better for stealing not only the future away from your grandchildren, or was it great-grandchildren, but our lives right here and now.

"I am going to earn my salvation tonight and shed this dead skin of guilt off my soul by giving you the choice of how you want your last act in this life to go. I'm going against my promise to Hannah to not allow you any control over this situation, but I'm not here for Hannah anymore. I'm here for the love of my life, my dead wife and child, and my soul.

"Do you believe you deserve mercy and a quick, painless death, or do you need to suffer a death that might help atone for the carnage you called life?

JOE?"

Joe is now almost completely sober from adrenaline. "Fuck you and Hannah for judging me and my life. I provided my family with a good quality of life and did it legally or at least what is acceptable in the greatest country on God's green earth. So, to answer your question, I don't give a shit how you're going to kill me.

"You're all the same, jealous of those of us who made something of our lives while you toil to just survive. I knew what we were selling was causing people to get sick, but for every person that got sick, tens of thousands could afford food, and if it weren't me earning six figures, it would have been someone else. Why would anyone who has more than the two brain cells you seem to have choose to live in squalor with multiple families if they had another choice?"

Amazingly, Josh has not lost control and become violent with Joe. "Well, Joe, I'm glad to hear you say that, because it bugs me not to keep my promise to Hannah. You've allowed me to keep my promise and release myself of everything I've done based on the lies told to me by those who were just trying to provide their families with a good quality of life and use what is acceptable deception in the 'greatest country on God's green earth.' I used to believe that last part for most of my life, but I am seriously questioning it the more I learn about how that country came into being and how it has risen to the top."

Aggressively grabbing Joe with both hands, Josh tells him it's time to end the chit-chat and get the interrogation underway. Joe goes limp and doesn't resist, but he doesn't make Josh's job any easier. Once Joe is leaning against the table in the incline position, Josh swiftly swings him horizontal. In what seemed like a single motion, Joe's head is now tied down to the table, and his hands, elbows, knees, and ankles are zip-tied down to the table so he cannot move.

Josh says, "I'm not exactly sure how I want to do this. My two brain cells are divided into torturing the fuck out of you or giving you a quick, painless death. You almost had me going with your wanting-to-be-a-doctor story, which I think is probably closer to the truth than the egocentric, power-mongering personality that has allowed you to dominate your life.

"But then I remembered my conversations with Hannah. We talked about you for hours and how manipulating you can be. She, too, almost believed your stories because she thought maybe you weren't a bad guy deep down. So, those stories have some truth in them, making it believable. The part you leave out, which we talked about most of the time, is that your biggest motivation was power over others and accumulating a fortune. It's all right in that folder, and it will be nailed to your body when I am done.

"For Hannah, Ashley, our child, Ashley's parents, and the tens of millions your companies have caused pain, suffering, and death, I want the former to be your final act, which means I torture the fuck out of you because you deserve to suffer and have a painful death. But for selfish reasons, I want to show mercy and allow your death to be quick and painless. First, I want some answers from you. Not the bullshit you've been spewing for the last sixty years and much of tonight giving you a chance to come clean. I'm no priest or connection to God, but I believe being honest and vulnerable to another person is a way to atone for wrongdoings. So, big boy, this is your last chance if you want to give it a try. As I have already admitted, I'm doing this for myself and the rest of my life."

"I got nothing left to say, you hillbilly, inbred, stupid, motherfucker."

The first jug of Kill-All is not so gently plopped onto the table next to Joe's head, and the clear liquid splashes up onto Joe's face. "Can you read that label?" Joe refuses to acknowledge anything that is said to him. "This is from your company and is your product that killed my wife and her parents. Most likely, it killed Hannah and her husband, Bob too. Guess who else it is going to be the death of? That's right, it is going to be the cause of *your* death.

"Nobody knows I'm here. The only evidence of whether you received mercy will be how much of your poison will be used. Do you know where I bought these two containers of poison? At the fucking hardware store—over the counter. It should be illegal in and of itself to sell known poison over the counter."

Josh now has the rag in Joe's mouth and his head covered with the paint strainer, but he keeps talking. He can tell by Joe's shaking and body temperature that reality is setting in—he is about to die a death he could have never imagined.

Josh pulls out the syringe of morphine and tells Joe, "There isn't enough to kill you but enough for you to be unconscious." Next, he pulls out the little bottle of morphine and shakes it next to Joe's ear. Joe flinches with the few muscles that can move. "This is more morphine that can easily be enough to end your life painlessly.

"When I think of our conversation here tonight and what's in the folder that will be left behind, outlining your lifetime of death and destruction, it makes me want to forget about this morphine idea. But my two brain cells are working overtime, and I don't want to be like you in any way. So, I am torn. What to do? What to do? Fuck it, let's get started."

APRIL 30, 2011—9:25 P.M.:

Josh departs Joe Sinclair's house, leaving all the evidence behind: an amount of two full syringes missing from two 1.33-gallon containers of Kill-All, the capture tote placed under the head of the table for the runoff is empty, the table, zip ties, tape, an empty syringe dripping pink liquid onto the table, and a folder in a plastic covering nailed into the chest of the dead body of Joe Sinclair.

Josh gets into the truck and asks himself the age-old question: What music does this occasion call for? Rifling through Bob's CDs, an oldy-but-goody jumps out: "Pat Garrett & Billy the Kid" by Bob Dylan.

* * * *

APRIL 30, 2011—10:25 P.M., NEW YORK CITY, ROUGHLY ONE HOUR AFTER JOE SINCLAIR'S DEATH IN INDIANA:

Minister Tim has been drinking soda water all night, waiting for Raymond Morgan to walk toward the museum's exit. He has already used his burner phone, which has a phone-number preset, to arrange for a driver to take him and the Morgan family members to the tent city or, more specifically, to The Lounge. Olga and Robert have set this up earlier in the week. The challenge is to get to Morgan and redirect him to a side exit, where the black town car will be waiting.

Raymond Morgan's attending this naming celebration is the best gift Minister Tim could ask for. Paintabs was Raymond Morgan's baby, and as disgusting as his family members are, Raymond Morgan is the man responsible for Jonathan's addiction, and ultimately, his death.

As Raymond Morgan gives a few hugs and kisses to his wealthy friends and bids them good night, Minister Tim intercepts him on his way to the front door. "Mr. Morgan, we have a car waiting for you parked on the side of the building. I guess there was a parking issue out front."

Raymond is a little tipsy from a few generous house pours of wine, and doesn't question Tim's directions. He follows him out the side door and sees the black town car and the driver opening the door for him. Morgan gets in just like the thousands of other times he has had cars pick him up for various events, airport runs, or even the country club. The driver tells him their arrival address as Morgan ducks into the car. Slightly drunk, Morgan says, "Right." It is second nature to enter the vehicle when a driver holds the door open for him.

Minister Tim goes around and sits in the front passenger seat, hidden from Morgan by the plexiglass barrier. The driver pulls out into traffic at 10:30 p.m. In New York, the only difference in the hustle and bustle between 10:30 a.m. and 10:30 p.m. is that it is dark at night and a different demographic inhabits the streets. Raymond Morgan treats himself to a two-finger pour of top-shelf cognac for the ride home. He notices they are not taking the usual way to his house and taps on the divider. The driver slides open the window just enough to hear instructions. Morgan asks, "Which way are you taking, because this isn't the way to my address?"

The driver replies, "I'm sorry about the detour, sir. Dispatch has warned me that there's some road construction, so we're taking a different route."

"Okay, very well." Morgan responds and continues to sip his cognac.

At the next stoplight, Morgan hears a car door open, and then the door across from him opens and the man who escorted him out of the museum slides in next to him. A bit surprised but in a good mood, Morgan asks the man, "Do we know each other?"

Minister Tim responds, "We used to run in similar circles a few years ago. I was a partner at Case Brothers before the crash and went down with the ship."

"I'm sorry to hear that; it must have been a big blow for your family. I can only assume you've landed on your feet, since you were at the event tonight. Why are you in my car?"

"I'm sorry about that, Mr. Morgan. There was a mix-up, and they gave the same driver two pickups from the same event. That's why I was waiting for your departure before I approached you. Since you were the guest of honor, it was fitting for me to wait until you were ready to leave."

"Very kind of you, sir."

"Since my home is on the way to yours, the driver decided to take me home first. Do you mind?"

"Not at all. I just wish he had said something before we got in the car—but I guess everyone still has to tighten their belts, and I'm sure the company is short-staffed. Well, look—who am I telling that news to? You know better than anyone. Can I pour you a cognac? It's very smooth and an excellent ending to a good night."

"No, thank you. I have a bit of a problem with addiction, so I've sworn off it for good."

Morgan now scoots sideways to get a square look at his ride partner and says, "Good for you. So many people in this country don't have the strength and faith needed to identify their addictions and like to blame it on society." Morgan can't help himself and enters Adicta Pharmaceutical's talking-point mode. "Abusers of drugs ruin it for the vast majority." He repeats, "*the vast majority* of people who take medications. Not you—you've looked your vice in the eye, wrestled with it, and won. Good for you." He finishes his cognac and asks, "Do you mind?" as he holds up the bottle.

"No, not at all. Go right ahead."

Morgan pours himself another and is already taking his first sip before he places the bottle back. "How rude of me. I really should introduce myself properly. I'm Dr. Raymond Morgan. Whom do I have the pleasure of sharing a ride with tonight?"

"Timothy McGee, but nowadays most people call me Minister Tim."

With a strong buzz from the alcohol settling in, Morgan points at Minister Tim with his nearly full glass of cognac still in his hand. A little bit splashes onto the pant leg of his carpool pal, which goes unnoticed by Morgan but very much noticed by Tim. "Now, there must be a good story behind *that* career move," Morgan says with a slight slur. "You don't often hear about a career change from an investment banker to a minister."

"No, Raymond. Is it alright to call you Raymond?"

"Of course, but I prefer Dr. Raymond or Dr. Morgan, if you don't mind."

"Well, Raymond, the addiction wasn't my own. It was my son's. That was the event that changed my life forever. He ended up taking his life by accidental overdose. He was a sophomore at NYU."

"Oh my, what a horrible story. I'm so sorry for your loss. Please call me *Dr.* Raymond."

"Yes, Raymond. His overdose was the beginning of the end of my marriage of over twenty years and my career at Case Brothers."

Another gulp of cognac was downed, and the glass was almost empty. The more intoxicated Morgan got, the less he could keep up his facade of being a caring person. Now he is feeling a bit uncomfortable. "I can only imagine the toll losing a child must take on a marriage. And please, if you don't mind, you can call me *Dr. Raymond* or *Dr. Morgan*."

Minister Tim tells him it is the most pain a human can endure, the loss of their child, especially when the loss didn't need to happen. "Do you have any children, Raymond?"

"Yes, I have two. I hate to be petty, but could you refer to me as a doctor from now on? It was hard work to earn my medical degree and license, and it is what I identify with in my life." Morgan is getting increasingly uncomfortable and looks out the window. He taps on the divider again and asks the driver, "Where are you taking us?"

Minister Tim answers the question. "We are almost at my home, Raymond."

The dividing window is still cracked slightly open, and Morgan is now panicking: "Would you please take me home first? I'm afraid I must demand it!"

With a calm voice, the driver says, "We have already arrived at our destination for Minister Tim."

Morgan looks out the window and sees a sea of tents, an underpass, bonfires, and hundreds of people living in an illegal campsite. He is seized with real fear and pleads with the driver to take him home immediately.

Minister Tim now turns to look Morgan squarely in the eyes and says, "Well, Ray, I'm sorry for a couple of things: The first is that you became a medical doctor, and the second is that my son took that first tablet of Paintabs that caused his eventual addiction and overdose."

Morgan is now screaming for help, and some of the campsite's population start to surround the town car. Pop! The doors unlock, and the tent city occupants open the doors, pull Morgan out of the car, and drag him screaming into The Lounge, where they proceed to tie him to a chair. Minister Tim has dozens of people around him thanking him for delivering his promise—and assuring him that they, too, will deliver their promises to him.

As Minister Tim walks into The Lounge and kneels so he is at eye-level with Raymond Morgan, everybody shuts up except Morgan, who continues to scream for help. Minister Tim says in a calm, soothing voice: "Raymond—quiet, quiet. Nobody can hear you and nobody calls the police in our part of the city anymore. This is what you and I have created. The difference is that I have repented and have tried my hardest to help as many people as possible kick their addiction to alcohol, gambling, Paintabs, and opioids—and help them find a way out of poverty. And you still covet money and prestige over other living beings and all their loved ones. In your gated castle on the hill in your little bubble of a life, you genuinely believe you're a good person. But you're not."

Morgan now starts pleading with the tent city residents. "I have money, and if you untie me and help get me home, I will give you whatever you want."

Someone replies, "We don't have any use for money. We deal in Paintabs, cigarettes, alcohol, heroin, and many other things, but nothing as trivial as money. Do you have any of those things to give us?"

"Yes, yes—I can get you all the Paintabs you could dream of. Just let me make a phone call, and it'll be delivered within the hour."

This answer gets a few residents debating as to whether to allow him the phone call. A massive man standing at least six-foot-ten, called Stretch, says, "Hell, even in jail, you get a phone call, man."

In his loudest sermon voice, Minister Tim yells, *"NO!* My brothers and sisters—I promised to bring a wicked wolf back with me, and what is right here in front of us? The biggest wolf of them all when it comes to the opioid epidemic. Just think of people who you once loved who have died because of Paintabs—or have disowned you because of the same drug. How much suffering and carnage is this wolf going to be allowed to inflict on God's innocent lambs? We are all born sinners, but along the way, we can atone and repent for those sins and change our lives to being people who live and preach the teachings of Jesus Christ, Our Lord."

Morgan is still trying to talk to some of the people in the tent into letting him go, and how he will not get the police and will bring back as much Paintabs as they would like.

Minister Tim rings a bell and gets everyone's attention. "Even now, the trapped wolf is still trying to eat us, instead of changing his ways. Now I ask those of you who would like to try and gain salvation to contribute just one tablet of their Paintabs for Raymond, here. He believes this drug is so good, and we are going to give him all he could ever dream of. Aren't those the exact words he used just a minute ago?

"So, brothers and sisters, we will pass around the collection plate, and no matter what dosage you can afford to donate, it all counts the same in God's eyes. It is the gesture that matters." As the collection plate makes its way around the room, most residents put in donations, and some take them. This is a normal phenomenon inside The Lounge during services. Minister Tim never makes a judgment but warns those who withdraw, "God sees all, and the more you take, the harder it will be to earn your place in Heaven."

As the plate makes its way up to Minister Tim, he is pleased. "This is a record number of donations. God will be very pleased. Raymond here likes cognac. Does anyone have any cognac they can donate?"

A woman in the back of the room says in lilting Bronxese, "I got some Four-Flowahs . . ."

Minister Tim replies, "Let that woman come to the front to donate. In the meantime, I need God's helpers right here in front to start wiping off each tablet so Raymond will get the full effect of his pain relief drug."

Morgan is now trying to drown out Minister Tim with his screams and begging people to let him go. A man known to be on the violent side punches Morgan in the mouth and tells him to shut the fuck up. That single punch knocks a few teeth out, and Morgan's mouth is now streaming blood. His begging has turned into crying and spitting out blood.

Minister Tim rings the bell once again, and it becomes silent except for Morgan's moaning and begging for mercy.

Then Minister Tim plops an 80 mg pill in the glass of "Four Flowers" bourbon. "I have a question for you, Raymond. Will you answer it honestly?"

"I'm sorry, I'm sorry, I will stop selling it," he cries, pleading for his life.

Minister Tim addresses Morgan while looking at his congregation: "No question has been asked, and you've answered it. You must listen to scientists and patients as you listen to my questions. No, Raymond. My question is: Do you feel pain right now in your mouth? On a scale of one through ten, with one being mild, five being moderate, eight being severe, and ten being the worst pain possible, which one would you call the pain you're feeling right now?"

His voice shaking, Morgan says, "Five—I would call it a five."

Minister Tim looks down and gives a gentle nod. The violent man punches Raymond Morgan in the mouth again. This time, no teeth come out but much more blood.

"How about now, Raymond? Is your pain about a five, or has it increased?"

"It's worse—I don't know how much, but it's worse."

Minister Tim exclaims: "How are we to know what dose you need if you cannot correctly describe the level of pain you're in, since pain is subjective? Isn't that how your scientists and paid spokespeople talk about your product?"

"Yes, that's what they say—I don't know—maybe a seven."

With his arms up like a choral conductor, Minister Tim leads the congregation. A chorus in the packed tent chants, "We all know what that means—*Double It*!"

"Isn't that correct, Raymond?" Two more tablets get plopped into the glass of the inexpensive bourbon.

CHAPTER TWENTY-SIX

DEATH IN SAN FRANCISCO

**SATURDAY, APRIL 30, 2011—2:00 P.M., SAN FRANCISCO, CALIFORNIA:
SAN FRANCISCO STAGE IV CANCER GROUP MEETING**

In a room of about three dozen people, Russell says, "Welcome. I'm Russell. If this is your first meeting, then I am sorry you're here.

"For time's sake, we no longer have an introduction at the beginning of our meetings. This group is made up of people who have been diagnosed with metastatic—or Stage IV—cancer.

"This is a safe space, and no criticism of another person's experience is allowed. We are here to help one another navigate our convoluted medical system and deal with adverse side effects and possible treatments that have been proven to work. If new people can wait until after the meeting, I can help answer any questions you might have about almost any topic of concern.

"I am the one who heads most of these meetings, and the city pays me to do so, not only because I need the paycheck but because I, too, am a Stage IV cancer patient. I have a form of bone cancer that is caused by excessive exposure to depleted uranium. Amazingly, I've been in remission for some time and can live a relatively normal life. As we all know, 'relatively normal' doesn't mean much.

"Today's focus is on how to control our perceptions of what it means to live with metastatic cancer. Our guest speaker will walk us through exercises we can all do at home to help keep our minds away from negative spiraling and toward the positive as much as possible.

"One last thing—Juan, would you be available to speak with me after the meeting?"

"*Sí*, I can stay," says Juan.

* * * *

Juan Santa Cruz is a dark, medium-build, and medium-height man in his late-forties to early-fifties with the infectious personality of an always-pleasant shepherd of the downtrodden. He is a fifth-generation potato farmer from the region near La Paz, Bolivia. Recently, he was diagnosed with advanced blood cancer, most likely caused by a long migration for work on farms situated along a route between his hometown in Bolivia and Pacifica, California. Unfortunately for Juan, this period was during the early stages of the Central America Free Trade and North American Free Trade agreements that allowed chemical or bioengineering agriculture to invest enormous amounts of money and infrastructure throughout the Americas. During his migration, Juan worked on farms that had no regulations or understanding of the new way of farming. When asked, he could name at least a dozen chemicals he used without protection over the years. Despite his recent diagnosis, he retains his joyful personality and love of working with the soil.

Russell Triplet is a retired civil engineer who has worked for Wasser or one of its subsidiaries for twenty-five years. He and his wife, Lisa, loved the freedom to travel to different regions and learn about new cultures. Russell's job took them to countries in Europe, the Middle East, Asia, South America, Central America, and his home base of San Francisco, where Russell headed up his department. In 2007, his wife died from carcinoma of unknown primary cancer, also known as CUP, which had spread to her brain. That is how Russell became involved in the San Francisco Cancer Support Team (SFCST). In 2008, he was diagnosed with Stage IV bone cancer that had metastasized into his lungs. Considering Lisa's history and Russell's exposure to post-war infrastructure rebuilding projects, depleted uranium and numerous other chemical warfare products used by the US Military were the most likely culprits.

Wanting to ensure that his two grown children have ample future income, Russell settled out of court for a sizable chunk of money, shares of stock, and a lifetime of Platinum Health Insurance that Wasser executives receive. Russell and Lisa's children both live in rural France and are married with children of their own. Russell will be cashing in all his Wasser shares on Monday morning, May 2, 2011. He currently resides in a small rental apartment in Daly City, California. He has kept enough of his settlement and his salary from SFCST to live comfortably. The rest has gone to his children through many untraceable channels. They don't understand why such actions were taken but trust that their dad has his reasons. Russell's children and grandchildren hope he will visit them this spring, but they cannot get him to commit to a date.

* * * *

4:00 P.M.:
Russell calls out, "¡Hola! Juan, thanks for staying after today. Are you going to the shareholders meeting tonight?"

"Sí—yes, I'm going. Are you?"

"Yes. Do you want to go together? You can park your truck at my place in Daly City and ride with me there. If I decide to stay on at the meeting and you want to leave, you can take a taxi to my place to get back to your truck. We can get something to eat along the way there and then be at the meeting early so you can get to the podium quickly. I've been to many of these over the years, and they're boring, but I know you want to speak to the board and CEO of Wasser, who is obligated to be at the meeting. We can talk about it a bit more between now and then."

Juan says, "That sounds good, but why will you not be with me after the meeting?"

"Well, I have something planned afterward, which I'll mention to you beforehand to see if you're interested. Knowing your story, I think you should be, but given these last few months of getting to know you, I don't think you will be. While we're eating, I'll fill you in on what I have in mind."

7:00 P.M.—WASSER CORPORATION SHARE HOLDERS MEETING:
While they dine and take a walk before getting to the meeting, Russell shares his plan with Juan. When later on, they are near the podium for open comments before votes are taken. Juan looks over and says, "Mr. Russell, I don't think your plan is so good. You might not want to go through with it."

"Thanks for your concern, Juan, but I'm going through with it. Another person in another SFCST will be doing something similar. That person may have contacted two other people."

Looking worried, Juan tells Russell, "This isn't about the law. This is about your soul."

"Although never this severe and personal, my actions for my job with Wasser have done much worse things that my soul has to account for. What happened to your family and fellow SFCST members is common wherever Wasser does business. I fully accept your position and will give you my time at the microphone to tell your story. If they allow it, which they should, you'll have six minutes. It is not a lot of time, but you can say quite a bit in six minutes if you stay on point."

"Gracias for giving me the time. But as we talked about earlier, I only want an apology for what they did. It costs them nothing, so I don't know why they wouldn't apologize." Knowing Wasser intimately, Russell knows Juan will not get that apology but wishes him luck and hopes he gets what he came for.

The Full Board and CEO Roland Durstig are in attendance. They have just finished reporting the first quarter results and putting forward fiscal year 2011 proposals. The meeting facilitator announces a break for people to stand up, go to the bathroom, and drink in the lobby before the open comment segment starts.

Juan stands up and goes straight to the podium. Russell points to the bathroom and mouths, "I'll be right back." Juan gives him a thumb-up.

Juan doesn't know that Russell is hustling to the parking garage to set up a remote-controlled speaker and to spray paint the security cameras. Once he returns, a bit out of breath and sweating, he asks Juan if he wants a drink of water or to go to the bathroom.

"No, I've waited ten years for this moment. I do not want to miss even one second."

The lights flicker on and off like during an intermission at a show, signaling everyone to return to their seats. Juan lets Russell get in front of him at the podium. For such a large audience, few people are lining up for open comments. Russell is very nervous, not for himself, but for Juan. Juan is his typical self—confident, calm, and focused.

The facilitator announces that open comments will begin with each speaker being allowed three minutes. "Please be respectful of the time-keeper's signals."

Russell steps up to the mic and taps it to see if it is on. Nothing happens. The facilitator tells him he needs to turn the switch on the microphone. Russell turns it on and thumps his palm over the microphone. The amplifier is working. Before the facilitator can indicate that his time has started, Russell says, "As a shareholder and employee for nearly twenty-five years, I would like to donate my time to Juan Santa Cruz. Thank you."

The facilitator looks at the timer, gives them a sign of approval, and says, "Can I assume you are Mr. Santa Cruz?"

In a strong voice, Juan says, "Yes." The facilitator instructs him to either talk softer or back away from the microphone a bit. "Okay, is this better, Juan asks."

"Yes, go ahead, Mr. Santa Cruz."

"If I did not have such a long story to tell, I would spend more time thanking each board member and CEO of Wasser. But anyhow, thank you all. I traveled here today from La Paz, Bolivia to tell you this story."

Roland Durstig and a few other board members squirm a little in their seats when they hear Juan is from Bolivia. They know what this story is going to be about: *Water!*

"My two brothers and me are fifth-generation farmers on our land in La Paz, which is considered a highland region of Bolivia and is about a three- to four-hour drive to the large city. The three of us have relatives who live in the region and in Santa Cruz.

"I don't know how many of you here today remember the International Bank policies in Bolivia starting in 1998. They stripped our country of public services and enterprises that kept many of our resources in Bolivia or sold in the interests of the Bolivian people. One of those public enterprises was our water agency. So, we formed a group to deal with our government, the International Bank, and any privately owned international companies coming into Bolivia. We were called, In Defense of the Water and of Life.

"We were promised many things over two years, but none were ever done. El Agua es Nuestra Company was given a no-bid contract for over $2 billion to control the Bolivian water system in a meeting we were not allowed to attend. El Agua es Nuestra is a company that Wasser Corporation owns. Our group and the people of Bolivia did not like this contract, and we opposed it. Despite our opposition, your company received a forty-year contract to control drinking water and sanitation.

We opposed this contract even more since the services we had been paying for in the past increased too much. Many people had to choose between water or food. There is no life without water.

"We organized a general strike in the city for several days to let our government and your company know we did not agree with their contracts. It was very peaceful; we used no violence of any kind. At this time, those of us who helped organize not only in the city but also in the surrounding areas started getting threats from people who worked for your company. We are not a big country like the United States, and we all talk with our neighbors, so when we started getting threatened, we would ask around. We would get told over and over again it was your company hiring these people to threaten us and try to scare us to stop our opposition to these contracts that prevent us from being able to live."

One of the board members rudely interrupts Juan and starts making false accusations. Then, the member asks Juan if he owns any shares of Wasser stock, or if he is even in the United States legally.

"Yes," Juan yells into the microphone, "I own one share, and this is my time as a shareholder, and I am telling you the history of what happened."

He continues. "I can see that many of you on the stage know this story, but I am not sure how many in the seats know. I will make it quick. As we protested peacefully, we were met with extreme violence. In exchange, our side became violent, but at first it wasn't toward anyone we knew. All of us who helped organize didn't know any of the violent people. And violence made more violence. None of this was discussed at a single meeting I had ever been to at that time.

"Eventually, your company, El Agua es Nuestra, and our government called us in for a meeting. We heard rumors but didn't believe a company would act so viciously towards people who are not military and just regular people who couldn't afford water any longer. As a farmer, I know that these policies affected us greatly, and my relatives in the cities also could not survive or live. The rumors had it that if we did not stop, they would find the homes of the organizers and burn their houses down, or worse."

Members of the audience begin to tell Juan to shut up and sit down. He went on: "I was an organizer but lived so far away that I thought your company couldn't know where I lived or would have any reason to burn my home. That's what I was thinking when I said goodbye to my wife and three children, who were all under ten years old. You're safe here, and I will be home in a couple of days. That is what I told them.

"At great time and expense, we went to this meeting in the city. But we found that there was no meeting. It was a trick to get organizers away from their homes.

"When I returned home, I could see the smoke from a far distance. At first, I thought it must be someone with a burn pile or field. The closer we got, the more scared I got, and I went faster and faster to get home. When I got there, my house was burned, my fields were burned, my animals were burned, and my wife and children were dead and burned. For what? Because we organized against your company's policies that had made it impossible for us to afford to live?"

Now, Juan is speaking louder and louder into the microphone so the board of directors can hear him over the irritated and noisy audience. They are calling him a liar, a filibuster, and a crank who is there to disrupt the shareholders' meeting.

Juan tries his best to be heard, "I spent many years making my way up to San Francisco—" when he is interrupted by CEO Roland Durstig in a condescending voice of superiority.

"I think I can speak for the entire board. We have heard enough of your story. Your time is up, and you need to sit down or leave."

Juan cries out, "*No!* I have time left. I just want an apology from your company for killing my family and burning my farm."

Durstig says with authority, "Sit down, Mr. Santa Cruz, or I will have security escort you out."

Juan ignores the warning and urges the board, "All I want is an apology for doing this to my family." He is so focused on getting an apology that he doesn't notice the four security guards surrounding him. Trying to protect Juan, Russell is grabbed along with him. Both men are roughly removed from the auditorium and into the lobby. They are man-handled by two guards each to the point that their feet are dragging along the ground despite their efforts to stand up.

Shareholders seated in the auditorium encourages security not to take it easy on these troublemakers. "*Crack their skulls!*" one woman yells. Another shouts, "A few good kicks in the ribs will shut them up!"

Once they reach the lobby, the security guards wail away at Juan and

Russell with their wooden batons. Once Juan and Russell are both on the ground and unable to protect themselves any longer, they are dragged out into the rain and told that if they try to reenter, they will be arrested.

Russell yells back, "*That's a good idea—maybe I'll call the police and have you assholes arrested for assault!*"

One of the security guards pulls his club out of the holster again and walks back toward them. "If you want to see what assault feels like when I do it, I'll show you." Another guard grabs him and says, "It's not worth it. Let these fucks figure out where they went wrong while they're lying in bed for the next few days."

Juan is lying in a pool of rainwater and blood, looking up into the sky, asking Russell, or maybe God, why Wasser would not apologize. Russell stands and helps Juan get to one knee. Crying, Juan keeps repeating, "Why would they not apologize for killing my family and burning my farm?" After this question's third or fourth repetition, it turns into a scream. "*WHY WOULD THEY NOT APOLOGIZE?!*"

Now standing and looking directly into Russell's eyes, Juan says, "Let's do it."

Russell is a bit scared because the person whose eyes he is looking into right now is not the Juan he has known over the previous months. "Are you sure?" he asks, dropping the direct eye contact. "You were so against it earlier. What about your soul? Remember your soul and reuniting with your wife and children, isn't that what you were telling me?"

"Mr. Russell, I now know I will meet my wife and children again no matter what I do. If there is any morality in God's plan, He would not allow those people to have success and an easy life while making the lives of others impossible and filled with suffering. No, He would not allow it to happen. I thought these people didn't realize what their company did in Bolivia, and once they knew, they would apologize and stop doing business in this way. But no, they behave the same way here in San Francisco. The people in the seats said to break my head and kick me in my ribs. For what, telling the truth? Let's do it."

"Okay. I wish I could say I'm glad you changed your mind, but seeing you like this makes me feel the opposite. You now understand how I feel about Lisa and, most likely, my two children. This company lies and kills everything and everyone to make money for people who don't care—those people in that room tonight. I want somebody who makes the decisions to finally be held responsible. Roland Durstig is the type of person who pays others to write the laws that allow them to legally lie to and kill their victims if it means more profits and money for their shareholders. That is all they care about—more money at any cost."

Russell goes on to tell Juan that Roland's car is parked in the garage. "We'll wait for him, and he'll be held accountable. Follow me."

The rainfall has intensified to the point that the gutters and downspouts are overflowing, and there is not enough room in the pipes for this enormous amount of water to pass through. Juan is moving better than Russell when they reach the correct parking-garage level. He asks Russell, "Are you okay?"

"Yeah, I'm fine. I'm just sore from being hit with those clubs. A few shots hit directly onto the bone."

"Me too, but I'm too mad to worry about being sore. Where is your box with the supplies? How much longer do you think it will be until he comes out?"

Russell points to the elevator and stays behind the wall in the corner. Juan goes over, and a waterfall is pouring down onto the box, a black twenty-seven-gallon tote with a yellow lid. Juan is already soaked, but his years of working hard labor on farms and odd jobs have made him immune from bad weather stopping him. He dives into the waterfall and feels around for the box's edges while getting pummeled with a massive overflow from the downspouts and concrete from the level above. He finds the edge and drags out the box. By now, Russell has made his way over, and they open it.

Amazingly, everything is relatively dry despite the amount of water and the force hitting it.

Russell says, "Everything is here and dry. I'll give you more details of the plan. First, I have spray-painted all the cameras that can see Roland's car. Hey, are you paying attention?"

Juan is in a daze, just watching all the rain and the excess creating the waterfall. It causes him to have a flashback of his farm in Bolivia. His cousins, who lived just outside the city, used to collect the rainwater from their roofs, just as Juan did on his farm. He remembers the first time they received a bill for the rainwater they collected, since it belonged to El Agua es Nuestra. From the company's standpoint, the rainwater was being stolen from them. At first, his cousins thought it must have been a mistake. They went to the company and told them about it, and it was no mistake. It was illegal to capture rainwater. El Agua es Nuestra, *or Wasser, owned the rain in Bolivia.*

Russell asks again, "Are you paying attention?"

"*No!*" Juan says firmly. "I have a better plan."

"We don't have time for this, Juan. I've covered all the bases on this plan, and it will work."

Once again, "No. My plan is better."

The elevator light clicks on, showing that the elevator is moving up from the first floor. Juan yells, "*There is no time!*" He dumps the contents out of the tote and slams it back down where it sat before, but this time without a lid. It fills in seconds, and Juan starts dragging it towards Roland Durstig's car. At this point, the elevator is on level 3, and they are on level 5.

"How were you going to grab him in your plan?" he asks Russell.

Russell starts to explain, but Juan cuts him off and orders him, "Just do it—there is no time."

The elevator door opens, and Roland Durstig walks alone to his car. Hiding behind another vehicle, Russell presses a button on a remote. As Roland Durstig approaches his SUV, a strange animal noise comes from under the car next to his. Roland stops and takes a few steps back to look under the car without getting on his hands and knees. To him, it sounds like a puppy whimpering. He doesn't see anything."

Russell presses the button again. The speaker hidden next to the tire cannot be seen, but the puppy's cry for help is heard again. This time, Roland Durstig puts his hands on his knees to bend over and look under the vehicle. Russell is too slow to grab the man from behind, so Juan flies past him and grabs Durstig. Now, in a choke hold, Juan is walking Durstig between the two cars, whispering in his ear.

Russell is shocked at how quickly Juan moved to attack and at his strength despite being so ill and beaten. He tries to listen to what Juan is whispering. With Juan's accent and how softly he is speaking, he can only make out certain words.

Once Juan gets Durstig to the water-filled tote, Russell hears Juan say, "Your company values fresh water over life." The next thing Russell sees is Juan dunking Roland Durstig's head into the tote of freshly captured rainwater. He holds him down for what seems like minutes, but it is probably more like ten seconds. Juan asks Durstig if this tub of water is more valuable than his life.

Roland cries out, "*No, it's not!*"

Juan is now enraged beyond control. "But it's worth more than my wife and children."

Durstig cries out once again, "*No, it's not!*" Juan slams his head into the water again for a long time and then pulls it back out.

"Is this tub of water more important to you than apologizing for killing my family?"

Before Durstig can speak, his head is back in the water—and this time, Juan, now speaking in Spanish, is saying a prayer.

CHAPTER TWENTY-SEVEN

JOSH/DAVID

MAY 1, 2011—5:00 A.M.:

Josh sits in Bob's patio chair outside the workshop and hears the roosters crowing at each other in the distance. The morning sky goes from black to cerulean-blue, to a golden-pink sunrise reflecting off the scattered cloud pattern that Ashley would have found a story in, somehow.

This morning is different. There is something very different about this morning for Josh, and not only Josh alone. At this moment he can feel a shift of energy in the world. Something has shifted, and he doesn't know if it is just inside of him or everywhere. Either way, he'll take it.

He has been sitting watching the stars through the night. When he returned from Joe Sinclair's, he showered, changed into clean clothes, and opened the bottle of wine Ashley had bought for them to drink once she came home from the hospital with their newborn child. Then, Ashley's diagnosis changed the wine opening to the day Ashley is declared cancer-free. This bottle now represents saying goodbye to Ashley's earthly life and letting her spirit go—to set off on her next journey.

Through the night, Ashley overwhelmed his thoughts, and he gradually began to feel less guilty about visualizing the remainder of his life without her by his side. He was beginning to understand that Ashley will be alongside him as he begins to live life again, appreciating the small things in life and leaving his baggage of the military and his family behind. Now, while sitting next to Bob's workshop contemplating the receding night and the remainder of his life, Ashley comes into his thoughts again. And whenever she is the focus of his mind's eye, he will ask for her forgiveness, say a prayer, and take a sip of the wine.

Josh's mind is not only calm but also clear. For the first time in years, he can think without having to block out millions of other things that kept his mind continually racing. He thinks of Hannah and how she must have been a guardian angel for both of them. Without Hannah, Josh knows he wouldn't have been able to handle Ashley's cancer and death with any amount of control. Hannah kept him centered and focused by allowing him to relish his last days with Ashley instead of having to go numb. He was allowed to feel and be with the love of his life instead of filling out paperwork and spending hours on the phone trying to organize appointments and understand why one treatment was approved and another was not.

Hannah understood all of this, and now, so does Josh. With this understanding, he knows how and why the Kesshitai plan is the only way things will change for ordinary people. So many loved ones aren't allowed to be *present*. They are stuck dealing with the nightmare we call the health care system in the United States.

Unless a person wants to dive deep down the rabbit hole, it is almost impossible to find these connections of interlocking boards, but once it's found, it cannot be unfound. Doctors are trained to pass exams and be licensed by what many now call the Medical Industrial Complex (the MIC). Once a noble profession has become distorted through corruption, many older practicing doctors leave it in droves to avoid the paperwork and helplessness of being unable to treat their patients properly.

For patients and caregivers, there is all the paperwork, appointments, medications, side effects, and more appointments. There is also worry about adverse symptoms related to either the disease or the drugs and knowing when to ignore them, when to call the doctor for another appointment, or whether the emergency room is needed. Josh wonders if it evolved into this, or if it is by design.

There is a labyrinth of code words, redundant paperwork, and a waiting-for-approval-game from an underpaid and undertrained insurance agent who may be coerced into overriding medical doctors' opinions and protocols. Those who have the unfortunate job of telling patients and doctor's offices one treatment is approved over another aren't the ones making the big money. They are the employees of a system where most patients, caregivers, and advocates are consigned to interact. It is a buffer zone that protects high-salary employees from feeling the wrath of their customers. This bubble of separation allows them to make heartless decisions.

Hannah knew how to navigate this labyrinth and allow loved ones to spend that time with each other instead of adding the stress of dealing with a system they did not, and could not, possibly understand. For that, Josh is forever grateful. The biggest gift Hannah gave him might be a purpose and a way out of a life he no longer wanted if Ashley wasn't to be part of it. Hannah opened a door he could never have found on his own. As the sun's rays break the horizon—first, he tells Ashley he loves her and will make her proud, and then he thanks Hannah from the bottom of his heart for saving his soul and giving him a new chance at life.

MAY 1, 2011—9:00 A.M., INDIANA "MAYDAY":

Josh knocks, holding a cup of coffee and a thermos filled with warm water. Scott comes to the door, looking like he is hours away from death. "Good morning, Josh."

Josh thinks, *we are odd creatures—here's a guy with one foot in the grave, and his first words are a nice greeting: "Good morning."*

"Good morning, Scott. You're still here, but it looks like you had a rough night."

Rubbing his eyes, Scott says, "I did get some sleep and I'm feeling better than I have in days, as strange as that might seem based on how I look.

"Maybe I'm glad I didn't come over last night, if this is *feeling better*. Dude, do you need me to take you to your doctor or the hospital?"

Scott laughs. "*Dude.* I didn't realize people still used that word. No, I think I'm over the hump on feeling bad. I left a message with the 24-hour call center last night for Doctor Evans, and he's going to stop by this morning to check on me before heading to the cancer center.

"He's a good man, Dr. Evans. He seems to really care about his patients. I remember that we never had a single appointment with Ashley that had good news, but now looking back on it, I see that he made them bearable and was always concerned about Ashley's needs. The same thing with Hannah."

Scott, wrapped in a blanket, skin peeling off the sores on his lips, and his face pasty white, tilts his head, looks at Josh for a second, and says, "There is something different about you today that I've never seen before. It's a good change. I don't know what it is—but hopefully, it lasts."

"Thanks for that; I feel different today. More than I have in a very long time. Hey, I brought you some warm water because I had no idea what you can eat or drink now. I was just happy you answered the door. I remember you said your chemo makes it so you can't eat or drink anything colder than like 80 degrees."

"Yep, good old Oxaliplatin and its side effects," Scott replies. "Sure, since you went to all that trouble of slaving over making me a thermos of warm water, it would not be polite of me to refuse it. It will feel good going down, but first, I will put some sea salt into it. I'm not sure what it does, but it makes things feel so much better when they are this bad."

"Look, Scott, I'm not sure if you're up for it, but I'm going do a bonfire this afternoon and early evening. You're welcome to come over, feel the heat, and stare at the fire. I'll have a small bottle of whiskey, toasting everyone I've lost over the years. Hannah had a pile of stuff she wanted me to burn after her death. I'll let you bring whatever you can handle for drinks or food. In case you don't come over, I'm warning you about smoke and fire next door today at some point, so don't worry about it."

"As nice as that sounds, I won't make it over. Smoke from a fire probably isn't on Dr. Evans's list of things to do, and during chemo, I can't stay warm enough unless I'm in direct sunlight or inside. We'll skip the four-o'clock call this afternoon."

Josh says, "I'm doing really good right now. How about *I* call *you* at four for a change, until you finish this round of treatments—just to make sure you're okay? I can't thank you and thank everyone from the cancer group enough for all the help you've been over the last month-and-a-half."

Scott looks sad when he responds to the last comment. "Our leader—our rock, Hannah—will no longer be here to help keep everything going. I'm still figuring out who will step up and take over the group. With Hannah's treatments being so spread out and being a palliative approach, it allowed her to stay on top of everything for quite some time because she didn't have the crippling side effects. All cancers are different, but her quality of life and how many years she got out of her approach . . . Many of us wonder if that's the best approach to deal with everything. But then you get someone who has a five-percent chance of living, and amazingly, they're cancer-free within a few months. We never know. Anyway, I'm glad you're looking and feeling better. Let's hope you continue to improve."

Josh begins to say goodbye, and he gets butterflies in his stomach. Looking at the ground, he says, "Scott, I love you and everything you meant to Hannah. She became like a grandmother to me and had nothing but good things to say about you. I wish the world had more people like you."

4:00 P.M. — INDIANA BONFIRE:

Josh sleeps through most of the day and wakes up at around 3:00 p.m. Feeling refreshed and full of nervous energy, he begins to get his remaining journals ready so that the military cannot confiscate them in the event of a possible incarceration. He has been unsure what to do with them, but he now has a feeling they should have been part of Hannah's folder labeled Bonfire. One journal is specifically what he is looking for. Buried in the midst of what seems like daily entries of babble is the list of names from every single one of the seventy-two interrogations he performed while in uniform. Many, primarily men, he interrogated were multiple, which meant they would have to come back for numerous torture sessions on the rack, the table on which they waterboarded detainees. In total, there were seventeen names in his journal, and one name that wasn't: Joe Sinclair. Amazingly, he knew most of their names without looking at the list. He began to write each name down on its own piece of paper. In the workshop, he had everything Hannah instructed him to have: the folders of each executive she had done research on, his clothes from the night before, gloves, and the folder, which was not to be opened until he was ready.

Josh hasn't eaten since dinner with Olga, and now he is hungry. He doesn't think he can stomach any more lasagna or casseroles. As nice as it was for the cancer group to make him so many days of food, he craves a good old-fashioned steak cooked over an open flame. He will need to head into town to pick up some briquettes, lighter fluid, and of course, a nice cut of filet mignon.

He jumps into his car and drives into town. While standing in line at the grocery store, he hears two people talking about how Joe Sinclair was found dead in his garage this morning. It was his friend George who found him. One of them asks, "Was it a heart attack or a stroke?"

The woman doing most of the talking replies, "I don't know. You know, my husband works in the Sheriff's Department—and he hardly ever discusses any of his job stuff with me—but I did hear on his walky-talking thingamajig that *foul play* was involved."

The man asks, "Does that mean he was *murdered*?"

"Not necessarily murdered, but there could have been a fight or something, and an accident happened. At this point, they don't just don't know."

The two notice Josh listening in on the conversation and ask if he has heard any information on the radio or TV about it. He replies calmly, "No. This is the first I've heard about it. What's the name of the person, again? I'm relatively new to White County, and I don't know very many people."

The woman says to Josh, "I recognize you from the paper. I don't mean to be rude or to overstep, but what is your name? I'm so sorry to hear about your losses and them coming so close to each other. Do you have anyone helping you out? My name is Darlene, and this is Jeff."

Josh nods to them both, saying, "It's good to meet you. Did you see me in the paper?"

Jeff starts to talk, and Darlene cuts him off, "Yes, there was an article and photo of Hannah Cassidy's funeral. She was such a treasure to our community for many years. And you had an entire paragraph written about your wife passing away from cancer just a few days before Hannah did. That's just too much for anyone to deal with on their own."

Just days prior, this statement would have triggered a crying episode that Josh would not have been able to rein in. But today, tears come to his eyes, and with a trembling voice he replies, "You're right there, ma'am. Just a day or two ago, that statement would have had me curled in a ball on the ground crying, but if it weren't for the cancer group and the church folks fixing meals and checking in on me, I wouldn't even be able to stand up, let alone come do some grocery shopping. When I think I'm all cried out, more tears come. I suspect there are many more days and moments when the grief will overwhelm me." Tears stream down his cheeks, and without shame, he wipes them away.

"To tell you the truth, today is the first day I've had an appetite in what seems like months but is probably more like weeks. Normally, I don't buy high-end beef. But today is my birthday, and I feel like eating a nice rare steak. And to answer your question, my name is Josh."

"That's a good sign, Josh—you havin' an appetite. Your body is telling you what it needs to begin healing from all the stress and grief. God Bless you, and I hope to see you around town more often in the near future."

The man chimes in with a careless remark, not knowing what else to say. "Nothing like a good rare steak to make a man feel a bit better. God Bless."

Josh checks out and gets back into his car. He thinks maybe coming to town today was a mistake. He drives extra carefully back to Hannah's. He goes into the workshop, uncovers the BBQ, and brings it next to a burn pit that hasn't been used for months and has spring growth and flowers around the edges. Both Ashley and Hannah pop into his mind. He talks to the flowers and then finds a shovel to dig them out and put them into pots so the bees have something to come to while they still have life in them.

By this time, it is after four, so he goes inside to give Scott the check-in call. Scott is doing better, and Dr. Evans has stopped by to give him some concoctions to help with his sores. *"A doctor making house calls on a Sunday,"* the two men joke. "Well, Scott, I'm about to fire up the grill and start that burn pile. No pressure—but the invitation still stands if you feel up to it."

"Thanks, but I'll pass today. Hopefully, I'll be back with the living soon. Have a good night, and don't stay up too late."

Josh has the salt and pepper-seasoned beef covered and sitting out on the countertop, with his bottle of bourbon right next to it. Then he goes to the hall closet where all of Hannah's files and items to be burned are stored. Taped to the top box is a folder labeled: Bonfire—May 1. He thinks, *Hannah, you must be the most organized and thorough person I have ever met.* He rips the folder off the box and opens it. There are two typewritten pages in chronological order, categorizing by importance which files should be burned. There is a reminder to use the stirrer stick to make sure every piece of paper is totally burned, and for the same reason: "Do not throw them all in together."

Within these two pages, Hannah suggests that Josh visit town and be seen. There is also an order and one more suggestion. The order is to check in with Scott, and the suggestion is to take this time to release all the negatives of his past life while visualizing Ashley's illness and her suffering, and eventually, a life she would have loved to have lived with him. "Live a life that would make her proud and make you content, and if you want to shoot for the bonus, a life allowing you to be a happy man again."

In the few short months Josh was being mentored by Hannah, he learned quite a bit without even knowing it. He has done everything Hannah suggests or orders him to do. To him, that is a sign that he is already beginning to shed his insecurities and perceived failures as a human being and making healthy, positive decisions.

He heads back outside, prepares for a kindling fire in the pit while he pours the briquettes into the BBQ and douses them with the lighter fluid. Finding no reason to waste any of it, he squirts the remainder of the can onto the fire pit and kindling.

With a single match, the night of letting go starts, and flames rise up quickly in the BBQ and the burn pit. He has a stack of wood of different sizes next to the pit to get it nice and hot before he can start fueling it with the folders, journals, and the list of names that need to be released from his consciousness. His prayer for each one, except for the last one, is: "I'm sorry for my actions, that I performed my duties as a soldier first, and that I forgot about my humanity. Please forgive my actions. I will try to create more positive than negative for the rest of my life. I have a long way to go, but I will do my best to keep this promise because I see you now as a human being before anything else."

The pit is ready to go much quicker than the BBQ, and he starts feeding the folders as fuel and stirring them up so they all become ash. So many folders, information, hours of Hannah's life and preparation are being burned as if they never existed. At first, he feels like he is burning away her existence and life energy, but then he realizes after a few folders that this burn pile isn't for getting rid of evidence but to release her. Removing the weight of all that negative energy will allow her to move more freely and with fewer obstacles on whatever journey comes next. They burn at a speed that makes it seem the universe wants to rid itself of them as fast as possible. As he gets to his journals and list of names, the briquettes are just starting to get red hot. He adds more to give himself a few extra minutes. Those minutes allow him to fully concentrate and say his prayer for each detainee with complete focus. For Josh, this is the key to the long journey of recovery and to fulfilling the promises he has made.

Eventually, the red glow of the pit and the BBQ lights up Josh's face as he watches the same sun set in the western sky that he watched this morning rise in the east. May 1st will be a day of cleansing for the remainder of Josh's long life.

With his bottle of bourbon by his side half empty from all the toasts for the people he prayed with and for, Josh is feeling pretty loose right now and damn hungry. He takes his one-hundred-and-eighty-second-cooked, rare filet mignon and makes his first cut. The knife slides through like it is warm butter. He takes the first bite, and with the juices filling his mouth, he can feel a sense of well-being rush through his entire body and mind.

MAY 2, 2011—JOSH AND MOM:

After his night of eating steak, drinking bourbon, and burning his past in that bonfire along with Hannah's demons, Josh feels like he needs to hear one more person's voice before he can move on—his mom's.

It's Monday morning in a mining town in Logan County, West Virginia, where miners are just either getting off their shift or going down into the mines. Josh is sitting at Hannah's kitchen table, his hands shaking and his heart racing. He waits until he knows she will be home alone. Dialing his childhood phone number, his childhood memories come flooding back. The phone rings three times, and Josh is about to hang up when he hears his mom say, "Hello, this is Loretta." When there is no answer she says again, "Hello?"

Tears pour down Josh's face as he tries to speak but can't. In a very soft, broken voice, trying to break through his emotion, he says, "Mama, it's Josh. Are you alone?"

She replies, "Who is this? I didn't quite hear ya."

"Josh—Mama, it's Josh."

Now he hears her begin to cry, and for a good minute or two, both mother and son do not speak another word but cry alongside each other on the phone. Eventually, Josh breaks the silence. "I'm alright, Mama. I'm going to be okay, and I just wanted to let you know."

She is still crying but speaks through it. "*Where are you?* I hadn't received your letters in months, so I thought something happened to you."

"I'm in a small town in White County, Indiana."

"Indiana? What in the—"

Josh cuts her off because he just needs to get it out. "*Ashley's dead!*" He begins to wail, holding the phone away from his face.

Loretta's tears of relief turn into cries of grief and disbelief. She says, "What happened? Do you need me to come to help?"

Once again, in a soft, very shaky, broken voice, Josh answers: "No, we met a nice woman who ran a cancer group, and she helped us through everything. She even helped me with all my PTSD stuff. I ain't fixed or nothin', but I feel better than I have in years, and I think I'm on my way back to being myself."

Loretta listens, with a hand on her heart. "God Bless her. But was it cancer that took Ashley?"

"Yeah." He starts to break down again and spurts out the words between sobs. "She was pregnant, and when the miscarriage happened, they found a tumor, and the cancer had already spread to her liver. She died quickly, and that is why I haven't written you in the last couple of months."

"Oh, baby, I'm so sorry to hear this. That girl was the best thing that ever happened to you. She was so lovely and nice. I wish I could be with you, give you the biggest hug and never let go. Are you coming home?"

"Nah. I have other plans. That's one of the reasons I'm calling you now. In the next few months, you'll receive a postcard from someone in Vermont. That will be me. I'm starting my life all over again, Mama. It will take lots of hard work, but I'm going to do it for Ashley, for you, and for the woman I mentioned before. Her name was Hannah."

"What do you mean her name *was* Hannah?"

"It's a long story, and right now I just wanted to hear your voice and tell you I love you. I also wanted to say that if things go well, I would like you and Dad to come up to Vermont and visit me. I'll let you know when I'm ready. For now, we'll keep my letters as our only communication. Keep checking your PO box. I love you, Mama, and I'm going to be okay."

Crying again, "I love you, Josh. It makes my heart swell to hear you say those words. I believe you, son—you will be okay. But there is so much I want to talk to you about, and I do have the time."

"Not right now. I tried to get you while you have the house to yourself."

"That's a hard thing to do. In fact, your Aunt Dory should be here any minute."

"You won't tell anyone I called, okay? Promise me you won't say a word."

"I promise. When will I hear from you again?"

"There are lots of logistics that need to be ironed out, and even more work for me talking with a counselor who specializes in veterans and PTSD. I can't tell you about it right now, but I will tell you everything one day when we are all sitting at the same table. I love you, and I've got to go. Wait for the postcard. I promise it will bring us back together again."

Josh doesn't wait for a reply and hangs up the phone. He is now sitting at Hannah's table crying again, but these are different types of tears—tears of hope for a better future. He looks down at his list. Olga and Robert are next on his list of people to call.

MAY 5, 2011, WHITE COUNTY, INDIANA

Drinking his coffee and eating a piece of toast, Josh sits at Hannah's kitchen table, waiting for Olga and Robert's morning call, concentrating on a story in the *the Journal* while he waits:

> The cause of death for Joseph Sinclair, 83-year-old former CEO of Fulcircle Company, has been released. A criminal investigation is underway and was determined when foul play at the crime scene was established. The White County Coroner's Office report confirms that Sinclair died of acute combined drug toxicity. Citing the coroner investigator's report, the former CEO of Fulcircle Company's death was caused by high concentrations of opiates, alcohol, isopropylamine salt, polyethoxylated tallow amine, and trace amounts of prescription drugs commonly used with cardiac health issues.
>
> The White County Sheriff's Office states that there are no suspects as of yet regarding the death of Joseph Sinclair case, and adds that they cannot comment about an open investigation. The Journal will continue to follow this story as further details become available.

Josh has no idea what isopropylamine salt and polyethoxylated tallow amine are, but he would bet the farm they are found in Kill-All.

Ever since Olga left Indiana after Hannah's funeral, either she or Robert has called Josh every morning at 9:00 a.m. Today is especially important—it's the day Josh finds out if his new identity has been completed and mailed. During these calls, they never refer to it as "new identity;" it's always called "the package." No details are discussed. It's simply referred to as "the package" or "the check."

In reality, the package and the check are the two main topics of their phone calls woven into conversations about how everyone is coping with life without Hannah or Ashley. This precautionary measure is taken because Josh or Olga may be considered potential suspects in Joe Sinclair's murder, and they suspect that their phone calls are being monitored. Since September 11, 2001, the newly formed Department of Homeland Security and the Patriot Act have stripped American citizens of the privacy of their phone and computer conversations.

"The check" refers to the life insurance payout that was filed within twenty-four hours of Ashley's death, which occurred seventeen days earlier. Hannah expedited the death certificate so she could mail everything immediately, fully aware that her own time was limited. The hospital obliged her request, and she believed that the insurance claim process couldn't be more straightforward. When she mailed Ashley's death certificate along with a copy of the policy, she included a note outlining Josh's situation, emphasizing that he needed to receive a lump sum as soon as possible since he was an unemployable veteran with special needs.

Starting on Monday, May 2, 2011, Josh began the grief counseling that James and the City of Bridges Hospice Center offered. The other counseling he started on the same day was for the David Edwards whom Olga and Robert set up, using his new Macbook Pro. The counselor resides in New Hampshire but does sessions through online sessions. His primary practice concentrates on veterans' PTSD issues, which was a way for Josh (a.k.a. David Edwards) to be introduced when Josh/David begins his new life in New England. Olga and Robert have set the whole thing up while completing the paperwork for the sale of their Vermont property and home to David Edwards.

Once Josh Bush receives "the check," he plans to take a trip to Costa Rica and check it out. Part of his therapy is attending the White County cancer group with Scott and others who know his current circumstances. Everyone in the group agrees that getting some different scenery, especially Costa Rica, could be a wonderful place to relax and heal from the past few months. Another topic Josh refers to in group sessions is feeling somewhat guilty about staying at Hannah's when she is no longer alive. Scott reassures him anytime it is brought up that Hannah wouldn't have had it any other way. He continues by saying Josh was helping Hannah's extended family get the house and property ready to sell.

In reality, Josh's plan is to fly to Costa Rica, send everyone in Indiana and his mom postcards, purchase a four-wheel-drive vehicle, and start heading north on the Pan-American Highway. He will sell the vehicle for cash once he makes it to the Mexico/United States border towns of San Ysidro and Tijuana. When he returns to the United States, David Edwards will become his new identity. Once again purchasing a vehicle with cash, he will use his new papers and ID card to give birth to David Edwards and leave Josh Bush back in Costa Rica, where he went on a road trip through Central America and never returned.

CHAPTER TWENTY-EIGHT

HEADLINES

MAY 8, 2011—THE *TIMES* SUNDAY EDITION:

Michael Bennett pulls up in front of his house in a new, blue, all-wheel-drive SUV. During the week after meeting Hannah, Michael traded in his Mercedes. He grabs the newspaper off the front seat while talking to his daughter, Amelia, on the phone.

"I know, honey. The cake has been ordered, and I talked to your mom. We'll all meet at the restaurant and then return to her place to celebrate with cake and ice cream."

While listening on the phone, Michael opens his front door, plops the very heavy Sunday *Times* onto the table and sees the headline down in the bottom right corner of the front page: Stage IV Cancer Group Goes on Killing Spree.

"Amelia, I need to go, honey. No, there's nothing wrong. We'll talk later, okay? I love you, and please give our girls a hug and kiss for me."

The introduction to the article reads:

> An alarming trend is happening nationwide, and there are reports indicating that it is not confined to the United States. The Times has confirmed that at least ten other countries and dozens of high-ranking corporate executives have been murdered in what seems to be an international uprising.
>
> Continued on page 17.

Michael pours himself a cup of coffee and has jitters of excitement and knots of dread in his gut as he flips to page seventeen:

Stage IV Cancer Group—continued

Numerous individuals have voluntarily surrendered to their local police stations, and it is anticipated that more will do the same. In several states, including: New York, California, West Virginia, Florida, Texas, Louisiana, Arizona and Indiana, multiple high-ranking executives from various industries have been murdered. Each victim was left with an identical message and a personal dossier. The perpetrators have not claimed any specific affiliation. Still, all the victims in what seems like a well-coordinated international revolt called the "May Day Massacre" were found with a typed-out message bearing the name "Kesshitai Exit Stage IV." The term, "Kesshitai," means the unit that expects to die, and may have been inspired by the Japanese teams of elders working on the Fukushima nuclear disaster. The statement left behind promises more press releases to come to explain these acts, using the words of Thomas Jefferson's Declaration of Independence to denounce 21st-century forms of despotism, particularly targeting corporatism and globalism.

The statement in its entirety:

Kesshitai Exit Stage IV
May 1, 2011

The concerned people of Earth are exercising our democratic right to self-determination and disassociating ourselves from the corrupted political, judicial, legal, and economic structures that safeguard and endorse corporate mass destruction.

We hereby withdraw our consent for the exploitation of our environment for financial gain, the theft of our physical and mental properties, the mass experimentation of products without prioritizing the Precautionary Principle, the undue influence of accumulated wealth on public policy and the deliberate creation of laws to shield the wealthy and powerful, enabling them to oppress, suppress, and repress the individuals who toil for the essential functions that uphold society.

We, the victims of the corporate ideology that prioritizes profits above all else, have united and made sacrifices for the betterment of the world today and for future generations to come. Decisions made decades ago for the benefit of a few at the expense of many have condemned us to death. Our numbers are increasing every day. We will not rest until this form of despotism ends.

This is not a new fight but a continuous struggle since the beginning of civilization. As industrialization advances, so does the destruction and death it leaves in its wake. We will draw inspiration from Thomas Jefferson's powerful words in the Declaration of Independence. Our cause is just, and we will remain vigilant until corporations assume their rightful role as subservient entities, serving the needs of all life on Earth instead of the dangerous ideal of dominion over it.

...WHEN in the Course of human events, it becomes necessary for one people to dissolve the political bands which have connected them with another, and to assume among the powers of the earth, the separate and equal station to which the Laws of Nature and of Nature's God entitle them, a decent respect to the opinions of mankind requires that they should declare the causes which impel them to the separation.

We hold these truths to be self-evident, that all men are created equal, that they are endowed by their Creator with certain unalienable Rights, that among these are Life, Liberty and the pursuit of Happiness....

MAY 9, 2011—THE *TIMES* HEADLINE: KESSHITAI EXIT STAGE IV CONTINUES TO TARGET EXECUTIVES

Statement #2: Kesshitai Exit Stage IV
May 8, 2011

The executives of industries that pollute the air, land, and water—as well as corporations that produce products that pose a severe risk to consumers' health when used as directed—are hereby notified that we know their names and have addresses. There is nowhere to hide.

As Stage IV cancer patients, we have had our lives and quality of life stolen from us due to these actions. Executives and companies prioritizing profits over people have led to a dramatic increase in chronic illnesses and have also created a profit-driven system for treating these diseases.

This immoral economic model will be held accountable, not within a political or legal system that serves the interests of these corporations, but by the victims of these corporate crimes against humanity who will be the judge, jury, and executioner. No longer will guilty verdicts result in monetary fines. A guilty verdict will be a death sentence, effective immediately.

Will you be next?

MAY 16, 2011—THE *TIMES* HEADLINE: CONFIRMED NUMBER OF KESSHITAI STAGE IV VICTIMS CONTINUES TO CLIMB

Statement #3: Kesshitai Exit Stage IV
May 15, 2011

The pursuit of justice is the goal, not revenge.

If a company knowingly creates a product or toxic environment that results in disease and death, this is premeditated. In that case, that company and its executives must be held to account for these crimes against life.

We are targeting executives who are guilty of these crimes.

Forever chemicals, biological technologies and carcinogens are being used as ingredients that will be consumed or aerosolized. With the capture of our entire political and legal system, these industrial criminals create a breeding ground for authoritarian policies imposed on those without political influence.

The public cannot depend on Justice to be served, so we must lead by example.

We fully expect to be held accountable in a court of law for taking the lives of other human beings.

We are asking the same for corporate murderers.

MAY 23, 2011—THE *TIMES* HEADLINE: CANCER GROUP RAMPAGE CLAIMS OVER 2,000 VICTIMS

Statement #4: Kesshitai Exit Stage IV
May 22, 2011

Our mission is clear; our mission is resolute.

For decades we have relied on protests, petitions, civil disobedience, and lobbying, only to face broken promises and exploitation by our political system for their own gain.

Therefore, industries, rather than corrupt government and law enforcement, must create a new business model.

There is no more time to waste.

Symbiosis is necessary for the existence of aerobic life on Earth. The sixth mass extinction is upon us. Human beings are among the tens of millions of species at risk of going extinct.

As a global society, we must refrain from raping

the earth for resources to continue the toxic and deadly throwaway culture—displacing people, wildlife and the destruction of the natural world.

Profits over life will no longer be acceptable.

The concerned people of the Earth will no longer sit by quietly.

MAY 29, 2011—*THE TIMES* HEADLINE: DEATH TOLL SURPASSES 2,500

Kesshitai Exit Stage IV continues to spread around the world. Thousands of metastatic cancer patients located worldwide have been held accountable for exacting justice from over 2,000 top executives of companies that are household names and others the ordinary citizen has never heard of. In today's infant stage of a truly global economy, corporations are drawn to nations with the least labor and environmental protections. This has made the Exit Stage IV group international with no other interconnection than being made up of advanced cancer patients.

It has been 21 days since the conflict with corporate executives began, and there are still no more answers than on day one. Surprisingly, public sentiment has shifted in favor of the cancer groups, with many now blaming governments around the world for prioritizing the economy and their political careers over public health.

Rallies and protests organized around the world are increasing in size daily in support of the reforms demanded by the Exit Stage IV group. These events are being held in front of government capitol buildings, legislatures and the headquarters of major corporations.

On June 4, 2011, a non-violent rally in Washington, DC, will focus on corporate accountability and the end of corporate personhood. Participants will march on the National Mall and proceed to the steps of the Capitol. More than 100,000 attendees are expected.

The Federal Bureau of Investigation (FBI) has not released any information about the murders and asks all journalists and news outlets not to speculate until concrete evidence is found. "This action is unprecedented, and we need to keep all information within the international intelligence community," said Ronald Boles of the FBI.

"With only one public statement concerning the actions of Exit Stage IV, it leaves us all with incredible number of questions and zero answers," Ronald Boles continued. "We are working around the clock to gather information that connects the suspects to any terrorist group. So far, we have come up empty-handed. If anyone has information, please do not hesitate to contact the FBI. Any details could help us save future lives."

A single question was asked and answered. The question was from a victim's family member, and elicited an out-of-character response: "How can a group of this size and scope fly under the radar of every intelligence agency worldwide?"

Mr. Boles responded, "We have been collaborating with intelligence agencies worldwide, and nobody has 'Kesshitai' or 'Exit Stage IV' on their radar or has even heard of that name. This lack of insight is unacceptable according to both the FBI and international intelligence agencies. We are all working tirelessly to uncover any connection aside from the cancer aspect. Please know that we are investigating these murders 24/7 until we can identify the master cell."

Currently, those who have surrendered only communicate through their lawyers and group statements. Despite numerous attempts to locate family members, friends, or relatives of the perpetrators, no information has been found beyond hearsay and speculation.

Memorial Services are being held around the world for the victims of these murders.

HARDWICK, VERMONT

MAY 1, 2016—7:00 P.M.:

Loretta and Henry Bush, and Jeannette and Jonathan Sands finish singing "Happy Birthday" to David Edwards. As David blows out the thirty-five candles on the cake, they all clap and congratulate him for overcoming so much adversity over the last decade.

David, with a grin on his face, feels whole for the first time in years. He thanks everyone, as each of them influenced his healing journey on some level. "I wish another person were here for me to thank, but she didn't know if her ninety-year-old body could handle the trip from New York City." Serendipitously, there is a knock at the door just as the cake slices are being served. Nobody was expecting another guest, and for Hardwick, Vermont, it is incredibly late to make unannounced calls to people.

When David opens the door, Olga is standing there alongside her son, who is holding a beautifully-wrapped birthday present. Acting like a huge wind blew him back, David says, "Wow! I wasn't expecting you at all."

"Do you think I would miss your thirty-fifth birthday? No way, José. This is my son Robert Jr. I could not have made the trip without him. Are you going to invite us in or what?"

"Of course," David says, still in shock. "Come on in. We're just about to eat cake." He gives Olga an enormous hug, and when it ends, he reaches out and gives Robert Jr. a firm handshake. "Thanks for taking such good care of your mom."

As the three enter the cottage kitchen, David introduces his guests: "Mom, Dad—this is Olga. She helped me so much. She and her late husband are why I can live in Vermont. I owe my life to her. Jeannette, Jonathan—you both know Olga and Robert."

With tears streaming down her face, Loretta Bush rushes over to hug Olga. "Thank you, thank you, from the bottom of our hearts for giving our son a second chance. We thought we'd lost him forever."

Olga squeezes her and says, "You've got an admirable and loving son. You both did a great job raising a good man. I wouldn't make the long trip for just anybody. David holds a special place in my heart."

Robert Jr. hands the birthday gift to David. "Happy Birthday. I wish I could say I had something to do with it, but it was all my mom. I have no idea what's in it."

"Thank you. Your part of the gift was bringing your mom here. When did we last see each other? Was it at your dad's memorial? I appreciate you coming today more than you can imagine. Your parents are some of the most amazing people I have ever met. I owe my life to them."

For the next hour or so, David opens gifts from everyone, and when he reaches for Olga's, she says, "Not now. Open it later—by yourself. Oh, everyone, get your mind out of the gutter. Nothing like that in that box!" she says. Everyone laughs. Olga hasn't lost her sense of humor.

MAY 1, 2016—9:00 P.M.:

Olga and Robert Jr. say their goodbyes long after everyone else has left. "I was so shocked to see you at the door," David tells Olga. "Thank you for everything. You look great, and your spirit seems as strong as ever."

Robert Jr. says, "That's the truth. Come on, Mom. You need to get some rest. It's been a long day."

Olga replies, "Okay, okay—I can't get enough of this handsome man. I remember the stones—and to think, from that day until now seems like a lifetime ago."

David pats his heart. "Always. I will never forget it. We did it, didn't we? *We did it!*"

"Yes, we did. Hannah's gut instinct and ability to strategize worked a miracle. They broke the mold after God created her."

David agrees, "I've never met anyone like her before or since."

Robert Jr. is standing in the doorway, not understanding the cryptic conversation, but is patiently waiting for his mother. David and Olga embrace for possibly the last time. Then, he watches the elderly mother and her son walk down the pathway to their car. He waves goodbye as they pull away.

David Edwards closes the door and returns to the kitchen to open Olga's present. Sitting at the table with another piece of cake and an honorary cup of *cawfee*, he removes the top. The box is filled with articles from newspapers, magazines, and online printouts.

He reads recent headlines one by one until he gets to the article in The *Times*, which has done the most extensive reporting on Hannah's plan.

5th Anniversary of May Day Massacre
Unthinkable economic reforms from private sector with over 5,000 executives killed

Earth Says: Thank You Exit Stage IV
Ten ways the biosphere has recovered since May 1, 2011

Exit Stage IV Creates Dramatic Reduction of Billionaire Class
The number of billionaires has been reduced by 50 percent since 2011

Industries Across All Technology Fields Dry Up
Top five ways tech industries are disappearing from our daily lives

Highest Juvenile Salmon Run in Over 70 Years
Fish populations continue to increase across oceans and rivers

Biodiversity Reversing Course
A significant positive trend in biodiversity for the first time in 15 years

Global Happiness Index Breaks Record
Since its inception, the Index has reached an all-timehigh

Extraction Rates of Rare Earth Metals and Minerals Has Dropped

Decreased demand leads to 40 percent drop in sales

Air Quality Reaches Highest Levels Recorded Since Measurements Began

Air pollution has largely decreased in developing countries

Finally, David gets to the article he wants to read in The *Times*:

United Nations General Assembly Approves New Economic Standard

UN statistical commission to implement alternative formulas for assessing the global economy

April 29, 2016: On Thursday the United Nations General Assembly voted in favor of a new economic model for evaluating the global economy's health. This model intends to move away from traditional metrics such as output, production, consumption and economic growth. Assembly members encouraged the nearly two hundred sovereign states to adopt these revised methodologies.

The new formulas will be derived from the research published by the Potsdam Institute for Climate Impact Research, drawing upon studies conducted in 2009 and 2015 regarding planetary boundaries. Even with the best intentions, the idea that we can ignore Earth's natural cycles while living the current industrial lifestyle has proven faulty. The Earth is in the process of the sixth mass extinction, which is universally agreed upon by climate scientists and driven by human behavior.

Planetary boundaries are the conceptual framework that outlines a safe operating space for humanity. They emphasize our symbiotic relationship with all life forms on Earth. There are nine specific boundaries;

regrettably, humanity has exceeded safe limits in several categories.

In addition to these critical indicators, the Global Hunger Index, Happiness Index, and Personal Consumption Expenditures Price Index will be utilized to evaluate global equity in access to essential resources and the necessities required for a healthy lifestyle.

As a global community, we are on the cusp of the fifth anniversary of the Exit Stage IV Mayday Massacre. The newly established metrics and priorities are directly linked to the ramifications of May 1, 2011, when over 7,000 metastatic cancer patients targeted corporate executives and government officials. Official estimates indicate that nearly 5,000 lives were lost due to these targeted actions.

The loss of these 5,000 lives precipitated an unprecedented global reform of business practices in the private sector, which few had anticipated. In this new economic model, profits, over all else, no longer sit atop the priority of a corporation's charter. What social good can be achieved with the least environmental degradation has replaced the top priority. Unlike the private sector, governments often do not possess the capacity to implement reforms within a reasonable timeframe. Nevertheless, we are currently observing the emergence of initiatives, propositions, and legislative measures worldwide that incorporate the Precautionary Principle, a key demand arising from Exit Stage IV.

The Precautionary Principle states that "regulation is necessitated whenever there is a potential risk to health, safety, or the environment, regardless of whether the supporting evidence is speculative or if the economic costs of regulation are substantial." Furthermore, the United Nations World Charter for Nature, established in 1982, asserts that "if potential adverse effects are not fully understood, the activities should not proceed."

A more stringent interpretation adhered to by many environmentalists is the maxim "Guilty until proven innocent."

For over two centuries, business and industry have dictated acceptable safety practices based on capitalism's flawed ideology and purported capacity for self-regulation. The developments initiated on May 1, 2011, have catalyzed an unraveling of the business norms that have historically governed society.

In the coming months and years, we'll continue to feel the ripple effect of Exit Stage IV global revolt, for better or worse.

NOTE TO THE READER

In October 2002, part of western Montana was designated as a National Priorities List (NPL) Superfund site due to the mining of vermiculite contaminated with asbestos, which had exposed an entire town to the toxic substance from 1919 to 1990. Despite awareness of the associated dangers in the early 1960s, mining operations continued for three more decades until the mine was finally shut down in 1990.

The Fukushima nuclear disaster in Japan occurred in 2011, and as of 2023, it remains unresolved. The Japanese government has announced plans to release 1.3 million tons of radioactive water into the Pacific Ocean.

In 2010, the Gulf of Mexico experienced an oil spill that lasted eighty-six days, releasing 210 million gallons of crude oil into its waters. It is also believed that the chemical dispersants used for cleanup were more harmful to the environment than the crude oil itself.

A chemical revolution that began in the 1940s continues today with C8 compounds, known as PFOA and PFOS. Found in products like nonstick cookware, waterproof clothing, cosmetics, dental floss, and plastics, these "forever chemicals" are valued for their nonstick properties and their ability to repel water, oil, and stains. Studies show that 99 percent of the human population tested retains these substances in their bodies, and that corporations have known about the associated diseases, birth defects, and environmental hazards caused by "forever chemicals" since the 1960s.

Plastics release harmful compounds into our air, food, water, and the environment during their production, everyday use, and disposal. There are over 16,000 different chemicals used to create various types of plastic, many of which are known to be carcinogenic, hormone disruptors, or linked to obesity. Additionally, some of these substances can harm the liver, brain, and kidneys—as well as the cardiovascular, immune, and reproductive systems. Many other chemicals used in plastics remain unstudied.

During the 1980s, the Iran/Contra Affair and CIA death squads in Central America were being funded by secret arms deals with Iran despite a US trade embargo associated with the Iran Hostage Crisis.

Prevailing chemical agriculture that began in the 1960s with the biotech name "Green Revolution" has accelerated damage to topsoil worldwide through the widespread use of synthetic herbicides and pesticides together with new farming practices. According to a 2014 study by the United Nations Food and Agriculture Organization, the rapid degradation and loss of topsoil worldwide could result in the global population having less than fifty years of food production left if these practices continue. Furthermore, known cancer risks and other health concerns due to herbicides and pesticides have been concealed from the public by biotech agribusiness companies, which have reaped significant profits and gained considerable influence over public policy through corruption.

The Bolivia Water Wars of 1999 were a violent uprising against the privatization of water resources.

Mountaintop removal is a modern method to access coal.

The opioid epidemic has been widespread and increasing since the late 1990s, with Big Pharma playing a major role under the guise of pain medications.

ACKNOWLEDGMENTS

Thank you to my friends and family by blood, marriage, and activism— who have informed, inspired, and helped shape my political ideology and spiritual belief system.

ABOUT THE AUTHOR

Benjamin Emery is a loving son, brother, father, husband, and friend.

After three decades of activism focused on various issues, primarily government corruption and electoral reform, Ben has dedicated much of his time to community volunteering and coaching athletics. Over the last twenty years, he has also studied and practiced the science of regenerative agriculture while attending nursing school part-time. During his tenure as a co-chair of his home county's political party, Ben campaigned for election to partisan public office—first, as a candidate for US Congress and later, for State Senator. In the end, he determined that it is nearly impossible to change the two-party political system from within, and our focus needs to be setting up peripheral systems that support regional and local economies.

In the spring of 2014, at the age of forty-four, the trajectory of his life was altered by a diagnosis of advanced colorectal cancer. As a result, Ben chose to focus his energy on ridding his body of cancer; caring for his elderly parents, who suffer from chronic diseases; and managing a permaculture farm. Though considered cured of his cancer in September 2019, he continues to live with disabilities due to lasting side effects from treatments and surgeries.

For years, Ben has participated in online cancer support groups and has offered mentorship to those who are newly diagnosed or are inflicted with his same disability.

His lifelong goal is fostering a more cooperative and compassionate nation—from Washington DC, and on down to his local community.

www.ingramcontent.com/pod-product-compliance
Lightning Source LLC
Chambersburg PA
CBHW020427030726
47495CB00006B/1691